WOMAN ON THE WALL

Woman ON THE WALL

THE SIBYLLINE CHRONICLES
VOL 1

ROBIN RIVERS

AMYNTAS
PRODUCTIONS

Copyright © 2022 by Robin Rivers

Library and Archives Canada Cataloguing in Publication
Title: Woman On The Wall / Robin Rivers
Names: Rivers, Robin, author.
Description: Paperback Edition
Identifiers: ISBN 9781778135729 (softcover) | ISBN 9781778135712 (ebook)

Edited by Claire Mulligan & Bevin Clempson
Cover art and layout by Ken Henderson

ISBN 978-1-7781357-2-9
ISBN 978-1-7781357-1-2 (ebook)

Printed by Ingram Sparks

www.thesibyllinechronicles.com

To my husband, who always believed.

ACKNOWLEDGEMENTS

No story comes to life without a collective of creatives. I am humbled by the many who came together to make *Woman On The Wall* possible. First, I must thank Alison Wurts for enduring the first-draft writing process with me. She is a patient gem of a human. The creative vision of developmental editor Claire Mulligan deeply shaped the structure and characters in the novel. Copyeditor Bevin Clempson's literary sensibility and poetic touch made the words on the page shine. My gratitude also goes to editor Mikaela Pedlow for her keen editorial eye. I must thank Janie Chang and Lissa Marie Redmond. Thank you to Beatriz Brenes for early draft reads and guidance with the audio book, and to all of those who read the early drafts of the novel, including Joelle Fine, Robin Blackburn, Samantha Peterson, Dave Kotlan, and Lisa Garrett. I cannot forget the very real Maurine Soudier, whose provocative tour of Château Gaillard in Amboise, France inspired the character of Maurine in the story and brought sixteenth-century Amboise to life.

Never to be diminished, I thank my husband Ken for the endless nights of brainstorming and hashing out of storylines, the ability to withstand the crashing waves of my worries and doubt, and being the workhorse of the novel visuals. His artistic vision shaped the website, cover design, and so much more. Without him, this project would still be locked away in my mind.

Beyond the process of storytelling, I am so grateful to my daughters Quinn and Mhari, for tolerating the mercurial nature of my writing process. Absolute support from our families & friends is ever precious. And to my KKMF ladies cheering me on at every stage. It kept me going even in the darkest moments. I thank you all for your part in bringing the Sibylline to life.

Finally, I acknowledge the women throughout history who were deliberately erased or demonized by those seeking power over truth. The Sibylline live within us all.

Me-kädmen anina il-ati.

Robin

THE ORDERS OF THE SIBYLLINE

The Sibyl (*Great Mother*) - Oracular prophetess who serves humanity for 1,000 years.

The Mother Abbess - Head of all Orders. This woman serves the Orders in this capacity until the Sibyl rises and replaces her. At that point, she returns to her original Order within the Sibylline as its head.

The Ba'alat - Guardian of the Seals of Annach. Eight women are chosen for this service. Each pledges a single vow—to wear and protect their individual Seal at all costs. To ensure the security of the Seals, no two Ba'alat can be in the company of one another.

The Metradora - Sibylline who determine the best matches to produce the next Sibyl.

The Iphegenia - Divine Birth Priestesses whose purpose within the Orders is to create a stronger genetic line and possibly serve as the womb of the next Sibyl. Untouched by men, they became the basis of the virgin birth legend.

The Asu - Order of priestess physicians who preserve the sacred healing passed from mother to daughter. One must be born into this Order.

The Heliades - The alchemists. Keepers of the light.

The Harimtu - The spy network of the Sibylline.

The Amyntas - The warrior order of the Sibylline. These women are recruited into the Order and then separated from the rest of the sisterhood to not taint the Sibylline with the violence of men. While the Amyntas are considered a necessity in order to protect the women from those who would seek to harm them, these warriors are considered outsiders, and no Amyntas was allowed to rise as the Sibyl.

CAST OF CHARACTERS
(IN ORDER OF APPEARANCE)

1945

Marie Guerrant

Cloutille Seydoux

Colonel Philip Millar

Noam Marchant

Oberführer Karl Diebitsch

Iné Soudier

Simon Faubert

Yara Paquet

Serah Izem

Rafidah Qabbari

1519

Aesmeh de la Rose

The Mother Abbess, Renée de Bourbon

Francesco Melzi

Lady Marguerite

Sister Maurine

Tommaso d'Arced

Leonardo da Vinci

WOMAN ON THE WALL

Chapter 1

MAY 2, 1519
AMBOISE, FRANCE

*D*ear One,

How awkward this must be to have a dead woman about to declare the direction of your life. It is unclear to me, even at this crucial moment, how I should address you. Alas, as time can no longer keep us apart, let us dispense with being strangers and begin.

I am the Sibyl of Amboise.

I died here.

You have arrived in this tiny commune because of a five-hundred-year-old pact to find you and bring you home.

As I write these words, I wonder what you know of my kind. Do you know the names Hypatia and Lubna? Does history speak of Shushandukht and Shajar al-Durr? Or, are the Sibyls little more than mythological prophetesses painted upon the ceiling of the Sistine Chapel? In truth, we are ancient, once powerful, and nearly vanished.

Born of the Great Mother's very womb, each Sibyl's sight gave men a glimpse of what might come. We predicted wars, warned against the rise of tyrants, shed light upon the fates of many. In the great capitals of Badari, Olmec, Xi, Khemet, the Jiroft, even the wilds of Scythia, we served humanity for more than eleven thousand years. And, then . . .

What do you know, Dear One? It pains me. What kind of world did my failures leave you? In the glimmers of your time, I saw only fire and death. Without the Sibyl, men know not the cost of their acts. Power is a seductive demon. Have I left you with the tyrants?

I must assume the world is well enough that Sister Maurine stands at your side in fulfillment of her vow. My regret is not being there beside you as well.

You are the hope of the Sibylline. I once was that hope, the first to complete training and enter the temple in more than one thousand years. Such care was taken to protect me. However, a malicious enemy lived amongst us. By the time I knew, my throat was nearly slit. It lays upon you now to do what I never fully could—to rise and serve the world.

Yes, Dear One, your coming has been foretold for five centuries. In those fifty decades, such knowledge has hung in the halls of the men who thought us eradicated. They celebrated that sublime smile, all without the fortune of knowing whom they kept safe. You are the oracle they could never burn, lying in state until this very moment.

Listen, Dear One.

Listen without fear.

Your life is an amalgamation of so many others. As you gain the sight, Amboise will return our memories to you. You shall reclaim them as your own. You may feel as if you have gone mad. Know that you are coming alive. This is where your service begins.

In the moments to come, others will attempt to strip your sovereignty. Such war is inevitable. You must prepare for it. Train. Fight as a warrior. Remain devoted to your purpose alone. Do not concede.

Then, call the Sibylline to your side. Step beyond the seven bridges of paradise and into hell in the forest beyond Gaillard. There, in the temple of the Sibylline, you shall rise and take my place at Amboise. That you might watch over humankind in beauty and justice as the Great Mothers before you intended.

Eternally in your service,

Aesmeh de la Rose

Chapter 2

MARIE

MAY 2, 1945
PARIS, FRANCE

Marie fidgeted with the strap of her brassiere that chafed against the welts on her back. The street lights faded as she rushed down the cobblestone streets toward the Louvre. A whiff of light morning rain mingled with that of cinnamon and sugar. She stepped quick and easy as the cloud-speckled sun streamed through the last of the cherry blossoms and storefronts transformed under the pink light.

She spotted the baker and eased her way through people waiting for bread. Women smiled and waved as they took their place in the ration line. A child scooted toward her with a bundle of delicate muguet blossoms left over from the first May Day celebration since the occupation. Baked goods and blooms would draw anyone back to Paris. That's what she needed to believe.

"Salut, Dr. Guerrant? What do you think awaits you this morning?" The boy knew Marie as one of the art historians repopulating Paris museums with treasures hidden during the war.

"It is always a mystery, Monsieur." She smiled and winked, taking the flowers.

Marie's attention turned to a crowd gathered down the street. The morning's pink clouds seemed to gray.

"Qu'est-ce que c'est?" asked the boy.

She dodged the question and ushered him back to the safety of his mother.

Two men had hauled a woman into the middle of the road, her heavy veil yanked back. Marie noted the heaps of hair piled on the ground and guns slung over shoulders. Boys were filling their pockets with rocks.

"Femme tondue." She heard women whisper. "Collaboration horizontale."

Femme tondue, Marie thought, a shorn woman. Stripped down to her slip and placed on her knees, the woman neither howled in protest nor stiffened in defiance of the men claiming she'd fathered a German soldier's child. Marie knew this state of brokenness and had no tolerance for it.

She pulled her fedora tight to her head and rushed over. "Get away from her!"

The men kept shaving the woman's head. Marie snatched the clippers. "I said to leave her alone."

"Maybe we should shave your head too, whore." A man with a gun approached. Others closed in around her.

Marie pulled her fedora off to reveal too-short curls and pushed up a sleeve to reveal the numbers tattooed onto her left forearm. "The Nazis already did that."

The men retreated, sucking in a collective long breath. Marie leveraged the pity in their eyes, gathered the half-shaved woman's clothes, and helped her to her feet.

The crowd had gone quiet. Marie paused, her heart pounding as she held the woman's hand tight. "We are better than this. Go back to your families."

As everyday life resumed, Marie hustled the woman into the alley behind the boulangerie, and helped her back into her dress. "Are you okay?"

Without response, the woman covered her head with the veil. Her eyes brightened, familiar but then not. Marie noticed markings on the woman's arm, a single line with a crescent moon on each side. A shiver shot through her body as she offered a cigarette.

"That's contraband, you know?" The baker stepped out from the back door of the boulangerie.

Startled, Marie turned towards him, disoriented for a moment.

"Got any more?" The baker winked and pointed out to the street. The woman had vanished into the crowd.

Marie passed him a smoke and he disappeared inside.

She tossed the clippers into the rubbish heap, fished fifteen cans of Rinderbraten out of her portmanteau bag and placed them in the delivery bin.

The baker returned with a one gallon metal thermal container. "Are you sure you can carry this?"

"Just made room for it." Marie banged on the bin lid.

"Sardines?"

"Roast beef."

The baker's eyes drooped. "Well, at least the Nazis left us something to eat."

"Any news on Serah?" Marie asked.

The old Maquis Resistance fighter glanced past Marie's shoulder before handing her a stack of metal cups and a baguette. "You know how it works."

She sighed.

"Don't worry," the baker said. "You'll find her."

Marie handed him the last of her cigarettes and pulled the watch from her pocket—nearly six o'clock. The guard at the Louvre awaits.

Picking up her pace, she pulled papers from her coat pocket and attempted to focus on work rather than the scene she'd just broken up. Quickly noting the stamp of the British Special Operations Executive, she read through the inquiry received the night before.

The words Mona Lisa stood out.

"La Joconde," Marie whispered. "Why can't they just call it that?"

The painting was French, even considering its origin, she thought. Da Vinci finished it in France, and the French had guarded it with jealous hearts for five hundred years. Ages ago, Marie hand-picked the French team that hid the masterpiece from the Nazis. Having British Intelligence inquire about the status of its return would surely cause unnecessary delays. She admired the Allied effort well enough. However, she knew that painting and those recovering it better than anyone. The Brits weren't going to change that.

She relieved herself of the pointless internal argument. As far as anyone knew, a transport truck was moving the painting down a French farm road at this very moment. Yes, it was a vital re-acquisition. It would also be the last re-acquisition, at least for her. Marie already declined an offer to return as the Directéur of Provenance Research at the Louvre. As soon as the piece hung upon the very museum wall from which it had been removed, she planned to step aside and focus on finding her daughter.

As Marie continued, her ivory oxfords slipped a bit at the heel which showed signs of a new blister. The enormous portmanteau bag in her right hand weighed her down. Shades of day breached the tops of the apartment blocks lining Rue Saint Martin. She paused to stuff cotton in the back of the ill-fitting shoes. A pair of young men wearing work shirts and leather caps walked down the sidewalk toward her. She pulled a photo from her pocket. "Salut, have you seen my daughter? Her name is Serah Izem. She would be about twenty years old."

They shook their heads. How many times had Marie asked that question? How many women were searching for daughters after the war? She'd had a few leads, rumors of sightings in the Var department near Aiguines. Old Maquis whispered of catching sight of a woman fitting her description just south of the Paris ring. It gave Marie hope. Yet, the shaking heads and silence reduced her devotion to little more than the hope of a grieving mother.

Marie considered how she arrived on the street she disappeared from two years earlier wearing a borrowed suit and scratching wounds that would never heal, in search of her daughter. Her mind flashed to 1943. Her husband shot in front of her. Serah's screams echoing as the SS hauled Marie away. Then, to the years after. Bodies piled in pits. Piercing howls of women. She stiffened as these memories overwhelmed her.

"Four hundred and eighty days." She reminded herself she'd survived more than a year as a political prisoner in Ravensbrück. Marie's in-depth knowledge of how to spot a key in art and old manuscripts made her valuable to the Nazis as they forced her to translate every hand-written piece of history dumped into warehouses behind the barbed wire circling the concentration camp. Their intended prize: a powerful modern prophetess hidden somewhere in France.

"Goddamn Sibyl."

Marie hated everything about those ancient oracles—their ability to see the future; their grip on men who saw them as the key to ultimate power.

The Nazis were obsessed, but never found a single piece of evidence. The oracles proved nothing more than myths like Hercules, mermaids, or Atlantis. Yet, Marie witnessed thousands of artifacts and countless lives destroyed in the quest.

The weight of the portmanteau bag forced her to move in spurts along the route. At each stop, she fidgeted with the hem of her skirt and fussed with her hair streaked with the first hints of gray. She glanced at her reflection in the windows of the dress shops along Rue de Rivoli. She poked at the dark circles under her eyes and the odd bend of her collarbones. The sharp angle of her jaw still startled her.

A cotton dress would have suited the weather. The butter-lemon linen suit given by her co-worker proved hot enough, even without the trench layered over it. Has this city always been this hot in May? Or did her time away erase such simple memories? A cracked coat of arms on the cornice of a building read *Fluctuat nec mergitur*. She snorted as she translated the Latin, as quick as breathing: "Tossed but not sunk." The official motto of Paris. It might very well be her own.

She wiped the sweat from her face and began reciting the alphabet in Attic Greek. The repetition served as a constant ritual to determine whether she suffered mental deterioration. It calmed her. Marie shot through the letters in record time, congratulating herself for keeping a sharp mind despite constant thoughts of Serah combined with the heat.

All of this Sibyl nonsense, she reminded herself, would soon be done with. The treacherous beasts would disappear into history. The Nazis were on the run, imprisoned, or dead. Marie would soon complete the task of keeping La Joconde safe. Workers would hang the painting where it belongs. Marie will have done her duty for France, and for the world. She was desperate for it.

Yet, a nagging sense curdled her stomach. Recent coordinates put the painting in the Loire Valley, only three hours south of Paris. Good news. But, she also knew that field updates had stalled.

She slid a hand back into her coat, pulling out her pocket watch. Six o'clock sharp. She'd have to deal with those discrepancies later.

Marie looked up towards the records room on the second floor of the Louvre. There was a dim light. A single figure. Marie noted the feminine silhouette and smiled. "Bonjour, Cloutille."

A series of barricades blocked the museum's Department of Statuary archives. It was tight. She traced back through old Maquis training on how to bust blockades, weaving her way through and wondering how any thief could navigate fast enough without getting shot. When the guard gave the signal, she hurried through the side entrance.

"Salut, Dr. Guerrant." He took her leather portmanteau.

"Your payment." Relieved as he took the heavy piece of luggage, Marie passed him the loaf of bread. It was their quiet contract for letting her team inside early. No one was supposed to enter the museum before 9 a.m. However, starting at 6 a.m. ensured her small crew, specializing in detecting reproductions, could work without interruption before the museum got busy with workers and officials.

"What about you?" The guard said as he attempted to split the baguette in half.

Marie declined the offer as they crossed into the storage room, normally stark and empty, but now packed with enormous wooden crates.

"The French Masters are back." The thick-mustached man flashed his light towards crates five deep in some places. Several had already been opened to reveal their contents. "I can't believe these statues have been locked away for so long."

Marie ran a gloved hand over the white drop cloth covering a statue. "From Château de Brézé?"

"Oui," he said.

"Any word from . . . our friends?" Marie had been waiting for the Maquis to make contact with her after requesting a meeting about Serah with fellow Resistance fighter Noam Marchant. However, she understood that scheduling reunions with friends whose political leanings did not settle well with any government must be done off the grid.

"Non, madame, désolé."

"Any word on La Joconde?" She could barely contain her enthusiasm for the end to come.

The guard shook his head again. "More manuscripts arrived, though. Professor Seydoux had the young men from the Sorbonne place them in the upper gallery. They should be ready. I hear the pieces are real gems."

"Well, the 'real' part of your claim is yet to be determined." Marie winked at him as shouts echoed through the halls. "I guess I better get to the party."

He offered an easy smile, returned her portmanteau, and opened the lock to the first-floor exhibition halls. "You really ought to consider hauling less around with you, Dr. Guerrant."

"Okay." She passed him the last two cans of Rinderbraten from her bag and winked again.

Marie pushed open the heavy door and moved quickly. The long walk through the lower galleries to the warehouse rooms prickled her skin every time. She breathed in the museum air. It stank of fetid gunpowder, ersatz soap, and disuse. Warehouses over enemy lines smelled exactly the same. She scratched one of her calves against the other. The memory of lice-filled wool suits she was forced to wear while translating documents made her skin itch. The Nazis never liked to think they weren't civilized.

Before the war, she admired the Louvre's bold choice of dark walls and how the masterpieces radiated their own magnificence against them. Now, as she walked, empty picture frames were stacked along bare walls. And where La Joconde once hung, shards of frames and tools lay piled below.

The outline of the painting flung her mind back to 1938. Her connections to the Resistance and Parisian Communist Party members served the museum's subversive plans well.

While men secured the original La Joconde, she hired reproduction artists to produce a series of decoys. And they had remastered Leonardo da Vinci's sublime portrait to near perfection. Only a handful of people knew which was the true masterpiece. From there, Marie used her skills to encode each one with a tracking marker and plotted routes for each. Maquis Resistance teams set off, with their cargo, to ancient castles, cloistered abbeys, and private homes across France. They'd done it all to stop the Nazis, but . . .

She scanned the galleries beyond. Thousands of artifacts had been returned. Workers would arrive later that morning to wheel crates down corridors lit with spotlights and hoist them up stairs using makeshift wooden ramps. Finally, she reached the end of the corridor and moved through the door to the workrooms.

Her mind shifted back to La Joconde. She regretted waiting for the painting to arrive in Paris. She should have gone to meet the Maquis team, overseen the delivery herself. That way she could have made contact earlier and gotten a jump on finding Serah.

It was unconscionable, she thought, having to sit around waiting for so much to return to normal and not having the ability to change that fate. She was grateful, though, for her team. They made it all bearable.

Marie pressed the handle of the workroom door and entered. She raised a delighted eyebrow as the men and women greeted her. This moment had become the happiest part of her day. Cloutille and an American linguist from Boston took the portmanteau and set up the coffee on the long, wooden table. A worker Marie only knew as Bert sliced pears.

"I brought bread." The guard walked in waving the baguette she had given him. She took his arm, offering him a place at the table.

"Is that cheese?" Marie asked Cloutille. "Wherever did you conjure that from?"

"Probably the same place you conjured this coffee." Cloutille passed her a drink and they toasted. "And, you got that baker of yours to give you more cups, I see."

Marie admired Cloutille Seydoux, a professor of art history at L'École des Beaux-Arts. She knew Cloutille had her own war-time ties. Those appeared to be a little closer to Allied forces than Marie preferred to keep company, but she had no doubt of her loyalties. She found herself faintly envious of the woman's effortless style and beauty. Cloutille always smelled of roses and had a complexion to match. She wore her amber hair in a victory roll, a style that was all the rage.

"Settle in please." Marie waited while everyone took a seat. "I want to thank all of you for your efforts. Without you, none of this work would get done."

"De rien et merci Dr. Guerrant, for bringing us together," Cloutille said. "Each day here is another day we grow closer to returning to normal."

"And, there's coffee!" Bert saluted before shooting back the remainder of his drink.

"To Dr. Guerrant and her contraband coffee," Cloutille said as they all raised a cup.

"And to France." Marie's chest warmed as she glanced around the room at each of them. For so long she'd been unable to offer a single comfort to anyone around her. She relished the sense of togetherness in that moment, even if her shoulders had paid the price.

With full bellies, they went to work on the arrivals.

"What do we know so far?" She requested an update.

"Monsieur Thompson has uncrated those we anticipated, including several Renaissance pieces from François premiere," Cloutille said.

"La Joconde?" Marie hoped the guard had not known what exactly came in overnight.

"Not yet." Cloutille passed along a series of billets.

"That's nine crates. I thought there were ten?"

Cloutille's eyebrow raised; her voice lowered. "Hildegard de Bingen."

"Ah! I heard the Maquis got those pieces out of Austria."

Cloutille motioned for her to keep her voice down. "And a truck full of children."

Marie's eyes lit up.

"Too young to be Serah. I'm sorry."

"No, that's so good." Marie shook her head and offered a smile. "Save that crate until last. We'll have some explaining to do. Those shouldn't really be in France."

The rest of the team showed her what they uncrated. Marie sent Bert, along with a new Sorbonne research student she hadn't seen at breakfast, off to sort and repair. Cloutille and the American linguist drew orders to decipher, localize, and date. The process never varied, and garnered all of their devotion. Precise and undeterred by the detailed cataloguing, the team reviewed the lots. They kept to her strict process. Every necessary review was completed for each piece.

Confirm or deny.

Real or fake.

Repatriation or reproduction.

Marie slid on her work gloves and became preoccupied with a Renaissance piece—a palm-sized, gem-encrusted sixteenth-century book of hours passed from King François I to his niece. She unlatched the ruby clasp. With a turn of the first illuminated page, her senses lit up.

"What is it?" one of the workers asked.

"These were functional prayer books made mostly for women to foster reflection and devotion." Marie pulled a work light closer. "Many of the greatest paintings and drawings of the Medieval period were preserved in these devotional texts. Did you know that there were more books of hours produced from the fourteenth to the sixteenth-century than any other type of text?"

Grammar, syntax, dialectal variants—how she loved words.

"No two are exactly alike. But, there is a set of prayers to recite at regular intervals throughout the day." She showed the team the layout of the palm-sized book. "The Hours of the Virgin, said in praise for the Virgin Mary."

Marie drew from her proficiency in Latin and Greek, and from French and Italian medieval and renaissance dialects to translate the perfect handwriting. Her mind settled on it all when a slight notation in a line of text piqued her attention. She called Cloutille over, pointing out the heavy line of ink, different from the lettering beneath it.

"This shouldn't be here," Marie said.

"No, you are right. It shouldn't." Cloutille slid her glasses on as she joined Marie at a worktable. "The whole piece shouldn't be here. I'm almost positive the original hasn't left England since the eighteenth-century."

"Why is it in the de Brézé lot, then? Did the British have access? Were they storing pieces there too?"

"Possibly." Cloutille continued her examination. "You understand it all. Resistance crews and civilian teams moving anything to keep the others off the trail."

"Who uncrated it?"

"Paul."

"Who?" Marie searched the room and found a young man sitting at a back table. He was cutting the last of the pears. "Monsieur! Are you Paul?"

"Oui, Madame," the young man said, his mouth half-full.

Marie noticed Cloutille stiffen. The others signaled for him to get rid of the food.

"Are you eating on a table next to a priceless manuscript?" Cloutille raced towards him and slapped the fruit out of his hand.

"It's over there." He pointed, still chewing, voice lilting upward.

She grew terse. "Did you touch anything?"

"I was just checking manifests." He picked up another pear. "I missed breakfast."

Cloutille glared at him. "I don't know who you are or who educated you so poorly. If you ever bring your flippant attitude or sticky breakfast within range of another artifact in this warehouse again, I will personally ensure you never work on a research team anywhere in Europe. Is that clear?"

"Very clear," Paul slid the knife and the remaining food to a corner of the table, stood up, and got to work.

Marie noticed an odd exchange of looks between him and Cloutille, and made a note to ask later if they knew one another. She put her hand on the woman's arm to ease her back. "Let him be. He's so young." She handed Paul a towel. "If you want to eat, arrive on time. Now, wash your hands and return. We have a forgery."

The team gathered around her to listen as she wove the clues together for them. "Twelfth-century handwriting does not look the same as sixteenth-century handwriting." She pointed out the differences in the scripts of an illuminated manuscript from the renaissance era laid out on the crates. "And both would certainly be very different from what a twentieth-century writer would pen just in terms of tools used."

Marie asked Paul to retrieve a reproduction of a book of hours off a nearby rack. She flipped to a marked page. "Look for ink quality, any variances in scripts, the jagged edges a quill gives versus a smooth metal implement. Do not ignore details others would not know to consider. This gold on the edge of each page is too well preserved, the colors too crisp. Either someone snuck into the de Brézé catacombs to restore a five-hundred-year-old book in the dark, or this is a fake."

Cloutille went to document the evidence when Marie stopped her.

"Let Paul do it. This will be good for him to learn."

Cloutille pursed her lips, the air audible as it escaped her nostrils. Marie coaxed her to oblige with a shake of her head. Paul took the ledger and pen, and began scribbling the details.

"As paleographers, we are among the few who understand the differences in writing and dialect." Marie led them through the process. "Medieval French made use of complex abbreviations and ligatures that varied depending on the document. This is where forgeries become most apparent. An untrained reproduction artist may understand the nuances of the language within the period but . . ."

"--they would not understand the codes." A voice at the doorway interrupted.

"They would not understand the codes." Marie repeated the words and made her way towards the man now standing in front of them. He was dressed in a fine suit, but his air was that of a soldier. No, Marie thought, an officer.

"Colonel Philip Millar." He tipped his cap to the crowd, showing off his cropped mane of thick auburn hair, then bowed toward her. His Kensington accent was smooth in her ears.

Marie noted the smart, well-shined state of his shoes, his bright, well-bred smile, and turned to Cloutille, who shrugged, before addressing him. "You'll have to excuse me, Colonel. We weren't expecting you."

"No, I suppose not," he said. "I just came in from London."

The quality and perfect press of his suit told her he hadn't just gotten off of a plane. Why would he lie, Marie thought.

"Go back to work. I've just come to admire your process." The colonel sat in her chair, right leg stretched while observing the team.

Marie signaled to Paul to pour the man a coffee.

"You might have given us at least an hour. We've hardly made it through the first crate." She waved at the circle of linguaphiles to break apart and return to their duties.

"Have you not been here since dawn?" Philip chuckled.

Marie stiffened. She knew her early hours were an open secret, but this stranger's knowledge concerned her. "Insomnia has its benefits."

The team continued, preparing documents for transfer to the Bibliothèque nationale. Others returned several palm-sized prayer boxes from the 1200s to their original glass cases.

"I hear you had a nice little surprise this morning," Philip said.

Again, Marie paused. He knew about the de Bingen crate. "So you're here to investigate me?"

Philip chuckled again. "Whatever could you mean, Dr. Guerrant?"

"Well, you know, saving German history."

"From the Germans." His matter-of-fact tone followed by a shoulder shrug disarmed her.

Marie continued working. "Hildegard de Bingen was one of the most brilliant women of the Middle Ages. To saddle her with such, such . . . I knew we could get them out. Just didn't want anyone destroying her work."

Philip held a hand up and looked around. "I couldn't agree more. The sooner this Sibyl nonsense ends . . ."

Marie's heart began to thump hard in her chest. Who was this man? How did he know de Bingen had been tied to the Sibyls by the Germans? "Can I see your orders, please?"

Philip passed her an envelope with the mark of the British Special Operations Executive on it. "Did you not get my inquiry?"

Marie eased and considered the SOE communique in her pocket. He must have come to her warehouse because of La Joconde. It made sense arriving unannounced and with knowledge of the Sibyl, as the Nazis had always considered the painting a potential Sibylline artifact.

"My office is upstairs." She stood. "However, maybe you can help me with a mystery first. It will just take a moment."

Philip gave an almost inaudible huff, but obliged her request with a smile.

"I'm assuming," Marie tapped a finger, "that you've been in the middle of efforts to recover artifacts."

"That's fair."

They gathered around the book of hours. Marie's spectacles, fitted with small magnifiers, sat on the point of her nose. They sharpened her gaunt features as she recounted the evidence for him. "Did your teams go through the pieces at Château de Brézé outside of Saumur?"

Philip cleared his throat, bending to look closer at the jeweled piece. "A fake?"

"I'm surprised, really." Marie leaned back in her chair, arms crossed. "There is no equal to the original of this. No other metalworks like the book of hours from François premiere exist. I'd have thought we'd have stronger documentation on its movement or at least the placement of replicas."

"There are reasons we rely on masters such as yourself," Philip continued. "I suppose it's good then that you found this one."

"Or bad. I suggest you put men on it as soon as possible."

"I'll cable and determine the whereabouts of the original." Philip cleared his throat again and stepped in to whisper. "Doctor, I really do need to speak with you."

Marie offered a perfunctory smile. "Of course you do."

Chapter 3

AESMEH

APRIL 30, 1519
FONTEVRAUD ABBEY, FRANCE

A missive from the royal court at Amboise fluttered in my hand as I broke into a run toward the chapter room of the Royal Abbey of Fontevraud. I attempted to blacken my mind, to halt the glimmers—visions I alone could see. Fire, ash, so many dead. I recited dull passages from manuscripts and formulas from the kitchens to block out the faces of men marching, the twisted pain of mothers, children ripped from their arms . . . I rushed through the cloister, faintly aware of the narcissuses, tulips, and yellow roses blooming, the wisteria transforming the arches and long, covered walkways into tunnels of purple.

At the ancient stone cistern on the edge of the cloister where the waters of the Royal River sprung up, I forced myself to stop. My hands burned as I washed—a requirement for seeing Fontevraud's Abbess—amongst the silent sisterhood. Twenty-seven in all, they stood robed in the violet tunics of the Sibylline Order, all but their plain faces draped in heavy linen. Behind their reverent stares, I sensed a grave concern for my panic. For a moment, I mistook it as doubt in my abilities. However, they knew, as well as I, that knowledge of what shall come to pass was as much my curse as it was my calling.

"Fire." I repeated the word as my hands lingered in the sacred water of the circular basin and the glimmer shot through my mind. The burning ramparts of the French King's royal residence at Château Amboise filled my thoughts. That had to be what I saw. There was no other explanation for it. My bones ached from the effects of the vision, and my breath came in stutters. The unopened missive tucked under my arm left me dreading all tomorrows.

I dashed past the refectory and dormitories into the gardens that kept the population of Fontevraud fed. The low sprouts of red amaranth and delicate spring lettuces had just begun poking through the soil. I tore through them, chaperoned by an elder sister. We moved, wordless, without pause, until we alighted upon the kitchens and a door leading downward. Renee de Bourbon, the Abbess of Fontevraud, waited at the bottom of the catacomb stairs.

Even for those such as myself, with whom she took immense personal care, a call to her side proved rare and cause for my full attention.

"Come." She waved me down into the cool stonework where our dead had been interred for ten centuries. The Abbey built atop it had long sheltered our activity, cloistering the Sibylline from a world that tried to end us.

As we approached, the sister accompanying me offered the Abbess the parchment I'd received. "As soon as it arrived, the glimmers rose up," she reported. "Since then, Sister Aesmeh speaks of nothing more than fire."

The Abbess refused the paper and thrust a leather glove onto each of my hands. She stared at me with vibrant blue eyes, so different from the near black shade of my own. The visions in my head had settled enough for me to speak.

"Désolé, Mother Abbess. I intercepted a rider from Amboise on my walk this morning. He said Monsieur Melzi sent for me. All I see is Amboise. It is burning." I refused to accept what had risen up in the glimmer. "This cannot be correct."

"Did you read the message?"

"No." I trembled. "As Sister Thumé shared, the moment I laid hands on it my mind was set ablaze."

"You, of all of us, know the sight does not betray." Her strong words echoed against the cavern carved from tufa stone as she went to open the missive. The Sibylline had begun to gather, their foreboding eyes watching, their keen ears listening. "I fear . . ."

A woman with hair as white as her skin, cloaked in an emerald green robe made from velvet, interrupted. The Abbess took from her another unopened parchment. She broke the seal, read its contents, and sputtered, ashen-faced. "The Harimtu spies have confirmed it. Master da Vinci and our Dear One have vanished."

My spirit sank. Two Amyntas guards caught the Abbess as her knees gave out. It pained me. I forbid myself to consider her less capable of guiding me in a state of such fragility. I'd always seen her as a brutal woman. She fought against the corruption of men, traveling the length of France building alliances to secure the place of the Sibylline once again. Those at Fontevraud not initiated into the Sibylline mysteries despised her rule of silence. Her oath of loyalty, if broken, meant certain death. The Abbess had sent our armies of all-female Amyntas warriors after kings. She had negotiated holy edicts with Popes. Few, beyond the sisterhood, did not quake at the mention of her name. She was revered and feared. At that moment, however, she stood before me as a scared, old woman despite her forty-three years.

An Amyntas brought the Abbess a drink from the sacred cistern. With one sip, her strength returned. The violet-robed women moved into the crypt, surrounding us. Their silence pierced me like thorns through my skin, as they communicated to one another without words. I was never spoken to directly, not allowed to enter the quiet.

I stood while their eyes darted back and forth. Several stormed off. The others nodded at me. "Me-kädmen anina il'ati," each whispered, one-by-one, before the Abbess sent them away.

How many times had those words fallen from my lips? "Me-kädmen anina il'ati," I whispered to each as they passed. In service to the Great Mother, indeed. At that moment, I understood they acknowledged not only our collective service to the Sibyl, but also their service to what I would soon become.

The Abbess and I moved quickly through the tunnels, side-by-side, without even a single torch to light our path. I kept my hand in position along the wall, letting it move across the lines carved into it. Every so often, it ran over a circle with a carving of a crown inside it. I knew the Abbess led us both to the Royal River. My ears perked at the constant rush of water. I stepped down a narrow, steep set of stairs. At the bottom, torches lit the stone dock, and a flat-bottomed boat awaited us in the underground waterway.

"You must go." The Abbess fit me with a wool cloak. Cinching the hood tight, she pressed my obsidian curls back behind my ears.

I understood her haste. All my life, it had been my duty to keep our Dear One safe because I, alone, had the ability to reveal the identity of the one who would take my place. Long ago, the Sibyl would simply name her successor at the appropriate time. Since the Schism, the women who came before me toiled with such effort to find me. Such knowledge could not afford to have to be rebuilt again should something happen to me.

"Women died," The Abbess said. "So many women died so that you could rise, so that you and the Sibyl after you could rise. We cannot risk anything at this precarious moment."

She adjusted the clear, crystal seal that hung around my neck. The Seal of Amərətāt, the only one of the nine Seals of Annach that remained at Fontevraud after the Schism. It activated my glimmers, and its impact on me was, indeed, why I was brought to the Abbey; how my path became that of the next Sibyl.

"We cannot fail," the Abbess said. She knew my life was in jeopardy, but far more important, she knew the knowledge of the Sibyl to come after me was at an even greater risk of being lost.

"Surely, it is more prudent for Maurine or Tommaso to conduct such a search," I told her.

The Abbess thrust the letter from Melzi, along with that from our spies, toward me. "This goes beyond a simple search. The Harimtu believe a traitor is amongst our people in Amboise."

"You cannot believe a woman of the Order . . ."

"Of course not. This is a man's doing." The Abbess grew terse.

A pair of Amyntas entered. The women had traded the velvet tabards they wear at the Abbey for thick peasant capes, heavy boots, and reinforced leather vests with brass buckles. Such protection spoke to the grave nature of our plight.

"I am not prepared for this." I knew otherwise. My skills at manifesting the glimmers had become formidable. Some women with such abilities could tell if a man lied. Some knew what herbs to combine for healing. I had always known a person's past by simply touching what they touched. I had begun to see their futures as well. It was not the visions from which I wished to keep myself. The Abbess knew and ignored my concerns. I slipped on a pair of leather boots for the first time since the winter festivals of Saturnalia. "Desolé, Mother Abbess. I will do what you ask, but how am I to face Melzi again?"

"You understood the cost that came with the vows."

I did, indeed, understand. Francesco Melzi was never mine. His duty was to Master da Vinci. Mine, to the Sibylline. Yet, my heart remained tender.

"Can it not wait two more sunsets?" We were, indeed, just days shy of when I was to leave Fontevraud in a day-long ceremonial procession that would see me from one sort of isolation to another. At that time, I would enter the great temple of the Sibylline to train for a year and then emerge as the Sibyl of Amboise—the first oracle to rise up and serve humanity in one thousand years.

"This break in your confinement is more than a mere interruption. I send you forth because, if I do not, it threatens our very existence." The Abbess' eyes flashed with anger. "La Joconde is the key to our future. Without her, the Sibylline will most assuredly die out."

"I thought I was the key."

"You are, for now. But, tomorrow is never guaranteed." The Abbess grew quiet. "We must serve the collective."

I knew better than to provoke her ire and attempted to distract us both from my impertinence.

"Maybe Master da Vinci is just off exploring a curiosity," I lied. The missive I intercepted had told me enough. The memories left behind on it from Melzi lit my insides.

The Abbess sighed. "One is never truly prepared to undertake the difficult work of the just."

She often spoke in this manner when my mind wandered to places that did not align with her requirements. It irritated me. "No riddles. Not now."

"There are no riddles, my dear, only truths that you alone have the ability to reveal—and change."

Her acknowledgment of my powers and responsibilities lay like a boulder upon my chest.

"I know how important he is to you." The Abbess seemed to read my heart. "But he knew the risks."

"It is not enough time," I said. "Maybe we should delay the ceremonies."

The Abbess did not let my increasing sense of overwhelm sway her. "Retrieve our Dear One, then Master da Vinci, if possible. Lady Marguerite and Sister Maurine will steer you clear of Melzi. You must enter the temple at the prescribed hour. We cannot wait another five hundred years."

Along the river, women of the Heliade Order lined its banks. The light which illuminated the water rose from their palms. The scent of damp limestone made me light-headed. So many depended upon me. "What if I fail?"

"Know that I would never send you ahead if it were not our only option. You alone can find our Dear One and get her to the temple."

The Abbess placed her pale hands upon my olive cheeks and drew me in. We spoke in the manner she had done so with the other sisters—without uttering a word.

You knew there would be tests.

Her voice echoed in my head.

I had said my farewells. It is cruel.

I cannot trust anyone else. The Abbess continued. *Others think they know the power of the Sibylline. They will try to control it as men always have. They will fight us for it without remorse. You are the only one strong enough to remain beyond their reach.*

I bowed and kissed her cheek. What more could she expect after condemning me in such a way? She heard my thoughts and placed a hand on my heart.

Trust in your sight. Only then will the Sibylline be released from our occupation and all will pay reverence to the Great Mother once again.

Chapter 4

MARIE

MAY 2, 1945
PARIS, FRANCE

Marie wrapped up assigning tasks to her team. The light streaming through the windows of the warehouse grew in intensity as Philip waited for her in the hall, his back to the half-open door. She filled two tin cups with coffee and made her way into the foyer.

Philip took his cup with one hand, placed the other on her shoulder. He then slid another small envelope into her clammy palm.

"What is this?" Marie took it.

Suddenly, a crack and a shatter rocked the hall. A man howled. Others shouted commands. A pair of soldiers dashed across the museum corridor. Another wail erupted. Marie tucked the papers hard under her arm and broke into a sweat. Her lungs seized; her breath caught. Her mind spun out . . . It is February . . . Dogs chased down a woman, an Allied spy, captured in Belgium . . . A gunshot went off . . . The woman collapsed after soldiers tortured her for an entire day . . . A hand on Marie's arm brought her back into the moment.

"Colonel." She cleared her throat and straightened her suit jacket.

"Ghosts spooking you? And, it's Philip." He turned toward the main hall. The crate holding Michelangelo's Rebellious Slave had collapsed on the makeshift wooden ramp—constructed to get it up forty stairs—and then slammed onto a worker's foot. "Looks like a slave rebellion."

"Very funny." Marie welcomed his easy manner.

"At least I got you to laugh." Philip offered his arm.

Marie took it and smiled. He made no fuss over her nerves and, for this, she was pleased and grateful. She had meant to ask about his own injury—a limp that explained his plain clothes rather than a uniform. However, her attention turned to the crowd rushing toward the worker yelping in pain. She relaxed. "There are still a few things that get me."

"It'll ease in time."

"Of course." Marie fidgeted with her suit. Again.

Philip stopped in the middle of the hall and pulled a picture out of his pocket to show her. "My sons, Henry and Benjamin."

"Soldiers. You must be proud." Marie admired the photo of the young men in uniform. "Where are they now?"

"Dead," Philip's voice was soft and tender.

"I'm so sorry." She put a hand on his forearm.

"Please, no pity." But Philip did not retreat from her touch. "I just wanted you to know that I understand. I know what . . . What others are capable of. You were beyond brave."

"I'm not so sure any more." Marie scratched at her neck, eyes turned away. She couldn't bear the thought that her imprisonment may have caused Serah's death.

The pair headed to the staircase leading to Marie's office. Along the way, several smaller statues were being uncrated. A worker removed one of the panels from a wooden box less than a meter tall. Marie released Philip's arm and moved in to inspect.

"May I?" Peeking inside, she sized up the contents.

The worker stepped back to let her get close. He picked up the piece with his gloved hands to show her. "It's a Jean-Jacques Caffieri. She arrived this morning with the others."

"The Erythrean," Philip muttered.

"You know your Sibyls." Marie's curiosity piqued. It was little more than half-past ten and already the Sibyl had consumed too much of her day. "I didn't realize you were a scholar."

"Not even close," Philip said. "Only privy to, well, the impact of belief on the minds of others."

Marie noticed a retreat from his previous warmth, but who could blame him? If he read even half of what she reported to the Allied teams on the Nazi effort at Ravensbrück, he knew of the unspeakable acts committed.

They stood, silent and drawn in. The statue was no taller than a young child, but its marble features were commanding.

"You know, it's rumored they controlled the fates of kings and war-lords with their predictions," Marie recounted. "Their power proved so great that even Michelangelo immortalized five of them on the ceiling of the Sistine Chapel. I used to tell Serah stories of them. The great oracles of ancient history who each lived a thousand years. She couldn't get enough."

"Your daughter?"

"Yes, she . . ." Marie cleared her throat. "I haven't seen her since the day the Nazis put me on a train."

"It looks like we have much in common," Philip said. "Don't give up hope."

Marie stepped back from the statue, heavy with all that the day's events had forced her to remember.

"Do you mind if I ask you some questions about what you discovered?" Philip clicked his tongue and grimaced. "Did you ever find anything that could have bolstered the Nazi belief that the Mona Lisa was the key to this modern Sibyl?"

They began walking down the wide, marble-tiled hall. Marie exhaled hard. "Nothing other than what I've already stated in my reports. The SS was obsessed with obtaining the journals of Francesco Melzi."

"Why?"

"They thought the journals could decipher a key the painting is thought to contain."

"And?"

"And what? They don't exist."

"You are sure?"

"What is it you need from me, Colonel?" Marie watched him, worried about what came next.

"Are you up for some field work?" Philip nodded before offering a salute. "I've got a job only Dr. Marie Guerrant can handle."

"I doubt I'm the only paleographer in your circles."

"Dare I say, the only one with any true skill." Philip paused outside her office.

"Don't butter me up, Monsieur. What do you want?"

"Your mind, of course." His eyes blazed.

"There is news then?"

"A bit." He grimaced. "It seems our beloved beauty with that sublime smile has gone MIA."

"What do you mean?" A sick panic settled over Marie. "She's on a transport. I have communiques."

Philip shook his head.

Marie read over the orders. Her eyes shot up to Philip's. She had to get to her team, sort out what they could do. "You'll have to excuse me, Colonel."

"Slow down, doctor." Philip reached for her. "No one's finding her by themselves."

Chapter 5

AESMEH

APRIL 30, 1519
ON THE LOIRE RIVER, FRANCE

I caught my shoe on the edge of the toue cabanée as it bobbed in the underground canal leading out to the Loire River. Reaching out, I anticipated the smack of my hands against the boat's damp deck. Instead, one of the Amyntas caught me and a glimmer lit up as my cheek brushed across her bare arm. A simple, fleeting moment. Yet, it was enough for me to have borne witness to her life, so very different from my own.

Sibylline warrior women have always provoked enough discomfort in me to keep my distance. They are the only faction of the Order allowed to fight and procure weapons. The Asu, Metradora, and women of my own sect, the Heliades, cultivated our mental faculties, abilities to forge bonds with the elements, and those of the healing arts, while the Amyntas cultivated the physical. The Abbess, and all Abbesses before her, insisted on the clear delineation between the weapons—mental and physical—with which we fought. Amyntas did not live on the grounds of Fontevraud. Their mindset, the Abbess reminded me often, was cultivated to defend against the rage of men. However, a mind that perfected the art of killing had no place amongst the day-to-day lives of the Sibylline.

I ran my hand along the water to clear the Amyntas' memories from my mind. The natural current guided us through the darkness of the caverns. The canals had been carved out along the route of the waterway thousands of years earlier, even before Fontevraud—the true Royal River. In the darkness, the seal around my neck allowed me to become our sight, leading us out into the low morning light at Candes-Saint-Martin.

We weaved through the union of the Vienne and the Loire onto our regular route. For a moment, I was startled at the sight of a small boat. It seemed to be crafted from material I could not recognize, the two women in it bloodied. The light grew intense around them, then faded quickly. Another glimmer. Have I just seen tomorrow?

We could not waste the hours investigating, and caught the wind. The twelve leagues to Amboise would take much of the day. Most people made the trip by horse, a far faster means of travel. Despite a desperately short time to secure La Joconde and find da Vinci, prudence dominated our lives. The flat-bottomed boat was the safest mode of transport. I watched a line of rose-laden light widen across the horizon, and pulled my cloak close, redirecting the rays of morning sun. My birthright Heliade gifts for manipulating light had never been strong, and grew less so once the Abbess began my training. Though I adored using the small cache of light-keeping I maintained. Local fishermen familiar with every boat on the Loire caught the sun in their eyes and waved us on. We must have appeared as a cluster of nuns in tunics out for a morning fish. It was hard to question hungry, holy people, I supposed.

The sun lapped up the fluffy rolls of clouds. It played with the swans as they landed amidst dozens of cormorants that haggled over fish hatchlings. I breathed with ease and pricked my ears for the wind. I let my fingertips glide along the water once again.

"Stick to the starboard shore," I instructed. The Amyntas had de-cloaked in the growing heat. My eyes grew heavy. I could see the condition of the waterway well beyond our actual sightline, projecting myself to the very position in question; a skill I'd developed using the Seal, but only in recent months. "There's been a blockage in the river overnight."

"How far up? We cannot delay today, Sister Aesmeh." The Amyntas knew, as well as I, that our three-woman crew had no ability to handle major snags. "It would be charitable to know before we reach Tours if we require horses or not."

It was the first time beyond the grounds of the Mother House that I had projected my mind into the near future in such a way, and I could not center myself. "You shall get your answers soon enough."

The pair glowered at me. I did not doubt their concern for delivering me unscathed at such a crucial juncture. My journeys between Amboise and Fontevraud had once required little planning. I had lived an anonymous life. The men who unlatched the gates of castles had known nothing of me. Rivers on which we sailed had whispered nothing of my name.

No more.

Nearly all of France knew of the coming events. The Abbess had negotiated an alliance with the French King, securing his loyalty.

However, my very presence on the river, having abandoned the protection of Fontevraud, made us obvious prey. The future Sibyl was a gift to some, a threat to many. Those in power feared my abilities as much as they sought them out.

A disquiet shot through me. My otherwise silent guards moved the boat upriver with heavy poles to make up for the wind easing back. "I'm sorry. We should be clear up to Tours. Let us hope the river beyond does not find us contemptible."

It seemed I spoke the future with each word. Hours later, the sun that still bobbed high in the west disappeared as the boat navigated toward Île d'Or. A gray thunder cloud loomed over Amboise. The Amyntas grew in their silence as we approached. Their leather became damp from efforts to dock the boat on the island in the rain. Men bickered on the shore, determined to unload their catches and crates for inspection. A chill in the air and colorless skies drove us all to seek shelter.

I secured my gloves. The Amyntas helped me as we scrambled into a rowboat for the short ride to the main shore. The oarsman shoved off before I found my balance. I wobbled and breathed in. A thick-sweet, pungent zing of energy cut at my nose and made me jump from the fire it shot through me. It told me the scene was about to turn grim. We had to get off the island.

"Last boat. Storm's comin'," the oarsman said in English. "I'm not fishin' ya outta the river."

An Englishman along the Loire? The oddity struck me, but the wind whipped at my cloak and I had not the will to respond.

Not a minute later, the clouds unleashed. The oarsman's eyes flashed. His arms shot out from under his wrappings, gripping and twisting the tiny boat. The Amyntas stood balanced and steady amidst the waves. The woman to my left snapped the oar back and caught the Englishman in the head. The other Amyntas second oar and rowed us to shore.

A pair of women howled and rushed us. The Amyntas struggled to control the rowboat long enough to tie it to a dock ring. The rain punished me, its chill raking the skin beneath my cloak and tunic. The women tried to board, reaching for the oarsman when the boat bucked. I was pitched into the water, the river pulling me out past my waist.

"Sister Aesmeh is in the water!" One of the Amyntas shouted as she tossed me a rope.

I grabbed for it, but the undercurrent swept me end-over-end down the river.

A voice pierced the sound of rushing water as I attempted to surface. "She's past the bridge. Make haste."

I lost my breath, my head sinking below the waterline. Within moments, I was lifted from the water by strong arms. My eyes cleared. The Amyntas were chest deep in the Loire fighting the current to get me to shore.

"Aesmeh." The madrigal song of a voice I knew well bubbled up. "Aesmeh! Breathe."

My arms were stiff. My legs limp. The Amyntas laid me on a shore just feet from where the Amasse and the Loire rivers became one. Then, his touch. His warm, gentle breath lingered on my cheek. I didn't need a glimmer to tell me who was at my side.

"My Dearest Melzi." My words fluttered into the air. My heart filled my breast at the sight of Francesco Melzi. I reached to brush back his russet hair so I could admire his sea-green eyes.

"My Asfoora." He pulled away and wrapped me in a wool blanket.

I loved hearing him speak the name he'd given me in the privacy of his bed.

My bird.

I let the words in the language of my people echo in my mind. Not realizing the over-coverings on my hands were missing, I coughed out the remains of river water and tugged the wrap tight to my shoulders. A glimmer from the blanket shot through me. I was relieved to find it little more than the thoughts of a chambermaid who yearned for Melzi. I understood her fascination.

"Did you toss yourself into the river with the intent that the Fates would relieve me of both you and Master da Vinci?"

His words forced my mind back to the issue at hand. "The Abbess was right, then. He is gone?"

"Not gone," came a voice from behind me. "Taken."

I shot up, tossing the blanket aside. The Amyntas snapped to attention as the King's sister stood before us.

"Lady Marguerite, I pray, you leave her alone," Melzi said. "She almost died arriving here."

As much as I adored his devotion, Melzi's defense made me cringe. To speak in such a manner to one of our closest allies was foolish.

"Do you not have a Master to find, Monsieur Melzi?" Lady Marguerite never hesitated in her reproach of others. "The very one that vanished from the room next to yours, in a raid you slept through."

Her accusation stunned me. "Melzi! Master da Vinci is the only task we left under your care at Amboise."

Lady Marguerite nodded at him, lips pursed. "Leave."

"But, I . . ."

"Leave! Or I shall have you strapped to a pole in the middle of town, charged with conspiracy."

Melzi didn't even look at me. He stomped off as Lady Marguerite's maids rushed me from the shore and into a passage beneath the streets.

As soon as the dark of the walkways settled in, they cut the wet clothes from my bones. Before I could protest, the light of the Heliades surrounding me penetrated my limbs. An emerald velvet bodice and a shimmering golden gown took away the chill, and a wrist-length pair of soft leather gloves covered my hands. My skin warmed as two women secured my sleeves and others called the light. I took a linen cloth from one of the servants and blotted my hair. Within moments, my being was restored and I once again found myself speeding through corridors. "What do we know?"

"Master da Vinci was attacked in his workshop." Lady Marguerite shooed the women off, pulling me to the side. "But you already know they were after far more than him."

Chapter 6

MARIE

MAY 2, 1945
PARIS, FRANCE

Marie could hear Philip's boot heels clicking against the marble floors in an odd rhythm, as he raced down the hall after her. She didn't want to concede to him. He was, however, correct. She didn't have enough information or the manpower to do anything about this herself. Philip could get her men, weapons, whatever she needed. She stopped near the door to a gallery where workers were re-installing Persian funerary masks and flipped around.

"Stolen?" she asked. "I thought she was being monitored."

Philip tried to back up too fast and stumbled. He caught himself and swept dirt off his pants. "More, well, we lost her."

"And the difference is?"

He sighed as they continued walking. "Where to begin?"

"I read the files. La Joconde was in the south."

Philip cringed and shook his head. "Not since August of last year."

"She's been missing for nine months?"

"She's been moving for nine months."

"Why did you not tell me sooner?" Marie steamed, marching back toward her office. "That's why we made all of those copies to begin with. What was the point of committing forgery, letting good people die, if you are just going to go and misplace the original? For Christ's sake, Philip, half of Europe's great works have burned. What if she is a pile of ash?"

"You've got to settle down." He stopped. The gentle pressure of his hands on her shoulders calmed Marie. "You were recovering. We thought we had her in hand, but last week all teams went dark and my men in Amboise were attacked."

"Amboise? Just get the army to oust the Germans." Marie hated having to delay her search for Serah any longer. "I'm sure it will be a quick fight."

"There's more activity in Amboise than them. It's why we need you." Philip stopped and leaned against an empty wall as workers pushed a series of ancient Sumerian tablets past them on old medical gurneys. "We're pretty sure all reproductions of the Mona Lisa, as well as the original, still exist. But, no one with a heartbeat seems to know where she is."

"And what am I good for here? I can read the words of the dead, not raise them."

"Don't sell yourself short."

"A séance then?" Marie raised an eyebrow at Philip.

"The team with her was Maquis," he said. "Maybe you can fire up your connections and track them down?"

"Introductions to Maquis leadership, that's quite the request, Colonel."

"I wouldn't ask it if it wasn't imperative. The Maquis must be looking for their people too. No one abandons a deep-cover mission like this without leaving some sort of trail behind."

"Unless they are dead." Marie entered her tiny office.

"Let's hope to hell that's not the case. I want you to take a look at these." Philip pulled out a chair for her and they settled around the round wooden table in the middle. He pushed a file toward her. "We think they may be notes from the team moving the Mona Lisa."

"This is all you found of them?" Marie noticed the imprint of a sword and the odd-shaped letter V of the British Special Operations Executive stamp. She slipped off her suit jacket and rolled up her sleeves. She thought of who may have been on the team. Did she know them? Were they prisoners? Were they dead? Did they know anything about Serah? "Looks like you need soldiers, not scholars."

Philip cleared his throat. "I need scholars who know what soldiers do, especially soldiers with certain goals."

"You mean the Sibyl." She backed away.

"The fact that you survived is a testament to your abilities."

"Or men's obsessions."

"You had a few things in your favor, others did not."

"How can you say that?"

"I just mean you were, well, more valuable."

Marie hated that it was true. "I may not have worn a yellow star, but Nazis value no lives but their own."

"Of course. I'm sorry." Philip's voice dropped low as he opened the folder in front of them and spread out the photos. "The Maquis codes in these documents, would you know them?"

Marie straightened and bristled, her palm gripping her forearm. "You cannot expect me to go back in after everything."

"You'll have every resource at your disposal."

"Philip, stop! This is too much!"

He paused, but would not relent. "Who am I supposed to get? We need your smarts, your connections to the Resistance."

Marie shuddered. "You understand this Sibyl myth has no merit at all, right? No one can see the future."

"For a fake, she's cost us all a hell of a lot," Philip said, patting the pocket with his son's pictures in it. "You know as well as I do what we risk as long as the Mona Lisa isn't hanging in the Louvre. Men will never stop as long as the Sibyl is out there."

"The Sibyl is not out there." Despite her words, Marie understood. She and Philip had lost all that they loved to this obsession.

"Please." Philip stood and again offered her the military orders to join the next convoy. "We need you."

Marie snatched the paper from him, stuffing it in her suit jacket pocket. "Get out. I've got work."

"You're in, then?"

"I'll think about it."

"That's all I can ask."

Chapter 7

PHILIP

MAY 2, 1945
PARIS, FRANCE

Philip never believed in ghosts. Floating specters appeared only as petty superstition, the sort of cockamamie story told to children and those susceptible to religious flights of fancy. The walking dead, though, he knew them quite well. Men lost themselves in the horrors of the trenches. Not him. Not ever. The mantra played over and over in his head.

He kept the bullet that had shattered his femur on a keychain. He made the field surgeons save it. He wanted to remember who shot him, and why they murdered his sons as he watched.

Philip grumbled under his breath. Running a finger along his collar to loosen it in the late-morning heat, he stood looking out over the Seine River along Pont Neuf. He knew those who had stolen Henry and Ben's lives, and what drove them to it. That's why Marie was so important to his plans. She hated this Sibyl business.

He had followed her across the bridge on foot hoping she wouldn't notice him. Philip's leg aches more than usual, the stifling humidity wobbling his knees. With nowhere to conceal himself above the calm waters of the river, his usual efforts at a straight gait proved too much. It helped, he told himself, that Marie also intended to remain anonymous.

The Eiffel Tower shimmered in the distance and he stood for a moment, heaving a sigh. Dr. Marie Guerrant made so much sense to him, yet none at all. He ticked through what he knew of her SOE records. Once married to a high-ranking member of the French Communist Party. Captured as a political prisoner and shipped off to Ravensbrück. Then, there was the issue of Marie's daughter, Serah.

Philip understood what it was like returning home to find little more than memories. It was, in a way, why he remained in Paris—to avoid a return to nothing. Henry and Benjamin were dead. A pat of his pocket assured him the last photo of them remained secure.

He rubbed at his eyes, attempting to keep the scene of the soldiers, and the beast that killed them for the ridiculous relic he'd sent them to retrieve, from replaying in his head. That day, Philip learned more than he'd ever considered plausible about the oracular Sibyl. He'd also learned the only way to make sure the deaths of his sons mattered was to destroy every remaining trace of the Sibyl. He counted on Marie to see it that way too.

Philip admired her. Men were savage, especially men who lusted after something. Ravensbrück was hell. All the reports he'd read noted Marie's efficiency at tracking military activity, how she'd thrown the Nazi's off-track with forgeries and false translations. Thoughts of the Nazi torture chamber at Ravensbrück made the bile rise in Philip's throat.

Marie's forced service to the Third Reich resulted in reams of intel along with dozens of people, parchments, and journals successfully smuggled out of the warehouses at Ravensbrück. It proved her brilliant and fiercely devoted to France. Philip also knew her wounds were raw, dark shadows. She had the fortitude to survive and get on with life. A determined woman, however, might not suit him well, depending on whom she served.

He flinched at the sight of Marie hailing a pousse-pousse as he stood just feet from the end of Pont Neuf. He watched, purposeless and panting, as a man got in beside her and the driver pedaled them down the street.

Philip sat on a bench and loosened his tie after crossing to the edge of the Left Bank. A black Citroën Traction Avant pulled up beside him moments later.

"Waiting for someone?" The perfect auburn victory roll announced Cloutille as she hopped out of the driver's seat.

Philip kissed her on each cheek and got in. "Let's see what she's up to."

The car sped past row after row of Haussmann-style buildings, and turned off down a nearly empty roadway. Philip pointed at the pousse-pousse rolling down the road. "She's obviously hiding something."

"You can't expect her to come back and ignore everyone from her old life."

"I'm counting on her not ignoring anything at all," he continued.

"Do you think it's Marchant?"

"Of course it's Marchant."

Noam Marchant had been a Paris cop turned Resistance leader. Philip knew his reputation and counted on Marie's loyalty to old friends.

"He hasn't been seen in more than a year," Cloutille said.

"If there's anyone that man would surface for . . ."

"What if he tells her?" Cloutille stopped.

"All the better." Philip considered the potential fall out if Marchant got his hooks in Marie first. "We need access to the Maquis to find Serah Izem and the painting. Besides, do you really think Marchant is going to tell her what he did?"

"It's her daughter."

"Marchant needs Serah just as much as we do at this point. She is the only leverage any of us have. And, even if he does tell her . . ."

"You can't just kill people indiscriminately," Cloutille interrupted.

"Of course not," Philip said.

He understood Cloutille's warning. No one liked messes. She'd been an efficient watchdog, recovering bits and pieces of Sibyl lore that needed to be destroyed from raids through her well-developed channels as a former SOE spy. He liked her demeanor; always bound to duty, playing required roles. She took calculated risks and, after helping him escape the compound where his sons were killed, had become his second in command.

"I'll keep us out of sight," Cloutille turned the car along narrow cobbled streets.

As they drove, Philip watched a crowd gathering around four men busy shaving the heads of two women. Three gendarmes stationed nearby ignored it all.

"Horizontal Nazi collaborators," he whispered. "They get what they deserve."

Smoke from a smoldering fire in the courtyards of the Sorbonne clogged the air. Philip wondered what exactly they were burning. The French had taken to punishing anyone who worked with the Germans during the occupation. It was public, swift, and violent condemnation. He shuddered, then applauded the raw justice the French afflicted upon traitors and abettors. The chaos had made it easy for him to set up his own teams and stay off the radar of commanders who may have otherwise presumed him dead.

The pousse-pousse stopped near an open pit past the southern edge of Luxembourg Gardens. Philip watched as two men approached, took Marie by the arm, and made their way through a cut fence.

"There she goes. Double back," Philip said. "Stay alert."

Within minutes, he spotted another pair of men. They moved through the crowds at the Medici Fountain, then skittered into alleyways near Saint-Sulpice. "Stop!"

Cloutille pulled over, straightened her gloves, grabbed her handbag. "Shall I come?"

Philip nodded. They walked arm-in-arm, appearing as a military man and his young bride. He wished his wife, Alice, were at his side, then recalled the writ of divorce accompanying her last letter. She'd long abandoned him, he deduced, for her version of grief. Lost love, however, had to wait.

This time, the heat and discomfort sharpened him. He counted four Maquis skulking down a thin roadway and followed, catching a glimpse of their black boots and tweed caps.

"Do you see them?" Cloutille whispered in his ear as he pressed her gently against a wall near Château de Colpach.

"Lunchtime rendezvous with the dead." Those caps and boots belonging to Maquis members piqued his attention. He and Cloutille had lost Marie. However, Philip didn't need to follow her to know who she was meeting as she slipped into the city's underbelly. "What are you doing with such men, Dr. Guerrant?"

Chapter 8

MARIE

MAY 2, 1945
PARIS, FRANCE

She checked the time. Quarter 'til twelve. Perfect. Marie's team had left the Louvre for a midday break. She headed out a side entrance leading toward Pont Neuf. The long morning lent itself to a long, quiet walk along the cool, flowing waters of the Seine despite the noon heat.

As she walked, Marie sorted through the news Philip had delivered. What had actually happened to La Joconde? Learning of the painting's disappearance left her mind churning. The Nazis had always coveted the piece, believing it housed the identity of a modern Sibyl. Had they decided to make one last attempt at acquiring the painting and a living prophetess? There was no one to find, she told herself. However, the Maquis didn't go dark without a reason.

Marie's blistered feet ached. She hadn't hailed a pousse-pousse, but one stopped right beside her.

The driver of the covered rickshaw handed her a bunch of muguet from the bucket in the back. "Black boots are moving."

She looked down. His pant cuff was turned up to reveal a red Cross of Lorraine stitched into the lining.

"Now? Here?" Marie knew the code words.

She recognized the baker, whom she knew had Maquis ties, as he waved at her from a nearby bouquiniste. Under his arm was a package of books wrapped in paper and secured with twine. He moved in and helped—more like commanded—her to take a seat in the rickshaw. Marie took a deep inhale, pressing the flowers up to her face, and glared at him.

The baker kissed her cheek and whispered in her ear. "Les murs ont des oreilles."

Marie knew better than to react to his warning: the walls have ears. Others were listening. The Maquis only went to the trouble of pulling someone off the street when something serious needed attention. She smiled at the baker, who retrieved a book from his pile and thumbed through it. Fiddling with the paper that held Philip's orders, Marie noted how the colonel had tried to remain charming while delivering them. However, she understood what the military orders inferred. Military orders, she repeated in her mind. Refusal proved tantamount to insubordination.

Marie tugged at her hair. Dismissing his offer was neither sensible nor smart. But there was no way she was going to Amboise, not as long as it meant going back into a war zone. And not as long as the whereabouts of Serah remained a mystery.

She scanned her surroundings, caught a glimpse of a pair of tweed caps, suddenly realizing they were near Jardins du Luxembourg.

Youth loitered with cigarettes hanging from their lips, pistols stuffed in the fronts of their pants, machine guns over shoulders. She shook her head. Marie had done the same with Jules years ago, albeit without the guns, long before they went off and got married without her father's permission.

Not that her father minded. Jules had been twenty-two when they met at the slaughterhouse where her father took her to learn to fight. She had been nineteen. They'd sneak out late at night, smoking, discussing politics and the proletariat.

Marie forced herself back to the present. The youth in front of her shot their guns into the air, shouting "Vive la révolution!" The pousse-pousse slowed.

"Conducteur." One of the men yelled at the pousse-pousse driver. "Conducteur!"

He pushed his stained jacket back to reveal a pistol before muttering. "Just stay quiet."

A Pistolet automatique modèle 1935A, she thought. His holster had a hand-stitched red cross. Everyone around her was Maquis. They came to a halt near an abandoned field just past L'hopital Cochin.

"Get out, now," the driver told her.

Two men rushed up, each taking her by an arm. The baker hopped out and took his pile of books in another direction.

"The catacombs?" Marie tried to confirm the meeting point. The driver didn't bother to respond and the pousse-pousse pulled away.

The tweed-capped pair grunted and walked her to the opening of a quarry where Marie shook free of their grips. "I know the way from here."

One of the men handed her a shoulder holster and waited. She knew it right away as she strapped it on and covered it with her suit jacket. Marie was pleased to have her weapon of choice back.

"Marchant?" she asked. The return of her blade confirmed who she was meeting. The man who delivered the weapon offered a single nod and retreated.

Marie hustled through a wide, hand-dug opening leading down into the catacombs. The heat of the day gave way to the sharp scent of urine and rotting potatoes. Too much like a tomb, she whispered to herself.

Feet first, she slipped through a hole and dropped into the tunnels. Makeshift orange lights made them appear more narrow than their true width. Limestone walls coated with graffiti, bullet holes, and dried blood made her think she was in the right spot. She turned a corner to land at a dead end lit with dozens of tall votives.

"Blessed Mother." Marie exhaled, crossing herself. "You snuck up on me."

Her skin itched at the sight of a life-sized statue of the Virgin Mary. Slowly her eyes adjusted. With its thousand years of graves and grottos, the catacombs had never lacked altars to the divine. She'd forgotten that people still prayed.

She doubled back and headed down another corridor. The sensation of watchful eyes weighed on Marie. An unexpected warmth of a phantom hand laid upon her shoulder; the low din of a far-away hymn; the faint scent of violet and rose mingled with piss and rot.

She made her way through the "streets," staring up at vertical shafts leading to manholes on Paris roadways above. Some had metal rungs. Some had remnants of grenade damage. Marie followed signs staked into the walls. She knew she'd be able to walk almost all the way back to the edge of the Left Bank remaining underground. Soon, the floors began to muddy her work shoes. The rush of water and chirping of rodents accompanied her in this deserted space.

"Where the hell are they?" Marie thought. Her ears perked at the hint of whispers down the corridor.

A head popped out from around a corner, a figure waved her down a better-lit corridor.

She hurried toward the man. "How far did you expect me to go before you showed up?"

"As far as needed." He pulled off a cap to scratch through his tight salt-and-pepper curls. Four others worked on maps. Piled behind them were German munitions, neatly stacked with their swastikas burned off. The tweed-capped pair from aboveground were already there.

"I told you she survived the camps." One of them punched the other in his arm.

Marie nodded with a warm smile.

Her host shewed them off and turned back, "Are you alright?"

"You could have come to the museum." She resented his nonchalance at forcing her underground. She had been locked up long enough.

"Ha, and get hauled off by Vichy disguised as victors?"

"You don't trust me?" Marie grew hot as her words came.

"Good Lord, woman. I don't trust them. We liberate Paris, the Allies hunt us down because we prefer communism over capitalism."

She knew he risked more in the daylight than she did in the dark. Politicians on every side wanted all Resistance factions brought under military control. "Grown paranoid of your own people, then?"

"Yes."

"Noam Marchant! I'll go then." She turned to leave, heels sinking into the muck.

"They didn't beat the spirit out of you, I see." The man's pale blue eyes, almost translucent against his dark olive skin, softened as he tossed her a pair of rubber boots. "Shit, you look terrible."

Marie smirked at him. "This is a lot of fuss for a reunion."

"I didn't expect to have to," Noam's gaze met hers, watery and bright. "How'd ya do it?"

"I followed our old route." She quickly switched her footwear to boots.

"No, I mean Ravensbrück. The guys bet me we'd be dealing with the boogeyman."

"Entirely corporeal." She pinched him. "They found uses for me."

"I knew you'd prove useful." Noam grinned. "I heard you got traded for Germans."

"Just like cattle," she said.

"A lot of women left behind?"

"Yes." Marie understood her fortune. Being French and Catholic had kept her out of the worst of the torture at Ravensbrück. She lived because of her smarts, yes, but also because she wasn't a Jew. That had brought her home while thousands of others continued to suffer or be killed. It made her sick. "Where'd you come in?"

Noam pointed down a newly dug corridor. He motioned for her to hand over her street shoes and began cleaning them with a rag. "It pops out at Rue Servandoni."

"More emptied Nazi bunkers?" Marie took her shoes back from him and set them on an empty crate while the men unloaded and cleaned weapons. Noam looked like he'd aged twenty years. She remembered him as a young father. He'd married a seamstress named Vera and had their daughter, Capucine, when Serah was twelve. Jules and Marie were Capucine's guardians. Serah had taken up the role of big sister and doted on the child as if she were family.

"More ways to get our work done without as many eyeballs," Noam said.

"Looks like you've taken up gun running."

He laughed. "There's a lot of people out there trying to save their own asses. You really should be more careful."

Marie shook him off, lifting the hem of her jacket back to reveal the shoulder holster with the knife strapped in it.

Noam nodded and grinned. "You know, a gun is a lot quicker."

"I'm better with a blade." Marie wasn't going to wait for him to get past the small talk. "Before you tell me why you dragged me down here, I need to find Serah. Run a line out to the Maquis down south or the FTP."

If anyone could get it done, she figured, it would be Noam. Her every hope was pinned on him having gotten her out, or at least knowing who did.

He kept cleaning and stacking weapons. "I heard you had a guest in your warehouse today."

Marie stiffened and nodded. "A British Colonel."

"SOE?"

"Yes."

"Wanted you to make contact with the Maquis?"

"He said the Maquis team with La Joconde had gone missing. That he needed me to go to the Loire Valley to help figure out what happened and get the painting back. Why?"

The men in the corridor stopped working for a moment until Noam gave them a hard nod. They each took guns and ammunition and left.

"Honestly, I really don't care about him right now. Where is Serah? Did you get her out?"

Noam grimaced. "She's in Amboise."

Marie shuddered and backed up. "What is she doing there?"

"I put her on a team."

"The transport team? With La Joconde?"

Noam hesitated. "It's not like she had parents who didn't teach her how to fire a gun or cut a man. Besides . . . "

"She's a child!"

"She's a twenty-year-old woman and a damn strong-willed one at that." Noam set the gun and rag down. "People were drawn to her. She had good instincts for avoiding the Waffen-SS. No one thought you were coming back after the first year at Ravensbrück. Jules was dead."

"Is she dead?"

Noam softened as their eyes met. He stepped out of the room and ushered her down the corridor. "Don't do this to yourself. I couldn't have stopped Serah from fighting if I'd put a gun to her head."

"I've been around your kind long enough to know otherwise."

"My kind is your kind. Remember that." He collected a pile of maps from the worktable in a room he stopped in as they walked. "Do you think any of us went looking for you?"

"It's not the same. You had to assume the Germans would . . . "

"Kill you? Yeah, we did."

Marie's heart pounded. "Serah wasn't with the Germans."

"We were all with the Germans. They ate off our dishes, lived in our houses, fucked in our beds. They held everyone in France hostage."

"You didn't return to the same world," Noam continued. "The Germans during the war were easy. We fought. We won. Surviving was the goal. Now, everyone is judge and jury as to whether you survive, whether you're the right kind of fighter."

"What about de Gaulle? He has good people."

"No, Marie. There are people. Goodness is circumstantial." Noam tossed guns from a pile to a man stacking them neatly, cautious of his left shoulder. "Allied or Axis, no government wants men with their own minds and the ability to fight."

"Unless, of course, those men are on their side." She smirked and picked up the last rifle, tossing it into the man's right hand.

Noam snorted. "Thank God you're coming around. I thought we'd lost you to those bureaucratic buffoons."

He pulled out an old, loaded Luger and handed it to her. Another man handed her a towel. Marie took it to wipe the weapon down. "Are you telling me Philip Millar has my daughter?"

"No. I'm telling you that Philip Millar thinks you can lead him to Serah."

"What use is she to him?" Marie recalled the file of Maquis codes Philip had given her to decipher.

"She'd been with us for a long time running reconnaissance on missions."

"She found something?"

Noam nodded. "Millar's men tried to take her in a raid three nights ago."

"He told me they were attacked?" Marie passed him the clean weapon.

"That, uh, might actually be true."

"How?"

"Last week, the Maquis team was set to handoff the painting. We'd turned over writings that had come up from Chenonceau to a British group led by Millar, at Amboise, a couple weeks earlier. After that, he told my team to only report to him."

"This is taking too long, Noam. Tell me what's going on."

"Millar thinks Serah knows something about some kind of ancient prophetess linked to the painting."

Marie's spirit sank. "The Sibyl?"

"He thinks they are connected," Noam said. "Serah, this Sibyl, and the painting."

"You've got to be kidding me?" Marie turned to face Noam. "All that kept me alive at Ravensbrück was knowing that Serah was not mixed up in this. I enabled the Nazis, ran rescue operations, endured all of it for the slightest chance to come home. And now you're telling me she's right in the middle of all of it."

"We can still get her back. Don't do this."

"Don't do what?" Marie asked. "That man stood in front of me this morning and told me not to give up hope. He showed me the pictures of his dead sons. Made me believe."

"She's not dead, Marie," Noam said.

"How the hell would you even know? I contacted you a week ago. You knew where she was. You knew I was here." Marie scanned the walls in search of markers to get her out. Now. She raced past the hanging meat, bins of potatoes, onions. She reached the metal rungs hammered into the wall that led up to the street, breathed in and turned to confront Noam, close behind her. "You thought I was one of them."

"No. It's just that we couldn't put an operation together until he made contact with you."

Marie settled, slightly, to hear Noam out. "Everything is heavily controlled," he said. "The military authorizes the convoys. They make deals with teams in the field. The Maquis, we're vigilantes. They're rounding us up. Putting us in prison."

Marie knew the French military had forced all Resistance factions to fold into one unit controlled by de Gaulle's Free France government. Still, Noam, a member of the newly-formed French Forces of the Interior, surprised her. "They can't have thought you would all join?"

Noam thumped his chest and turned up his pant cuff to reveal a red cross of Lorraine. "They didn't. I'm dead. Vera, Capucine, my whole family thinks I'm gone."

"Them, too," he continued. Three men down the corridor raised their hands and waved. "All vanished because men of power are men of power. It doesn't matter what side they're on. But we don't stop. We get back to work."

"I see." Marie sped through a series of strategic options. "Doesn't that make it easier for us to move undetected?"

"You're the only one that can get inside his operation," Noam said. "The Maquis can help, but our resources are spent and we've lost all contact with Serah."

"Does she have the painting?"

"No idea. Seeing this through with Millar and finding La Joconde is the only way any of us are ever going to get deep enough to get her out."

"You want me to go back in and play his game?"

Noam nodded.

"What if he has my daughter?" Marie's exclamation shook the men in the tunnel to attention.

Noam tried to pull her close.

"No!" Marie shook him off. "You don't get to comfort me right now."

The improvised metal sign pounded into the wall read Rue Servandoni. She started up the metal rungs hammered into the wall in front of her, then hesitated and climbed back down. "Give me your gun."

Noam handed her his Luger and shouted at one of his men. "Get her a box of bullets."

"Amboise is where you last saw her?" Marie tucked the gun next to the knife and emptied the sixteen bullets from the box into her suit jacket pockets. All sixteen. "Get your men organized. The convoy leaves in the morning."

Noam watched as she started her climb to the street. "It's good to have you back."

Chapter 9

PHILIP

MAY 2, 1945
PARIS, FRANCE

Philip and Cloutille moved through the crowd of uniformed French soldiers chatting up red-lipped women along the Seine. The heat, Philip thought, never stopped men from their pursuit. He wished the wispy clouds might cool the steamy air.

"Her Resistance ties are dangerous," Cloutille said.

"Possibly, but you can't tell me Dr. Marie Guerrant doesn't want the Sibyl gone. She's got reason to help us." Philip considered whether Cloutille's concern was warranted. He'd been right, Marie had lied to him. The men who'd gone down the hole at Rue Servandoni were deep-level Resistance fighters. Reservations or not, she remained the quickest route to Serah and the painting.

"I know you saw things, Philip. I know you believe something more than a bunch of trigger-happy Nazis killed your sons."

"They were obliterated," he said. "Nothing in this world could have done that."

"I get it, but Marie is not going to buy into destroying the painting and turning over her daughter to you."

"It's an issue, I agree." Stepping off Pont Neuf, he caught sight of Marie heading back to the Louvre. He pulled Cloutille into an alley to keep them out of sight and lingered on Marie as she made her way toward the Grand Palais. Philip noted the hat she never took off. Her bony fingers and sharp elbows. The high-necked suit covering brutal scars. This he knew from her file. "Such savage things. Is there no cure for this infection?"

"She's sure got you whipped up." Cloutille adjusted her victory roll and fixed her lipstick in the window behind them.

"You and I both know how important this is. Do you not want to be done with it all? The world has suffered enough for a thousand lifetimes."

"Is it the world, or you?" Cloutille asked.

Philip bristled. "If you are so underwhelmed by my intentions, why are you here?"

Cloutille paused. "We all want this done. It's also important that Marie Guerrant doesn't find you staring her down on Rue de Rivoli at one o'clock in the afternoon."

"Give me a bit more of your confidence, will you?" Philip knew Cloutille kept one eye on him, the other on Marie.

"I just want you to be smart about this. Not get caught up in any personal loss."

Philip gripped Cloutille by the neck. "Did you watch my sons die? Did you see their brains turn to mush? Did you see their limbs removed from their bodies?"

Cloutille shook her head, gasping for breath. Philip released her.

"All we have to do is make sure everything she needs is ready. Marie Guerrant is a brilliant, calculated woman. She's not going to take any risks, especially if she knows she's got her freedom at the end of it all." He kissed Cloutille's cheek. "If she does, we take whatever action necessary."

They reached the main hall of the Louvre and moved back into the gallery. Cloutille's eyes had grown serious. "I'll go prepare."

Chapter 10

AESMEH

APRIL 30, 1519
AMBOISE, FRANCE

Lady Marguerite and I made haste to get from the banks of the Loire up the lengthy hill toward Château Gaillard. To our right towered Royal Château Amboise, looming in its grandeur over the crowded cluster of merchant carts and shop fronts that struggled to feed, clothe, and arm the ever-growing number of French soldiers amassing in the fields beyond.

"Why so many men?" I asked.

"Your ceremonies have provoked a fervor." Lady Marguerite ushered me to a staircase that led to the corridors beneath Amboise. "Master da Vinci's disappearance is the last of many incidents of late."

I found the cool tunnels much more familiar than the commune above us. Bins of onions and potatoes, stacks of textiles, and loom benches lined the halls. Our footsteps echoed as we hurried along a torch-lit path. Although dimly lit, it was possible to use the etched lines along the walls to guide us through just as they did at Fontevraud. My sight landed upon what appeared to be an orange carved into the stone wall. Then another, and a third, all leading us to the safety of Château Gaillard, lying at the edge of the forest on the northern border of the commune.

Lady Marguerite remained silent, leading me up into the inner stone courtyard where the gates could be locked behind us.

The smell of hen's broth floated from the kitchens beyond us. Lady Marguerite ordered servant girls to set a simple table in the courtyard. Within moments we sat sipping the warm soup, nourishing ourselves with the meat of the birds.

"I advise we consider this as Charles scheming." Lady Marguerite turned to me, as if we had already spent hours in consultation with one another. "The valley floor shakes from the march of his sycophants."

"I feared as much," I said. "These petty skirmishes between King François and the Spanish whatever-he-is have shifted into threats of all-out war. The Mother Abbess should have known better than to assume those two would forgo power mongering in the light of my ceremonies."

"I do not believe a slight of her attention is the cause. My brother has turned desperate for this. The pope and his cardinals will soon declare the future Holy Roman Emperor," Marguerite continued. "With Master da Vinci missing, everyone is distracted."

"Classic strategy. Are the Sibylline interests secure?" I asked.

"Other than the obvious, yes."

"How does that not include La Joconde?" As I eased back in my chair, full-bellied and heavy-lidded, I spotted the emerald velvet robe belonging to a Harimtu spy. I waved her in to deliver her message.

"Me'kädmen anina ilati, Great Mother. Men are gathering outside Master da Vinci's workshop," she said.

"For what purpose?" Lady Marguerite inquired of the Harimtu.

I did not wait for her reply, and moved down the stairs, through a corridor I knew would get me closest to the walls of Close Lucé without being spotted. My host gave chase without another word. We rounded a corner. A figure blocked our path. It was the first person we had come across since moving beyond the river. I held my breath as the figure came out of the shadows.

"Mademoiselle Soudier." Lady Marguerite said, clearly relieved.

I could not be bothered with formalities. I flung myself into the arms of my dearest friend. Her burnt umber curls were pinned tight against her head, her tawny skin perfect and glowing, her hand warm on mine. "Sister Maurine!" I cried.

I indulged myself in the conviviality of our relations for a moment. However, it was not to last as I realized the women grew impatient with my delay.

"I missed her." I shrugged off their rolling eyes and tapping feet. "Am I no longer allowed to miss her?"

"Me-kädmen anina il'ati." Maurine handed Lady Marguerite and myself a blade. "Just forged. Nothing that will force you into one of your glimmers."

"Where did you get these? You know such implements are forbidden."

"The Mother Abbess cannot admonish us for protecting ourselves," Maurine said. "What if you had been wandering down here and came across a garrison rather than me?"

"I could have taken at least three. Lady Marguerite surely could handle two in that unwieldy dress of hers." I laughed and posed with the knife. We all burst out laughing. "It's you whom I would never want to cross."

The three of us locked eyes, sheathed our weapons, and spoke nothing more. Maurine was not wrong. The conditions at Amboise had deteriorated. We needed to protect ourselves at any price, even that of disobeying the Mother Abbess. We followed Maurine back the way we came, up a narrow, steep set of stairs. They opened onto the tall, narrow interior courtyard of Gaillard. The rain had come again, pouring down upon us. Yet, I found the thirty-foot-high walls, potted palms, and cherry-red doors leading to the wings of the house soothing, if only for a moment. As servants approached, the fierce, low voice of a man echoed violently against the stone.

Showing nervousness, Lady Marguerite whispered, "I shall see to my brother. Take the garden route to the Clos."

I retrieved a fresh cloak and a pair of high boots from a well-stocked alcove. The rain continued to lash down. I pulled the cloak tight against my shoulders, hoping for warmth.

"Great Mother." A young postulant holding a cup appeared along the walkway. Her left forearm bore two crescent moons separated by a single line—the mark of the Sibylline. She offered me the steaming tincture smelling of peppermint, honey, and lavender.

I took the soothing drink, but balked at the name she called me: Great Mother. No one could convince me to grow comfortable with such a name. It was a title I may have earned through twenty-five years of tutelage, yet to hear it used reverently chilled me. "Why must they do that?"

"Why deny them respect for you?" Maurine positioned herself beside me and we walked the grounds. "You are the firstSibylline who is not a Ba'alat to wear a Seal of Annach in twenty lifetimes. Let them have hope."

I pulled my sleeves tight on my wrists as we crossed the gardens and moved along the stone wall surrounding them. "I believe I preferred the cloister."

Maurine chuckled. "Your Amyntas are waiting for us, Great Mother."

Her formal words shook me.

"The postulants, I understand. Why, pray tell, are you so formal with me?"

"Will you please cease your challenge of this?"

"Will you please cease pretending like we have not pissed in those very bushes over there and tortured nuns with our games, and swam bare-breasted in the Amasse. You treat me as if we don't know each other's hearts."

Maurine, more than any other, understood. She, too, had trained the entirety of her twenty-five years under the tutelage of the Abbess. Her gifts were no less profound.

"Now is not the time." She pointed to the Amyntas standing guard at half a dozen points along our route. The horizon beyond the river was illuminated by the glowing campfires of troops, giving off the air of men in search of blood and wine. "Others must witness the Sibylline in full support of you. Do not be fooled. The Harimtu believe our position with the royal court to be far more precarious than The Abbess wants to believe. And I suspect you shall develop your own concerns after what you are about to see."

Chapter 11

MARIE

MAY 2, 1945
PARIS, FRANCE

Marie popped the manhole cover at Rue Servandoni, looked back down the hole at Noam, and straightened the jacket of her suit. The air slapped her with its heat. She moved quickly, staying tight to the buildings to avoid the brunt of the afternoon sun. Her eyes adjusted. She glanced up and oriented herself in the direction of Église Saint-Sulpice. Then, made a quick right, heading back toward Carrefour de l'Odéon to find another pousse-pousse to take her back to the Louvre.

Noam's words echoed as she moved beyond Pont Neuf. She wandered a bit, trying to make sense of it all. He was logical, and she preferred reason. Serah, trapped by Philip Millar, however, left her anything but rational. Marie knew Noam was right. She had to go back to the Louvre and play this game with Millar. She'd get on the transport to Amboise and do whatever it takes to find Serah.

Her chest ached. Marie hurried off the bridge and made a quick left up Rue de Rivoli. Within a block, she passed the red doors of Basilique Notre-Dame des Victoires. The urge to step inside overwhelmed her.

The handle unlatched with little effort. Her mind switched to Latin, pulling up Hail Marys and Our Fathers from her mental catalog. The scent from thousands of burning candles and myrrh wrapped her in comfort. She knelt beneath a statue of the Virgin Mary. Her eyes traced the ex-votos that covered every inch of the walls. She'd heard stories from the baker about the engraved bricks. The man spoke of soldiers devoting themselves to the Virgin Mary after facing death, having begged for miracles on the battlefield, which the Virgin granted. More and more war medals had appeared lately, army men and their wives giving thanks for returning home. It irritated her, this devotion to myth. It smacked, she thought, of the Sibyl. Yet, the desire to believe overtook her.

Marie knew it was foolish, this sort of hope. Prayer, she thought, never saved her from the whipping post at Ravensbrück, never spared a woman from the mad doctors who injected them with gangrene or drained their blood. However, she needed to keep hold of this hope that Serah survived. If she lost that, how far behind was madness? She lit a votive, scribbled Serah's name on a piece of paper, and slid it beneath the candle's base.

"Maybe," Marie whispered. "Just maybe."

Just as in the catacombs, a warmth that felt like invisible hands laid upon her shoulders offered comfort and an assurance no man could. She attempted to pray but gave in to memories instead.

Marie recalled moments spent in that very spot near the front vestibule. For forty-one years she upheld her Catholic duty. Before the Nazi's invaded, her mother and father owned a flat just beyond the Grand Palais, mere blocks away. She hadn't been back to see what remained. She hadn't even returned to see her old place in Belleville. Only four weeks had passed since her return, yet an eternity of loss enveloped her. For a moment, a vision descended upon her. A woman, a shadow, a tomb. She sobbed.

Three plump women in cotton headscarves and musty shawls cleared their throats as they waited their turn on the kneeler. Marie ignored them. Since the occupation began, she had not allowed herself to cry. Now tears offered such relief. One of the women stomped her foot until the priest near the main altar took notice, and frowned at Marie. Just past him, standing in the flickering light of the church vestibule, stood the woman from the incident in the street that morning. She lifted a hand in recognition, a soft smile forming on her face.

Marie wiped her tears and commanded herself to stand releasing the occupation of the kneeler to the women. She would not retreat into self-pity.

"Maybe." She locked eyes with the six-foot statue of the Virgin in the alcove and crossed herself, grateful, yet awkward, in the ritual after so long. "Just maybe."

Chapter 12

PHILIP

MAY 2, 1945
PARIS, FRANCE

Over his shoulder, Philip found himself being stared down. Cloutille had disappeared down the hall. A worker swept remains of straw and wood slivers from the floor. Philip turned to find the two-and-a-half-foot-tall Erythraean Sibyl, the one Marie had admired in the hall that morning, on a pedestal in the middle of the room.

A fog settled over Philip's eyes. He tried to follow Cloutille as she disappeared into the museum, but a disorienting scene manifested before him. He caught the scent of rain, of dead fish on the banks of a river, of fresh blood. Memories from the night his sons died never dulled. His ears rang. His pulse raced. His mind flashed to men in British uniforms lined up in the cloister of an abbey, and shot down—no, electrified—one after another. Ghosts.

He fought the weakening of his knees, gripped his fists, and let out a short shout.

It all vanished, leaving Philip and the marble Sibyl nose-to-nose. He fought a longing to know what prophecies she held on the stone tablet in her arms. Was she Herophile? The one said to have predicted the coming of Christ? Was she another, much older Sibyl? The one who foretold the destruction of Troy? Was she the same woman, somehow immortal? He studied the carved folds of the simple, elegant gown. Her marble face grew bright. So small, she was. Yet, she commanded the room. As a tear trickled down his cheek, Philip charged at her. He lifted her with all of his might, then slammed her against the floor of the gallery until her head split from her body. He stared at the marble pieces scattered across the floor. The Sibyl, he told himself, would never again be the most powerful woman in the world.

"Colonel Millar!" Cloutille rushed into the museum gallery. Hands on her hips, she looked down at the pieces of the statue. "We have trouble."

The sound of his name forced Philip to retreat from his rage. Cloutille handed him a sidearm and tucked a handgun in the back of her skirt. "That Sorbonne student you had me put on Marie's team, he came back early with one of the quay workers who unloaded a caravan last night. They claim to have the Melzi journals." Philip's eyes flashed at the Erythraean Sibyl a final time. "We best go, then."

The pair moved silently through the halls of the Louvre and into the storage room near the Department of Statuary. There, the student whom Cloutille had scolded for eating in the warehouse and another young man stood.

"Salut, Colonel Millar." Paul wore a tweed jacket and pants. A gray cap set jauntily on his wavy hair.

Philip had inserted Paul on Marie's team to watch for anything Sibyl-related coming through. He had been one of his snitches keeping tabs on rich bankers who moved items of interest through back channels. Young and brash, he was well connected and had a reputation for being able to find anything that had certain value to very certain people. The kid next to Paul smelled like rotting fish and garbage, despite his tidy work shirt and clean-shaven face. Philip figured he must be the quay worker Cloutille mentioned.

Paul set three journals on top of a worktable. "My friend and I, we want in."

"You work fast. May I?" Philip eyed the books; all properly secured in the original leather sheaths he'd seen them in before they'd gone missing. He let Cloutille examine each one. She nodded. "Where did you find these?"

Paul stood, arms crossed, waiting.

"What'll make your lips move, my friend?" Philip asked.

"I figure there's something about the Sibyl in those journals or you wouldn't want them so bad. Is she real?"

"That's classified. Where did you find them?"

"That's classified." Paul smirked. "We want half of whatever you're getting."

Philip contained his urge to knock the young man to the ground. "And you think that's fair?"

"Pretty sure my father is having lunch with Major General Gubbins tomorrow," Paul said.

Philip considered the threat. Gubbins is the Director of the SOE. Paul had moved his chess pieces with skill.

"Alright then, half it is. Where were these?"

"Amboise."

"You took them from Maquis fighters?"

"It got rough. I even shot one."

Philip steamed. If these fools had driven Serah deeper and darker, this whole thing might be ruined. "You made a bit of a scene this morning."

"Just playing dumb."

"Of course." Philip resealed the bags. He handed Paul and the quay worker the journals before nodding at Cloutille. "Get these on the caravan this afternoon. I'll make sure you get the best deal possible."

He put a hand on the young man's shoulder and walked him toward the gallery where the Sibyl statue lay in pieces. Cloutille moved alongside the quay worker. They chatted as the foursome dodged crates and shards of marble.

"What happened here?" Paul asked.

"You two head out. We'll take care of the arrangements," Philip replied.

The quay worker spasmed and stumbled through the door. The light of the afternoon glared overhead when two of the journals dropped to the ground. The worker careened into Philip and Paul, blood pooling around him as he collapsed.

Cloutille's gun had been fired. She shouted, "Get down! Everyone get down! We've got them cornered."

Philip firmly pressed his wide palm into Paul's shoulder, took the third journal, and tucked it in the back of his pants. Seconds later, a single, muffled shot to the young man's gut. He collapsed at the colonel's feet, leaving a crimson handprint on his coat. Philip holstered his gun.

"It seems the Louvre has their thieves." Cloutille unloaded a shot into his chest.

Philip removed his coat, placed it over her shoulders as museum guards and gendarmes flooded the scene, and whispered, "Well, that was no trouble at all, my dear. Was it?"

Chapter 13

MARIE

MAY 2, 1945
PARIS, FRANCE

Marie snuck up a flight of narrow stairs in a side hall at the Louvre. She flung open the window to let in the sticky breeze. She needed to analyze whatever Philip had on La Joconde's disappearance. It would help her settle into this ruse, get ahead of the colonel.

The contents of the manila folder turned out to be very detailed. From manifests to telegrams sent through various means, the path of the painting appeared to have been documented just as Marie had planned before it left the Louvre seven years earlier. As anticipated, the manifests also included the journey of each reproduction.

Nothing in the stack seemed out of order. The codes from the Maquis teams who moved the fakes were standard, basic coordinates exactly what anyone might expect. Marie experimented with different puzzles and word combinations to see if they could be deliberate distractions. She spread out a map of France on the wooden worktable to match notations on the photos with manifests detailing the original painting. The markings to that point rendered themselves as perfect matches for coordinates where the true masterpiece made stops. No hint of Serah's role surfaced.

Tossing her hat on the table, she pulled her fingers through her hair. It bit at Marie that she'd spent so much time planning for the safety of this painting only to see it gone. Now, Serah was mixed up in it as well. "Bastard. Did you really think I was that broken?"

Obviously, Marie thought, Philip did. The heat rising in her chest made her strip back her suit jacket. She laid a hand on the hilt of her knife, the one Noam had saved all this time, and wondered if she was still capable of stabbing a man. Confident that the current moment was not one to get caught meditating on murder, she slid her jacket back on and buttoned it up.

Marie rolled her stiff neck side to side. She was exhausted. With a handful of photos to go, the points she mapped out continued on a haphazard, yet clearly documented course. Halfway through the stack, she stopped. Her mind brightened, interest lifting with the discovery. The new ones were heavily coded markings—ones reserved for emergency communication and critical details. She'd developed this code herself. Jules, Noam, and the others relied on her skill at making and breaking codes to adjust the beats when they'd been compromised. She knew of five, maybe six, Maquis teams who might use them. On top of that, the ink looked fresh, even in a photo. Hadn't Philip said these were from last year?

She kept reading. Her body tensed. There. The words rose clear and clean from the page as she translated the Resistance code: φΛ. Σίβυλλα. Mére. Maison.

"This can't be right." Marie set everything down. The breath grew heavy in her lungs. She shook her hands and began to pace. Greek lettering was used for one thing only: to alert those in the know that there had been a breach of loyalty amongst the Maquis. The symbols φΛ equaled La Joconde.

The second word was clear: Σίβυλλα equaled Sibyl. She stopped herself and reached back to feel the welts along her shoulder blades.

"We were strapped to a pole in the middle of the camp. They shot her, whipped me." Marie recalled what she'd reported to the Allied team debriefing her after her rescue from Ravensbrück and return to France. She'd been helping other prisoners escape for months. That night, one was caught and ratted her out.

"Why did they not kill you?" The psychologist had asked.

"I have no idea." Marie really didn't. She had always wondered why Nadine died and she survived.

"You're a known communist, high-level Maquis."

"Yes."

"A traitor."

"I made sure the Germans trusted me."

"And what did the Allies get for that trust?"

"I got eighty-four women out of the camp. Alive." Marie's irritation grew as the recollection played out in her mind.

"What did we learn?" The psychologist had asked her.

"Nazis are assholes."

Marie tried to block out the beatings she'd taken when the Germans believed she was hiding evidence of the prophetess. Her mind circled around days chained to a chair, arms bloodied and infected from being injected with Pervitin, and forced to decipher stacks of handwritten journals and thousands of pages of notes scribbled in books. Her calves burned as she recalled being summoned, stripped naked, and told to lay over a stool. Marie's answers earned their trust. Her silence earned her a whack with a stick, sometimes a metal rod.

"Dammit." She read the words again. La Joconde and the Sibyl, from all that she'd been forced to decipher, had no direct connection to one another. She told herself this, again.

"They intended to capture and control an oracle." She had told the Allied psychologist a month earlier. "If the stories of the Sibyl had been true, the Nazis, or anyone who got their hands on such a creature, would have been able to predict every move the Allies made and set strategic counterattacks. A prophetess controlled by the Third Reich would have . . ."

"Allowed them to take over the world," Marie interrupted her own memory.

She wondered if that's what Philip Millar wanted as well. She scoured the new notations placing the two ancient women together. They were perfect. No awkward lettering. No obvious marks from specific types of writing implements. It felt too convenient. Like those making the notes knew she'd find them.

Marie gathered the file and headed into the hall to find Philip.

"Dr. Guerrant." The guard from the morning lumbered toward her. "You better come with me. There's been an incident."

Shouts echoed throughout the corridors as she wove her way through guards and museum workers. Some appeared bloody. Marie rushed through the galleries until coming across pieces of the Erythraean Sibyl statue across the floor. The guard had been explaining, but all she heard was the colonel's name, then Cloutille's. Marie broke into a sprint, only to find the two of them being treated in the street by medics.

"Paul?" She stared at the wrenched face of the young Sorbonne student whom she'd taken under her wing just that morning, along with that of another young man. They lay dead in the street.

Chapter 14

APRIL 30, 1519
AMBOISE, FRANCE

My feet landed on a giant compass set in the stone at the main entrance of Clos Lucé. A garrison of soldiers bearing the standards of King François awaited us at the ornate, carved wooden doors. Accompanying them were five men equipped with parchment, ink and quills, and investigatory tools. I recognized Tommaso de Arced, another of Master da Vinci's apprentices. Unlike Melzi, he had failed, with much drama, at painting, but he excelled at politics with just as much flair. He led the way.

"My friend." I rose on my toes to offer the customary kiss on each cheek. A lacing from his doublet caught on my glove, snagging it long enough for my hand to touch his. My senses piqued. He had grown wide-shouldered and tall. In the year since he had garnered a position at court, he seemed to age far more than a man of twenty-four. Tommaso commanded the guard as if he were their master. "You have risen in the king's favor."

I caught him focused on Maurine, who had turned into nothing more than a hasty blur headed north toward Château Gaillard. The two estates seemed almost as one, with the ramparts of Château Amboise dominant to the west along the twisting roadway that ran in front of both. For such a modest house, the twenty-foot-high stone wall enclosing Clos Lucé and the expansive trees and grasslands surrounding it never failed to surprise me with their grandeur.

"No time for nattering like maids," one of the men accompanying Tommaso interrupted, staring at the seal around my neck. "We need your sight."

The pair of Amyntas with me stepped forward to block him from laying his hand upon my arm. The other men skittered back, hissing. Tommaso offered a perfunctory smile, straightening his doublet and rolled his eyes before waving me through the door with a sophistication that went beyond courtesy. He had been mentored, groomed even. But, by whom?

"It is good to see you," he whispered. "Steady yourself for this."

Master da Vinci's workshop appeared as if a wild boar had been trapped inside. The Amyntas entered first, ensuring the space free from intruders. I climbed upon broken cupboards and stepped over slashed canvases to get inside. The room stank of Venetian turpentine. Buckets of lacquer diluted in gum arabic and flour paste had been overturned. I bristled. Amongst the violet and cinnabar powders lay a length of white hair caked with blood. "Has anyone entered since your discovery?"

"Your Amyntas can attest, we secured it as soon as we understood the seriousness," Tommaso said.

His assurances proved vague. My women arrived with me and could not have known of the chaos until that very moment. I found myself quizzical. I contemplated the truth of his words in the presence of so much destruction. I knew the others, including Tommaso, would expect my worry to be for Master da Vinci.

I traced the edges of every splintered piece of wood for a hint of La Joconde. We moved through the wreckage, searching. I relayed the details of my observations, careful to keep my true task private. The men scribbled incessantly, lingering on every element. Each time I moved on, they rushed to my prior locale, mumbling and sketching.

"What else do you envision in your mind's eye?" one of them asked. His breathlessness bit at me. I saw nothing. A foreboding concern overcame me.

"Do they have to dwell on me so?" I needed Tommaso to assuage their assumptions. People no longer saw the merit of my mind, only the divinity they believed I possessed.

"You have us all under your spell, Mademoiselle," one of the men said. "You have grown powerful."

Indeed, powerful, I thought. I needed to concentrate. The Amyntas nodded at me and I turned my back on the others for a moment. Concentrating on the space just beyond the open door, I gathered the light beams shining through the panes of glass and moved it back and forth, creating shadows. I threw my voice, calling out. The men were startled. The Amyntas snickered under their breath. These were slights of hand we often used to delight ourselves while at court. Nothing more. However, the men found them unsettling enough to skitter off into the hallway.

Tommaso must have taken note, as he stepped in to relieve me of their attention.

"The blood is browning. It is sprayed, not pooled. Our conspirators did not stab but rather punch." As he overwhelmed them with details, their quills furiously scratched against their journals. "All of this has been here for a while. The paste in the buckets, however, is relatively fresh. Less than half a day."

I spotted Tommaso as he rolled one of the buckets back with his foot to show it still moderately sticky and wet.

He had dutifully distracted the men. I let them continue and slid my gloves off, proceeding with the inquiry that fortune saw fit to bestow upon me. As I placed my hands on the table, the glimmer offered itself as proof. I began my own collection of notes.

"Master da Vinci was here at his worktable. I doubt he even knew his attacker. This was ransacked after the captors made off with him."

"How can you tell?" a bearded man rushed back in, only to be stopped by an Amyntas.

"Any indication of those responsible?" Tommaso returned as well.

I heard them, but was lost in a glimmer: a calm scene with nothing more than the Master quietly reading.

"Aesmeh," Tommaso grew louder as I moved us into the Master's study. It had endured the same sort of ravagement. "Do you see the men responsible?"

I hesitated, trying to sort through what manifested as blackness in my mind. I tried to move forward in the glimmer. Why, pray tell, could I sense nothing beyond Master da Vinci reading?

"Aesmeh." Tommaso kept prodding me, but I slipped deeper and deeper into the empty space. Finally, he took my hands from their grip upon a shelf and I had to fight my way back from the vision.

"The room seems to have been cleansed somehow." I had not meant to tell him.

This was deeply concerning. It seemed even more treachery was at hand. La Joconde was surely the target. Otherwise, no one would go to the trouble of cleansing a room of its memories. The only reason to do so is to stop someone like me from learning the truth.

Tommaso shooed the remaining men away. "How can that be?"

I stammered a bit. "Such a thing is nearly impossible."

"A traitor then?" He knew as well.

"If so, a very powerful one, but a tender moment such as this cannot give way to assumptions." My words slowed and broke down. As my hands traced the lines of a worktable in the library, I caught a new glimmer. The table had been cleared other than a single puzzle box placed at the very back of a cubby. I tried to pry the box from its hiding place. It refused as if it had a will of its own. I yanked again.

"Is that the dodecahedron?" Tommaso recognized the old brass implement consisting of twelve equal sides marked with Roman numerals on each panel.

"Yes. This one was the Master's favorite." I took it, sentimental in having retrieved it from the chaos. I wrapped my bare hands around it. In an instant, my mind traveled to a place we knew well. My heart soared at the memory—thankful.

"What is it?" Tommaso asked.

"Those early days after you all arrived in Amboise from Rome."

"Is it three years past now?" Tommaso noted. I nodded. "Those were amongst my most precious."

I savored the chance to relive such happiness. "I remember when the Abbess conscripted me to Master da Vinci's side. I thought it the worst fate, yet it brought me to all of you."

The glimmer led me to the grove of Gary Oaks above Château Amboise. There, I had begun long practices harnessing glimmers; the Master taught Melzi, Tommaso, and Salaì how to lay color on canvas; and Maurine would join us to spark spirited debates on every manner of concern. I relayed it all to Tommaso.

"We were family," he said.

His words rang true. That grove, those moments, were where I conjured La Joconde, pulling her visage from somewhere in time. They painted the woman from the details I spoke just as we had once done years earlier in Milano. The memories carried such strength. Again, I had to fight my way back to the current concerns.

Tommaso quieted while the past poured through me. Another glimmer appeared: Master da Vinci filling the dodecahedron with playful messages before sealing them inside. I realized I could open it.

I fidgeted with the top of the mechanism, following the exact motions shown in the glimmer. It twisted until the layers of the box fell back to reveal a cryptext nested inside.

"Do you think he left it for you?" Tommaso twirled his finger, his eyes ablaze. "Spin it on its brass handles."

That was indeed how it worked. Seven characters across. At least a thousand combinations. Numbers, not letters, which I might have anticipated. My senses soared, then dropped. If I got it wrong, I would lose a potential clue. I held the metal puzzle. The ache of the glimmer reached the tips of my fingers. A series of numbers began forming before me.

The patterns ceased in an instant. My attention shot across the room. I made my way to a heaving door leading to the living quarters. I ran my fingers along the crease of the threshold and the combination of numbers again appeared in front of me. They ordered themselves in my mind.

Tommaso stood, pacing as I moved the dial into position until a click announced success. Inside the cryptext was a single piece of vellum. It had yet to yellow, the ink was sharp as if written yesterday. I flipped the scrap around to show him the writing upon it. We both let out a heavy sigh.

A series of shouts coming from down the hall interrupted us. The Amyntas charged after a figure running straight toward me.

"Aesmeh, will you not order these beasts out of my hair?" Melzi begged as he tried to drive them away with his hands.

As my hand raised, the Amyntas stopped. They stood firmly gripping their swords close behind him; sentinels obeying my command in severe silence. Tommaso backed into the workshop, attempting to close the door blocked by the debris.

"Where is Master da Vinci?" I asked Melzi.

"I cannot tell you what I do not know myself," he said.

"You cannot or shall not?" I held my hand out displaying the solved cryptext. In an elegant scrawl: the strip of paper bore the word 'Melzi'.

"Che cazzo!" He fussed with a note that proved the source of my fury. "Now this."

Chapter 15

MARIE

MAY 2, 1945
PARIS, FRANCE

Marie sat in the stiff metal chair placed outside the doors of the curator's office. Hours passed. Gendarmes, men in military uniform, and investigators moved in and out in an endless stream. She tried to glean anything from the shouts coming from inside the room. English. French. No matter what language, three words kept piercing the leaded glass and wooden door: "Nazis. Capture. Dead." She'd rubbed the skin of her forefinger and thumb almost raw. How had Paul ended up shot? How?

A French officer finally approached.

"I'm sorry, Dr. Guerrant. This is taking longer than expected."

"I'll wait," she said.

"I've been ordered to send you home. You would do well to stay clear of the museum until our investigation is complete."

His sharp tone annoyed her. "I do not take orders from you, Lieutenant. I deserve to know why one of my team members was killed today."

She spotted Philip leaving a warehouse room across the hall. "Nevermind."

Marie headed toward Philip who sat himself on a bench, clothes still bloodied as workers and police rushed past.

"Finally! Are you all right?" she asked. "What the hell happened?'

"Paul was a plant. I need you to pack," Philip said. "We either go get her now, or we lose the Mona Lisa forever."

Marie shook her head, trying to get words out. At that moment, it seemed all but impossible to not confront this man about Noam's accusations.

"If you're worried about Serah, my officers in Paris will continue the search for her," Philip continued.

Marie nodded. "Should you not rest?"

"Look how easily your team was infiltrated. Everything you sacrificed to hide the Mona Lisa years ago, everything you are doing now will not matter if others get to her before we do. We can find a pillow when it's all done."

"You're hurt, though." Marie pointed out the stains on his jacket.

Philip opened it and smiled. "Turns out your colleague is one hell of a shot."

Marie realized he had been keeping tabs on her through Cloutille.

"Paul pretty well killed himself. If Cloutille hadn't shot him, the gendarmes would have laid him out in the middle of the square."

"What was he after?"

Philip glanced at the file still tucked under Marie's arm. "Did you read through everything?"

"Of course."

"The journals that disappeared along with the Maquis team in Amboise, somehow Paul had them," Philip said. "Cloutille caught him and a quay worker in the warehouse. I was just coming back from lunch. It was all done in about five minutes."

Marie was startled, wondering if Paul, or others, had taken the Maquis team prisoner or, worse, killed them.

"I didn't realize we needed to run around with guns tucked in our handbags." She thought about the gun and knife in her own shoulder holster and worried Philip would notice the bulge in her jacket.

"Or I'd wager a member of your team was an informant."

"That's not possible." Marie spotted forged identities as easily as she spotted forged artwork. Paul came off as a a hapless fool, not a Nazi plant.

Philip seemed irritated. "Maybe he was sneaking in Hildegard de Bingen pieces."

The assertion triggered Marie's nerves. Her pulse raced. She tried not to fidget. Has her trip into the catacombs been discovered? "Are you asking me to defend against my past?"

"I'm just saying, he must have betrayed a whole lot of people to get those journals. We both know what becomes of men who sell out Resistance cells. You were around in '41 when the Maquis marched twenty of their own into the mountains outside Langogne and just left them to die."

"I'm aware." Marie knew Jules had been a part of the team that ordered the Langogne march. Traitors were worse than the enemy. "What was in the journals?"

"I don't know. We never saw them," Philip said. "If Paul went to anyone before us . . ."

Marie understood. Paul's acquisition of the journals was a problem. If he had known how to get to the deep-cover maquisard, then he would have known how to get to the painting and Serah. Her throat seized up and her jaw ached as she mentally reviewed the details from the photos. She couldn't refuse Philip. "Thank goodness those pieces are in our hands now."

"The caravan leaves at 0500 hours. I expect you'll be on it?"

"Of course."

Chapter 16

AESMEH

APRIL 30, 1519
AMBOISE, FRANCE

Melzi rushed me into the chapel at Clos Lucé, sealed the door, and unfurled a formal parchment. I turned my back on the Virgin Mary staring down at us from the archway painting above. Standing alone, I longed to reach out and take him in my arms. The watchful eyes of the mother of Jesus kept me from committing such an act. The storm had broken, a bit; the sun shooting fragile rays through the stained glass above the diminutive altar. As we stood in the quiet, shivering, I peered at the parchment in Melzi's hand and recognized the handwriting of the Abbess.

"A communique arrived three days past beseeching me to secure the Master's work." His voice cracked. "Do you think the Abbess suspected an attack?"

I read it again, relieved that she had instructed Melzi to hide La Joconde. I could complete my task of retrieving the painting and begin the search for Master da Vinci by nightfall. His knowledge meant that I could speak freely. "You have everything, then?"

"I secured all of his writings in the smithy's hut at Gaillard."

"What about La Joconde?" Only those within the folds of the Sibylline called the painting our Dear One.

"The painting?"

At Melzi's words, my tongue stilled and I could not form a thought. I rushed out of the chapel and out of the house, unwilling to let myself breathe until I looked upon it all myself. I ran out the back gate of Clos Lucé where the ducks nestled and swam along the Amasse. The Amyntas moved swiftly to catch up as I made my way toward the eastern edges of Gaillard. I stumbled once I reached the arches in the wall surrounding the King's Garden, but still managed to outrun them to the hut.

"Cut the lock," I commanded.

Inside, I released the latch of a door in the floor and descended a set of stairs into a secure room carved into the stone foundation. There sat stacks of journals and loose drawings. Botany cases held plants and creatures, the likes of which I had never seen. They were stacked ten high. I ripped through them, the glimmers coming forth. Master da Vinci's memories poured through me at once. I nearly collapsed from the rush. Melzi caught up to me, his face stupefied.

"Is there nothing more?" I could hardly stand beneath the weight of realizing that our Dear One was not amongst Master da Vinci's hidden possessions.

"What more could there be?" Melzi gazed at me. His eyes damp.

Oh, those dazzling dark eyes I fell in love with so long ago. I refused to return such a gaze—not at that moment when our fire stood overshadowed by the one about to burn the Sibylline to the ground. The wall of fire raged in my mind. Melzi had misunderstood the Abbess. Could this glimmer be of a future far beyond?

"I had no idea they might commit such a ghastly offense over a single unfinished painting," he said.

I could offer no solace. If he didn't know the power and purpose of our Dear One, it proved safer to let him remain ignorant.

Chapter 17

MARIE

MAY 2, 1945
AMBOISE, FRANCE

Marie arrived in Amboise via overnight convoy. Perched atop a transport truck, she scanned the landscape through binoculars. Soldiers and the townspeople worked to rebuild the bridge that connected the two sides of the tiny commune divided by the Loire River in the distance. The convoy entered along a more circuitous route and disembarked at the top of the main road, near Clos Lucé. Château Royal d'Amboise was nearly uninhabitable and much of the riverfront town, including its ancient stone bridge, lay in ruin. She wondered how she would ever find Serah.

As Marie followed military transports up and down the main street, she thought it the oddest place one might expect an Italian master artist, like Leonardo da Vinci, to complete his life. The sun transformed the hills beyond town. Palettes of rose and lavender painted the morning sky.

She'd traded the work suit for a khaki skirt and matching cotton shirt. Even in the heat, Marie wore long sleeves. The tattoo on her arm required too much explanation, a distraction from her true purpose.

Philip had demanded that she wear a heavy flak jacket and bulletproof apron over the top. Despite its weight, the brown, collarless vest offered protection. The helmet was well secured and she had already begun to help soldiers unload the vehicle. She hoped her respect for the men and the appearance of taking her orders seriously had left Philip without a sliver of suspicion. Marie knew the dangers of being in the field, but Philip needed to keep her safe—at least for now.

Two men, their black boots giving them away as Maquis, had kept close to her since the caravan arrived. The pair looked normal enough to the untrained eye. Woolen gray flat caps and the usual work shirts under aged tweed jackets. They shared smokes a block down. A single motorbike tracked her along the route from Paris as well. A third tail—a woman whom the lieutenant with Marie couldn't get close enough to identify—followed the caravan on foot.

Marie knew Philip needed the Maquis to protect one of their own. They'd made sure the transport marched along without interruption, despite radio traffic warning of German Werwolf squads operating in the vicinity. But, she noted, he had not doubled down on secondary troops along the route.

She knew, too, that, no matter how the newspapers hailed them as heroes, Maquis still held communist values and treasured their sovereignty too much. No one negotiated with them. That would play in her favor.

Suddenly, a mine exploded with a shattering boom. Rock and metal flew upwards. The anti-personnel device took out half the street. Marie waited for the debris to settle, then moved through the smoke and mayhem. Her ears rang, machine-gun fire and howls from the wounded were no more than a din. She pushed on, her senses sharpening just as she came upon Philip near Tour Hertault, the north tower of the castle.

"Let's go!" He hurried her along. "Now."

Marie looked over her shoulder at the Maquis tails. The men had already pulled black bandanas over their mouths. Hats tight over their heads, they proved unrecognizable. One had a gash in his leg that his partner tended. However, the moment Philip's hand met Marie's, the man jumped up and ran toward them. Crumbling walls and choking dust slowed everyone down.

Another blast went off. Marie lost sight of everyone. Her eyes burned. She fought her failing ears. The explosion slapped her against one of the transport trucks. She lifted her head from the dirt encrusted brick road. Time slowed. Arms and legs like jelly. She reached for the weapons in her shoulder holster, but couldn't get to them under the weight of the flak jacket.

A man was down in front of her, his sidearm on his belt. Marie shimmied over to him, staying low and close. She felt hazy, like time was suspended. Someone grabbed for her. A hand. She gripped it, leaving the gun behind.

"Dr. Guerrant!" A man helped her off the ground and pulled her away from the fighting.

Another device went off, rocking the ground beneath them. Machine guns. She had to run. Marie searched through the smoke and debris for cover, and slipped into an alleyway.

Suddenly, two hands pulled her by the shoulders, guiding with calm deliberation through the chaos. The hands of a woman. She turned to see a figure, wearing an odd cloak, whose steady, brilliant eyes seemed to defy everything going on around them.

"You are Marie Guerrant?" She asked.

Marie nodded. In the solitude of the alley, the woman took a deep breath and pressed her cool palms onto Marie's eyes. Within moments, they cleared and her hearing sharpened.

"You are well now?" The woman's eyes appeared clear and bright like those of the woman Marie had pulled away from the men shaving her head in the street in Paris. "Come."

They almost made it to a low doorway near the looming, massive castle when something, or someone, caught the woman's attention.

"To hell." It was all Marie heard before the woman abandoned her.

Another voice faded in and out. "Marie, move!"

Noam took her hand. She felt him shudder. Time slowed, again. They moved as if the air had turned thick as cotton. Bullets. Smoke. Screams. Gunfire. Noam's hand jerked away. Someone yanked her back. Inside the castle tower was a stone path spiraling upward, wide enough for six horses across. Nazis, Marie thought. She refused to go in. The soldiers forced her inside, propped her against a wall, and returned to the fighting. Marie couldn't catch her breath. She tried to focus on the stone gargoyles, the warlocks and ogres, mad monsters, and dragons staring down from the masonry of the ceiling that oversaw her capture. The black smoke from the village filled the tower and stung her eyes.

A hooded figure swept down from the spiral path above. Marie looked up to see the same cloaked woman from the street. She hoisted Marie up by the armpits.

"Good, you are safe. Let us get you out of this."

Marie welcomed the strong embrace. The scent of anise and ash filled her nose. The woman's dark, lustrous skin seemed to shimmer in the darkness. Marie's head cleared, once again, as her new companion unbuckled the chin strap of her helmet. A pair of women in gas masks and civilian clothes slipped a mask over Marie's head and bolstered her on either side. One wrapped a blanket around her shoulders. The other offered water and a clear, powerful stare.

"What are they after?" Marie asked.

"Great Mother," one of the women said. "You look so much like your daughter."

Chapter 18

MARIE

MAY 3, 1945
CHÂTEAU ROYAL AMBOISE
AMBOISE, FRANCE

Marie wondered how she came to stink so badly. All she could smell was rubbing alcohol and old sweat. Every other question swimming inside her head mattered so much more, but body odor and the irritating itch from the scaly rash left over from Ravensbrück were a fine distraction.

Forehead bandaged and ribs taped, she stood in the afternoon sun fiddling with her short tufts of hair. She sniffed, half-expecting the smell of German ersatz soap, black bread, and wet SS field uniforms. Only rubbing alcohol. Still, she wasn't convinced the incident hadn't left her captive.

It was the first time she'd been awake long enough to get out of bed. The medics outfitted her with men's pants and an airman's white dress shirt. Ah, she realized, the shirt was the source of the pungent smell. She cinched the belt around her waist. Pants, she thought, smoothing her hands down her legs. Marie preferred them. Only a few circumstances allowed a woman to wear them and not be deemed 'fast.' She supposed enemy attacks counted as one such instance.

She peered over the side of the tower balcony and took stock of teams clearing away the last of the destroyed transport vehicles. Her eyes shot up and down the streets on the off chance that Serah might use the attack as an opportunity to emerge from hiding to resupply.

That is, Marie thought, what she would do in Serah's shoes. Long lines at the village farmstand clogged the roadway with people in farm trucks full of early lettuce and overwintered apples. Men and machinery worked at restoring the long bridge spanning across the Loire. A woman bickered with another near a blackened building before they laughed and hugged each other close.

Marie drifted back to an outing at a castle along the Loire. She and Jules took Serah when she was nine or ten. They turned back almost immediately when the girl began wailing, terrified, shouting that she had seen a hooded woman roaming the halls. Serah's unmoored imagination as a child proved challenging. For a moment, though, Marie wondered if she too had encountered that old, hooded specter in the violence of the morning.

She sorted through spotty details. Had Noam been there? And Philip? Her right hand still trembled. The scene triggered old losses, ones that first cost her Jules, then Serah.

Marie looked around. Men in Allied uniforms ran drills over on the dry grass of the castle yard. Clearly, this was a safe zone. She breathed deeply, eyes closed.

"You better?" A woman's voice caused Marie's eyes to flutter open. She too donned the standard-issue pants and shirt, but with the addition of a rose-pink cardigan overtop. Her black hair, braided tight to her head in a circle, swept Marie back to Tunisia and the coastal streets of Mahdia with Jules. The woman's skin was deep amber and clear, just like his.

"Je m'appelle Iné Soudier. Prenez-vous un café?"

Marie took the tin cup and gulped the bitter, lukewarm coffee. For a moment, she worried whether the baker had delivered the morning coffee to her team left behind at the Louvre. She'd paid him with another case of Rinderbraten before leaving Paris. "Merci. I am . . ."

"Marie Guerrant. Yes, I know."

Marie paused, but figured others knew of her arrival. "Has anyone been briefed on what happened?"

"No, and we probably won't." Iné afixed a bandana around Marie's head and ran her hand over the forehead bandage. "Good thing they gave you a helmet."

"And the vest, yes. I didn't even know they had those." Marie patted her ribs. "Bruised, not broken, thankfully."

"The British."

"Does everyone wear them?"

"You seem to be the only one." Iné pointed to the row of bodies near the burned-out castle gardens.

"How many?"

"Three soldiers. One maquisard or maybe FTP." Iné took a cigarette from a case on the stone banister.

"Just one from the Resistance?" Marie begged herself not to ask about Noam.

"Should there have been more?"

"They usually don't go it alone."

Iné eyeballed Marie. "We get strays down here from time to time. Lots of folks don't trust the government, even with the Vichy gone. Plus, the Nazis have small cells running reconnaissance or continue tracking whatever high command ordered them to track since the liberation. There's always plenty to shoot at."

"Werwolf?" Marie whispered.

"You know some?"

Marie slid the sleeve of her shirt up past her elbow and held it out for examination.

Iné's eyes grew wide at the sight of the numbered tattoo. "May I?"

Marie stepped in and let the woman run her hand over it.

"How long behind the wall?"

"Too long."

Iné nodded before leaning on the banister and offering the smoldering cigarette in her hand. "Every once in a while one group or another gets blamed for blowing something to bits. Troops head out on raids . . . kill a few people."

Marie took a drag of the smoke and handed it back. "You don't think it's Germans?"

"I don't know if it is. And that's the trouble, isn't it?"

Marie wondered how much Iné Soudier knew about La Joconde, the Maquis team, or Philip Millar. "You sound a lot like a friend of mine."

Iné tossed a glance over at the dead Maquis soldier. "Be careful to whom you mention those sorts of friends."

Marie pondered this woman who, somehow, seemed especially familiar. How could she casually make her way through military zones? She didn't dare ask about what took place in the castle tower. "What do you do here?"

"I'm . . . ." Iné's sparkling eyes darted around, never landing on Marie. "Looks like we've got company."

"Hello, ladies. How are both of you feeling after this morning? Healing?" Philip and a small cadre of soldiers made their way onto the balcony.

Marie hadn't considered that Iné might also be injured. She tried to shift her body to stand at attention, but the pain in her ribs caused her to double over.

"Take it easy, my dear," Philip continued. "The Germans made quite a scene."

Marie gave Iné a quizzical look before turning to Phillip. "So much for being safe."

"Well, you're off the street. No one is getting in here." He offered his arm. "We've got to find the old girl and get her back to Paris before anyone else. Ready to head inside the treasury caves?"

"Les Greniers de César." Iné repeated it in French. She rolled her eyes at Philip and turned to Marie. "Why can't the British ever just speak our language? Or even attempt to?"

Taking Philip's arm, Marie gave her a crooked grin. She knew the royal history of Amboise well enough to understand his reference was to the caverns beneath the castle. They once held the riches of rulers. "Underground? Why Les Greniers?"

"That was the designated handoff point for the Maquis," Philip said. "My team was attacked there. Whoever did this fled into the network of tunnels beneath Amboise."

"You think they are still there? In the tunnels?"

"There are a million places to hide down there. I'm just hoping you can make sense out of the bits and pieces we have left, so we can get to the Maquis in time."

Marie agreed. The clock was ticking against the Germans, or whoever the attacker was. Getting a clear picture would surely allow her a better sense of the players.

"Are you up for getting to work?" Philip asked.

"Please. Boredom is torture."

"Good. Iné here knows the underground network better than anyone. She will be your second, if I may be so bold as to pick your team for you."

"Of course." Marie noted the authority given to Iné. It seemed odd, she thought, out of place. "But I'm afraid I lost my tools in the attack."

"Ask the men for whatever you need," Philip said. "We'll do our best to accommodate."

They crossed the lengthy yard in a small Jeep. Marie tried to ignore Philip's duplicity and imagine the high walkways and dirt patches of the castle as more of an elegant courtyard than a bombed-out pile of rubble. The once-green grass now burned black from a recent Allied initiated bombing. Barricades cordoned off massive pits where bombs had landed.

They took a circuitous route along the outer edges, passing St.

Hubert's Chapel, small, yet elaborate and decorative. Marie noted a mix of military personnel and civilians helping to recover steeple segments adorned with metal deer antlers. They were arranging the massive, carved scenes of the ancient hunt and medieval crosses, attempting to match them. She choked up as they slowly maneuvered past the remains of crumbling ramparts that half-heartedly stood as sentinels over the handful of streets in the commune and the majesty of the Loire. The Jeep headed toward the only building still intact.

"They're going to rebuild it," Philip gestured to the chapel. "The church, I mean. Even the stained glass in the upper windows, I'm told."

"So much is lost," Marie said.

"So much yet to be found." He patted her on the leg as if she were an army buddy. Her stomach soured.

They stopped at the edge of the wall, near the entrance to the main hunting lodge—the only major building left standing. Marie had once seen drawings of the original Château d'Amboise dating back a thousand years. It once stood five times the size. She let Philip escort her and Iné to the door where he stopped, along with the soldiers.

"You aren't coming in?" Marie asked.

"Miss Soudier knows her way around. You don't need an old man like me." He winked at her. "I admit, you don't have anyone else with your smarts down there in the hole with you on this mission, but the guys work hard. I'll have the lieutenant bring dinner."

Marie hesitated. All she could think about was Serah. Was she suffering? Was she injured? Was she, heaven forbid, dead?

She and Iné moved inside, past boxes of munitions and stale Nazi rations, the walls bare. All marks of history before the war had been stripped away in the attempt to claim France for the Third Reich. Passing through a series of desolate halls, they stopped in a room that housed an enormous, carved bed. Tapestries hung from walls and ruby-red velvet curtains covered the blasted-out windows. Heavily starched uniforms hung neatly in the open wardrobe. Such perfection.

"The Nazi commander slept here." Iné ran her hand along a wooden interior wall. "Used to be the king's quarters. Pig didn't even realize where he laid his head."

With a single flick, she released a latch hidden within the latticework of a wooden interior wall. "The servant's passage. It will get us right where we need to be."

Marie held her breath and confronted the narrow, dark stairwell that led to nowhere. She had never been more certain of what mattered to her. "Let's go find our girl."

Chapter 19

AESMEH

APRIL 30, 1519
AMBOISE, FRANCE

"You fool." I slapped Melzi across the face. We stood in the smithy's hut, amid specimen boxes and Master da Vinci's journals. He stared at me, wide-eyed. His hand moved to his cheek like a little boy reprimanded by his wet nurse.

"What are you doing, caring about journals and sketches?" I rushed out of the hut to the edge of the river. Pacing. Seething. Untethered. The sun hung low along the horizon, warming the garden. "Where is La Joconde?"

Melzi did not bother to respond.

I left him standing in the field and called out to the Amyntas and insisted that two more attach to my guard. We rushed to the workshop at Clos Lucé. The moment I laid hands on the brass handle of the front door, a glimmer revealed itself. Explosive, violent rage shot through me. My ears went deaf, a wordless fury overtook my mind. I sought out a face. Nothing. I flung my way through the workshop, tossing anything upright, in search of the painting—attempting to recreate an event from someone else's mind. I snatched up a jar of paintbrushes and another glimmer seized me. Again, I sought out a face; it was nearly in view when another touch pulled me back to the present.

"Overcome, are we?" Tommaso stepped back when I was startled.

The Amyntas stood on alert at my side. I waved them off. Tommaso turned and took two goblets of wine from a servant boy standing just behind him.

"You are presumptuous." I breathed for what seemed like the first moment since I entered the smithy's hut, and snatched the cup.

"The situation is far worse than you expected?" Tommaso righted a stool for me to sit on, choosing the floor for himself. He always put me at ease, even as a boy in Milan. Him, a courtier, perched cross-legged in the debris proved comical enough to cut the tension. "Master da Vinci's disappearance is a big loss. I know you wanted him at your side when you entered the temple."

"That may not happen." I hesitated. The Abbess instructed me to speak nothing of our Dear One outside Sibylline circles. However, Tommaso's trust was implied.

"What do you mean?"

"I cherish Master da Vinci, of course," I said. "I do not know how I would have survived the loneliness of a silent childhood at Fontevraud without his letters and visits, or my years in Milan without his gentle guidance. He is almost a father, I suppose."

"An old, odd, cranky bastard of a father." Tommaso raised his cup and drank.

"Indeed, but . . . ." I hesitated.

"Aesmeh, you cannot hold this in. Have I not known you for too long?"

My head spun. I kept blabbering. "The Abbess trusted Master da Vinci with a crucial task. I swear she would have trusted him with her life."

"You are senseless. I never have seen you this flabbergasted."

I tried to sort through my thoughts. "You know who we are, what the Sibylline have endured to reach this point, oui?"

Such a question proved ignorant. Tommaso knew better than just about anyone. He had been a boy of twelve, maybe, thirteen when the Master took him as an apprentice in Milan. He was raised alongside Melzi and myself. Quiet and observant, he remained on the fringe as we explored our blossoming talents and undisguised passion. We brought him everywhere. Salaì once referred to him as our pup, trailing along, loyal and true.

He grinned. "Do you recall when the Abbess held Melzi in a cell at Fontevraud for six months after she found you two half-naked in the Forêt de la Morte?"

"I recall how you tried to sneak him out in a habit and a wimple." I winked.

Tommaso took another sip of his wine. "What a blessing that the Master came to use the Fontevraud kitchens for one of his experiments."

"Him stinking up the Abbey with his putrid wolfsbane allowed for your escape from the Abbess' whipping board."

I appreciated Tommaso's attempt at calming my mind. Alas, the issue at hand dominated. "Master da Vinci is not the only thing missing."

"I gathered that." He gestured at the twisted canvasses, pools of paint, and emptied drawers—the result of my frantic search.

"He was working on a piece, an important one. I have to find it. But, aside from the dodecahedron, almost everything I lay my hands upon has been cleansed of all imprints."

"You told me. Can anyone really do that?"

"Master da Vinci could. One of the Harimtu taught him. He was quite proficient at it."

"Your spies are talented. Melzi and I once . . ."

I bristled. We sat for a while, staring at each other until a seeming truth crystalized between us.

"No," Tommaso said. "Melzi would never do such a thing to you."

"You just said it. Master da Vinci taught him everything. The only other people capable of it were not here."

"I refuse to believe Melzi would turn on the Sibylline." He stood. "You must not either."

To accuse Melzi pained me, but the evidence led in one direction. The Master's disappearance destabilized our position. With La Joconde gone, too, it left ten centuries of sacrifice and planning at stake. Was he playing dumb? Had he denied his part in this as I stood at his side? "I suspect we should . . . I mean . . . ."

"Round him up and hold him?" Tomasso asked.

"Tell the guards not to harm him."

"Are you sure?"

"No, of course not." My heart ached. "There is no other choice."

Chapter 20

MARIE

MAY 3, 1945
LES GRENIERS DE CÉSAR
AMBOISE, FRANCE

Marie's heartbeat quickened as she moved down the stone stairs into the cool, dim passageway that led from the king's former quarters at Château Amboise into the tunnels.

"Are we headed toward the river?" she asked.

"Oui," Iné motioned. "Follow close."

The light from the open door dissipated with the first turn, and they moved in utter darkness. For a moment, Marie stiffened.

Do not fear.

She heard the words echo in her mind. Iné took her hand and illuminated the space in front of them. The dust seemed to shimmer and swirl, as if being pushed aside to make way for the women. The cool air caressed Marie's skin. For the first time in ages, her scars neither itched or ached. She searched for the source of light—a flashlight, even a lantern—dismissing her own sense that Iné was creating the glow herself.

Marie almost gave into the urge to retreat back up the steps and into the castle when a memory of Serah descended upon her. The serious child intensely watches Jules and the men map routes through which they smuggled Jews; then helps Marie prepare coded commu-

105

niques. How many times had Serah obeyed our instructions? Riding her bike through the Bastille to Maquis drop-off points along the Seine; standing watch as teams moved women and children from cellars to storage sheds to the backs of farm trucks then driven into the countryside until the gas ran out. Marie then realized she had trained Serah as a maquisard. She'd created this, leaving her own child prone to men like Philip. She owed Serah her respect and devotion.

With a heavy sigh, Marie blindly followed Iné. She anticipated a single, rugged pathway devoid of any life other than an occasional sconce or face-to-face encounter with cobwebs. Instead, the tufa stone walls were smooth and adorned with intricate frescos of women. Some in heavy robes, and some in ethereal, shimmering silk dresses. All emanated light. Marie stepped close to a wall for further examination. If she read the cues right, a shell gold technique created the luminescent effect. "I haven't seen this in anything beyond Islamic manuscripts," she said to Iné. Usually, Marie thought, any sort of mural project involved gold leaf. This, however, was different. It was as if the gold had been applied with a quill, or other writing implement, to be so precise and elegant. "This must have taken decades."

"Or more," Iné whispered.

"Do you know, did the men use gum arabic or egg whites?" Marie imagined herself walking through corridors designed by Leonardo da Vinci.

"Why do you assume men created these?" Iné asked.

Marie remained silent, unable to conjure a reasonable response. The pair pushed on and the complexity of the network became clear. One corridor led to what appeared to be a series of small rooms. Another led up a set of stairs. A third gave no information about what lay beyond. All adorned with shimmering artistry beyond Marie's imagination.

They walked for another few minutes until the passageway seemed to drop off. The women scrambled down a precarious ladder. In this passage, the walls turned dark as coal, as if they'd been burned. In the complete darkness, Marie kept focus on Iné's back and counted her steps in Greek. At five hundred and twenty-seven, they arrived at a sealed wooden door. Iné banged. A uniformed man gave them entry from the other side. The unnatural glow of floodlights and the hum of gasoline generators hammered Marie's senses.

British soldiers moved up and down cockeyed stairs that appeared to have been hastily constructed. Marie's eyes followed them to the top of the tall cylindrical space. She tried to envision men planning battles, trysts, and tyranny in here. Though narrow, the silo was more than three stories high. Not unlike the grand cathedrals of Paris, it echoed in spaciousness—only, stark and monotone. At least ten men labored, several on each level of recently-built scaffolding. They moved crates of which Marie could not immediately determine their origin. Could this have been where da Vinci perfected his designs for cannons and catapults, even his massive ballista crossbow? She lost herself in history.

"Impressive, no? They were once used to store the riches of France," Iné said.

"One silo, how underwhelming."

"Ha. The ones in front held the grain. The rest held everything from gold to human remains."

"How many?" Marie knew about the treasury, but had no concept of its vastness.

"At least a dozen more out past the ancient temple," Iné continued.

"Temple?"

"The French were the last people to settle the Loire, not the first." Iné smirked.

"They are perfect for preservation."

"Yes, the temperature stays the same no matter the season. They are clean and sealed away from rats, cockroaches, and even those evil silverfish."

"The perfect secret hideout."

Iné winked. "Everyone needs a place to commit treason."

"And what are we committing here?" Marie admired Iné's blunt manner.

She glanced around at the operation. There wasn't a French soldier to be found. De Gaulle, Marie thought, would never have authorized such access to the British. Her senses sparked as she considered the chaos above. Entering the commune earlier that morning, she'd been told to take care for it had become a stopover for troops making their way home or taking out the last of the Nazi holdouts.

She looked up. Men were moving in and out at the top of the silo.

"Why didn't we come in that way?" Marie asked Iné.

"Too many eyes."

Marie realized they didn't have authorization to be in the silos. It was the perfect cover: soldiers from everywhere and, more than likely, no distinct chain of command. Millar's men could move freely with little suspicion. A woman could not.

Marie's shoulders tensed. She needed to gather information. She could see the men were trying to clean up a major preservation disaster, that much was clear. Marie could start there.

At the second landing, papers hung from makeshift drying racks. Frayed edges and yellowing marked their age, but the intended restoration was likely leaving them in worse condition than when they arrived. On a nearby table, men appeared to be removing stains from old journals.

"There are a lot of dismembered documents here. Was there a larger recovery effort taking place?" she asked. "I thought we were going to the exchange point for the painting?"

"I get paid to take you from point A to point B," Iné told her. "Anything else comes from them."

Marie understood. Iné wasn't a part of Millar's inner circle. She spotted several pieces where covers had been cut off with what looked like sewing scissors. It drove her mad, almost to the edge of booting everyone from the silo.

"You can't do it that way? These aren't coffee marks, A stain could make a single piece of paper priceless." Marie shooed the soldiers and sat down to work. "What did you use to dislodge the pages? The back half of these are destroyed."

"Talk to the lieutenant." A thin man wearing the typical olive drab battledress and round spectacles shrugged and pointed to the second floor.

"Only one sheet is irretrievable. The others are fully intact." Another British soldier spoke as he made his way down the stairs. The pair of Bath stars on his uniform identified him as an officer.

"And you are?"

"Lieutenant Alexander Berry. Her Majesty's Armed Forces. I'm in charge down here."

Iné let out a short laugh.

The lieutenant's snort and glare told Marie all she needed to know about Iné's place amongst the men. The woman seemed unfazed. She left them alone, and positioned herself in strategic proximity to the only way in or out that didn't involve scrambling out the top of a giant silo. If Iné did so out of worry for her safety, it didn't show.

"Dr. Marie Guerrant." Marie shot out her hand. "Now, I'm in charge down here."

Lieutenant Berry reddened and shook her hand hard. "Of course. We were hoping to have this in better condition for you."

"It may have been in better condition before you touched it." Marie gave him a concerned smirk.

The lieutenant cleared his throat, remaining red in the face. "Let me show you around, then."

He stood a full head's length above the women, his blond-haired, blue-eyed youthfulness at odds with his rank. Marie noted his calm willingness to concede to her authority, which meant he was part of Philip's inner circle.

Iné pulled a pair of glasses and a folded bundle from the canvas bag slung over her shoulder. Marie watched her as the lieutenant spoke. She recognized the underground newspaper—*Défense de la France*. Iné either held great faith in Allied support of French leftist politics or great faith in most Allied soldiers' inability to read French. The eyes of the two women met. Such willful confidence, Marie thought.

The lieutenant offered her a small metal table to work on. She started poring through pieces the men had already tried to salvage.

"Why didn't you wait for me? We might have been able to deal with it if you'd at least bagged them." Marie glared at him, tossing down the pages. "Where did they come from?"

"From an earlier attack, a few days ago," the lieutenant said. "Thankfully, the others that came with you from Paris were unloaded before the events of this morning."

"I didn't bring anything from Paris other than the files the colonel gave me."

"I'm sorry to bicker with you, Dr. Guerrant, but I unloaded the pieces myself."

His assistant retrieved a crate for them to examine. He tripped on the way, dumping the contents. Marie slowly bent down, stiffened from her bruised ribs. As she labored to pick up three leather carrying cases, she caught sight of an old script inside one.

Before she could investigate further, coins dropped from the open case and caught the light, blinding her and the men, who seemed to slow, even freeze. She reached down and flipped one over. They carried an image of Our Lady of Sorrows—a veiled Virgin Mary with seven swords piercing her heart. The Blessed Virgin kept showing up at the oddest moments. Marie read the inscription, "Mater Dolorosa." Then, below it, "Me-kädmen anina il'ati."

She shuddered. The first reference was to the Virgin Mary. The second seemed like gibberish—a possible mix of Hebrew, Urdu, and ancient Summerian.

In your pocket. Marie, again, heard a voice in her head. She looked around. Iné read silently. The men were somehow unaware. *Pick them up and put them in your pocket, quickly.*

Marie scooped them up and shoved them into her pants pocket. She closed the case and returned it to the man, who took it and nodded.

The light diminished. The soldiers didn't even notice what had transpired. Marie's stomach went hard. She whipped her head around to confront Iné, who was still reading her paper. Unaware. Questions mounted.

Marie could hear soldiers hauling boxes, the low echoes of their conversations from above. She needed to understand her circumstances better. "I should meet the team. How many?"

"There are fourteen," said Lieutenant Berry.

"Fourteen?" Marie knew that was an excessive number of soldiers to assign a non-military operation.

"Plus your . . . negro friend here." The lieutenant flung his finger at Iné.

Marie was caught off guard by the slur used against Iné. Jules had endured endless harassment from police and everyday French people alike, having come from Tunisia as a child. She'd tried to shield Serah from her own differences, but hatred never grew uncomfortable with being seen.

She stared at Iné for a moment, but the lack of attention the woman paid to all of it allowed Marie to return her attention to the box. "Are these part of the larger investigation into La Joconde?"

"Did the colonel not brief you?" Lieutenant Berry asked.

"Are you unable to answer?"

"I'm sorry, Dr. Guerrant. There must be a misunderstanding."

"There's no misunderstanding, lieutenant. Are we not all here to determine the whereabouts of the painting? Are these not pieces that could help us find her?" Marie grew suspicious. "Relay your orders to me now."

He pointed to his chest. "I was given orders simply to help you.

Anything from the colonel is classified. You're the only one with authorization to know the details of this investigation."

Marie knew he was lying. She picked up the leather cases and turned them willy nilly. The coverings were plain, not a stitch of adornment, and relatively new by historical standards. Inside, she found much older leather-bound journals. Why would Philip send them back from Paris with her? She didn't have time to decipher these types of documents. Besides, nothing so old would lead her to Serah. It was time to get her strategy mapped out. Marie looked up and realized that slivers of sunlight shone down from up above. She shifted toward the stairs. "What's up there?"

"The hatch. We drop everything in from the top," the lieutenant said. "It's easier to get the trucks up on the high ground where there are roads, and just send it all down via a rope system. Everything at the base of the silo is still blocked in from bombings."

"What about the tunnels from the castle?"

"That . . . person over there is the only one who can figure out how to get through them." The lieutenant waved a finger at Iné. "The colonel would have had you go in with us, but there are Allied troops moving through. We thought you'd prefer discretion."

"Hmm." Marie paused. "Indeed."

She and Lieutenant Berry moved up several sets of stairs onto a platform high above. Four soldiers sat on bedrolls, smoking. There were crates piled on either side of them. They snapped to attention at the sight of their commanding officer.

"What's in the crates?" Marie asked.

"Spare equipment," one told her. "We tried to cobble together everything we thought you'd need, but there isn't much left."

"What exactly happened?"

"Werewolf squads, more than likely," the lieutenant said. "We've had four or five attempts before the recent attack. That's why everything is locked in here. We installed the hatch to seal it from the inside."

The ache in Marie's shoulders doubled. At the bottom of the silo, where the journals remained, she would be trapped if anything happened. She took a moment to assess liabilities and the chance of another attack. "Any other way in or out?"

"Just the door you came in." He pointed back down to ground level. Iné was situated at the door's threshold, still reading. "Most everyone is on patrol up top. You're damn safe in here."

"How'd they get inside last time?" Marie stared at the hatch and back at the lieutenant. She wished she knew how to arrange some Maquis backup.

"Not everyone is loyal," the lieutenant said.

Fourteen soldiers. Constant attacks. Limited supplies. No more time. This had to be done, Marie determined, in less than a day. Otherwise . . . "I need the files from the colonel. You said you got everything out of the Jeep that brought me here?"

The lieutenant ordered one of his men to retrieve them.

Marie hated to wait. However, there was plenty of work to keep her busy in the meantime. Nearly everything in the silo was old and potentially valuable. She took four soldiers down to the second level where the pages of a manuscript hung. There, she showed them how to spot important pieces. "Look for any signatures or artwork."

"It was challenging to create a manuscript," she continued. "One had to start with very specific tools. Treated animal skins, or parchment, were cut, stacked, and folded. That was one process. A scribe wrote the text, an enlumineur painted the sheets. Then, they were sewn and threaded through wooden boards. Journals were a little less complicated, but not much. Anything that looks like it was made with more ease than that is not authentic. Set it aside. We'll deal with forgeries later."

The men appeared captivated.

"Does anyone know French?" she asked.

Three soldiers raised their hands. Marie assigned them to order the pages. The other unloaded crates. One was full of ration packs, the men looked longingly at the food.

Marie doled out a ration pack to each of them. "Try to keep the sardines off the papers. Lieutenant, you're with me."

She headed to the lower level. The leather cases pulled from the first box sat uncrated on the wobbly metal table. Marie considered taking a look, but wanted to be ready to start on the colonel's files.

Lieutenant Berry came down the stairs. "I'm sorry, doctor. I should have sent for the files earlier. It's going to be a while."

Marie felt herself unraveling with worry about Serah. Keeping herself in check, by staying busy, was the only way to avoid breaking down or giving herself away. "Well, let's see what else you think came from Paris with me."

The first of the leather cases contained several journals. The initial journal held a series of manifests in Latin. The French notations on wheat, corn, and gold written in a dialect common of the 1400s and 1500s, offered insight into their age. She tingled as her energy returned. Marie kept reading, noting the details of Amboise, travel on the Loire, even a reference to King François I.

She dug through a bin searching for small brushes, blades, anything that might gently separate pages. The toolbox, thankfully, was well-stocked. She reached for her glasses, remembering they had been destroyed in the attack. The lieutenant passed her his own set of magnifiers. He, Marie thought, knew exactly what Philip Millar wanted from her. Nothing was classified.

The noise of the men above abated. She looked up at Iné, but the woman ignored her. With a huff, Marie shook her head and moved on. She opened the other book from the satchel, read over it for a moment and held it up to the light to show the lieutenant. "Are you religious?"

"Every Sunday."

She pointed to the lettering. "Look hard."

"Latin?"

"Good eye. How about this?" She pointed to another passage.

"Is it backward?" the lieutenant asked. "Like da Vinci?"

The mirror script was not the wonder the lilt in the lieutenant's voice made it out to be. Marie had seen dozens of manuscripts and journals that used the same code. However, it was curious. "This is . . ."

"Really old." He smiled and winked. He walked away, snatched up a sheet from another box, and rushed it back to her. "We have a few of those. One with a year on it . . . 1519."

Given the script, they were written on split sheepskin parchment with iron gall. Incredible. The writing had almost made Marie forget about the circumstances that forced her into the silo. She returned to the pages of the journal in front of her when a name jumped from the pages. Her face flushed. Her chest burned.

"Asfoora," Marie hadn't meant to say it outloud. It was the name Oberführer Karl Diebitsch had been obsessed with at Ravensbrück. He was convinced she was the ancient Sibyl during DaVinci's time. Marie had read dozens and dozens of journals and pieces of ancient correspondence looking for that single reference. To see it—to actually read the name Asfoora written on paper—after searching so long and finding nothing, sickened her. "Does this show up in anything else you have read?"

"I told you, doctor. I don't have clearance."

"Of course." Marie noted a quickening in the lieutenant's breath. He knew, she told herself.

"What does it mean?" Lieutenant Berry asked.

The name roused Iné, finally breaking free from her paper. "It's Urdu, for bird."

Marie was taken aback. She wanted to ask the woman if her knowledge of Urdu meant she was Tunisian. However, her hands shook fervently. Here sat a priceless artifact. One she hoped never to find. She clenched her teeth and refused to let the memories of Ravensbrück win.

Iné continued, "Some believe da Vinci's man Melzi called a woman he'd had an affair with by the name Asfoora."

"I thought they were Italian?" The lieutenant sounded like an actor playing a part.

"The woman was North African, probably Berber. There are many rumors." Marie relayed enough detail to see if she could draw more information from one, or both of them, as to how the long-missing journals of Francesco Melzi sat in front of her; sent across France without an ounce of fanfare to a silo where it's probable the man once stood. "Most of the writings after his death portray her as some sort of witch or courtesan who tried to infiltrate da Vinci's inner circle."

"What happened to her?" the lieutenant asked.

"Melzi's writings have been missing for hundreds of years," Marie continued. "All mention of her stopped right after da Vinci's death."

"She vanished?"

"As most women did," Iné said.

Marie stopped herself from saying more. The historical recollections came easy to her. She'd known many pieces of lore through her work. These details, however, she knew from her time at Ravensbrück. They must be, she thought, the reason why the journals sat in front of her.

The pages were astounding. Marie spent a moment running through the catalog of Sibyl information stored in her head, but, again, she stopped herself. To pursue this line of questioning about Asfoora distracted from the goal of finding Serah. The name's appearance was dangerous. It told her that Philip Millar might be no better than the Third Reich. Yet, she also knew the Sibyl wasn't real.

Whatever the medics had given her for pain was wearing off, making it difficult to concentrate. Marie forced herself back to the task of locating Serah and turned to the lieutenant. He was the only one who seemed to know the history of the teams tracking and moving the painting. She had to probe him.

"Did you ever interact with the team moving La Joconde?" she asked.

"I did the work on the ground for the colonel."

"How did the painting end up back here?"

"They'd had her in an abbey in the South, but Mussolini tossed everyone into a tizzy. So, a Maquis team brought her back up to the Loire after Allied troops began bombing occupied castles, and the Germans ran. Guess they figured they'd put her back where she started."

"And?"

"And, nothing. Everyone thought she was at Chenonceau. When they started moving everything back to Paris, they discovered that one down there was a fake."

"You sure?"

"I couldn't tell them apart, but the colonel's woman before you said so."

Marie straightened, wanting to confirm more details. "What was her name?"

"Say . . . Sow . . ."

"Seydoux?" She tried not to react to Cloutille's involvement.

"Yeah, I think so. Dark hair. Curvy."

"Yes, I get it."

"Anyway, the colonel brought me in to collect the fakes and work with Maquis to get the real one back," he said. "That's as much as I know. I have all of the reproductions, though."

"Really?"

The lieutenant moved toward a dark part of the silo and opened a wide, flat crate. He pulled the paintings out. Three were framed. The others had their wooden casings removed. One was half burned.

One severely water damaged. All were exactly as Marie remembered them. The sight of six smiles, the sfumato expertly reproduced in every instance, left her breathless. She could see the slight flaws, the eye a tiny bit off, a tree in the background too green, but that was only because she'd known what the flaws were. The modest beauty with chestnut eyes stared back at her. So familiar, and not because Marie had spent so much time with the original. To the eye of an everyman, each one was the original La Joconde. She knew better.

Marie turned the framed ones around, not even looking at the painted figure, and ran her fingers over each set of markings she'd left encoded on their backs.

"This is your work, right?" the lieutenant asked.

"Partly." Marie thought of the people who had worked on these reproductions, these perfect decoys for the Nazis to take as their prize, while the real masterpiece remained secure. "I simply made sure attention was duly diverted. How could you have found everything except for La Joconde?"

"Honestly, I thought we were done. The rendezvous was set. When I arrived at the exchange, the woman never showed."

"Woman?" Marie sputtered. Serah? "Did you see her? Did you know her name?"

"No. Just a code name, Rose."

Marie noticed Iné shudder. "And the documents you found. The photos I received in my report? Do you have the originals?"

The lieutenant looked puzzled. "We never took any photos."

"I received at least a dozen in the SOE file. Several with handwritten Maquis notations on them."

"That's bizarre. I put that file together myself." he said. "Well, they'll be here momentarily. What about the journals with that Asfoora mentioned in them? Are they of any help?"

"It's very unlikely they have anything to do with this." Marie wasn't going to give anyone a reason to go after a Sibyl instead of Serah.

The soldier finally returned with the colonel's files. Marie showed the lieutenant.

"I never saw any of these spaces or documents," he said. "Colonel Millar must have had them taken."

Whatever suspicions Marie had, she set them aside in order to concentrate on Serah. They went through the military documents, setting out potential scenarios as Marie had done at the Louvre just days earlier. She ordered Lieutenant Berry and Iné to look for simple location notations they already knew were from the teams moving the reproductions and the original. Another soldier brought them a map of France so she could re-plot where the reproductions and the original had crossed paths.

One scenario put the original too far north for it to be plausible. "Too much military contact," the lieutenant told them.

Four other scenarios had teams running up and down the Loire, which the lieutenant reported wasn't possible because Saumur, about fifty miles to the west, had been repeatedly attacked and roadways had been inaccessible for a year.

One scenario put all the decoys and the original within reach of Amboise. The only problem was that Marie and the team were in possession of all the decoys with no trace of the original.

After hours of running scenario after scenario, Marie dropped into her chair. "We're exactly where we left off, aren't we?"

The lieutenant paced the room with his hands behind his back. "What about the photos? There's got to be something more to them."

Marie knew there was, but couldn't risk giving away the position of the Maquis. For a moment, she considered hauling Philip into the silo and putting a gun to his head. It occurred to her, though, that he'd been so desperate to get her to Amboise because he, too, had so few answers. The pair in front of her flipped through the remainder of the manifests, dejected and, in truth, not much help.

"Go get some food," she told them. "I'm good down here for a while."

The lieutenant and Iné left. Marie stretched for the first time in much too long. Her ribs ached.

She stared at the notations she hadn't told the others about. Marie translated the code again: **φΛ. Σίβυλλα. Mére. Maison.**

A scream welled up inside her. All of this led nowhere. All of this, that was, except the journals—Francesco Melzi's journals. The greatest find of her lifetime. They were, however, leading her to a place she had no desire to go.

Nonetheless, they were all she had. Marie slid the second one out of its leather casing and turned straight to the colophon. These coded details at the back of the book usually recorded information relating to how a manuscript was produced and the people involved in its production.

The cipher, one favored by Anglo-Saxon scribes, was relatively easy to break. It replaced vowels with nearby consonants. She hadn't expected the date to be right there, but it almost slapped her in the face: January 1516.

A second cipher used a more concerning technique. Those lines appeared as Greek numbers. She knew otherwise. It took her a while to break a simple line into the Latin phrase "caute age".

"Act cautiously." She caught herself explaining it out loud.

"Why?" Iné had just returned. Marie could hear the lieutenant talking to another soldier in the passageway.

"Not you, the book." She held it up to show Iné. "This was a technique for warning people of traitors. It's most common in medieval pieces, but it persisted well into the Renaissance with some of the more secretive sects."

"Can you tell who wrote it?"

"The book is damaged beyond that. But our author was definitely worried about being exposed." Marie carefully paged through, showing her what she meant.

"The whole book is in code just like the first one," Iné said.

Marie looked at her, bubbling over with surprise. "How did you know about Asfoora earlier?"

"My family is from the Maghreb."

"Desert people," Marie smiled. "I wondered if you were Tunisian."

"You know it?"

"My husband was from el-Jem."

Iné lingered on Marie for a moment, her eyes growing soft. "These books are important, then?"

"It's just a personal journal."

"Can you break the code?"

"It'll take some time." Marie found herself at ease with Iné. "Let's see what Melzi had to say."

She dug into the translation, mumbling to herself and jotting down combination possibilities. About an hour later, she looked up to see Iné staring at her.

"Sorry. Have you got it yet?" the woman asked.

Marie read what she could.

"I regret, however, to report that while the King finds his company charming, others continue to plot to use him. An old man filled with more vanity than sense at times, the Master has taken to such sycophantic attention. The servants whisper he meets with generals to design grand devices of war. The nobles speak of revolt. I hardly encounter him now, little more than an overseer of his affairs."

"Castle intrigue," Iné jokes. Shifting back and forth on her feet, she rubbed something on the inside of her forearm with her thumb

"This had to be an apprentice of some sort." Marie hedged on the details. She kept reading: "The girl knocked upon my door last evening to alert me to the Master's state of mind. We'd arrived at the royal residence without most in France knowing what we carried with us and for whom."

Marie continued, "I found myself envious of the Master's lack of concern at our delicate situation. I isolated myself to the point of utter loneliness and longed for simple joys. How could he not be fearful once stepping outside our living quarters? So many traitors."

She abruptly closed the book. Strange. Why did she feel so guilty for reading a journal penned more than four hundred years earlier? Why did she feel like an intruder back in sixteenth-century France at a precarious moment in a man's life? She tried to return to the investigation of details.

"Any more?" Iné asked.

"A bit." Marie sized up the woman who had inched closer for the next installment.

She found herself compelled to keep going. "I found the underground passages near the Gate of Heaven, the gardens of Château Gaillard just beyond. Oh, Dom Pacello's sublime creation! Within moments of entering, the warmth of the torch-lit corridors offered up the least of the surprises. Life flourished in such a space. There, in the hills of Amboise, it seems an entire civilization lives. I shall have to write to my Asfoora. She will be able to decipher all that my eyes took in."

Marie caught her breath at the mention of the name again. She took in the date, the references, and the name of the woman into consideration. These were Melzi's journals. She was sure of it. That meant the woman named Asfoora was real. No, Marie told herself, she had to be wrong. Yet she couldn't stop translating the backward script out loud, "There he was, at the Treasury, demanding I follow him just past the grove. We tucked ourselves behind the stone wall and the Master commanded me to listen. One of the veiled maidens spoke of Herophile's declaration. Surely, they could not mean the Sibylla Erythrae. Yet, these women laid out the Tilia leaves in the falling snow with the reverence of those awaiting a prophecy from my Asfoora."

A notation in the margin clipped her words short. Marie snatched a photo from the files. She pressed the two together, laid one on top of the other, examined the script of each searching in disbelief. There it was: φΛ. Σίβυλλα. Mére. Maison. It was penned in ink that she knew was less than a week old.

An exact match.

"My God." Serah had sent her a message. She was alive and well enough to make sure the message was slipped into top-secret SOE documents. She thought of the guard, of others, who served as go-betweens to make this happen. Serah knew they were looking for the Sibyl, and she sent for Marie to help her get La Joconde back to Paris.

She read the final passage out loud, "A single horn cried out in the night. A strange chorus echoed in Latin, Hebrew, the tongue of the Arabs and those of the Far East, the light above the grove growing luminous. The hymns called for the coming of a beast of burden, one who would bear the duty of healing others in devotion, and the prophets sang in unison an Alleluia to the long-sought Sibyl of Amboise."

Serah, Marie thought to herself, you amazing girl. Marie pushed herself back from the small table.

"What is it?" Iné asked.

Marie had just read the passage that, for hundreds of years, kings, clergy, and Nazis had killed to track down. If Serah had found it, she knew its importance. If Serah had left the Maquis code referring to the painting and the Sibyl in the margins of that passage, it was deliberate. Marie still didn't know what it all meant in terms of finding her daughter. She took a duffle from a corner and started shoving the journals into it. "Can you get me out of here?"

Iné cleared her throat, discreetly pointing to the stairs.

"Only one way in or out, Dr. Guerrant." The lieutenant marched down them along with several armed men who flanked Iné. He set his pistol down on top of the journal on the table. "I'm going to assume you found something."

Marie was no stranger to threats. The last time she was cornered, she lost Serah. She had to find a way around the soldiers. "Why don't you tell me what you really know about these journals?"

Lieutenant Berry stared her down. "Don't be foolish."

Iné eased away from the conversation.

"Even if this Asfoora existed, she's been dead for half a millennia," Marie said.

"We're not looking for a dead woman." The lieutenant continued to look through the forgeries. "Tell me where your daughter is, Dr. Guerrant."

Marie lost her words for a moment. Noam's warnings from Paris echoed in her ears. Her eyes shot around the room. She noticed his pistol was gone from atop the journal on the table in front of them.

"Your goddamn brothers-in-arms thought they could hide her from us," he continued. "The Sibyl is ours."

"You're not going to find Serah. You're not going to find a Sibyl either."

The lieutenant picked up the journal and stroked the numbers tattooed on her arm. "You are keenly aware that many believe otherwise."

Marie yanked her arm back and buttoned the sleeve of her shirt. "I'm keenly aware that men covet power above all else."

"Some men," he continued.

"All men," Iné interrupted.

Marie heard a series of thumps. She whirled round.

Iné moved in behind her, gun pointed at Lieutenant Berry. "Give Dr. Guerrant the journal."

"Whoa, now." He took a step back and reached for his sidearm, hand landing on an empty holster.

"Give her the fucking journal," Iné barked.

The lieutenant offered a crooked smirk. "I've got men at every entrance. How do you think you're getting out of here with those, you bint?"

"Pretty sure you've lost a few." Iné kicked at something. Another pistol slid across the floor toward Marie.

Marie glimpsed a motionless boot, then a leg, then a hand. There were two dead men slumped in the doorway. She picked up the gun. "Did you think I'd come down here and turn my daughter over to you?"

A shot fired. The lieutenant collapsed, blood pooling beneath him. He gurgled and choked until his eyes clouded over, staring straight at Marie. She turned to face Iné. The woman had shot the lieutenant in the chest.

Chapter 21

PHILIP

MAY 3, 1945
CLOS LUCÉ
AMBOISE, FRANCE

Philip stood in the worn-down chapel at Clos Lucé, about to brief a unit on the morning's landmine explosion. He congratulated himself. Marie had fallen into line so easily. She was loyal to those who watched out for her; those who kept her safe. He shuddered at the memory of her face. The fear. He'd been a prisoner for eighteen days. What had she endured in four hundred and eighty?

He considered the morning's losses. Necessary. Philip had to be sure that, when details of the Mona Lisa's location surfaced, Marie would bring Serah back along with the painting. Too much hung in the balance.

Soldiers filed into the room that once housed da Vinci's workshop next to the chapel. Before heading in to greet them, Philip crossed himself in front of the Virgin Mary looming above in a half-faded fresco that reached the arched ceiling. As he entered, his satisfaction turned to unease. He shook it off, briefed the soldiers, and dismissed them for the night.

He waited for everyone to leave before lighting a cigarette. A window perch offered him a clear view of Château Amboise across the commune and the flickering stars that filled the sky. With the team at work in the silo, Philip could no longer play an active role. All he could do was wait for others to complete their tasks.

The lieutenant would keep Marie on track, he told himself. Philip's faith in him ran as deep as his respect. Both men knew Marie was the key to the whole operation. With Iné adding a sense of French camaraderie, it all came together rather smoothly despite the set-backs of the past week. Although, thinking of it, Iné was due for their evening brief. He was anxious. A second cigarette failed to settle him.

The grounds of Clos Lucé were tightly packed with military vehicles. Portable washing stations were set up along the Amasse River. It was the stopover between Nantes and the east. Still, so much fighting. With no commanding officers on the route, men hooted and howled. The air stunk of tobacco and booze. Tents filled what open ground remained available.

Intense loneliness struck him. Philip made his way outside and stood in the intricately carved stone foyer of the Clos; a stone compass that once adorned the courtyard walkway now rubble neatly piled to the side. He walked down the path, through gardens that had become makeshift toilets, working through the pieces of his plan that still needed to be moved into place. He required access to the Maquis in order to find Serah. Marie was well on her way with that. And, there was the regretful job of relieving anyone having knowledge of this of their memories. That would have to come later.

Near a pond where ancient willows watched over the troops, he caught a whiff of meat cooking and made his way toward the smell. A group of men were clustered around a campfire, while two pheasants turned on a spit. They invited Philip over and offered a seat. As he joined in the backslapping and whiskey drinking, two other men sat down. He recognized them.

"Privates," he shouted. "Didn't you pull patrol duty at the silo tonight?"

"Sir." They shot up and saluted. "Lieutenant Berry sent us back to camp, colonel, sir."

"At ease, Gentlemen." Philip passed them the communal canteen. "Just you who got sent back?"

They sat.

"No, sir. Everyone," the one said. "The doctor gal wanted us all gone except the lieutenant and that Iné lady."

Philip's mood turned. Marie must have found something. It explained Iné's delay.

"All right, boys, enjoy yourselves." He needed space. "Watch those birds. They're finicky. They'll burn you if you don't tend to them."

The night air was comfortable and cool. Philip decided to walk. What would have provoked Marie to send everyone away for the night? Should he head to the silo and evaluate the situation? No. He forced himself to stick with the plan.

The questions in his head disoriented him. He'd walked well past the boundary walls of Clos Lucé. Philip knew better than to be out in the brush at night. His feet settled into the soft earth and his eyes adjusted to the moonlight. Peeking out from the canopy of chestnut and acacia trees, he could make out the half-collapsed roof of a massive château built into the stone hillside. Almost hidden by vines, moss, and years of neglect, it hadn't shown up on any of the town's maps. He was retracing his steps when he spotted shadows darting across the open field. They vanished at the very bottom of the rocky cliff, just as clouds covered the moon.

Did they just go into the rock cliff?

A theory quickly took form about the Maquis team that disappeared with the Mona Lisa: They went into those stone hillsides!

He ran across the field toward the derelict château. In less than a minute, Philip reached the wall. He wrenched back the ivy and morning glory to find a door no taller than half a man. It was propped open.

On hands and knees, he scrambled inside. Carved into the wall near the entrance was a single line and two crescent moons, a marker he'd seen on at least a half-dozen documents his men had confiscated.

Rage filled him. He needed to track those men down. However, the caves were complex, and Iné was the only one who knew how to navigate them.

Philip froze. Iné and his advice to the soldiers came to mind. Watch those birds, they'll burn you if you don't tend to them.

He sprinted back toward the Clos. He'd need troops. Near the main gate, he saw a woman running up the hill. Cloutille.

"The lieutenant's dead." She stood, hands on her knees, out of breath. "Dr. Guerrant, Iné. The journals. Gone."

Chapter 22

AESMEH

APRIL 30, 1519
AMBOISE, FRANCE

The edict I handed down to jail Melzi left me inconsolable. While I understood the haste behind my actions, I could not bear the thought that he betrayed Master da Vinci and the Sibylline.

With Tommaso having gone forth to confront him, I found myself listless and under guard in my room at Gaillard. My brain fogged as I fumbled with a plate of candied oranges on the small tin tray in front of me. I flopped onto the intricate brocade of the ruby bed covers. Any attempt at the glimmer sputtered and died out. It was as if the Sibylline Asu Priestesses had plunged me into a frigid river. Only, their healing light could not penetrate the depths of the water. I was locked in darkness. The Abbess had long warned me of such possible dampening of my gifts. It is why she protested the love between Melzi and myself. It was not joy—that brought clarity—but grief that tamped out my inner fire. I finally understood. The isolation which accompanied a Great Mother Sibyl's service was as much to keep one's mental faculties sharp and her heart devoted only to truth, as it was to protect the Sibyl from those who sought to profit from an oracle.

The urge to abandon this quest for La Joconde and Master da Vinci overtook me. I wanted to run, to feel safe once again despite the Amyntas standing guard right outside, keeping me secure. I had crucial Sibylline work to complete. However, my impulses would not let me remain.

"Might we please take stock of the preparations for my ceremonies?" I pressed my face and hands against the wooden door, knowing my Amyntas were just beyond it.

"The Abbess has ordered us, Great Mother. No one in or out."

"Of course." I slumped, concocting tales to ease their devotion to vows. "Alas, I overheard one of the elder scribes at Clos Lucé speak of sentinels in the forest down at the holy waters that flow from Caelmorney."

"Not a soul in or out. Desolé, Great Mother."

The adherence of the Amyntas to what I knew was wise infuriated me. I scrambled out a window and teetered on the ledge just outside, sliding my feet until I could leap onto the lower roof. As soon as my feet alighted upon the stone path of the courtyard, the Amyntas from outside my room flanked me.

"Shall we walk, then?" one asked. Her face remained unadorned with sentiment. However, I understood the concession.

We took to the path from Gaillard up onto the ridge above from which all of Amboise could be surveyed. There, outside the temple that stood carved into the rock not more than the length of four men in the distance, women moved in procession. They carried baskets of food and shimmering fabrics. A pair of Sibylline from the Heliade Order laid down radiant paintings of women in gold. All paused, soft and reverent, as I mounted the hill and stood before them. They worked in the open, even as soldiers gathered in the valley below. My heart leapt at the sight of my people once again as peaceful and productive above ground as we had been below. It struck me, the dire nature of ensuring our Dear One enters the temple with me at the prescribed time. I rushed off from the crowd, overrun by such delight and despair, searching only for a quiet, solitary moment.

The cool air of the evening filled my lungs. My eyes could not clearly see the blooming muguet along the river banks. My nose was unable to inhale the lilacs in the forest. It was not until I found myself amidst the circular columns of the sacred spring, guarded for more than a millennia by a trio of monks in the forest outside Gaillard, that my senses returned.

I tossed myself upon the stonework at the edge of the turquoise waters. A wall of stone shaped like a half-moon directed its gushing flow into the Amasse River. I wept. Peering into its depths, I contemplated what lurked at the deep bottom. Was it the serpent of death that villagers whispered tales of to keep children from inching too close? Was it a portal to new worlds that women, such as myself, had always held close in our stories, yet never confirmed?

I lingered, allowing the coolness of the forest to ease my spirit. I was alone, utterly so. Beneath the chestnut trees, the solitude swept away the fog in my mind. However, the solitude alarmed me most. No monks of Fontevraud, the spring's eternal guardians, joined me in the forest.

I stretched my renewed senses, trying to reassure myself that the brotherhood had not abandoned their post. Yet, the thorny pines whispered in the wind; the sparrows' songs grew weak and distant. Not even the Amyntas knew where I had gone. So, I set forth along the path back toward the smithy's hut amidst the groves of oaks, beeches, and wild cherry trees.

I sensed a presence, then two—a growing concern they were in danger, hunted even. I searched for signs of anyone, yet found nothing beyond disembodied footfalls. The Amyntas no longer took up their positions on the seven bridges leading from the hell of the forest into the heaven of the gardens. I drove myself to presume the quiet was a result of the late hour, my incursion at the smithy's hut, and the edict to lock Melzi down. Yet, I sensed a nefarious presence tracking us.

I bolted through the east gate of Gaillard, past the stone walls that protected the gardens from the rumors of witches, fairies, and goblins. Such stories of evil kept us praying to God for protection and I wished I might be granted salvation. It was too late. From the twisting path above me, two men in dark cloaks approached. I searched the balconies of Gaillard for the Amyntas. By the time I understood my hasty mistake, the taller of the men had backed me into one of the shallow caves just off the main forest path. Ones I knew well, having used them often to sneak off with Melzi.

I fought. As hands pressed over my mouth, I spotted a ring with the crest of Charles V. The smell of Valerian and clove overtook me as they tore the Seal from my neck and blackness set in.

By the time my head cleared, I could not see a thing. I was bound, tossing about in a cart in the dark of night. The weight of dead bodies pressed against me. All I heard was the men shifting on the cart bench and a slight snort from the horses, as the cart bumped along. Their silence proved one thing—they were no amateur abductors. I contemplated my options. My feet were not bound tight. This told me they either consider me dead or am no threat to them.

At that moment, I valued Maurine and her penchant for disobeying the Abbess more than ever. As children at Fontevraud, we often snuck over the ridge to watch the Amyntas train. Evading capture was one of our favorites. We'd even go back to the Abbey and practice tying each other up. I always got out.

The rope was pliable. I began to work the binds from my legs, twisting my feet back and forth until the rope started to stretch. I did the same with my hands until I could work each loop of rope over my hands until free.

Tugging at the sack on my head, I quelled my desire to gulp air. In the cart, on either side of me, lay the girls who clothed me earlier alongside

Lady Marguerite and Maurine. I placed a hand upon one of them and a glimmer shot through me.

"My God, no!" A collective voice screamed in my head, as if all of the Sibyls of eleven millennia witnessed the killings. The men had forced their way into the herbal stores demanding a valerian compound and murdered them as they prepared tinctures and poultices. The markings on their necks and arms, half-torn clothes, told me they had been ravished to death. I placed my hands on the other to relieve both women of the mark of such a woeful end. The pain seared my spirit, but it was the least I could do to quiet their spirits passing into the beyond.

I had to get away.

The cart pulled off the road. As far as I could tell, we had been moving south, and at a grueling, slow clip. The cart halted in a small grove. I felt it go over a heavy bump before settling. The stink of something rotting in the damp heat overwhelmed my senses. No man would be tolerant of such an odor. They would sleep far from the cart—hopefully the last advantage I would need. But, I also needed to retrieve the Seal I expect they still have.

I wriggled out of my position. As I hit the ground, I came face-to-face with a soldier who met his end long ago with a blade to the neck. He was heaped amongst at least four more—the bumps the cart had gone over. Those poor girls were no longer the foulest thing in the forest.

The cadavers proved useful. My captors, indeed, slept far from the dead. Holding my breath, I wrapped what was left of the dead man's slender form in my cloak. His remains were in such a state that I could not offer him what I had done for the women. However, I offered a prayer over him and the others, and plumped the space in the cart with his bones.

"May the light of the Great Mother, without end, carry you forth to the dawn of all tomorrows," I whispered the blessing and reached for the handle of the cart, which I hoped my captors had touched. A glimmer rose, showing one man wrapping it and placing it under the seat. Pleased at how easily men were outmaneuvered, I had it back around my neck in moments.

I knew that part of Amboise—a mixture of crops, sunken lanes, and dense hedges just beyond the Loire River. In the glow of the moon, the twisting lanes lined with birch and oak offered plenty of cover. However, the trees offered the enemy the same protection. I grew hot and stuffed my gloves in my belt. Collecting two small sticks, I fastened my hair off my neck.

Within the first stretch, my eyes adjusted to the darkness. I reached out, my hands landing on the trunk of a tall birch. This was much like taking stock of the conditions along the river that morning as we left Fontevraud. The Abbess had guided me in how to use this aspect of the glimmer as a guide. The natural world had its own imprint. One could use a tree as a way to grow taller in the sense that my sight could shoot up to the very tip of its top. The birch allowed me to see above the canopy.

It was as if I saw through the eyes of the tree, then my own. In the distance, the narrow, tapering flags of the castle carrying the Salamander coat of arms of King François fluttered above the forest.

"Hypatia as my guide," I said, eyes wide as the stars offered me a map. I was back on course to Gaillard.

My low spirits shifted to determination. I would find Maurine, and get word to the Abbess. She could rally the other Sibylline to search for La Joconde. As my foot fell upon the ground, the soft crush of bones startled me. I had stepped on the shattered skull of a man. From the picked-clean look of the skeleton, his death, such as the others, was not fresh. Flowers grew around it. I spotted a weapon in the underbrush. I reached for it, forgetting my bare hands. The instant the metal met my skin, a glimmer shot into my body and I relived the last moments of his life.

Never before had I immersed myself in the horror of reliving so much death. In the glimmer, people and animals lay bloated, their legs stretched up towards the sky. Master da Vinci once told me the graveyards were full of markers with no bodies beneath them. Out there in the forests, where the stench wafted through the night and scavengers came to pick at the flesh before it turned black in its corruption, most men found eternal rest. What I saw at that moment confirmed his thoughts. The glimmer showed man-after-man dying by the blade of the weapon in my hands.

My fingers traced the carving on the handle of the knife, then wrapped around it and gripped the metal. Again and again, I saw the dead man thrust the blade into the side of another. My mind flashed. Men killed one another over and over in the fields of Amboise. Fire rained down from the sky. The cacophony of screams and strange roars as if great beasts inhabited the sky loosened my grip. I could not focus on the face of the victim. A nose. Eyes, terrified, and draining of life. Blackened hair. Stained hands. Was I seeing the Master's abduction? He had only disappeared days earlier. This man had been dead for months.

Then, a face appeared. Voices in my mind.

"Where is he?" the dead man spoke to his victim. "Why are you protecting those whores?"

The bleeding man whimpered and begged, whispering as he faded away. My spirit ached. These men, so full of hate, as if the Sibylline were monsters placed upon the Earth to rid it of their very souls. From the memories forced into me by the blade, it was clear that not one of the men in that field ever lived or worked in the presence of a woman of the Sibylline Order.

"Such ignorance," I said, and that is when it struck me. The Abbess understood, as I had not until that moment, what the last thousand years in hiding had cost us. The few of us left after the schism retreated further and further into regular society. Yes, we had established ourselves secretly amongst queens, abbesses, domestics, and courtesans, where men and women who showed promise could be taken in by the Sibylline and instructed in the mysteries. Most, though, considered us vermin. "Unless I rise, unless our Dear One is found, we are lost in the minds of anyone beyond Amboise."

I slumped down into the morass of skeletons beneath my feet. The words of dead men cried out in my mind.

"Sorceress."

"Beast."

"Unholy."

We had become only what others told them of us. Men had been turned away from the light of the Great Mother. The gift of the Sibyl, her powerful voice and capacity to end the death, the fear, and the ignorance I squatted amidst on that battlefield could not be believed. A war of the mind had been waged. The plot to take out the Sibylline had been planned a thousand years before and raged to this very day. I had to prevent it from turning our world into nothing more than a myth.

Chapter 23

MARIE

MAY 3, 1945
LES GRENIERS DE CÉSAR
AMBOISE, FRANCE

Marie stared at Lieutenant Berry bleeding out on the floor of the silo. Dead men littered the room. She wasn't sure who had pulled the trigger that killed him and didn't bother to examine the guns she and Iné clutched in their hands.

She picked up the duffle bag containing two of the journals and shoved the third inside.

Once it was full, Marie emptied out the contents of a haversack propped against the wall: twenty-four-hour rations, full water bottles, wash rolls, socks, a gas cape, and a sweater. She considered picking up her gun and forcing Iné into the middle of the silo so she could make a run for it. But, Philip would torture and kill her. "We're going to need all of this. Repack it."

Iné didn't hesitate and grabbed a second pack.

"Whose side are you on?" Marie went through the loose papers on the table and those stacked in boxes. She took care to look at them for a few moments, then kept searching for another duffle, which she found in a crate. She shoveled as much of the room's contents into the bag as possible.

"We've got five, maybe ten minutes before someone gets here," Iné said. "What about the paintings?"

"They are useless," Marie said. Reproductions aren't going to help her find Serah. Besides, neither woman would be able to carry the heavy pieces far. "Just tell me, can you get a line out to the Maquis?"

Iné nodded.

"Good, let's seal this place up." Marie looked down at the bodies. "Help me."

They dragged the corpses of the two soldiers that had been with the lieutenant into the tunnel, closed the heavy door, and stacked the dead men against it. "That should give us some time," Marie said.

The pair moved into the dark corridors, back down the painted hallways. Iné broke the silence. "The tunnels can get us as far as Gaillard, but we'll be out in the open after that."

"Gaillard?" Marie asked.

The women moved into synchronicity, a sort of grace overcoming them, as they planned.

"The outer castle to the north," Iné explained. "There's a discrete exit point there, but we'll have to cross the Amasse River to get to the Maquis camps."

Iné moved with power Marie had not noticed before. Was she the same woman from earlier? Even her eyes seem to have shifted, a pearlescent green coming through the deep brown. An obvious plant, but from whom? What was she after? Would she shoot Marie as she had done to the lieutenant? "You planned to kill him?"

"Did you?"

The sleeves of Iné's blouse were rolled up. Marie snatched her arm and pushed the material looking for SS or Russian markings. Covering much of Iné's right forearm was a tattoo of a single line with two crescent moons on either side. "For Christ's sake. What are you?"

"It's the mark of my people." Iné tossed both duffle bags over one shoulder.

"Can you fight?" Marie was sure she'd seen that marking elsewhere, but she couldn't place it.

"Of course."

Marie rummaged through the second haversack, pulling out a knife. She took the lieutenant's gun from her waistband and handed it to Iné. "I prefer the blade."

"Hmm." Iné grinned and lifted her sweater to reveal a shoulder holster with a dagger in it. "Me too."

"The other soldiers?"

"Back of the neck. Didn't even squeal."

Marie spotted the woman catching the upturn of her smile.

"My father taught me how to use his Le Vengeur trench knife." She didn't really know why she rattled off her own history. "Never trusted the Germans."

"You sure you remember how to use it?" Iné asked.

"Like to find out?"

Iné sniffed and kept working. She put her trust in me, Marie thought. Odd. This level of loyalty was almost suspicious.

Marie gripped the double-bladed, seven inch dagger she'd pulled from the pack, which brought her father's words back to her.

"It's too easy to kill a person with a gun." Her father taught her the basics of elbow, neck, knees, waist, ankles, shoulders. "Too easy to see life as dispensable."

The F-S trench knife looked far more slick and deadly than the one her father passed down. She didn't ever want to point a gun at another person. However, the incident with the lieutenant gave her reason to rethink that. Marie reached her hand back out to Iné. "I'll take the gun too."

She sifted through the haversack and pulled out a pair of charges. An idea sparked. "Get into the corridor. Keep moving. I'll catch up."

Marie handed Iné the packs.

"What are you doing?"

"We need to blow the stairs leading from the castle. Then, there's no way in but from the top."

"Good call, but you should let me do it."

Marie admired the woman's sensibility. She wasn't going to get far in those dark corridors without her.

Iné pulled more charges from her bag. "Do not move from here. In all seriousness."

Marie hesitated. "You've got a lot of nerve."

"For getting you out?" Iné shouted back at her from the staircase above. "Do you even know what you signed on for?"

Marie didn't answer. The lieutenant's threats proved she had not properly evaluated what she'd walked herself into.

All of a sudden, Iné bounded toward her. As the charges went off, she leapt and landed on top of Marie. The tunnels shook for a moment, then settled. They moved quickly down a new corridor, again, their way lit by a source Marie could not determine.

"Did someone hire you for this?" Marie probed for answers.

"I'm . . . undercover."

"SOE?"

"Ba'alat."

"What the hell is that?" Marie knew Ba'alat only as a reference to Ba'alat Gebal, the goddess of the city of Byblos in ancient Phoenicia. She sorted through all the correlations to Egypt's Hathor, then remembered her Hebrew. The Ba'alat Ha'Ov was a sorceress. The connection sent shivers through her body.

"We, um, get people out of situations."

Marie knew what she meant by 'situations.' Philip.

"You are stupid, you know." Iné finally turned on a headlamp, revealing a ledge in front of them. She easily scrambled up it, as if having climbed it a thousand times.

"I'm sorry, what did you say?"

"All those degrees, more than a dozen languages. You even survived those bastards in the camps, but you almost let your desperation give everything away."

Searching for Serah in Paris, unable to uncover any leads as to her whereabouts, had left Marie frantic. Philip knew it. He gave her La Joconde. It was only because of Noam that she didn't hand the colonel everything he wanted. Marie's heart broke. "You know where Serah is ?"

"Not quite." Iné stuck her hand out to assist Marie up the jagged wall of rock.

"Then, why should I trust you?"

"This is a rescue, we've established that." Iné pointed out the dim shapes of footholds and handholds. "There's a small landing about ten feet up. I'll toss the rope down. You can cinch the bags and then climb yourself if you don't want my help."

"I don't need your help to find Serah."

Iné snorted, got to the next level, and sent the rope down. "He was going to kill you and all the rest of us once you gave us up."

Marie strung bits of knowledge about the woman together. The attempt to help her in the street after the land mine went off. How Iné reappeared in the tower, got her to safety. "You're Maquis?"

"You've got plenty of people who believe you have value."

Marie tried to construct an argument, but opted for silence. She had watched the route Iné took up the rock face. Had mapped it in her head and traversed the wall. She made quick work of the climb, even with a sore set of ribs. The pair, again, moved as if old partners, but silence hung between them. "Why were you in there, with the colonel?"

"The colonel, yes. It is better to stand at the side of your enemy than wait to find him at your back."

How very true, Marie thought. How often she had submitted to whatever Nazi whim needed dealing with in order to stay alive another day. To get back to Serah.

"I supervised the whole ruse around La Joconde in '38." Marie suspected Iné already knew that.

"We're all vulnerable when we love something."

"You seem to know a lot about this situation." Marie started to concoct a round of questioning.

"What did you find, I mean, in the journals?"

"Just get us out of here."

Iné stopped talking. They turned down a dim, musty corridor so unused it appeared as if it would never open onto the outside world. It revealed itself as nothing more than a single tunnel with no defining characteristics other than the rugged stone from which it was carved, so different from the other entrance. The women moved up a series of steps that led to another level of passages.

"How did you know?" Marie looked out over the five paths they had to choose from and shook her head. It was brutally black in the corridor. She had already started to gauge the time between segments of the walk. At Ravensbrück, a political prisoner, taken for blowing up bridges in Denmark, taught her how to gauge time to and from certain locations in the dark by the number of paces. They were five minutes from the rock they just scaled, fifteen from the silo.

"About what?" Iné glanced around, distracted.

"About the lieutenant? Philip? How did he know?"

"The lure of that sort of power changes a man. I've seen what she does."

"La Joconde?"

"The Sibyl." Iné kept walking, never hesitating. "Immortality. Control of one's fate. They test the best of us."

"You think she's real, then?" Marie's emerging trust for Iné came to an abrupt end.

"They do."

"Is that what the colonel's men were after when they were killed?"

"That's what everyone is after." Iné stopped.

They walked for a long time in the darkness.

"The photos the lieutenant denied putting in the SOE file," Marie finally spoke. "They had notations about the Sibyl and the painting."

"Like what?" Iné seemed to stiffen.

"Four notations in ancient Greek."

Marie caught the spark in Iné's eyes. It was the same glint she saw in the lieutenant's eyes. It was the one SS officers got when women in her barrack found a clue. Marie most definitely knew she wasn't in the presence of an ally.

That oracle drove everyone who came into contact with her mad. History proved it. Julius Caesar burned entire cities based on a single image reported in a vision. Croesus, the king of Lydia, asked the oracle if he should attack Persia. Believing she told him yes, he attacked and was annihilated. Himmler leveled oracle sites all across Europe and North Africa searching for access to her power.

"What did the notation say?" Iné had yet to look back.

"Please tell me everything happening here isn't about Serah."

Iné grimaced and remained silent.

Marie fumed. She waited until Iné set the duffles down. Elbow. Neck, she told herself. She'd had enough, refusing to go on another minute, chancing Serah's death for this Sibyl lie. The blade met the woman's neck in an instant. She directed Iné to open the first duffle. "Pull them out and put them in the middle of the room."

Iné fished stacks of papers and the journals from the bag. Marie pushed her away and rummaged through a haversack until she pulled out a book of matches. She tore the page with the notations from Serah out of a journal and tossed it on the ground. What she was about to do horrified her.

Marie lit a match. The superstitious horror of the Sibyl needed to die right there. Not one person would discover a single piece of evidence feeding wild theories ever again. No woman would be flayed, dismembered, or burned to death for this myth. Ever again. Each page had to be obliterated. She could find Serah without them.

"Don't do this," Iné said, on her knees. "You will be just like your colonel."

"I'm nothing like any of those bastards." Marie shook as she lit the first pages on fire. "I'm just doing what no one else will do."

Tears flooded Marie's cheeks. She bit through her lip attempting to remain steady and true. All she had to do was ignite the rest of the documents and let them burn.

"You're doing exactly what he wanted. Can't you see?" Iné looked at Marie with an eerie calm. Her hands went up. She swallowed. "Just stop. Please."

Men's voices grew louder behind them.

"Look . . . see." Iné pressed a hand against Marie's chest. A jolt shot through Marie. For a moment, the tunnels seemed to lighten and warm. The walls danced with intricate murals. Stacks of colorful woven blankets, tall amphorae filled with water, and bins of onions lined the corridor. The olive-skinned, youthful face of a woman not much older than Serah appeared. Then, more women, all with the tattoo that Iné had on her arm, rushed past.

"What is this?"

"The only proof I can give you. Please, trust me." Iné crouched next to her. She removed her hand and the corridor darkened again. She stamped out the burning pages and stuffed everything back in the duffle. "There are things at play, things you deserve to understand. However, they will get us both killed if we don't get out of here."

Chapter 24

PHILIP

MAY 3, 1945
AMBOISE, FRANCE

In the main silo, Philip stood over the lieutenant's body. A man he'd respected. Going out like this was unacceptable. The blood on the stone floor circled the lieutenant's head like a horrific halo. His filmy eyes offered astonishment, as if they had no clue what froze them in place. There was the stench of urine and shit. That was always the worst part of men dying, their bowels letting loose like those of babies. Undignified, incontinent, then nothing. Life ended in a pile of shit. Seemed just about right.

The silo was a hive of activity, with men hauling scaffolding and buckets of wood through a rope and pulley system out the top. Philip closed his eyes, tuning in to the boot-steps of soldiers searching the corridors beyond those that hadn't been jammed by rocks and bodies. All that remained were the replicas in boxes.

A throat cleared behind him. Philip turned around and sighed.

"There's no trace of Iné or Dr. Guerrant," Cloutille reported.

"The journals?"

Cloutille waved her hand across the mess. Philip quickly silenced her as another officer entered. He took note of the soldier's stocky, thick-shouldered build and jet-black hair. Hopefully, he was more durable than Lieutenant Berry proved to be.

"Corporal Davies, sir!"

"The women can't have gotten far with the load they were carrying, corporal," Philip said. "There are at least a hundred men on the ground at Clos Lucé. Arm and mobilize them. Everything else is need-to-know. I've given the coordinates of an entry to the caves that I found. Time the teams so units of four enter in fifteen-minute increments. This is capture, not kill."

With a salute and a pivot, Davies left. Cloutille lifted the lid off one of the intact crates and pulled one, then another of the replicas out.

Philip forced himself to calm down and studied them. His eyes traced the hint of a black veil layered atop the Mona Lisa's ringlets of hair. He examined the details of the background; the tiny bridge in the right half of each of the paintings—it looked remarkably like the one crossing the Loire at Amboise, perfect in each rendition. "You know, these really are very good. I'm no art historian, but I'd never be able to tell the difference."

"Her mouth is off. The eyes are too soft." Cloutille's victory roll and perfectly pressed khaki suit stood in stark contrast to the catastrophe that had just occurred. She stepped closer, arms crossed. "The sfumato is muddy in the first and the third one. The second is the best. I might have done better."

"You're sulking."

"I told you Alexander didn't have enough sense to run the operation alone. Dr. Guerrant is not as simple and broken as you assume." Cloutille eyeballed the dead lieutenant. "Why not let me go in by myself?"

Philip considered her offer when it occurred to him that Marie, and that conniving Iné, had given him an unexpected advantage.

"Have you ever been hunted?" He looked over the features of the woman in the painting.

"Not lately."

"The Nazis tracked us for almost two weeks in the early part of the war. They always knew where we were. We earned every yard. The pace drove us to the edge of our minds."

Cloutille watched as he drifted into the wicked memory.

"We woke up to barbed wire strung across our planned routes. Mortars were set to blow arms and legs in every direction." He ran a hand down the thigh of his lame leg. "I hated the sound of Spandau fire, but the short crack of a sniper's rifle was so much more deliberate. One pop and someone didn't make it home. Living and sleeping with the dead all around us, was far worse than being locked in a cell."

"You think a woman who survived a German camp will be drawn out by time and pressure?"

"Marie is vulnerable. I saw it at the Louvre. This will paralyze her."

"What about that woman Iné? You said yourself the caves are her domain, and I doubt she's innocent in this," Cloutille said. "The soldiers at the Clos are infantry. They aren't trained for a hunt. They'll never get on top of them."

Philip offered her a sardonic grin.

"You're not trying to capture them," Cloutille said, sharing a grin. "You're going to let those two get us inside the Maquis. They're going to find Serah Izem for us."

He took one of the framed decoys of the Mona Lisa and cracked it in half with his good leg.

"Then," he said, "you can empty an entire box of bullets into both of them."

Chapter 25

MAY 1, 1519
CHÂTEAU GAILLARD
AMBOISE, FRANCE

Sunlight dappled the velvet coverings layered upon me. I took note of the soft featherbed, what a delight. The modest living of the women at Fontevraud did not allow them. I considered determining how I had found myself returned to Gaillard, but the hours spent in the woods had left me chilled in body, uncentered in mind.

I could see the bright-blue day through the tall, thin windows. Two Amyntas stood on guard inside the doorway. A pot of herbs bubbled on the hearth. I detected coriander, smallage, henbane, and hemlock—the source of my spotty vision and heavy eyes. Maurine once used that herbal concoction to put a fellow Sibylline into a long sleep and cure her of ergot poisoning that ended in a bout of St. Anthony's Fire. I hoped I hadn't ended up in the damp rye fields tromping around in the ergot mold that often caused this painful malady. I must have returned to Gaillard rather incoherently for her to treat me with such an aggressive fume. The last moment I recall was releasing the dead soldier's blade from my hands, and collapsing amongst the dead.

What I witnessed in the fields beyond Gaillard confirmed what the

Abbess had deduced. Men were ignorant to our true purpose of guiding them to their truth. My mind returned again and again to a truth I didn't want to accept—the message in the dodecahedron. That Master da Vinci left such a message proved he suspected his abduction was imminent. Yet, the message did little more than implicate Melzi in all that passed. Was Melzi the traitor the Abbess had spoken of at Fontevraud?

The recollection of my glimmer gave me nothing beyond that. Every person left an impression that I could pick up. A lack of one was nearly impossible. All touch left remnants for me to read. The only plausible answer was that whoever took him cleansed the space. Yet, the dodecahedron still had the Master's imprint. Nothing added up.

My mind spun. I knew I had to get back to his study at the Clos.

"You shall lose your life if you remain buried much longer," Maurine spoke from the other side of the room. I poked my head out from beneath the bed coverings. "Come, I steeped a bath of linden, lavender, catswort, and ginger hot enough to soothe the devil's soul."

The Amyntas moved the steaming bath into the room after sending off the two servants who hauled it to the top of the stairs. I piled the blanket over my head.

Maurine stifled a giggle. "You look like a specter."

"How did I make it back?"

"I swear, you think you are the only one with any power," Lady Marguerite said as she entered. Her courtly robes told me she had just come from an audience of her brother and the king's advisers.

Maurine straightened up and waved me toward the steaming tub. "We found the dead femmes de chambre a few clicks down the road. The Amyntas discovered you in the woods, curled into a ball."

"Those who took me?"

"Gone, of course." Maurine broke in. "It was foolish for you to wander like that."

The heaps of bodies in the fields of Amboise dominated my memory. "Did you know about all of the killings?"

"Men have been fighting since the spring," Lady Marguerite spoke as if I should have known this.

"Who could have foreseen such a plot was underway?" Maurine asked.

"Me! I should not need to guess." I shook my ungloved hands at her. "The glimmer is the only undertaking I was said to have mastered in this life."

"You were at Fontevraud," The Abbess entered, everyone dropping into silence. The Amyntas locked the door. "Besides, the visions are not always clear or complete until your trials are done."

"They were after the Seal. Stole it right off my neck," I told her.

"Why? Men cannot use it properly." The Abbess questioned. "Did you catch a glimmer from it?"

"Very little, but I do believe someone paid them to destroy it."

The Abbess took a deep breath and held up the dodecahedron metal puzzle from Master da Vinci's workshop that set this all in motion. "What you did was utterly foolish. You risked all of our lives, but this is good information."

Maurine kept her eyes lowered and passed me a pad of Castile soap. When I refused the offer, she shoved it at me, plugging her nose, and commanded me to wash the layer of dirt from my body.

"You will remain under the guard of the Amyntas from this point forward, is that understood?" the Abbess commanded. "Lady Marguerite and I will request a private audience with King François. Move forward with your search for our Dear One."

She left me soaking, Maurine sulking in a wooden chair near the window. The sun had moved to the west before I broke the silence.

"What, pray tell, are you so sullen about?"

Shouts in the hallway roused us. I shot up from the water with barely enough time to grab a robe before Melzi and Tommaso burst in.

"Cazzata!" Tommaso shouted the expletive down the hall behind him, then turned to me and bowed. "I told him not to try this. Everyone is restless with the Master missing."

Melzi raced in after. "Aesmeh, I need to speak with you."

"This is not a good time." I stood, dripping wet.

"Can you not see she is hurt? Are you so simple?" Tommaso shouted at him.

"Yes, I'm simple. The more complicated I make it, the more likely I am to lose my head," Melzi said. "I quite like my head."

Maurine nodded at me as if I ought to let this intrusion go. "Most people do not enjoy the company of the executioner."

"Enough, please, I have nothing to do with the Master's disappearance," Melzi said.

"Yours is the only name the Master left behind." I voiced the accusation we were all thinking. "And where is La Joconde?"

Melzi gazed, his look one of confusion.

"The woman you have been painting since your fifteenth year?" I doubted his ignorance and resented having to offer up the reminder.

"The one the Master used to instruct us?" Tommaso asked.

The three women glared at him.

"Was it more?"

I shot a fiery glance and turned my rage upon Melzi. "The Abbess directed you, specifically, to clear out anything Master da Vinci worked on."

Melzi hung his head. "Heaven on Earth."

"Where was it?" I asked.

"On the Master's easel," he said. "I thought he was adjusting the midtones, fiddling around. He has painted very little in a year. Is it gone?"

"Of course, it is gone."

"Should you not be able to see who took it?"

I hesitated, not wanting to tell them, already spooked by my attempted abduction. My words would make a dire situation bleaker. "The workshop and study were cleansed."

"You could not read its imprints? Isn't that impossible?" Melzi said.

"You know it is not."

Everyone fell silent, heads down. Only Melzi and I held each other's gaze.

"You are the only one who knew that the Abbess taught Master da Vinci the technique," I said. "The only person to whom he would trust to teach such a skill."

"I would never," Melzi spoke gently. He stared at the rope burns on my ankles and legs. "They tried to take you? Who would do such a thing?"

He started to pace. I tossed out a hand and stopped him. He brushed it away. "How could you accuse me of this? That you might take me for such a perilous creature."

"That I might not, and meet the executioner myself." I remained still and focused. "You are amongst the few who know our plight, what we risk."

"You must return to hiding."

I considered what I had witnessed in the field of dead soldiers. "We have hidden for nearly a thousand years. Too much has been sacrificed, too much will be lost if I do."

"Then let me help you find the Master and the painting."

I stiffened. "For the last fifteen years, Master da Vinci has trusted you with every detail of his life. Now, you are clueless and mistaken at every turn?" I gave judgment, believing it might ache less to render it with haste.

"You must believe me."

"I have learned not everything is equal to the stories told," I told him.

Melzi watched me. Tears stained his perfect face. The Amyntas took one arm each and escorted him out. Tommaso turned as if to offer advice, but left without a word.

Maurine began the tedious work of dressing me. As she worked through each piece, slipping my arms through the embroidered gown at the end, we remained silent. She looked into my eyes, lips tight, holding back words. She gloved my hands and passed me the dodecahedron the Abbess had brought with her.

The silvery smoke from the hearth fire in my chamber rushed out and down the hall through the open door where Melzi and Tommaso had recently departed. I cringed. At that moment, I acted as a Great Mother. My first edict—to lock my love in a prison cell.

Chapter 26

MARIE

MAY 3, 1945
THE TUNNELS
AMBOISE, FRANCE

Marie fished a headlamp out of one of the haversacks and banged on it, trying to get its flickering, dim light to grow steady in the dark tunnels. Iné reached out and turned it off.

"That light is more likely to get us killed than anything we stumble across in the dark," Iné said. "You cannot depend on your eyes down here. You have to feel the space to navigate it. Your sight is a crutch. Use your other senses."

In her own way, Marie understood. She'd shown her team well-hewn techniques for analyzing handwriting in manuscripts, recognizing how certain inks laid on a page, the texture and quality of certain animal-skin parchments, and the stink that certain spores left on rotting books or paintings. Such discoveries could not be made with the eye; they had to be detected through smell, touch, even taste. She possessed other skills, acquired by less conventional means.

Marie put the headlamp back in the haversack and perked her ears, taking a cue from Iné that others might be near. She let herself be still, Then, the deliberate press of boots against the walkway announced itself.

"Three, maybe four, soldiers," Marie said.

"You keep surprising me, doctor." Iné whispered.

Marie found the approval satisfying. "The Nazi camps. I helped get a few women out. In the middle of the night, the only way you can tell what you're up against is to figure out how many men they sent after you."

As they crouched, backs pressed against the stone wall, she showed Iné how to listen for cues, how to get a sense of others approaching. Pay attention to a sudden, subtle push of air past your cheek. Listen for the sound of trousers crinkling, gun-belts rattling. "Boots are a dead giveaway. No one can sneak around in them. If a man picks up his pace, you will know it. If I start to run, you better run too."

"Clever." Iné laid out her plan. "We only have to make it about half a kilometer without being spotted. The tunnels are very straightforward once you get used to our navigation system."

"How does it work?"

"Give me your hand." Iné tugged Marie close. Her fingers glided along ridges carved into the wall. The marks were distinct, cut into the stone so that no one could mistake them. "Each pathway is noted with a stamp. It's not always easy to locate, but they are connected. Keep your hand running along the wall until you start getting used to the spacing between markers. It'll make sense after a while."

"What do the symbols mean?"

"Like street signs."

Marie understood, thinking back to how she knew to make her way through the Paris catacombs. Her ability to navigate the underground reaches of Paris translated well in her current situation pleased her.

"Trust me, we've been using it for a thousand years," Iné said.

Marie was startled by the time reference. Iné's hands pressed gently over her own, her warm breath on Marie's neck as they worked. It was rather like reading cuneiform on clay tablets or, in a more modern sense, the braille language for people who are blind. Marie's fingers tingled as they moved. She made a mental sketch of the tracing, as she often did while reading ancient languages until the picture was complete.

"Is it an orange?" she asked.

Iné's expression turned serious again. She pivoted and strode down the hall. "It's the route to Château Gaillard."

She stepped forward, pulled Marie along, before closing and latching a wooden door. The air seemed to shiver, then a warm light filled the room. Marie looked around for the source.

"Watch." Iné traced the orange counterclockwise and the lights dimmed. Then, clockwise to turn them back up.

"The tunnels are wired for electricity?"

"There's a current available."

Iné looked different, ethereal in the low light. She smiled. It must be the refraction of the light of the stark, stone walls. The moment seemed familiar. She could have sworn she'd stood in this very spot before. Yet, she'd never once been to Amboise. The sense of déjà vu set her on edge. She cleared her throat.

"I've never seen anything like it. Marie was transfixed by the room. It was neat and clean, as if someone had taken a wet cloth and a mop to it every week. Yet, the chest that lined the walls appeared as if they were hundreds, possibly thousands years old. She pressed one of the lids open. "May I?"

"Of course."

In the chest were stacks of velvet blankets in the richest shades of emerald, brandy, and indigo.

"Why an orange?" Marie developed a hypothesis of where they could be, but wanted a few more details about the carvings.

"Dom Pacello." Iné's voice was almost lyrical as she led Marie down a narrow hall. The light of the room behind them dimmed and went out.

"Who?"

"Dom Pacello da Mercogliano? Léonardo des jardins? I thought you were a historian."

"I am not an encyclopedia."

Iné paused, then huffed. "About five hundred years ago, the king brought a master gardener from Italy to grow oranges in France. The orange tree here was the first of its kind. He chose the orange as the emblem for Gaillard's standards."

"I thought the first orangery was at Château Amboise."

"Not everything is equal to the stories told," Iné spoke the words in such a way that they seemed like a warning. The woman cleared her throat and returned to her previous tone. "Gaillard was the true seat of power. The castle was more of a, well, a mask."

They walked in silence. Marie's hand followed the trail. She counted five orange markers before they had to crouch and continue on hands and knees.

Iné went to pass her from behind when Marie shot a hand out. "Stop."

It was black as tar in the tunnel. Boots thumped against the path. Marie caught her breath, realizing there were men in the corridors.

"Quick, this way." They scrambled deeper into the passage. The boots stopped, then hit the path again, harder, louder. Marie couldn't wait for Iné to take charge. She moved back toward where they came from, the sharp scrape of her knife being unsheathed the only sound other than the men. The smell of fresh dirt and a whoosh of air. Neck. Side. Up the middle, she repeated to herself. The first soldier fell. The second grabbed her arm and Marie's knife dropped. Boots thumped harder, louder, closer. She wanted to shout for Iné, instead cocking her ears at the sound of bullets being chambered. Then, a shove. She rolled as a foot kicked at her. Three shots. Marie heard a gurgle. A soldier sank against a stone wall. Iné grabbed one of the men's headlamps and showed Marie a ladder leading up into another corridor. They scrambled. Behind them, a gun fired as they ran. Something shoved Marie. Her face hit the dirt. Iné hit the ground and pushed her through an opening.

Marie breathed in; the air had turned velvet. They were out of the tunnels. Iné pulled her to her feet. Marie scanned the mossy rock walls of the cave where they stood. Her eyes landed on an iron door at the front of the space that swung back and forth in the windy, hot, dark night. The trees outside, lit by moonlight, looked like the middle or even the tops of pines. Were they on a hillside? Was it a cell? Were they trapped? Several German Sten guns were stacked next to crates in one corner. She assumed they had been leftover from the occupation of Château Amboise. Bones of small animals littered the floor.

"Are there Maquis in the forest?" she asked.

"There's a camp to the north." Iné pulled a pair of flares out of the haversack still on her back.

Marie shook her head. "We need to let them know we're out here . . ."

"There's a dead drop just down the hill, maybe a hundred meters. A metal box. They check it every day. Use the coins."

Marie had no idea what Iné meant.

"The Mater Dolorosa. The Maquis know them. They know those coins were in the silo."

Marie took the red handkerchief that had been in her hair. She tucked one of the coins that fell from a journal, earlier in the silo, inside and tied it tight. "Is there a rendezvous point?"

"There's a spring in the forest. We can make the drop and head there," Iné said.

Marie's eyes shot back to the small, low opening at the back of the cave. It was thin, barely visible. How had they fit through? That didn't matter. The shouts from men grew close.

"We've got to cover that hole," she told Iné. The pair scrambled to move a set of old supply crates and stacked them to seal the opening shut.

Marie wedged one open, sifting through it. She found another knife.

"Let's get out of here." Iné pushed through the door into the forest. Marie heard boots outside the cave. She yanked Iné back into the cave fast, knocking them both on their backsides. "Stay down. Where are we?"

"A jailer's cell. They're built into the caves all along the ridges north of Château Amboise."

"Not much of a prison if you can find the back door."

Marie peered through Iné's legs into the night. They were high on a ridge. She made a mental note of the terrain. There were the remains of a stone wall. She figured they were well beyond the castle. The forest looked as if the gentle hand of a gardener had groomed it to pristine perfection. The trails were cleared and even. Birch trees stood as upright as sentinels in the night. Earthy scents of pine sap and damp moss permeated the thick heat. Marie felt soothed.

Yet, the lumbering ruins of a three-story stone house surrounded by garden walls in the near distance told a different story. Time had done its work. Vines and weather had devoured the remains of a metal roof. Stone balconies teetered. Some had entirely collapsed. A separate entrance directly beneath the house was walled over, the door boarded shut.

In the middle of a massive, overgrown garden filled with horsetails, blackberry briars, and yellow butcher's broom stood an enormous, crumbling fountain. Closer to the river, a pavilion listed, its tattered awning shifted in the breeze, statues of Venus, Hebe, the goddess of youth, and a trio of headless stone cherubs laid scattered near a dilapidated one-room brick outbuilding.

Four British soldiers stood near a layer of heavy ivy that overran the garden wall protruding from the base of the ramshackle house. Marie and Iné waited and watched as the men paced back and forth, trading details via two-way radio. Within minutes, the soldiers had scrambled through a small entrance into the rock, behind the creeping vines, and another group of soldiers took their place.

"To hell," Marie said. "I totally misread it."

"Those are the men from before."

"That will bring trouble from that direction." Marie pointed toward the crates blocking the opening at the back of the cave. The repeated slams against the wood echoed like a drum call. She then turned to point outside. "They'll see us if we head for the dead drop. We'll have to adjust the route."

Iné moved towards the Sten guns. "We can use these."

Marie grimaced. "Those may be a bigger problem than the men."

"They're guns. Let's hope they're loaded."

"They're garbage. That's probably why the Germans left them. I threw one out a window once. It hit the ground and shot out enough bullets to take down at least ten men. I wouldn't carry a loaded one around on my shoulder."

"Then, they are useful." Iné took one of the guns and moved a crate away from the back opening. Men's voices grew louder.

Marie nodded. "I guess even a shit gun is a good gun when everyone has them."

She and Iné kicked at the hole in the box that blocked the tunnel. As soon as they saw soldiers, Iné tossed the gun through the opening. As soon as it hit the ground, it started to fire. The sporadic firing of the gun silenced the voices. Marie and Iné crept out onto the forest path. Men charged up the hill toward them.

Marie twisted around, looking for a way out.

Iné held up her pistol and an empty ammunition box. "There's no way we can overpower three men with daggers."

"You'd rather try your chances with those?" Marie looked at the two remaining Sten guns.

"I guess not." Iné pulled her knife from her belt.

Marie moved toward the front of the cave, pressed herself against the front wall and waited. The night seemed darker; she struggled to make out details visible only moments ago. The men coming up the hill had gone silent, but she could hear their footsteps just beyond the cave.

Marie tried to slow her breath. She knew that if she panicked, it would be the end of them. She thought of her father and their hours of training in the Paris meat locker, as she did before a fight.

"Picture yourself landing the knife exactly where you intend. Your knife is an ambush weapon," she heard her father say, as if he were standing right next to her. "It extends your hand, gives you an advantage against bigger, stronger, more deadly opponents. Very quick, very deadly."

Her back straightened. She took up the position. Her hand molded itself to the handle. It was comfortable, familiar. Marie traced the moves her father taught her, moves she'd honed through many hours of training. How her feet could shift to give her an advantage. How to spot overconfidence—men were always overconfident. As a prisoner, it had paid off. And it needs to pay off again. She whispered to herself, "The neck is the hardest to hit, but the most deadly blow. Five, six stabs in the gut, and your opponent will bleed to death before he can attack."

The first soldier came through the door, clean-shaven, blond tufts of hair damp with sweat. No more than eighteen years old. Marie hesitated. He was so young.

"Are you trying to die?" Iné shouted as she landed the blade in his left shoulder and wrestled with him. A stocky soldier with a wisp of a mustache barrelled in. Marie let her survival instincts overtake her heart. She stabbed his lower left side near the groin, getting in two good jabs before another soldier put a gun to Iné's head.

"Drop it," he ordered.

This time, Marie didn't hesitate. She loosened the gun from the hand of the soldier she'd stabbed and trained it on the one pointing his at Iné. She stood. The blond-haired soldier on the ground grabbed her ankle. Her back hit the floor of the cave. She lost her breath but kept a hold of the weapon.

Iné's hands went up, the knife rendered useless. Marie watched her move out onto the forest path, the soldier forcing her down onto her knees. The blonde she stabbed was up on his feet, limping, having left

Marie there with a gun in her hand. Overconfident men, she thought. Men are always overconfident.

She carefully slid the gun along the ground, shifted into position, and pulled the trigger. The blonde collapsed, while the other soldier spun around. Marie fired again.

"Let's go." She got to her feet and handed Iné the haversacks, the knife, and the handgun. She emptied the pockets of both men. Ammunition. Even a little money. The duffel was strapped to her back. "Now! We have to go."

The women moved off the path into the forest. Before they got half-way down the hill, a man howled from above. The blonde soldier charged out of the cave, his eyes shooting around searching until landing on Marie and Iné. Blood stained his shirt on both the chest and shoulder. He was heaving and began to shout. "I found them. Get up here. I found them!"

Marie and Iné broke into a run, scrambling into the forest. The bags weighed them down, but Marie kept pushing hard, her mind clear and focused on getting to the Maquis dead drop and to Serah. Iné snagged her ankle on the underbrush. She stumbled, crashing over tree trunks and through blackberry patches. She thumped down a portion of a thin trail and pointed.

"See that," Iné said. A water spring bubbling out of a rocky pool was about one hundred and fifty yards down a steep hill that fed into the Amasse River far below. "That's the rendezvous point."

Men's voices grew closer from both directions. Suddenly, someone charged out of the woods and slammed into Iné. They catapulted down the hill. Marie could see nothing in the dark of night, the grunts and gasps below leaving her helpless. She spotted the glow of a headlamp, grabbed the haversacks Iné had dropped, strapped everything to her back, and tried to make her way down the steep hill. Within a few feet, she was on her rear end, sliding out of control. At the bottom, Iné was on her back, breathing hard, the soldier dead beside her.

Voices above kept them from saying a word. A sliver of sun cut across the dark horizon. It had been almost twenty-four hours since they had slept, and they'd soon be prone in the light.

The pair hobbled down the trail, Iné showing Marie where to find the dead drop. She put the handkerchief and coin inside and they hiked along a short offshoot to the northeast. There, in the middle of the forest, a spring slowly bubbled up water. It filled a channel that looked as if it had been widened to keep water flowing. There were plenty of boot prints surrounding it. Marie figured the soldiers must use it for drinking water.

The remains of a circle defined by a set of columns surrounded the spring. Iné sat down on a low boulder and motioned for her to fill up the canteens from the haversacks. Then, Iné handed Marie a metal tin the size of a pillbox. Inside was a manilla envelope, folded once over.

"What's this?"

"Dried fungus. It grows on the rye in the fields here. Careful opening it. Don't get any on your hands or you'll suffer St. Anthony's Fire."

Marie knew the medieval reference to a burning in the hands and feet. It surprised her how Iné had an odd way of talking—a trained assassin one moment and a Renaissance woman in the king's court the next. "What am I supposed to do with it?"

"Dump it in the spring."

Marie knew what Iné was up to—contaminating the drinking supply. It was easy to do. Nazis had been dumping Pervitin into the canteens of its rank and file to keep them awake for a decade. She heard about experiments at Dachau Concentration Camp, where prisoners, before being interrogated, were given water laced with mescaline that caused horrendous hallucinations. She placed her hand on the crease in her arm scarred by needle marks. "Poison?"

"It'll slow them down," Iné said.

Marie pulled her sleeves down over her hands to keep from touching the contents, then took the packet and dumped it in. She noted that Iné could barely stand.

They moved off the trail and into the forest looking for a dense patch of brush to rest in. The attack in the cave and escaping through the trees, drove memories of Ravensbrück to the front of Marie's mind.

"Are you thinking about your daughter?" Iné asked.

Marie hesitated, sucking in a few hard breaths. "This just feels way too familiar."

"The camps?"

Marie nodded.

"Just talk it through," Iné said. "It'll keep us going."

Marie pulled her up and they made slow progress toward some briars. "We had to get across Germany. Three hundred women in Red Cross trucks. I don't know what we thought. The entire countryside was burned out."

The two of them looked around them at burned out swaths of trees and entire blackened fields, scorched by bombs or deliberate fires set to expose enemies.

"They let all the French prisoners go. We just drove away. I knew the rest of those women were dead." Marie found herself filled with guilt. Iné's eyes started to flutter, her breath growing shallow. Marie kept up with the details of her own rescue to keep Iné conscious. "We were starving, soaked."

"How'd you make it?"

"Shovels," Marie said. "The Canadian soldiers who drove the trucks passed them out to the strongest women. We were so broken. We all thought they did it so we could dig our graves."

"Really?"

"German snipers. The Nazis had retreated, but they hadn't stopped trying to kill us."

"Bastards."

"Many of the women wouldn't get into the holes at first. Honestly, we were all terrified that the soldiers might bury us alive. Then, a soldier—I remember him, he had a terrible scar across his left cheek and a disarming smile—he gave each woman a blanket to wrap themselves in and then he went into the hole. He'd be at the bottom, he told them. If they died, he died."

"Ha. So there are good men left." Iné shifted and moaned. Her knees gave. She stumbled and almost levered herself over a downed tree. "But you survived them all. Now, you can go find your daughter."

Soldier's voices echoed through the forest. They had no time for self-pity. "Can you move?"

Iné tried and collapsed near a blackberry patch. "Use the knife. Like a shovel. Dig a hole for me. Aesmeh is the most important person to save right now."

"My daughter's name is Saaayyy-raaahhh." Marie pronounced it slowly, a bit untethered by Iné calling out in such a way. It was oddly-timed, she thought, but the woman was in no shape to understand her words.

Marie cut through the briars, considering her next move. The ground beyond the brush was relatively soft. She got on her hands and knees, stabbed at the earth with her knife, breaking it up enough that she could dig with her hands. She worked fast, the rocks and roots coming up easily. Her arms ached, but Iné wasn't walking anywhere and Marie needed to get to Serah. She moved Iné into the hole. The briars provided decent cover. She grabbed a haversack and stuffed it with the journals from the silo, along with anything she knew was valuable. Then, Marie packed everything else next to Iné's injured leg, hiding her as best she could. The Maquis would find the handkerchief at the dead drop. They would come for Iné, Marie told herself.

Marie strapped the haversack onto her back, the two remaining guns and her knife into her waistband, and began the hike out of the forest. Her face was wet. Tears, she realized. She hated herself at that moment. She was leaving Iné to die. The faces of three hundred women flashed in her mind. Then, the soft, green eyes of that one Canadian soldier. Marie remembered the feeling of wrapping herself in the blanket he gave her, of wedging herself in that hole, believing for the first time in two years that men would not kill her. That a soldier valued other lives more than his own. She fought the urge to run, to get free of everything that had drawn her into Philip Millar's scheme. Yet, he'd drawn her closer to Serah. It struck her that leaving Iné wouldn't get her any closer to finding her daughter.

She ran back to the pit, slid off the haversack, and laid down. "If you die, I die."

Iné smiled as they settled in, face-to-face. "We'll find her, together."

The women gripped hands and Iné drifted off. As Marie watched over her, she began to hallucinate. Men seemed to be buried all around them, their boots sticking out of the ground. In the distance, sharp, short screams of women interrupted. Had she touched Iné's water-poisoning powder? Slivers of light. Faint blurs of movement. A pair of dark shadows hovered over her as her eyesight returned. She tried to scream, but a heavy hand clamped over her mouth.

Chapter 27

AESMEH

MAY 1, 1519
AMBOISE, FRANCE

The afternoon light sent the tall Queen Anne's Lace swaying back and forth along the walkways of the bustling courtyard at Château Gaillard. I could hardly maintain my composure as Maurine and I moved along the edges, avoiding attention. My actions with Melzi, the Amyntas hauling him off in such a manner, weighed heavy. However, the task at hand and the command of the Abbess required me to turn away from my heart.

I admired the grand fountain in the middle of Gaillard's formal garden. It proved immense and hid us well from the king's soldiers half-guarding the grounds on the other side. Maurine and I slipped out the south entrance to the garden and moved with haste along the river. The Amasse seemed to flow slowly and cautiously. I spotted tiny fish and frogs gliding beneath the surface. Every bit of the world moved at half-speed while we whisked ourselves toward, what I hoped to be, a reunion with La Joconde.

The day had grown oppressively hot.

"Why did you force me to wear such a . . ." As I struggled to breathe, I begged Maurine to explain why she insisted I strive to look like a member of the court. There I stood in a satin cobalt-blue gown, its sleeves embroidered with red roses and pink peonies. Maurine fussed with the neckline of her own poor dress choice, a marigold brocade gown with a pomegranate pattern. The stiff, hot fabric chafed my skin and made me long for the roominess of a habit. Thankfully, Maurine had seen to it that we both donned a pair of knee-high leather boots, a weapons belt, and a new blade—far more appropriate than satin shoes of courtly ladies, which would have made the walk much too slow and tedious. Even the river route was littered with soldiers and, dare I say, mercenaries who placed uneasy gazes upon us. Despite my previous protests, I no longer thought the dagger at my side unwise.

As we reached the grounds of Clos Lucé, life there continued without pause, as if Master da Vinci had simply wandered off for an unremarkable walk. We moved past men training with swords in a grassy quadrant under the heaving willows situated far from the house. As we approached, a youngish monk with the four-knotted cord of the Franciscans around his waist sermonized to a group of courtiers. A high-ranking nun lingered on the stone pulpit beside him. Her instructive and serious gaze never left the man.

She looks ready to devour him. Maurine spoke with her mind.

Those women terrify me. I turned away as the sister glanced at us. **I wanted to run every time one of them came near me at Fontevraud.**

We both watched as the nun remonstrated the poor Franciscan, who shrank from her.

That is why we live in the Madeleine and they do not. Maurine lifted the skirts of her gown to leap onto the long path in the grass when four Amyntas approached. They said nothing, but I understood that my lack of armed escort was not only unwise, but not an option. They took up position in the back and front of us and shepherded us along the creek where Master da Vinci and Melzi had built a stunning bridge to test the

Master's theories on suspension. We needed to avoid the nun if only to avoid her disapproval at our lack of decorum, and the Amyntas were not immune to the soothing effects of natural surroundings.

As we approached the Clos, two additional Amyntas approached. The four with us entered and returned within minutes, signaling it was safe for us to enter. No one other than Maurine, myself, and our beautiful warriors walked the halls under the elaborate frescos and stained-glass windows. The house was hot, the air acrid and stale, as if it had been sealed to never be entered again. Maurine reached the second landing and unlatched the tall windows in the hall. They creaked open. The hot breeze drifted in.

I slid my gloves off and ran my hands along the banisters. A glimmer rose up. A line of faces shot through my mind. With a deep breath, I tried to sort through the stories of the people who recently touched it.

Anything? Maurine asked without a word spoken.

I shook my head. My fingers continued to brush along the stone walls and tapestries, in search of clues.

I entered Master da Vinci's workshop. It was as if no attack, no thievery, no betrayal had occurred. Indeed I had never witnessed the workshop in such a state of cleanliness. It was too tidy. I shook my head as my mind remained dark. "Such a twisted sense of nothingness."

I entered Melzi's room. As my feet fell upon the stone floor, I felt more at ease. I could sense him. An odd smell of cinnamon and anise perfumed the air. My fingers lingered on his writing desk, drawing me into his memories and sending me backward to several days earlier. The glimmers came in an instant. He had wept here, head thrust back, hands gripped into fists. The sorrow flooded through me. The Amyntas stood watch at the doorway and I kept these visions to myself.

Maurine lifted quills, inkwells, parchment, flasks, and seals from the desk as if searching for something. "I know he had a key to this desk."

Finally, she spotted it under an inkwell and handed it to me. I slid it into the lock of a thin drawer located just below the writing surface. Shortly, I found a letter. My heart cracked in two as I read it out loud.

My Sweet Asfoora,

You have gone. Hence, I now become a man destined to live a plain life of endless obligations. Yes, that might make life so simple, so safe. Tell me how might I find safety satisfying if it means I must turn away from this service that led me to you?

I despise you. You caused this. Even from the time we were children, you broke me. You provoked my slide from the favored pupil of a Master to the caretaker of a mercurial old man who spent as much time running from his enemies as using his vast intellect.

Yet, since the moment we met, all I have known is your eyes, your smile.

If this is to be the only way for me to forever stand beside the woman I love, know I will do what must be done to achieve my ends.

You are the cause of my slide, but it is a slide into ecstatic joy. It seems I, too, am vexed. Your power over me will surely cause my very end, and I shall end it all for us willingly.

In faith,

Melzi

My hands shook. Maurine took the letter, set it on the desk, and held me close, although I sensed her distraction.

"Tommaso was right. He has gone mad." The visions in my mind revealed Melzi pushed to the very edge of his being. I could not rid myself of his disgust upon receiving the orders of the Abbess or of him ordering servants to bolster the weapons' cache at the Clos. I gasped.

"He snuck into the stores of herbs," I relayed, the glimmer repeating in my mind. "Do you think he gave the men who tried to capture me the valerian?"

"Steady yourself." Maurine took me by the shoulders. "He brought them to me two days past after struggling to sleep. I made him a tincture. You cannot do this. Melzi suffers only from heartbreak."

I pulled away from her, furious. I could no longer see inside his memories. Guilt overwhelmed me. "I should have attended to our hearts."

"Enough." Maurine tossed the letter on the floor.

I snatched it back. In the day or so since Melzi had fished me from the river, everything I found showed me that he hated me. "All I see is Melzi, him sneaking around. He has to know where La Joconde is."

"Do not believe that. Please, let us keep looking."

Maurine foraged through the desk, coming up with nothing more than ledgers, lists, and sugar cubes. I leaned against it, spent from the rush of emotion. A glimmer shot through me, which I relayed to Maurine. It was Master da Vinci placing item after item in a specific spot. Each time, Melzi retrieved the item. I followed the glimmer through time until a far more recent moment appeared. The Master became clear in my mind. He stroked his long, white beard, scratched his belly, and struggled with something on the desk. His eyes shot behind him. He scrambled away.

"Help me remove the lip of the work table," I told Maurine.

She could not, and called in the pair of Amyntas at the door. The top was loose. One of them jammed her dagger into its side until it popped off. I found what must have left such a potent signature. I pulled a torn corner of the vellum out carefully and read: *Our body is dependent on heaven and heaven on the spirit.*

My shoulders slumped. "I hate riddles. This is useless."

"No, it is good news," Maurine said. "Why would Master da Vinci have put a message in a place he regularly hid things for Melzi, if Melzi were the perpetrator of his demise?"

I wanted her to be right. Master da Vinci's note challenged the ideas of Melzi's guilt for the first time. Yet, I could not relieve myself of the words he had written. No matter how much hope Maurine found in this discovery, every clue in my possession contradicted the other.

Chapter 28

PHILIP

MAY 3, 1945
AMBOISE, FRANCE

Philip ordered the men in the silo to collect the reproductions of the Mona Lisa and whatever remained of the research. He wanted to burn it all to the ground, to be done with it, let his sons be at peace. Marie frustrated and thrilled him. If she had done her job and gotten the painting, as well as Serah Izem, back, he could just gas the whole lot. However, the game had changed.

A pair of soldiers approached and saluted.

"Colonel, Sir. Harris, Edwards, and Davies are down in the forest just north of an old château," one reported. "They tracked your women into a cave and were attacked."

"Attacked?" Cloutille asked.

"Edwards is dead. We can't find Davies."

"Harris?" she continued.

"Still in pursuit." The soldier held up more papers. "Harris said they have packs and weapons."

Well, that ended any hope of Marie making this easy, Philip thought. Cloutille pursed her lips. Her eyes bulged. Philip knew she was right. Marie was willing to fight, after all.

"Also," the soldier continued, "there's a man in your quarters. A

German."

"I see." Philip watched as the body of Lieutenant Berry was hoisted out the top, the same way all equipment and men got in and out of the silo so they would not have to navigate the tunnels. "Is that the only way to the surface?"

"Yes, Colonel. The women set off explosives in the tunnels. It will take a while to get through."

A pair of soldiers strapped Philip and Cloutille into harnesses so they could be lifted out of the silo quickly. It took less than a minute, yet Philip hung there, helpless, and seething. At the top, he clambered out of the harnesses and onto the hill above Château Amboise. A soldier handed Philip a paper report and a box of ammunition for his pistol. He and Cloutille raced toward Clos Lucé.

"Why is that man in your quarters?" Cloutille asked.

"It's a business transaction." No one could blame Philip for securing his interests.

"Oberführer Karl Diebitsch is not a man to bargain with," she said.

"Just Diebitsch, now. He got out."

Cloutille frowned. "No one gets out of the SS."

"You do when you report to the kind of friends he has made." Philip fiddled with the bullet on the keychain in his coat pocket. Cloutille might be right. But, Nazi or not, Philip understood his visitor was needed now more than ever. Diebitsch's resources proved endless. They were enemies on paper, yes. The Sibyl, though. Both of them wanted her dead and gone. And as long as that bonded them, he held the advantage and one he'd leverage it to its fullest extent. "We compromised."

"I thought the journals were the last of that."

"It's just practical. We're not finishing this alive if we try to hide our activity from his people." Philip straightened his uniform jacket and walked into the front hall of the Clos. A single man waited for him. "Karl. Welcome to . . . "

"Such formalities are not necessary for this sort of circumstance." The former SS officer looked like just about any other townsperson in Amboise. He wore well-tailored trousers, a crisp white shirt, vest, and a tweed jacket. His hair was graying, cut short beneath a wool cap. Philip spotted his cufflinks—odd silver runes with two triangles touching one another on either side. They proved unsettling, in exquisite condition, and bore the hallmark of the Munich firm of Gahr, the preferred silversmiths of the SS. Diebitsch greeted Philip as a friend. "I hear you have trouble."

"No trouble." Philip knew his visitor's people kept spies in place. "How was your trip, Karl?"

"I didn't expect you to find this woman so difficult," Diebitsch continued, running his hand along the frames of the Mona Lisa reproductions which had been moved back to Clos Lucé. "Alexander was one of our best soldiers. I thought you said Iné Soudier was . . . How could you not have known you had a collaborator embedded in your inner circle?"

Philip controlled his tone, knowing Diebitsch was trying to get a rise out of him. "She was rather convincing."

"Meddlesome. Shall I send someone in to take care of them?"

"Her sort of collaboration is exactly what we want right now," Phillip continued. "We need Soudier to get Dr. Guerrant deep inside."

"I wasted a lot of time, early on, because of her. You better hope she can get the Maquis outside, in plain view. Draw that girl out." Diebitsch put his hand on Cloutille's shoulder, then ran it down her back as her face remained emotionless. "They cannot be allowed to get in the way of this acquisition. Once that's done . . ."

"Once we've got the Mona Lisa and the girl, you can break down and rebuild the oracle in whatever ways make her more pliable." Philip's grip tightened around the bullet in his pocket as he watched Diebitsch.

"Let's hope for your sake she is worth it," Diebitsch continued. "Cruel filth, you are, letting a mother lead you to her daughter. My people would never have lost Serah Izem to begin with."

Philip and his guest stood in silence, arms crossed, and studied the reproductions. A trio of armed German men stepped inside from the hallway, keeping Cloutille from leaving.

"All this wasted momentum," Diebitsch said. "So many people moved the Mona Lisa over and over again, not knowing what they truly had. That she was the key."

"Indeed."

"Don't make me clean up after you again." Diebitsch clamped his hand down on Philip's shoulder. "You're just lucky Paul loved money more than the French. He was easy to turn."

"He was also easy to kill." Philip shook the man's hand away. "I'm going to assume you had nothing to do with him trying to shake me down."

Diebitsch guffawed. He took a cloth handkerchief out of his pocket and wiped down Philip's desk chair. Then, he sat, cleaning his finger-nails with a letter opener. "Who do you take me for, colonel, a petty thief? My people are not playing for a couple extra food ration coupons. Maybe Paul sensed a weakness."

Philip tensed, yet understood what the man implied. Serah and the Mona Lisa had vanished on his watch. The burden, he knew, was on him to find them.

"I did my job getting the journals back to you," Diebitsch said. "Now, do yours and get the Sibyl back, for me. You don't need another Oradour-sur-Glane."

Philip bristled. The town in Southern France had been leveled a year earlier. More than six hundred men, women, and children had been burned, some crucified, by Waffen-SS. A Maquis deep cover operation, including Serah Izem, had been hiding one of the Mona Lisas in the village church.

"If you don't," Diebitsch continued, "I will take care of this myself."

Chapter 29

MARIE

MAY 4, 1945
AMBOISE, FRANCE

"Crack the code yet?"

Marie bit down hard on the hand that pressed over her mouth. Her assailant snatched it back and shook it. A red handkerchief was tied around it.

"Jesus, Marie."

"You found the dead drop." Her terror dissipated. It was Noam. She sucked in a breath and realized she was still in the forest, damp from the morning dew. The pit had worked. Marie and Iné had made it through the night "What are you doing in the middle of this?"

"On the lamb?" Noam said. Dappled early-morning light cascaded over the forest. Two men charged up pointing their guns. He turned and called them off.

"Something like that. You were right about Philip."

"I told you to earn his trust. The forest is crawling with armed soldiers. What did you do?" He pulled back the brambles, trying to help Marie up, and found Iné, unconscious. "Oh, dammit."

Marie's shoulders and biceps burned as Noam guided her out of the hole in the ground. He tried to take the haversack she'd cinched across her body, but she refused. Marie watched Noam and the others carry Iné to a flat surface near the water spring, surprised at how deep the hole really was, when she saw one man pull out a canteen to fill it.

"Don't drink the water!" Marie shouted.

"She needs liquids," one of the men said.

"No! It's . . . it's contaminated. Trust me."

Noam stared at her for a moment, then ordered the men to back up. They propped Iné against a tree snag.

"Philip's lieutenant is dead," Marie said.

"That explains the friendlies."

"What did you think I was going to do? Assemble a council? Place a request with him to return Serah tout suite?"

"Tie him up? Knock him out?" Noam paced.

"He was going to kill us." Iné had regained enough consciousness to try and stand, but her knees gave way. "I told you it wasn't going to work."

Noam pulled up the woman's pant leg and whistled at the sight of her purple, bloated ankle which matched the goose egg on her head. "Painful?"

"We've got to get moving." Iné tried to get up again.

Marie realized the woman spoke to Noam as if they'd met before, but needed to keep focus. "She's right. We ended up on the ridge in a cave with soldiers coming from inside the tunnels and the old château."

"How many?"

"At least three on both sides."

As the sun rose, more men surrounded them. Each seemed to watch Marie and Iné, their faces appearing stunned and pitiful.

"You two took out six men?" Noam gave up a crooked grin.

"Seven . . ." Marie thought out loud. "Eight . . . Nine, actually, if you count the two Iné took out in the silo."

Noam and Marie broke into low laughter.

"It figures. You're a piece of work," he said, putting his arm around her. "We've got a truck near the Amasse."

"What about Serah?"

Noam hesitated, "We were hoping you'd figure something more out before you started killing people."

"Always the detective, no?" Marie referred to their first meeting somewhere around 1938. Noam had still been with the Paris police, recruiting Communist Party members as snitches. He had been ordered to arrest Resistance members, take them out. Jules nearly killed him for it. Instead, he recruited Noam into the Maquis. Seeing people fight for their country and beliefs made him hate the establishment. Frenchmen had all but opened their arms to the Germans as they trotted into Paris like tourists. Instead of turning them over to the Vichy, he joined the Maquis and rose to the highest ranks at the side of Marie's husband.

"I told you, it was our best shot at finding Serah." Noam's voice turned to a whisper as they walked.

"But, they didn't know anything at all," Marie said. "The lieutenant thought I was conning him, that I was the one who knew where she was."

"Really?"

"It doesn't make any sense? Why would Philip be so fixed on her?"

"She's got La Joconde."

"I don't think that's it. Everything they had in the silo had nothing to do with the painting at all. Yes, La Joconde and the replicas are a part of this, but . . . ," Marie sorted through the details in her head. "I think they believe Serah is . . . Important."

"In what way?"

Marie considered the markings on the photos, the possibility that they came from Serah herself, and the journals in which they were written. Time and time again, the Sibyls had proved to be the common thread. She didn't answer.

"I'm sorry I sent you in there," Noam continued. He paused but never stopped moving through the thick trees toward the river. "Let's get someplace safe first. Then, we'll figure this out."

Marie took stock of everything that happened. The museum. Paul. What had begun to unfold?

Noam walked ahead of her, a rifle slung over his shoulder, pistol in the back of his pants. Several men in black boots and square wool caps scrambled up from the banks of the Amasse. Marie could see Iné being helped into the back of a farm truck that looked as if it were loaded with sacks of lettuce. The woman helped a man secure the tarp over the top of her and gave a thumbs up from beneath. The circle of armed fighters broke up. Three got in the front of the farm truck. Two others jumped in the back as it drove off. Marie and Noam stood near the bank of the slow, broad river, their silence razored with tension.

She rummaged through the haversack strapped around her and pulled out the photo and the journal. "She's here, Noam. I know it."

Marie showed him the symbols on both: *φΛ. Σίβυλλα. Mére. Maison.*

"Part of it is Maquis code." Noam was stunned.

"Exactly. The only person other than you or me who could have known how to write this and get it to me, in Paris, is Serah. She wanted me to find it."

"That piece of work." Noam stared at the documents and motioned for Marie to tuck them away as a Jeep rumbled up.

"All I want is to walk the canals with Serah again. Chase cats, pick flowers." Marie spoke as if Noam wasn't sitting next to her in the Jeep as it headed down the road.

"I'm going to take you to see some people," Noam said.

She understood. They arrived at a temporary dock where the Amasse met the Loire. On the Loire side, Marie spied a traditional flat riverboat, the kind she knew had navigated the river since the Renaissance. It was positioned at a spot in the river nearly invisible to military patrols.

Marie boarded and stood on the deck facing the north shore. She took note of a series of small, similar docks along the shoreline at irregular intervals. It was hard to tell they were docks. However, she recognized the signs of old fishing weirs. And she certainly knew how to tie up a boat without others taking notice. She counted and marked little landmarks in her mind, a habit really, just to calm herself from the remaining agitation about Noam. Each tie-off had one boat docked. There was one just past the silos that made her grin. The Maquis always worked under everyone's noses.

As they slowly fought the current to get to the wide strip of land that cut the river in two, the morning cold bit at her bones. She stepped off the boat onto the island in the heavy, overnight fog. The mist hung between the thick weeping willows like sheets of cotton stuffing. The light remained low. Her exhaustion left her neck stiff, eyes crusty. She settled her gaze on the shore near town. Château Amboise loomed in silhouette, casting a tall, wide shadow over the waterfront. Her body shook.

The shore ebbed and flowed, but not with water. Marie thought she spotted a procession of veiled women making their way to the edge of the river. There, four across, four deep; their coverings shimmered; their eyes bright and visible in the distance. The cool wind turned warm and steady, carrying on it what sounded like a soft warble, maybe even chanting. Marie tried to perk her ears to decipher the words. The women overtook the shoreline, growing in number, their light burning away the fog until each one, in their veils of violet, indigo, crimson, and marigold, illuminated the riverbank. At that moment, the figures each raised a hand. Their veils flitter in the wind.

Her eyes cleared, the voices spoke in a dozen languages with no distinct message. Then, one phrase, "Dear One," echoed. Noam laid a hand on her shoulder. Marie flipped around and realized he was looking in the same direction, lost in thought, but it wasn't them the women keyed in on.

"Iné," she whispered as a light seemed to form on the side of the river opposite the women. Then, in an instant, the figures vanished. Marie took Noam's hand. They watched the shoreline fade in the distance and let their breath rise and fall, even and true.

Chapter 30

MARIE

MAY 4, 1945
AMBOISE, FRANCE

Once Marie and Noam were on the other side of the river, rain began to fall. Both remained lost in the vision of the veiled women on the riverbank. Marie wanted to ask him about them, learn if their experience matched up. A shame, however, washed over her. She was exhausted. The figures were a mirage, nothing more. She and Noam tossed on rain ponchos and climbed into the back of the open military transport. Marie noted the burned-out tracts of land and the pungency in her nose.

"I expected everyone to be thinner." Marie watched beyond half-crumbled walls as women tended to the lettuce and fava beans they'd cultivated in small gardens. A man in overalls and boots with holes in the toes waved at the transport before trading a handful of beets and asparagus with his neighbors.

"Everyone grows one or two small crops to share outside ration pools," Noam said.

Marie noted the familiarity the locals seemed to have with Noam and his men. The transport juddered to a halt in front of a two-story, stone building, abruptly dropped them in front, and sped away. The heavy metal gate hidden beneath thick vines of ivy made it look more like a bunker than a house. At one time, it must have been an artist's studio. Marie could see the faint lettering École de Décoration stenciled next to house number thirteen. Now, the pair of second-floor windows are boarded up and the pair on the bottom floor are barred. The only entrance, a plain wooden door. Noam knocked. A man with thick gray eyebrows peered out from beyond it. He shut the door in their face.

"Friend, right?" Marie asked.

Noam attempted nonchalance. "It's been a while."

"How long?"

"How long has it been since you've seen Simon Faubert?"

Marie's spirits soared. She had known the art restorer and his partner, Yara Paquet, for almost thirty years. They'd been an integral part of hiding La Joconde in '38, and close friends of her parents since her youth. To her left, the metal gate grated and creaked as it opened. The ivy moved with it. Eyebrows once again peered out from behind. "Get off the street, already."

They scooted through the crack in the gate. Simon held out a hand to keep them silent, pointing to a second-floor window across the street. They reached the shed, latched the door, and looked at one another with relief.

"What have you done, Noam?" the man asked.

"Bonjour, Simon." Marie slid her poncho hood back.

He stumbled back. Noam steadied him.

"Ma belle." Tears filled Simon's eyes.

He ran his hands over her face, before hugging her fiercely. Marie had forgotten how his fuzzy, gray hair smelled of sweet tobacco. She leaned in, smothering herself in his comfort. They hadn't seen one another since La Joconde went into hiding.

Simon pushed back from Marie and punched Noam in the arm. "You could have at least sent someone ahead to tell us. From the way Brutus was barking, I thought you were Germans. The stink of sauerkraut and gun powder has been wafting across the street all morning."

"Why are there Germans casually eating lunch in Amboise?" Marie asked.

"You tell me. They arrived in civilian clothes late yesterday, but I can tell a Nazi bastard by scent alone."

Marie could too. She watched through the open back gate as the transport with Iné rolled through the alley with its engine off. A better move, she thought, rather than coming through the front door like she and Noam just did. She wondered why he'd risked being seen.

Simon raised an eyebrow. "So, what the hell is going on here, I . . . "

Noam interrupted. "We require your expertise."

"I told you I was done." Simon turned to walk out. "Find someone else."

Noam spun him around. "I think you'll want to see what we've got."

"I am too old for this. I've done my part."

"Don't tell me a respected reproduction artist like yourself isn't interested in La Joconde?" Marie said. He did look older, worn, and yet, he was the man who had painted six copies of the masterpiece. Surely, he couldn't resist the call to help.

Simon pushed up his glasses that lingered on the tip of his nose, looked at Marie with curiosity, then turned away. "Not this time. I'm no good in the field, and the team . . . Too many of us are dead."

"What about Serah, then?" Marie asked.

"You've got news on her?" Simon responded as if he'd been waiting for such a moment.

Marie passed her haversack to him. Simon's eyes widened.

"Please," she said. "For me."

Marie pulled out the journal with the markings. Simon's eyes grew wider still. He rummaged out a pair of white cotton gloves, took the book with the tenderness of a man knowing its worth, and moved to a worktable. He slid open a drawer to reveal all manner of tools for delicate work, and chose a tiny, metal wand. How could one have this many tools at the ready amid war? Marie wondered.

"Oh, it's in a painful condition." Simon moaned at the sight of the flaking pages.

"I know," she said. "Two-thirds lost."

"Maybe not."

"That's what I hoped you'd say." Marie brightened. She'd always relied on Simon's skill and devotion.

"Stolen?"

"Recovered."

"From whom?" He peeled back the pages as he talked.

Marie hesitated.

"Philip Millar," Noam said.

Simon hissed under his breath, eyes raising to meet Marie's.

"I think these are Francesco Melzi's journals," Marie said.

"You are sure?"

She pointed to the mark on the first page of the second, less damaged book. She took the metal pointer and carefully flipped over five more pages. Each carried the mark.

"Ordre du Saint-Esprit." Simon stood back, cleaned his tool, and wiped his forehead with the red bandana from his pocket.

"I'm stunned to see them." Marie moved in next to him, two scientists examining specimens. "These were all the Nazis ever wanted. There were warehouses full of French books just outside of Ravensbrück. They confiscated everything they could in search of these."

Simon was now staring at her instead of the journals. His eyes grew watery before returning to his assessment. "I didn't know you were . . . home."

"A month. They reinstated me at the Louvre. You should see it," Marie told him. "Your work saved many masterpieces."

"I saw they got a few out of that Austrian salt mine," he said.

"Probably a lot of your fakes." Marie grinned and patted him on the back.

Simon used the metal wand to lift her shirt sleeve. "How did they treat you?"

Marie brushed him away and looked around the space. "Where is Yara?"

"She will come. I see three books. Were there more?"

"Not like this," Marie said.

"This is where Millar comes back into the story, isn't it?" Simon asked. "He has the rest?"

"I think I got what matters." Marie pressed the photo with the matching markings onto his worktable next to the journal. "This photo was in the SOE file Millar gave me. His lieutenant claimed to have never seen it."

"She thinks Serah may have gotten her a message." Noam interrupted.

"Is that possible?" Marie asked.

Simon examined the photo and the journal for a long while in silence. "I guess you ought to stay, then. Yara will not forgive me if I keep you out here much longer. Go, she's in the house."

Marie wanted an answer, but Simon didn't look up as he shooed her and Noam away. They stepped into the courtyard. A Mastiff bounded towards them, barking hard.

"Brutus!" a voice yelled from the house. "N'oublies pas de tu comporter correctement avec les personnes que tu ne connaisses pas."

"Don't play with strangers?" Noam shouted. "When did we get demoted?"

Marie spotted a diminutive woman approaching. Her kinky gray hair was elegantly swept up in a bun. She gestured for the massive dog to come to her side.

"Salut, Yara." Marie fondly studied this woman who'd fostered her love of languages, who'd vouched to get her into the Sorbonne at age sixteen, who'd even taken care of newborn Serah so Marie could keep her teaching position.

"Did you think you could just waltz back in here?" Arms spread wide, Yara waved them both in close. Marie noticed the deepened creases around her eyes, her thin arms, and the sharpness of her clavicle. "I cannot believe it. Miraculous." Yara cocked her head at Noam. "How is your family?"

He fell silent.

She put her hand on his shoulder. "I cannot fix what we must sacrifice, but I can feed you."

"Is that boulou I smell?" The scent of orange and anise tickled Marie's nose. She nudged Noam. "Who did you pay off to get flour and sugar?"

"We have our ways." Yara waved her finger over the wall where neighbors worked in the garden. "The loaves are just cooling."

Noam and Marie followed her back into the small, spotless kitchen. The condition of the building and the mishmashed collection of kitchenware stood in stark contrast to Simon's workshop. Marie then realized they were in hiding.

Yara cut two slices from the Challah-style bread and passed it to them. It was sparsely studded with dried fruit, nuts, and seeds.

"I love a woman who bakes." Noam looked over at Marie and winked. Marie felt as if she were at home with her family. She softened into the high-backed wooden chair at the kitchen table and laughed. She watched Yara twist and turn like Serah dancing around their old apartment in Belleville. As a child, Serah would make sure each person got the same-sized serving of boulou, then take to bandaging up their cat after its latest late-night fight. She finished every evening telling any adult who would listen about the events in her dreams: ends of wars, cool waters filled with sprites, maidens in castles . . . The happy moment shot pangs of guilt through Marie.

"Maybe you will stay this time, instead of bolting off." Yara poked Noam in the side. "The cottage roof leaks, and I'm not entirely sure the mice will enjoy your company, but there is a mattress."

"Where is Iné?" Marie asked.

"The men brought her to the upstairs bedroom earlier. Her ankle is swollen, but not broken. I can brace it and, hopefully, she'll be walking tomorrow."

Yara seemed as familiar with Iné as Noam. Marie wondered how that was possible.

"We'll get ourselves settled in," he said.

"Take your time, but Marie." Yara took her hand. "You being here again is not easy for Simon. The wounds are deep."

"It's hard for me too."

They held each other for a long while.

"What is Simon prepping for me?" Yara wiped her tears with a handkerchief, then passed it to Marie.

"Journals, from Melzi. They're in bad shape." Marie said. "I found something, perhaps about Serah."

"Oh, my. I'll put the kettle on." Yara shook her head. "I'll ring you when dinner is ready."

Marie and Noam stepped out into the courtyard and glanced over at the shed where Simon had first taken them.

"They look terrible," Marie said. "What happened?"

"Most of Yara's family died in the camps. They'd just come from Libya," Noam said. "She and Simon had to go into deep hiding after you and Jules disappeared. The Nazis were tracking down everyone they thought involved in any sort of resistance. They'd round up men and women into warehouses and just shoot them. Yara set up safe houses. They watched over the movement of the art, kept our teams fed, and buried our dead."

"Simon knows Philip?"

"Your colonel did a lot of work with the Maquis."

"And?"

"We trusted him for a long time. He almost had us convinced ..." Noam trailed off.

"He's got a way with words."

"I'm actually surprised we found you or Iné alive in the forest."

"Why?"

"Before we pulled you out of that hole, we'd been trailing a transport that dropped a man off at Clos Lucé."

"Why does that matter?"

"It was a German. The private identified him as Diebitsch."

"Oberführer Karl Diebitsch?" Marie's head went light. She felt as if she'd been turned inside-out.

"I think so. My men say he's not SS anymore. Gotten in with some group. Their leader makes Hitler seem like a spoiled princess. Do you know him?"

Marie fought the urge to run and hide. Instead, she unbuttoned her blouse and slid it back to reveal the whip scars on her shoulder blades. "He gave me these."

Noam eased the blouse back over her shoulders and straightened her collar. "The usual, then?"

Marie took his hand and held it to her chest. An understanding of the torture she'd endured blossomed between them. "Yep, the usual."

Chapter 31

MARIE

MAY 5, 1945
THE HOME OF YARA PAQUET AND SIMON FAUBERT
AMBOISE, FRANCE

"Me-kädmen anina il'ati." A voice crying out woke Marie from a heavy sleep. She lay in the lumpy bed of the tiny, one-room cottage that Yara had prepared for her and Noam. The eyes of the veiled ghost waking her lingered. She shook her hands in the air to make the vision disappear.

The metal frame of the bed squeaked. On the other side of the room, a mattress looked as if it hadn't been slept on. Her ribs ached, old wounds making it worse. Marie thought to call out for Noam when she was startled, her sight still foggy, as someone approached.

"Hey, it's just a dream. You're all right. You're safe." Yara sat on the bed. She stroked Marie's forehead. The short curtains billowed from the breeze coming through an open window. The bright May air was scented with wisteria, a hint of smoke, and a musty tang.

"How bad was it here?" Marie lifted her head.

"We found this compound deserted. The British flushed the Germans out a few months back."

"Ah, the smell."

"Ah, the smell." Yara took a deep breath. "The vinegar makes the constant scent of that damn fatty ersatz soap slightly more tolerable."

Marie tried not to recall the rumors that the Nazis made their soap from human remains. "How are you?"

"Let's not."

"Yara, please. Noam told me about your family."

"I cannot change it, and you sitting here is miraculous. Your mother would be so pleased." Yara remained emotionless. That is how Marie had always known her. "I didn't even know she had died until we made it back from the south and set up in Amboise a few weeks ago."

"I heard she caught a fever," Marie said.

"Yes, sometime around '43 I was told." Yara brought in a basin of water and a towel for Marie to wash herself. Then she set out a fresh shirt, pants, and undergarments on a nearby chair.

"What was Serah doing with your team?" Marie asked.

Yara sighed and looked at her as if she'd been trying to avoid the conversation. "Noam brought her south right after, well, everything. Simon taught her how to use the tunnels to hide Jewish families until caravans could get them down to Toulouse and on boats to North Africa. I've never seen a braver woman, Marie. She never once wavered when it came to choosing between what was easy and what was right. Serah always took the path of justice and compassion."

"Do you think she's . . . ?" Marie shook, trying not to assume the worst.

"I think, to save others, she risked what others could not." Yara wiped Marie with the dampened cloth and treated her back scars with a lineament. "Not unlike her mother."

"I am no hero."

"I never said you were."

They sat for a moment, Marie unable to express the hope and dread churning inside her. She could not pause with it too long, and changed the subject as she hauled herself out of bed.

"I can't believe the Sorbonne didn't try to help you." Marie knew

Yara had been one of only three women in her generation to earn a tenured teaching position at the university. Marie pursued her gift for languages with Yara's encouragement. Yara had even called in several favors to get Marie admitted. "There's not a man in that place who is a better preservationist than you."

"Brown is the wrong color and female is the wrong gender." Yara held out her hand. "And, few men care what women can do. Especially those from lands they took over to justify keeping us in chains."

Philip flashed through Marie's mind. He guarded his power jealously. She sat on the bed, hand-in-hand with Yara, and tried to make sense of everything that had happened since Noam told her about Serah. One moment she was quietly rebuilding her life in Paris, the next she was, once again, on the edge of death.

Yara pressed her thumbs down. Marie settled and her mind seemed to clear. For a moment, she wanted to wriggle free, but relented. She breathed deeply as the notations on the photo and the journal raced into her mind. Her hands, still in Yara's, began to itch. She could sense an echo.

Of La Joconde.

A deal made.

Women, just like those on the riverbank.

Of . . . Of . . . Was it Serah?

Marie stiffened, the series of visions connected her daughter to the Sibyl.

"What do you see?" Yara's whispered inquiry seemed to replicate over and over until it became a shout.

Marie yanked her hands free and shook so hard she nearly fell off the bed.

"What is it?" Yara appeared oblivious to what Marie just experienced.

"I'm worried," Marie said.

"Of course you are."

"It's not just Serah. I found something in the journals."

"More than the code?"

"After I'd arrived at Ravensbrück, that Nazi Diebitsch took me, and six other women, into his private quarters to put to work. His men forced us to pore through endless stacks of papers and books hunting down Francesco Melzi's journals."

"Looking for what?"

"A modern-day Sibyl."

Yara froze. "My God."

"Not God." Marie saw the worry in her eyes and guilt overcame her for driving such fear in her friend. She pushed Yara away gently. "He thought he could find a prophetess to turn the war in their favor. Now, I think Philip Millar is trying to do the same, but I don't know for whom. They may have been right."

The air between them seemed to vibrate.

"Serah found it, at least I think it was her," Marie continued. "The codes are written next to where Francesco Melzi claims his lover was the Sibyl of Amboise. She's one of the few who could have written them. What if Serah found this woman?"

Without pause, Yara stood, gathering up the bandages and the water basin. "I need to finish making lunch. Come into the main house when you're done. Stay low, though, Germans have been skulking around the village all morning."

Marie watched her go, stunned that was all Yara had to say. She called after the woman, "Me-kädmen anina il'ati. What does it mean?"

Yara paused at the door without turning around. Marie swore she trembled. "I have no idea, dear."

Yara had just lied, that much Marie knew. She wiped herself down with the warm cloth, dressed, and went in search of others.

It was much later in the day than Marie though. The sun in the courtyard baked Marie's back. The space was filled with simple gravel surrounded by potted trees and sorted boxes full of machine parts, broken pottery, and damaged cookware. She thought of what Noam had said about Simon and Yara setting up safe houses. The boxes made sense. "They're moving supplies," she whispered.

Stiff arms and bruised legs made walking a chore. The shed door stood open a crack. She paused. The journals sat under a yellowing cotton sheet on the worktable just inside. If Simon had gotten through a few pages, Marie might be able to figure out more about Serah's location.

She stepped in. The shed, unlike the cottage, was cool. It was carved from the tufa stone of the Loire. Dozens of empty frames leaned against the stone walls. Paintings were stacked beside them. Marie knew from the walnut frames dotted with gesso glue, the linseed varnish, and carvings hand-cut with forged metal tools that many were hundreds of years old, or, at least, meant to look that way.

Two paintings were blatant replicas, marked with the yellow and cyan colors she had designated as codes for reproductions of Louvre paintings long ago. She spotted two replicas of medieval pieces that had already been returned to the Museé de Cluny collection. She understood what paintings should be inside these frames, and if they had yet to be seen again in Paris. How many had Simon and Yara helped hide? How many had they lost or recovered only in part?

As she moved from frame to frame, her breath caught.

There stood Pilgrimage to the Isle of Cythera By Jean-Antoine Watteau. Marie peered at the hazy depiction of the legend of Aphrodite's birthplace. Such an idyllic landscape with its blue skies, green leaves, and soothing earth tones. Aristocrats drenched in silk and velvet. Hats, fans, and walking canes.

The glamor!

Flirtatious conversations, courtly scenes. It awed her to see it again. The reproduction was more than six feet by four feet. Enormous. Breathtaking. At that moment, her mind veered from the romance many claimed it celebrated to the worship of powerful women such as Aphrodite. More Sibyls. She was beginning to see the Sibyl in everything.

"That is a big one." Iné stepped into the space.

Marie smiled and helped her sit in Simon's work chair. "Simon started this one before he began the reproduction of La Joconde. The original had hung in the Louvre since 1795."

"Why is this here?"

"We hid the original at Château de Chenonceau. Didn't really need this one, I suppose. We hid most everything there. It's all back in Paris now."

"So, this was a decoy?"

"We had many. La Joconde, though, was the only piece we moved regularly. Her appeal, well, she had many unsavory suitors." Marie moved to the next frame and ran a hand over burnt canvas and wood. It was half a scene from a reproduction of The Concert by Vermeer.

"Have you gotten back to the journals yet?" Iné shuffled toward the worktable.

Marie watched her. "Your ankle seems much better."

"Yara is an excellent nurse," Iné added.

Marie pulled the cotton sheet off the papers and slipped on a pair of work gloves. She ran her hands over the leather cover that held one journal taken apart to dry. Noting its size—not more than a piece of stationary—she also noted the stains on her gloves from where the deep mahogany of the leather was damp and left a mark. She showed Iné the inscription she'd pointed out to Simon.

"What did he call that?" Iné asked.

"The Ordre du Saint-Esprit. It was a quasi-religious order formed after da Vinci's death. Lots of rumors around secret activity. Journals from its members often bore the mark, especially if the writings contained details of the Order's undertakings." Marie pressed her hands on the table and stepped back. She started to shake, and then, to quell her reaction, began to recite the alphabet in Attic Greek.

"Are you okay? What's going on?"

The symbols from the photos in Philip's files were jotted into the margins on several different pages than the ones she had already seen. They weren't in the same order or next to one another, but there. Marie exhaled and pointed them out: "La Joconde. Sibyl. Mére. Maison."

"This is why you took the journals?" Iné asked. Marie noted her surprise.

"See these symbols?" Marie nodded and explained to her: *φΛ. Σιβυλλα. Mére. Maison.* "The first two stand for La Joconde. I created that marker myself. The second word is 'Sibyl' in ancient Greek. I have no idea why the other two would be there. This was the code on the photos I had in Paris. They also seem to be all over this piece."

"Why didn't you show me these earlier?" Iné had gone pale.

Marie couldn't stop looking at them. She tried to decipher the rest of the page. It was written in a mixture of coded Latin and broken French. "What do you know of them?"

"Nothing." Iné shook her head, but Marie noted the worry lines on her forehead. "I'm a little woozy. I'm going to lie down."

Marie tried to get back to the decryption, but Iné's abrupt retreat left her concerned. She found the woman perched on the retaining wall in the courtyard, smoking. Marie sat down, snatched the cigarette, and took a drag. She closed her eyes, raising her face to the sun.

"What are you doing here?" she asked.

Iné took her cigarette from Marie and shrugged.

"You're not Maquis," Marie pressed. "But you know everyone here who is. You got yourself deep into the crew of a man everyone has figured out has personal motivations for finding La Joconde and my daughter. You gun down his first lieutenant and know every inch of the tunnels beneath an old commune that history forgot. You know Serah wrote those symbols, don't you?"

Just then, shouts from inside the house interrupted them. Simon stormed into the garage and started bagging up the journals. Yara chased after him.

"What's going on?" Marie rushed back in.

"The only way to stop this is for me to get everything out of here." Simon's glasses slid down his thin nose as he stuffed his bags full of ancient books and valuable letters from kings, monks, and revolutionaries from his private collection as well.

"They'll kill you." Yara tried to stop him.

Simon pushed past her and pulled a pistol out from his work drawer. He stuck it in the back of his pants. "I have to get everything back where it belongs."

Yara motioned for Marie and Iné to leave. They stood firm.

"I told you this would happen," Simon spoke as if he and Yara had discussed the journals a hundred times before. He charged the door, swinging back toward the alley. "I won't abandon her!"

"Simon!" Yara ran after him.

The back gate swung open. Marie saw four men pressing their index fingers against their lips to quiet everyone. They crouched behind the transport that Iné had arrived on, guns drawn. Maquis, she thought. Shouts at the front gate made everyone stiffen.

"Sonderbehandlung!" A German soldier ordered.

"Special treatment?" Iné asked, translating German.

"Execution." Marie knew Nazi code words. "Their commander just ordered his men to kill us all."

The rat-a-tat of a machine gun sounded.

"Get in." Simon passed the sack of letters and journals to Yara and helped Iné under the green canopy of the transport truck. Simon turned toward the courtyard.

"You can't go back there." Marie sobbed as she pulled a tarp over herself and the other women.

"Stay in the goddamn truck or they will kill us all." He put a hand on Marie's shoulder and then kissed Yara on the forehead. "These men will get you to Serah."

The driver released the break and they started moving slowly without any engines. Marie peeked out to see the others sliding open a heavy wooden door from a ramshackle building in the back alley. They rolled the truck inside and waited. Back at Simon and Yara's, the voices of German soldiers and gunfire told her they had broken through the gate. Shouts for Simon to get down echoed through the air. A series of gunshots rang out at once. Then, nothing.

Marie held Yara close in her arms. I've brought this on, Marie thought. She wanted to take it all back.

Another shot.

Footsteps.

The door slid open. Someone tossed something heavy onto the front seat of the transport. The ignition turned over. The truck roared down a long stretch of road towards a wooden bridge over a narrow part of the Loire, then back into the forest where Noam found Marie and Iné a day earlier.

Chapter 32

AESMEH

MAY 1, 1519
CLOS LUCÉ
AMBOISE, FRANCE

I lingered on the hard rain through the diamonds of leaded glass in Melzi's chamber at Clos Lucé. Maurine sat on the soft feather bed waiting for me to release myself from a glimmer that had not come. Outside, in the distance, I spied a twist of smoke curling up from the north tower of Château Amboise. I took a quill from its holder and rolled it between my palms until the glimmer finally began. Gentle, aching memories appeared in my head. I wondered how many times Melzi had sat at his desk, watching and waiting for me.

"Did you know his window looked out over Tour Hertault?" I asked Maurine.

I could see the fire flickering in the hearth of the tower. For years, the ancient flame of the Sibylline was lit at Tour Hertault each time the Abbess had business in Amboise. Lady Marguerite convinced King François that honoring the Abbess of Fontevraud would carry favor with Rome and the Sibylline, without drawing much inquiry. We understood its purpose—to let others who might challenge him believe we sided with France. Amboise was our ancestral seat in France, too. So, we conceded to

Marguerite's play and the king's vanity in order to procure our safety until the ancient flame could find its permanent home, just beyond the castle, when I entered the temple.

Maurine coaxed the quill from my hand. She leaned against the desk, waiting for me to calm myself. "Melzi wanted to be close to you, I think. Master da Vinci switched chambers with him in the winter."

"Is anything the same as it was before I left?"

Maurine smiled at me. "I suppose he simply longed for a way to remind himself that you did not leave him for another."

"Stop it."

"What? Like you two are not scheming to find a way to stay by each other's side for eternity."

"Tell me you could control your heart if Tommaso broke it?"

Maurine's silence startled me. She looked away, cleared her throat.

"Honestly?"

"You mustn't . . ."

It was then that my heart broke. Tommaso and Maurine had never hidden their love for one another as Melzi and I were required. For so long, I envied them. They had walked hand-in-hand through Gaillard's gardens, snuck from each other's beds with little care for who saw them. Their separation seemed unimaginable.

"What can I do for you?" My confinement at Fontevraud had rendered so much of my old life forgotten. Others had moved on. My memories could not be made anew. That was, indeed, the intent of the Abbess—to cut me off from the world my duties denied me. She meant it as a way to ease the ache of separation. The intrusion of reality stung.

"I am Sibylline. We cannot be together. That is all that ever needs to be spoken of it." Maurine gathered her weapons belt, and secured it around her waist. "My heart is not in the task at hand. Let us get on with the search for our Dear One."

I refused the dagger she pushed toward me. "We ought to take the Amyntas with us. Can you go fetch them from Gaillard?"

"Of course." Maurine left the knife on the table and tapped the blade. "Take care not to suffer this too deeply, my friend. I know where my loyalties live, and they will always be with you."

I admired her ability to set emotions aside. It made sense. Maurine trusted few to take care of the business of surviving. Her mother had been seized by Reformationists in Gibraltar. They forced Maurine to watch as they burnt her mother at the stake. At Fontevraud, we shared a modest cell of a room. She taught me to fight. I taught her how to read people. We did not need those skills to understand the depths of our devotion to one another and the Sibylline.

The door latched behind her and I pulled Master da Vinci's dodecahedron out of my dress pocket. The annoying letters remained perfectly written on the parchment inside. I placed it upon the desk and spread out his vellum note, contemplating its meaning.

"Our body is dependent on heaven and heaven on the spirit." I read aloud the inscription on the note again. Why would the Master play games at such a crucial moment? He made everything so difficult. I wanted to admonish him—if I ever found him. "Truth, indeed."

I slapped it all onto the ground. The contraption whacked against the tile of the floor. Several pieces slid across the room. I panicked, frantic at the thought of ruining the only piece I had of my old life, even if it incriminated Melzi.

"Are you all right, Great Mother?" Tommaso entered. He carried a tray of dates and olives, warm bread, and cheese.

The Amyntas waited for me to consent to his approach. I nodded and they closed the door.

"Do not call me that."

"Désolé." He halted at the sight of Maurine's blade on the table, running a gloved finger across it. He set out the food, collected the pieces from the floor, and fumbled with the dodecahedron, as the pieces gently fell into place. I sighed. "I thought you might be hungry."

"Please, sit. My heart finds itself a bit fragile."

"It is to be expected." Tommaso took his knife from its sheath and cut us both a slab of hard cheese. "Please tell me you have found proof that releases Melzi from these accusations."

I stopped him. "Accept my apologies about you and Maurine."

He set down the knife. "That is not the concern at hand."

His repetition of her words made me sadder for them still. I reached to remove the glove from his hand.

"Please, I beg you not to." Tommaso pulled away and put his glove back on. "Love, just as grief, is tender."

"Of course," I said, abashed. "However, I must seek your advice."

He raised his eyebrows and leaned in. "I thought the Seal gave you forward sight. Did you not know what was happening with Melzi these past months?"

"I have only recently started training with it," I showed him the Seal of the Sibyl, how it refracted the light. He went to touch it and I pulled away. "You must be careful. It will only confuse a mind not ready for it."

Tommaso raised an eyebrow. "Now, about Melzi."

"I only knew of anything in Amboise through the Abbess. He once wrote to me asking to relocate Master da Vinci to Fontevraud. Something about the poison of the royal residence. But, I never saw the recent schemes for myself."

Tommaso went rigid. "Did you respond?"

"Should I have?"

"I only meant that you have seen for yourself how Melzi has gone quite mad in recent days. You should just return him to Milano. Let him live a safe, quiet life."

"Is he that much trouble?"

"Worse than ever, I must say. Look at what happened today. Even I could not coax him to retreat." Tommaso stood and began to pace. He fidgeted, hands gripped behind his back. "Can you imagine if word of your abduction got out? Charles would surely set fire to the walls of Amboise before tomorrow's dawn."

I swallowed hard and realized I was gripping a bowl full of olives. The images of the castle on fire rose up again.

"We must find Master da Vinci." Tommaso stared into the hearth before continuing. "But, it will not serve you to go this alone."

"You know I cannot form alliances. The Sibyl must stand alone." My defensiveness, I knew, proved a poor mask for my pain. "I have one duty."

"As do I. Alas, Sibyls have a history of dying at these crucial hours. Hypatia died at the very moment of her crowning. Lubna vanished. And you are but moments from the ceremonies," he said. "You know as well as I do there has not been a Sibyl in more than a thousand years. They stood alone and died."

Tommaso's frank manner frightened me.

"Nothing has been prepared for with more care," I told him.

"Others see you as a threat. Why else would they take Master da Vinci?"

"Monsieur d'Arced, your tongue is too loose."

I expected him to heed my reproach. Instead, he seemed to find purpose in it. "Take an oath to his majesty, King François. His protection will relieve us of all of this unnecessary risk."

"I cannot bind myself to any king."

Tommaso leaned back in his chair. He spoke to me as if having prepared a speech. "You will let the outdated code of the Sibylline bring us to the edge of defeat?"

"Do not imply my unwillingness to form alliances is the cause of this war." My earlier reluctance to accept my role vanished as my ire was provoked. "You are not talking to a girl in Master da Vinci's workshop any more. You are speaking to the Great Mother."

"Please, you won't even let the servants call you that."

I was shocked by his dismissal. He would not let up.

"Did you expect to return and find two princes cordially dividing the Empire in the name of equanimity? You may believe you will rise and work for justice, that the dramatics between men will end. However, neither will stop unless . . ."

"Do not speak to me in this impudent manner, Tommaso."

"Why are you denying what you must do?" He pushed the chair back with his leg. "For the last half of a year, we fought to hold off Charles, waiting for you to return. The wealth of France has drained in your absence. While you prepare in your safe haven, our supplies, support, and gold flow as freely to France's enemies as the blood of our men. The loyalty of men such as me has kept others from the doors of Amboise, as well as Fontevraud. If it were not for us, this might be far worse."

"You blame the Sibylline?"

The Amyntas entered, weapons drawn, alerted by my shouting. I ignored them, as did Tommaso.

"Have you not had hundreds of generations to prepare?" he asked.

"Have you ever negotiated your freedom?"

"Indeed, I have."

I considered his rise in the King's court and conceded the point, raised my hand to coax back the Amyntas growing concern. "Then you know it is more than declaring victory and taking a throne."

"At least secure the throne." Tommaso hesitated, then reached out and set his hand on my shoulder. "It is time for the Abbess and you to do what you must to secure France."

"This is not a negotiation." I shook his hand away.

The Amyntas cleared their throats. Tommaso looked over his shoulder, and walked to the desk where he thumbed the note with Melzi's name on it.

"Who will others blame when you have found Master da Vinci dead and your beautiful La Joconde lost forever? Men will set you aflame because they fear you most."

I breathed in, attempting to cool the fury welling inside me.

"Do you even know who she is?" Tommaso said. "How many times have Melzi, Salaì, or I tried to perfect that nose, to paint the upturn of her smile with the perfection you wove into stories for us?"

I watched him. Tommaso's calmness sent a sickness through me.

"A woman on the wall is worth Master da Vinci? Melzi?" he asked.

I straightened and sharpened.

He stared at me for a moment, then handed me a small leather book pulled from his tunic pocket, detailing the contents of the workshop. "Well, if you must do this alone, at least be a bit more stealthy. The whole court saw my men chasing you through Heaven yesterday."

"Heaven? Is that not a bit much?" I took the ledger he left and thumbed through it.

"Dom Pacello would be hurt that you forgot his masterpiece."

I felt the full effect of my lengthy absence. Years ago, The Dom, Italy's greatest architect of royal gardens and Master da Vinci's closest friend, had deemed the gardens he created at Château Gaillard's gardens Heaven, and the forest outside the stone walls Hell. I had forgotten.

Tommaso's tone eased as he made his way to the door. "I am sorry for my behavior here. It is just that you and Melzi are all I consider family in France. I worry."

"Let us not linger on such errors and, instead, set our eyes only upon what needs to be done," I told him.

"What is so special about that painting anyway?"

"She will carry us into the future," I relented with my fury. Tommaso was, I thought, a friend. "So the Sibyl can be found when the time comes."

"As in the woman who will follow you?" Tommaso fussed with his gloves, straightening his greatcoat. "The painting, really? Not the Seal?"

The comment drew out a curiosity in me. I had never heard such a rumor, and it painfully matched what I had seen of my captor's motivations from my abduction a day earlier.

A spark of understanding struck me. Heaven. The Gardens. Gaillard. In the middle of it all was the Fountain of the Holy Spirit. The lettering from the scrap of paper that came from the dodecahedron popped from the page. I snatched it up. The script in Master da Vinci's vellum note left for Melzi was different. However, the writing on the scrap and that in Tommaso's ledger matched. I held it all close. A glimmer shot through me.

In an instant, all of the clues that appeared jumbled lined up. I tried to remain in control of my senses as an old friend's face settled in my mind.

"Indeed. The Sibylline nearly died out after the schism." I took a risk to see where my instincts lead. "The Abbess devised it so we will always live on."

A knock came at the door. The Amyntas allowed Maurine to enter. Tommaso looked up to find all of the women glowering at the sight of him. He said no more, backing out of the room with a low bow.

I tried to settle once again.

"Why was he here?" Maurine asked.

I fingered Master da Vinci's vellum note. Tommaso's voice lingered in my head. I held up the two pieces of writing. "I think I know where Master DaVinci is being held, and the identity of the one who betrayed us."

Maurine's lips tightened, her look stern as if she held the same suspicion all along. She pressed the knife on the table toward me. "Into battle we go."

Chapter 33

PHILIP

MAY 5, 1945
THE HILLS ABOVE CHÂTEAU GAILLARD
AMBOISE, FRANCE

Philip stood at the top of the hill just north of an old, run-down château where Marie and Iné had, somehow, overcome his soldiers and vanished into the forest. The tips of his boots were flush with the edge of a sharp drop-off where the earth had eroded, laying tree roots bare. Behind him, two men were dead, another injured. The body count on his end was far more aggressive than he intended or even thought possible.

He squinted in the afternoon sun, wiping sweat from his forehead. He poked his head inside the cave and walked over to one of the crates.

"German Sten guns," a soldier from the clean-up team said, as he pulled a body out of the opening at the back of the cave. "There's two more DOA underground. They must have dropped one down there and it went off."

Philip nodded, admiring the proof that Marie's reputation as a skilled Maquis fighter along with her smarts made her a worthy opponent. Worthy or not, he considered, she had gotten away. He knew the occupant of the Jeep roaring up the hill would force him to account for it.

Edwards' body was still laying there, bleeding out, when Philip got back outside. The Jeep screeched to a halt nearby. Diebitsch sauntered up. A silent man in street clothes stood at his side. Philip watched as he lifted the head of the dead man, inspecting it before letting it slam onto the ground. Diebitsch dusted off his uniform pants with the handkerchief cloth from his pocket, and folded it neatly before dabbing the sweat from his own brow. The man with him wore a torn jacket. His face was marked with dirt and he reeked of rubbing alcohol.

"They must have ambushed the men," Philip said. Manifests, photos, and folders were scattered everywhere.

Diebitsch took the gun from his holster and checked for a bullet in the chamber. His man passed him a canteen and he took a drink.

"I could use some of that," Philip said.

The man with Diebitsch took another canteen from the Jeep and gave it to him. All of the men drank.

"Your problems seem to have grown in my absence." Diebitsch stopped to listen to one of his men whisper a report in his ear. "Get this under control now, Colonel."

Philip was interrupted by shouting. Two British corporals came up the hill, pistols drawn on the German who arrived in the Jeep with Diebitsch.

"Stand down, boys," Philip said. "He's on our side."

The soldiers paused, but did as they were told. The German patted them on the back and offered the soldiers another canteen from the Jeep. Philip's pulse shot up. The scent of ersatz soap on the man was sickening, like rotten lard and chalk. He'd forgotten what it was like to stand so close to this sort of evil. It would all be done soon enough.

Philip heard sounds of a scuffle coming from the direction of the derelict château. He signaled to the soldiers to crouch and move low along the route to stay out of view. Philip stayed in place above the garden. Both men signaled those with them to stand down.

"I believe we've had a bit of luck. That's Yara Paquet." Philip pointed in the direction of an old woman who appeared at the south side of the garden. He noted the German's slight smile. "Original team member. She's been with the Mona Lisa since it was at Chenonceau."

"So predictable." Diebitsch motioned for his men to move down into the garden.

The trio of German soldiers had her at gunpoint within moments.

"Where is Doctor Guerrant?" one of the men demanded.

Philip had started to scramble down the hill when a gun fired. A bullet hit one of the German soldiers in the chest. A woman charged out from behind a tree while Yara whacked another soldier in the neck and disarmed him. He dropped to the ground, choking.

Philip's eyes grew wide as he spotted Marie holding her knife at the neck of the third German soldier who was on his knees.

"Where is my daughter?" she shouted.

He shook his head, grunting.

"Der Seher?" Marie kicked him in the ribs. "Bist du wegen des Sehers gekommen? Where is Serah Izem?"

Philip lit up hearing those words—*Did you come because of the seer?*—Marie had said it. She must have found it in the journals. She was asking about the Sibyl. He caught the hint of admiration in Diebitsch's face at her perfect German. He'd anticipated the familiarity between the two. Karl Diebitsch had overseen research on the Sibyl at Ravensbrück for years. But this was more than familiarity.

Four bursts of gunfire rang out. Philip whirled to look. Two men raced across the field from the west, firing Bren machine guns.

"This is better than I could have hoped." Philip recognized the man as Noam Marchant. He'd done it. He'd gotten Marie to confirm that the journals were Melzi's, that the Sibyl was in them, and she drew the Maquis out into the open. He would let the fight play out.

"You have delivered them, as promised." Diebitsch nodded at Philip. "We'll have Serah Izem, the painting, and the Sibyl before nightfall."

Philip tracked the fight. He watched as a mustached soldier on the ground ripped a knife from his leg sheath and swiped at Marie. She grabbed her ankle. The man kicked her good leg out from under her, then took Yara, holding his blade at her throat.

Another soldier moved in and pinned Marie's arms behind her back.

"You think you could kill us all and still find her?" she shouted.

The soldier shoved her down to her knees. Philip took note of a Maquisard man captured and face-down in the dirt. Two others lay dead at the edge of the garden.

"You bastards." Marie squirmed.

Soldiers started moving in from every direction. Where was Iné Soudier, Philip asked himself?

Diebitsch scrambled down the hill and walked up to Marie.

"Doctor Guerrant." He removed his leather glove and ran his hand across her cheek. "How lovely to see you again."

"These people don't have anything to do with this game of yours." Marie stared at him. "I'll get you the painting."

"Ha. You'll get me far more than that." Diebitsch turned to Noam. Their eyes connected. "Why don't you ask your friend over there on his knees why he got you into this mess?"

Soldiers pinned Yara face-down in the dirt. Noam glared at the man.

"I wouldn't want to play your hand either, Monsieur," Diebitsch continued talking to him. "Who wants to be the one to tell the woman whose husband you let die that you lost her daughter too."

Marie stared at Noam, the horror on her face clear. Philip relished the distrust building between them. It had all come together so neatly. Everything he needed to find the Sibyl and destroy her was his. Soon, the honor of his sons would be secured.

Suddenly, a light flashed. The wind blew. Philip's eyes shot upward.

Ears perked. From somewhere within the stone hills, a long, low sound rumbled, lilting up, down, up, down, up, down, then a triple blast until the tone settled low and steady like a French horn echoing in a canyon.

The pulse of the light overwhelmed his eyes. The horn called out again. The sun seemed to dip below the blue-gray horizon despite Philip assuring himself it was no later than half past one. His perception shifted, as if the sound were dragging him away from his feet, his legs. His eyes fogged. Then, the howl of the horn shot through him like a bullet forcing him back to the day his sons died. The fog had altered everyone's senses. He found himself twitching and anxious. Henry and Benjamin missed the rendezvous with him. The horn. The horn! It had kept Philip from hearing them, from hearing the soldiers behind his sons, until they were burning in the flames of a fire the likes of which he had never known. The horn, the boom of that woman's voice. She had come for them. The Sibyl, he told himself, had stolen his sons from . . . He turned. Someone brushed against his shoulder. He turned again. There stood two young men.

"Ho there. What do you think you're ...?" He gasped as their faces became clear. His sons. He tried to speak again. They were gone.

Philip's eyes cleared. A young British soldier near the Jeep jabbed at his companions. He panicked, tossing a canteen at the others. Men started to shout and kick at each other, spinning around with their guns. They shot at trees, rocks, and other men.

"Witchcraft!" Diebitsch shrieked, slapping at the air.

Philip looked over at him, panicked that the terror he witnessed in Belgium was happening again in Amboise. The man could hardly stand as he tossed his canteen away and stumbled over to a tree stump. He tried to think practically. The canteen! Philip had seen troops contaminate civilian water supplies. The villagers had literally beaten each other to death. If the soldiers had been exposed to this, he knew there was no hope. He kicked the canteen across the field. Philip only had a few sips of water. How much had Diebitsch and the other men drunk? Philip shuddered. "We've been poisoned."

The hallucinations mounted. The horn grew silent. Women's voices called out. Hymns, he heard hymns. They sang with fury. *Elohim. Ave Maria. Gayatri. Alláh-U-Abhá. Maranatha. Mitakuye Oyasın. Kyrie Eleison. Yá Bahá'u'l-Abhá.*

Philip struggled between wanting to linger in the vibration of the songs and needing to escape. He waited too long to decide. Diebitsch, caught up in a hallucination of his own, began to howl.

Philip's sons seemed to appear across the field. He knew they were a hallucination, but still he ran towards them. The heat, the bodies, the crowd of men fighting pressed in on him in the darkness. He fired his gun at anyone in his way. Soldiers collapsed. He was killing his own men. They were killing each other. What was happening? He fumbled, hacking away at the tree roots that appeared tar-black in the utter darkness of the forest. Anything to get to his sons. Closer and closer he inched. Philip had lost Diebitsch, but he cared for nothing but his boys. Tears wet his face as he pressed on.

A single feminine voice rang out with a chilling, wordless song. Then two. Then a third, making a melodic soprano within the harmonies.

Philip couldn't reach his sons. Then, everything settled. Rain fell. A cascade. A swirl. A twist. A gathering of breath. Peace. Was it peace? He couldn't tell if this was dying. A sparkling glow, that seemed almost sentient, illuminated the forest.

Out of the corner of his eye, he caught movement. A pair of large figures in midnight-blue cloaks ushered Marie, Iné, and Yara, even Noam Marchant, away from it all.

Philip was far from anyone now. Yet those two young men heading up the hill were his sons. He was certain.

"Henry! Benjamin!" It couldn't be the boys he'd watched shot and burned to death five months earlier. Never would they turn on him, help the women escape. Yet, his eyes defied his thoughts.

Their purposeful pace made Philip impulsive. He weaved through the crowd of veiled women and the soldiers laying on the ground. He shook. What, or who, had killed them. That stinging smell of ersatz. More and more dead soldiers in his path. He stumbled over them.

The women kept ahead of him, as they made their way into the forest. Philip turned back, desperate to find anyone alive. A veiled figure stood nose-to-nose with him. His hand reached out but landed on nothing but air. She vanished. In her wake, came the sound of a thousand voices. A thousand prayers, sung aloud. And now the glow from a thousand lanterns illuminated the perimeter. He saw his soldiers rimming the gardens.

"Take those women! They are getting away!" he shouted. "They're at the top of the hill!"

But his men stood entranced. Stiff. The women, along with the rest of the Maquis, had made it out of the gardens and into the forest. He'd lost them.

Chapter 34

MARIE

MAY 5, 1945
THE HILLS ABOVE CHÂTEAU GAILLARD
AMBOISE, FRANCE

Marie watched as the soldiers flailed and howled in the overgrown garden below. Those who weren't injured had stopped pointing their guns at each other. She watched their terror as each stumbled and bucked from what she assumed was the effect of the water she and Iné had contaminated. Yes, they were able to use that to their advantage. Yet, it shouldn't have been necessary. Why had Yara leaped from the transport and made a run for the old house?

It was dark. She had no idea how much time had passed, but the night was thick around them. The lack of light would prove a decent cover, Marie thought, but the questions in her head and the stinging of her heart kept her away from the others. Iné had hustled them into a sheltered area beneath an overhang of rock, moss, and pine. It was filled with wooden crates. Just inside, Marie spotted an entrance to the underground tunnels.

She tried to piece together what took place from the moment she was on her knees. She remembered Noam running in, Diebitsch collapsing, and Philip firing his pistol over and over. Did he kill his own men? She hadn't seen Iné until the very end. It made no sense.

Marie returned to the issue of Yara's nonsensical action. She stared at the old woman rummaging through the crates. Yara lit two portable lanterns, then fished out bandages, scissors, and alcohol. She had returned to the woman Marie had always known—calm, focused, even pensive in her devotion to getting the necessary work done.

Marie took stock of the injuries. A cut on Noam's forearm would need stitches. Yara had a gash across her temple that appeared rather deep. Marie suffered the least of the physical damage. She ached, but not from the cuts and bruises left by the soldiers. Her spirit felt crushed. She took the roll of gauze Yara handed her, along with a clean-enough cloth to clean up her scrapes. "How did we get out of that?"

"The water," Iné said.

"I realize that, but we walked right into an ambush." Marie acknowledged Iné's forethought, considering it saved their lives. However, what kind of woman was she to do something like that? "And what about what Diebitsch said. Were you even there?"

"Wipe down your wounds," Iné didn't acknowledge the accusations laid against Noam by the German. "We can't risk infection."

Marie ignored her own injuries and went to Yara, who was clearly hurt. She reached for Yara's forehead and pushed back her mound of silver hair. The wrinkles on her forehead made the gash across it stand out. "That's a lot of blood."

"Not bad, really. I'll be fine." The woman shook her off.

"But, it's . . ."

"I'm fine!" Yara's voice startled everyone. She dropped to a whisper and took Marie's hand. "Get yourself taken care of."

"Simon's fine. I'm sure of it." Marie tried to comfort her. Yara let her begin to bandage the head wound. "What happened to you out there?"

"You've been gone a long time," Yara said. "There have been many sacrifices. Simon only wanted it to be done."

Marie berated herself. She wanted someone to blame. "This is about Iné, isn't it?"

"Don't make assumptions, girl," Yara took Marie's chin in her hand.

"I'm not telling you this to give you an enemy. What happened here was going to happen whether you were with us or not. Iné is important to us."

"What about Serah?"

"What about Serah?" Yara snapped back. "You think you're the only one who has lost people!"

Her words were like claws digging into Marie, but she shoved the regret down and continued to bandage Yara's head in silence.

"Stop." The woman pushed her hand away.

Marie would not listen. "You know I always figured Jules would be killed. He'd leave for months."

"We never even knew what happened to either of you," Yara said. "Noam took Serah, hid her for a long time. I hope you don't think what any of that Nazi said down there was true."

"I used to think it was me." Marie squirted iodine in Yara's cut. "I second-guessed myself with an American operative, made introductions to Maquis. He was a plant. Jules and five other men were executed."

Yara put a hand on Marie's face again. "You can't take that on yourself."

"All I could think about was getting to Serah. How could I get out of that prison, get back to the house, to Serah . . . ?" Marie couldn't finish. Noam had been absent that day. He was supposed to have been at the meeting with Jules. She watched him now as she taped the bandage to Yara's forehead. He sat on a rock, head in hands, wearing nothing more than a bloodied t-shirt and ripped pants, while Iné stitched his arm.

The tears came again. Marie had trusted him from the moment they met. In the beginning, his duplicity as a cop trying to get inside the Communist Party seemed like conditioning he could overcome. Noam had proven he had a heart; that he cared about people, not power. He hid Jews in his cellar, protecting those who were stripped of their identity. Yet, she wondered what he had done to provoke Diebitsch.

"Don't dwell, my dear," Yara said. "We all did terrible things to survive."

Settling herself with a few deep breaths, Marie turned away from the group. A frosty white rat ran in and skittered past her legs. She tried to edge it aside with her boot. The rat stiffened and hissed, twisting itself up in her feet.

"Get away!" Marie snatched the rodent up and tossed it gently toward the entrance. "Get out, stupid beast."

Iné finished with Noam's arm wound. "Making friends, I see."

Noam reached out to pet the rat's back. It slashed his dressings and hissed. "Ah, an excellent judge of character."

Marie glared at him. Noam had never looked so beaten.

"You have to see they need us to be divided, afraid, hateful," he said to her. "We are cattle. They feed on our disconnection."

"I know the game—get inside our heads. Make us doubt. Classic divide and conquer," Marie said. "It's much easier to knock us off when we don't trust each other."

Noam sucked in a hard breath. His eyes grew sad. "I didn't betray you, Marie. I just didn't tell you everything."

Diebitsch's words rang in her head. "And what is everything?"

Noam's deep, wordless stare revealed his thoughts to her.

"The Sibyl." Marie's temperament turned bitter. "You're after her too?"

"No. Well, sort of," he said. "Look, Yara can tell you. She was with the team that got La Joconde as far as the Loire. When they got here, though, something changed."

Yara looked up from her work of sorting field rations. She nodded.

"Think about it." Noam kept going. "The painting hadn't been back at Amboise since da Vinci died. You, better than any of us, know its history."

"Sure. King François bought it from Salaí for something like four thousand pieces of gold. Then, he locked it away at Fontainebleau."

"It is a nice story, isn't it?" Iné tried to bandage up Marie.

"You know better?" Marie questioned, willing to take out her growing rage on anyone.

"We never intended for this," Noam said.

"I don't understand." Marie wondered if everyone except her knew what was going on.

"We didn't either." Yara passed out chocolate bars and gum. "La Joconde had been relatively safe during the occupation. The same Maquis team stayed with her the whole time. We spent a lot of years with her and never considered that the Germans were right about the rumors of her being the visage of an actual, modern-day Sibyl. We knew Himmler was insane. We thought we had to hold the outlandish theories at bay just long enough for the war to be over, and then get her back to Paris safely. Philip and his men were our handoff."

"And?" Marie had heard most of this story before.

Yara turned to Iné as if pressing her to say something.

"You know they're just stories, right?" Marie could not believe she had to talk her people through the difference between legend and truth. "The Sibyl. She doesn't exist."

"This afternoon in Simon's workshop you weren't so sure." Iné tossed her a tin of franks and beans. "Eat. Then, we'll get somewhere safe and talk further."

"At least explain what Diebitsch said out there." Marie felt helpless. The three of them, again, seemed to draw on familiarity with one another. They spoke without words. The isolation drove her deeper inside her head. She turned to Noam. "You can't expect me to trust you after that."

"But we should trust you?" Iné asked. "You're the one who hid the notations in the journals from us."

Marie ground her teeth. "You owed me assurances back then. You owe me them now."

"Not now," Iné said.

"How about you explain how we got up here? We were as good as dead twenty minutes ago."

"Not. Now." Iné said.

"When, then?" Marie leaped to her feet. She charged Iné and pushed her to the ground. The necklace around the woman's neck caught on Marie's sleeve and broke. Iné scrambled toward the broken chain and the small cylinder hanging from it. Marie scooped it up. "You want this back?"

"Give it to me." Iné was on her feet.

"Why? When do I get the truth from any of you?" Marie stormed out of the cave. Just as she reached the edge of the pathway, she heard a noise and her vision shifted, blurred.

"Dear One."

She searched the forest for the source of the voice from her nightmare a day earlier. Her senses burned. A pressure formed against her right arm. She stiffened. She turned to identify it. Nothing. Her feet moved, but she had no sense of the direction she was moving in. The words grew more audible.

"I died here."

"Marie." Noam's voice echoed behind her. The rhythmic thwack of his boots against the dirt path seemed so far away. The voice in front of her was a tether, pulling her toward it.

"Look . . . See," it called.

Marie had the necklace in her hand. She peered over the blackness of the overgrown garden below. In the middle of it stood a single veiled figure that seemed to radiate a dim light. Marie's mind flickered. Scenes of a woman on fire seared into her mind. Men in doublets crashed against the stone of the roadway. Others in velvet coats and leather boots watched from a tower. Rust-tinged marks staining the walls of the château turned to blood. The air bristled. A sharp scent of life violently exiting, of lilies, of vomit. She was sure she knew the voice.

"Serah?"

"Marie, get back!" Noam yanked at her. "What is wrong with you?"

"Do you hear it?" She couldn't clear her head. She tried to recapture the fading scene.

"Do you hear me?" he grabbed her hand. "Men are coming up the hill. We have to go."

"I died here." The formless voice now commanded the attention of them both.

"Holy hell," Noam whispered. "What is that?"

Marie bolted down the ridge. "It's Serah, I know it."

"Stop!" Noam chased after her.

"It's her. We have to get her."

The rustle of a boot. The snap of a twig. The sound of a rifle butt being repositioned. Marie heard a bullet enter a chamber. Led by her senses she made it across the briars, weeds, and vines, past the toppled heads of statues and old carved stone overtaken by mud and mold to the crumbled wall at the north end of the garden before the shot was fired. A glance back. Noam was gone. More footsteps. More guns firing. Marie knew she was about to die. Even if it were Serah, there was no way to reach her. No chance of gaining enough distance between her and Philip's men. Her chest heaved. Another bullet fired from behind the ruins of a towering old fountain.

Noam grabbed her hand from behind as she halted near a patch of blackberry briars. They threw themselves past the crumbled wall of the garden, their feet tangling in the masses of ivy and underbrush. They ran along a trail barely visible beneath the rocks and snags. Up. Finally, Marie spied the ramparts that ran all the way to Château Amboise. She panted and held her chest. Exhaustion. Heartbreak. She and Noam stood shaking. Beside them was a deep trench at the backside of the castle. The men searching below hadn't seen them run.

"It was Serah."

Iné came up behind them, her mouth gaping. "Give me the necklace, quickly."

Noam let go of Marie's hand, turned and tossed the piece to Iné, who took off back toward the others.

"You have to stop," he said, holding Marie. "She's not here. There is no way Serah could be here."

Marie couldn't feel anything but the weight of grief. Her hands were clammy. They rested on Noam's chest. He looked down, his arms around her. She snatched her hands back. "There are ghosts everywhere."

"I know," he continued, pulling her close. "They refuse to leave people like us alone."

Relief and fear overwhelmed Marie. She and Noam held one another a moment more. She caught her breath. He said nothing. He just held her, breathing with her. Their shaking gave way to a calm.

"He was my best friend, Marie. My brother, really," Noam said. "I loved Jules, would have done anything at all to have taken his place. You have to believe that."

"I know," she said. Surprised, Marie took notice of what looked like a servant's entrance to the castle. And there, in the doorway, a person stood, holding a lantern and staring at them.

Chapter 35

AESMEH

MAY 1, 1519
**THE COURTYARD OF CHÂTEAU GAILLARD
AMBOISE, FRANCE**

Maurine and I stood at the Fountain of the Holy Spirit in the courtyard of Château Gaillard. I had the Amyntas position themselves inside the orangery below the main house, as to remain less obvious. In the center of the immense, square sections of groomed grass, stood the marble, ornamental pool. Atop it, an angelic figure watched over the garden, her wings sculpted, her hair twisted and pinned in perfect rendering, her robes flowing from bare shoulders. I found myself taken by her radiance. Water arched elegantly from the shell cistern in her arms to the pool below. I marveled at the system that made the water flow. A summer earlier, Melzi and I had watched the Masters Dom Pacello and da Vinci map out and build it together. The mechanisms that made it work were stored beneath in an underground room with a coded lock.

"You are sure he is here?" Maurine asked. The Amyntas had disobeyed me and taken up positions at the east and west entrances to the garden. I admitted it did provide more immediate protection if something went wrong.

"Just pretend to admire the statue," I said.

"Such a travesty." Maurine grimaced. She never developed a taste for Italian frivolity.

"Can you do what I ask so I can concentrate?"

Maurine huffed. I took the dodecahedron in my hand. It seemed the most likely tool for revealing the combination to open the door. I studied it. Endless mathematics lessons from Master da Vinci took shape. I ran a finger over its lines. Twelve faces, twenty vertices, thirty edges, and one hundred and sixty diagonals. I slipped off my gloves.

"Can you not use the forward sight?" Maurine asked.

"That only shows me possible outcomes, not solutions." I twisted the mechanisms on the lock until all of the numbers were in place. It released. "Huzzah! The man is as predictable as he is mercurial."

I yanked on the door handle. It gave way with a stiff tug. Only a child could stand tall and walk across that threshold. My heart skipped as Maurine and I crouched and ducked in. I worried about what we would find. I had already succumbed to the most basic of deceptions. That Tommaso saw me as an enemy, or at least an adversary to be controlled, stung. I had told him too much about La Joconde. My error in judgment had sped up the need for this rescue. The unpredictability of Tommaso's ambitions made the situation urgent. I pulled the door shut and almost collapsed at what my eyes landed upon.

There sat Master da Vinci, happily eating roasted boar and fruit, bread and cheese—this beautiful, white-haired, wizened old man whom kings had sought out as their greatest prize.

"Ma bella." He looked up and grinned as he popped a piece of cheese in his mouth. "Sei venuto."

"Of course, I came. Your puzzles made it more difficult than necessary." I wondered where he got the food. He smelled unwashed. "How long have you been here?"

He patted my cheek and shook his head. "Too bad Tommaso is as blunt as a butter knife. His tongue shall get him into the highest of places, but the rest of his talents can fit on the top of my popper."

Maurine laughed uneasily and then glared at him.

"Why are you here?" I demanded. "Everyone is searching for you."

Master da Vinci leaped from the chair and pulled off his soiled tunic. I attempted to shield my eyes as well as Maurine's. His butt cheeks wiggled as he took a cloth. He picked up an old amphora, poured cool water onto it, and wiped himself down. He then opened a box along the wall, pulled out fresh hose and a tunic, and dressed in silence.

"Why must I answer my own questions?" I hated this duel of wits; it was one we had undertaken many times before.

"Because you already know the answers. I am not here to confirm what you can see without my help."

"You did this to yourself?" Maurine asked.

"Of course, I did. It is much easier to hide if people think you are dead."

"So, your intent was for us to find you dead?" I still failed to make sense of the situation.

"Arghhhh. Such a mind. Yet, still, so literal. Did your sojourn with the Abbess do nothing?

"I had to break my sojourn because of your little treachery," I said.

"There was no choice."

"You could have told Maurine."

"Why? I did not need a nursemaid, just a place to work away from all of the treachery at court." He ignored us as he fussed with a gadget on the table. "Tommaso set his eyes upon his rise in favor. Let the boy play his games for a few more days. He can do nothing more once you are safe within the confines of the temple. Besides, we all know the real reason for this."

I caught him staring down Maurine. She hastily brushed him off. "Master, there is trouble."

"When is there not trouble in France?" Master da Vinci guided us back into a room. It was lit from the slit windows cut into the base of the fountain. "I see you have not told Sister Aesmeh how you were entangled in this mess. Our Dear One is safe, though."

I breathed in for what seemed like the first time in a day, unable to clarify Master da Vinci's comments about Maurine. The eyes of our Dear One stared at me from her position on the tall wooden easel. A day earlier I believed the painting was gone forever. At that moment, she sat waiting for me. Dozens of jars, brushes, knives, and palette boards were strewn around the space.

"She is not ready for the key." I gasped at the simple beauty of this woman. Yet, her face lacked a lifelike glow. One of the many layers of glaze was fresh. He had not even begun to lay down the white highlights. I realized my outburst stung. "Desolé. I just thought you ought to have her prepared by now."

Master da Vinci stared at the face of the woman he had been painting for the last fourteen years. He wrapped his hand in a thin layer of silk, then set a leather and iron contraption on the table. He waved Maurine over.

I gasped, again, as he put his hand on top of the device. His fingers were twisted and bent, stiff as a bird's claw. Maurine pressed each finger straight and strapped them in, one-by-one. The cinch of each leather piece made Master da Vinci's breath catch. The tears in his eyes and ever-whitening face were too much for me.

I took his hand, allowing the fingers to return to their malformed shape. "How?"

"In the depths of last winter, he went cold and lost a few days." Maurine wet a cloth and massaged his hand until the color returned to his face.

"I was there one minute, to the heavens, and back," Master da Vinci said.

"The gods stole a bit of your mind and your hand." Maurine joked with him.

"Why did you not tell the Abbess?" I could not understand why he would suffer.

"I wanted so much to finish her for you."

"However." I interrupted him.

"However . . ." Master da Vinci pulled his hand away from Maurine. He cleared his throat. "Melzi can help me insert the key."

His words settled on me. For a decade, Melzi had guided others to learn the use of the Master's sfumato technique. He was the only one capable of such a task. I had just sent him to the dungeons.

"This glaze is drying. Just the highlights and the final step," Master da Vinci said. "Could you imagine that this beauty you envisioned when you were a twelve-year-old girl in Milano would lead us here? That face has graced the canvasses of apprentices more times than I could count."

I wanted to soften at Master da Vinci's devotion to this woman none of us would ever know, but whom we all loved. The time we all spent together bonded us. The men painted her and I shared every detail of her beauty and power. However, I could not overlook the consequences of the painting not being complete at this late hour. The Master knew that he was solely responsible for people finding the Sibyl who would follow me, five hundred years from now.

"Is there no other way?" Maurine asked.

"The Abbess and I have already debated this," I said. "She will be locked in the temple with me."

The irony of my declaration hung heavy in the air. I had only two days before the painting and I were set to enter the temple. The key could only be carefully inserted in the final stage. Master da Vinci could not do it on his own.

The Master snapped his fingers at me. "Enough. Have Melzi bring the linseed. I failed to escape with all of the pigments. Have one of the boys bring the other mixtures."

How could I tell him what I had done? My horror at accusing Melzi, having him locked in the cages beneath Château Amboise, silenced me. That Tommaso helped me do it made the grave error even more grotesque.

"Well." Master da Vinci stared at us. "Get to it."

As he repeated his orders, the glimmer in my head flared up. Once again, I saw the fires at the base of the castle ramparts, my death, that of the dead soldier in the clearing outside Château Gaillard.

"Master da Vinci." Maurine placed her hands in his. "As I said, there is trouble."

His uneasy glare ceded control to me. I stumbled with my words and thought it best to recount everything from the moment we received news of his disappearance. "When I got to your workshop, it was nearly destroyed."

He returned to preparations. "Yes, I told you what I did."

"Did you cleanse it?"

He paused. "That seems a little excessive."

"The room was cleansed of just about everything. I found the dodecahedron tucked in the back of your work desk. Your other message was wedged beneath the top of the desk in Melzi's room."

His pause grew longer. He began to mumble. "Yes, I knew Melzi would be able to help you find me if the situation grew dire. I need him. Go."

I knew Master da Vinci understood my error. "He slept through the attack, hid your journals instead of the painting. I thought he overlooked and therefore lost our Dear One."

He would not look up at me. His voice cracked. "All clearly explained if you had kept your head. Where is he?"

My face burned.

"Have I not always cherished what lives between the two of you? Even argued to keep you close after Milano?"

"You know what our separation caused."

"So you needed him to betray you." The Master still would not meet my eyes.

"You think me so petty?"

"Your broken heart is bloodying my floor, ma bella. Lies are too often told to end the carnage of loss."

"You know as well as I that the only reason to cleanse a room of its memories is to keep someone like me from reading them."

"Indeed." Master da Vinci exhaled loudly. He turned to Maurine. "Are you to tell her or shall I? You two and your hearts."

I dared not ask for clarity, but I waited for my oldest friend to offer it.

"We all underestimated Tommaso," Maurine finally spoke.

Master da Vinci drew back at her words. Chin in his palm, leaning on the table, he stared into the space between us. He was dozing off when he leaped up and slipped on a pair of stiff boots. "Did Tommaso offer any clues to his end game?"

"Only that he would prefer to see me bound to France," I said.

"I suspect he would see you bound to no one, but has promised you to everyone." Master da Vinci held back the heavy drapery covering the low door to the courtyard. "Tommaso may have caught us off guard, ma bella, but everyone underestimates an old man. Now, what hole did you stuff Melzi down? Because we are going to have to dig him out of it."

Chapter 36

MARIE

MAY 6, 1945
THE SERVANT'S ENTRANCE OF CHÂTEAU AMBOISE
AMBOISE, FRANCE

Marie gasped. The gray-haired man who'd stepped just beyond the threshold of Château Amboise's servant entrance reached for her.

"You look like hell." Simon wrapped her in a blanket.

"How are you here?" Marie could not gather her wits enough to think through his obvious escape from the Germans hours earlier.

"I still have a few tricks left in me." Simon grinned.

His left eye was thick with blood and black around the edges. She reached up to pat it. Simon leaned in to her touch and she pressed her palm against the side of his face.

"Did you think I'd let the Germans kill me? Please, give an old fighter some credit."

"Of course." Marie smirked at him.

"They thought I'd go with them willingly. Then, well, all of this." Simon waved his hand in the air.

Marie looked out over the soldiers lying dead or writhing in pain, as if they had fought on the front lines. "So many down there."

Simon turned to Noam. "The others?"

"They are coming. Is everything ready?" Noam quizzed him.

"This is your rendezvous point?" Marie asked.

"We've been anticipating some kind of encroachment," Simon said. "No need to die if we can help it."

"For what?" Marie asked. Neither man answered.

"I'll go get the others." Noam turned to leave. "You two have some things to talk about."

Marie took his hand and pulled him back. "I shouldn't have run off. I compromised everyone."

"We'll forgive each other for all of this later." Noam squeezed her hand one last time before turning to head back outside. He backed away, heading off into the night before Marie could protest.

She and Simon started walking down the narrow stone hallway. He handed her a stack of notebooks. "There's a lot you need to catch up on."

Marie expected they'd entered the castle, but it was more like an underground storage building. She and Simon walked down a cool, stone corridor that smelled of chalk and anise. The safety of the dim hallway allowed her to collect herself after the hallucinations.

"Turoni. Damn, it took me a while to get that," she blurted out, finally remembering the name of the ancient Gaelic tribes who had lived along the Loire. "People of the bulls, or thunder, or something like that."

Simon pulled aside a stack of wooden crates to reveal the remains of a glorious, colorful mural of a bull. They smiled at Marie's recollection. History had always been their connection, even when she was a child.

She mulled over the name—Turoni. It was hard, even for her, to break down the origins of it. Marie had read dozens of Gaulish texts in Greek and Old Italic written before the Roman conquest of southern France and northern Italy. Their stories, though, were passed down around the fire, never written. The mural though, much like the ones she had seen in the tunnels, made her wonder if those stories had somehow been destroyed.

Simon smiled at her. "Amboise has a way of reminding anyone of its past."

"You're not kidding." Marie thought back on the disembodied calls for help that drove her into the old garden just moments earlier. "I keep seeing things."

Simon perked up. "You've seen the pilgrimage then?"

They turned a corner. The light in the hallway grew far brighter. Marie discovered the imprints on the walls just like the orange symbols Iné had shown her, which distracted her from Simon's odd comment. She traced one. A wheat husk. Then, another. She coaxed her finger clockwise around the orange carving and the light in the room grew warm and clear.

"Iné?" Simon asked and Marie nodded. "She's a good teacher."

Wooden bins of onions and potatoes were lined against the side walls. Sausage and sides of pork hung from the ceiling of an open room. It made that part of the corridor smell musty and pungent. Along the sides of the hall, heavy, magnificent tapestries with horned creatures and women in medieval finery covered military crates. Marie assumed this was the remains of a Nazi cache of food, but couldn't shake the memory provoked by Iné's touch. The main space overflowed with generators, rolled-up tents, and other military equipment with French, Nazi, British, and, even, American markings.

"Your supply depot?" Marie was impressed.

"Survival has no allegiances." Simon patted her on the shoulder and helped her navigate.

They maneuvered across the wide, deep room, and climbed two sets of modest stone stairs. At the top, Simon unlocked an oak door. Inside, Marie saw a small space outfitted with intricately carved shelves. The ceramic floor tiles were painted with peacock feathers and the heads of unicorns. Slot windows brought in air and light. A small fireplace burned in one corner.

"Ohhhh, this is Marguerite de Navarre's library," Marie said. Her eyes widened at the thought of a queen holed up in here, writing treatises and letters that shaped the Humanist movement of the Renaissance. She noticed a pile of military rations on the table. "Is that coffee?"

"I'd say yes, but I can't find anything to heat water in."

"Cruel." Marie eyeballed the pile of army-issued writing pads stacked next to the undrinkable coffee. "What's in the notebooks?"

"Well . . ." Simon exhaled hard.

"I'm going to assume they have something to do with you throwing yourself at the Germans earlier?"

"About a week ago, a Francs-Tireurs et Partisans showed up, just before we were about to do the drop for La Joconde, and told us about Philip Millar."

"Paul," Marie said the name as she thought out loud, not remembering that Simon was listening.

"Yes, how did you know?"

Marie felt her face redden as the pieces. "You had the journals."

"For a bit." Simon was pensive, his voice low, his eyes staring off as if looking at nothing at all.

"Millar sent him in?"

"Paul figured out Millar and Diebitsch had a deal. We knew we had to get the painting and the journals out."

"The colonel killed Paul for them."

"We know."

"Did you know about the code?"

"Not until yesterday. Millar's team got the jump on us. We had to separate."

"Serah?"

"She's got the painting."

"Where?" Marie grew demanding.

"There's more to this than Serah and the painting, Marie."

"No, there isn't," she shouted. "Serah is the only thing that matters now.

"Can you just listen? You read the journals. They are authentic, we both know it, and they name her. Asfoora, Aesmeh, the great Sibyl of Amboise, she was here. No matter what you want to think, Melzi believed she was a Sibyl."

"Not you too?" Marie wanted to choke Simon. "Who cares about the Sibyl?"

"Serah. She was the one who found her."

"Oh my God. Are you telling me she found a woman?"

Simon opened a notebook. "We have a situation to deal with right now and you just have to trust that we've been in the middle of this for a very long time."

Marie closed her eyes, her teeth grinding. She let out a heavy sigh. "How far did you get?"

Simon released his own breath and a sense of relief came over the room. He thumbed right to a page, which he tapped his index finger hard against. "Far enough to know that Melzi had more than da Vinci on his mind while they were locked up at Clos Lucé."

"Are you saying they were in some sort of confinement?" Marie moved in as well, pulling the notebook close to read it.

"Come on now," Simon continued, showing her the passages. "You know the last few years of da Vinci's life were nothing more than the exile of a crippled, old eccentric masked in a French King's patronage."

"You make so little of such a great man." Marie had forgotten what a harsh view of history Simon held. Still. It seemed odd that, as a magnificent reproduction artist, history was his business, his art form, his muse.

"He was brilliant. That's not up for debate," he continued. "Yet, we tell tales about him like the world did not influence his choices. Like the wars between power-mad kings and the desires of the sycophants surrounding them played no role in shaping those stories."

"I've never been prone to segmenting individual histories and scrapping them of their context," she looked up at Simon, who was hunched over her. "You know that. What is your point?"

"What if da Vinci was caught up in something?" He stood. "What if Melzi was too?"

"That's one hell of an assertion." She went back to reading. "da Vinci as a traitor to France?"

"No, nothing like that. And, I'm not talking about him."

She knew, in an instant, to whom Simon referred. The stillness in the room prodded her to ask him, despite her own hesitations. "You mean the Asfoora references?"

Simon spread out new pages he'd copied from a journal, and put on his glasses. He moved a chair next to Marie's. "Melzi refers to her in his journals and letters almost exclusively by that name. However, he clearly requests permission to use Asfoora in an early letter. So, we can pretty confidently infer the name is not her given one."

"Makes sense. The love between him and a woman of the French court would be scandalous," Marie said. "Secrecy proved paramount."

"There's more, though." Simon pushed one of the notebooks toward her and opened it to a dog-eared page. "The first letters from 1506 show our Asfoora as a girl of no more than twelve, assigned to da Vinci."

"Assigned?"

"Yes, like to watch over."

"By whom? For what purpose?"

"I'm not sure, maybe an Abbess. Some of the pages are missing." Simon showed her the notes he had taken from several journal entries that spoke of this Asfoora's days in Amboise with da Vinci and Melzi.

He pulled out an old entry he'd retrieved from one of the original journals. "I think she's directly connected to La Joconde. She might even be her if the stories are to be believed. Read what Melzi wrote."

August 18, 1518

I fear today may be the last of my many summer hours upon the ridgeline above the Royal Residence with my Asfoora and the others. As we painted, the Master guided us. It was then that I spotted the standards of the Mother House. The Abbess' women descended upon the oak grove and plucked my Asfoora from her perch. We weren't even allowed to finish the last of our lessons in sfumato and the laying of the glazes. Now, I am comforted only by the wisps of woodsmoke coiling upward from Tour Hertault. As long as they remain, so does my love here in Amboise.

There they were, other words far more significant than Asfoora: *Mother House.* Marie stared at them, recalling the same words on the notes in the SOE file Millar had given her. "Could you have mistranslated it?"

"You're reading the original." Simon patted at the old parchment on the table.

Marie's eyes blurred. She'd translated the entire letter without even realizing she'd been doing so. She caught the table to stop herself from toppling out of her chair.

"What is it?" Simon helped her steady.

"The reference to the Mother House."

"I saw it too. Do you know what it is?"

She shook her head. "Someone on your team knew."

"That's impossible," Simon said. "There were only a handful of us who even knew the journals existed, much less could translate them."

"Who?"

"Me, Yara." Simon hesitated. "Everyone else is gone."

"Well, these two words were written next to the Sibyl on a photo that the colonel's second-in-command didn't even know the origin of."

"What do you mean?"

"Millar's team. They prepped the file for me. I'm assuming they figured I could help find all of you. But, when I told the lieutenant about the photos, he had no idea what I was talking about."

A click of the door latch interrupted them and Iné walked in.

"Could Serah have sent this?" Marie asked.

Simon opened a wooden box and, without a word, spread out a stack of ledgers, signed decrees, and other paper artifacts. He handed her two pieces of wood, each about the size of Marie's palm.

Upon the first was painted the scene of a woman swathed in white. She stood above a garden filled with veiled women, addressing crowds from atop a unicorn along a river. The second stole Marie's breath. On it was a woman, her dark hair coiled in a braid at the nape of her neck. Her bronze skin was shown in the golden tones of the painting. Her eyes the same as the one in the vision she had experienced on the boat ride to Simon's. They were aching in their familiarity.

The script upon it read: *The Sibyl of Amboise.*

Simon took the paintings from her and explained, "As soon as we got La Joconde to Amboise, Serah started having visions. The pilgrimages. She couldn't get away from them. We ended up finding her one night in some sort of a trance in a temple just past the old castle. She'd seen the Sibyl."

"What?"

"This Asfoora, she wasn't just Melzi's lover. She was the Sibyl here at Amboise five hundred years ago." Simon turned the second scene over.

Marie peered at the script. She struggled for a moment, and did not want to trust her eyes. However, the lettering proved clear, the translation, even from an unusual form of Medieval French, quite straightforward:

"From the woman on the wall rises one to serve justice to the many."

Marie felt her stomach drop as she read it. Her shoulders dropped.

"Serah figured out that La Joconde is the key." Simon took the piece from her, wrapped it, and set it back in the box.

"To what?"

"To finding the Sibyl. She's alive today."

"The Sibyl is a goddamn myth!" Marie slammed her hands down on the table. "A fictional story that men use to justify burning and murdering women."

"She's real, Marie."

"Stop, now! Do you know how many people have been murdered for this?"

Simon reached out to take her hand. "I can't fix what the Nazis did to you."

"You have no idea what they did to me, what she did to me, you stupid old man." Marie turned her back on him. "I came here for Serah. Where is she?"

He shook his head, chewed on his lip. "That's just it."

Marie grew irritated.

"Serah went out on reconnaissance. There was talk of movement in the area. She went to check it out and found Philip's team."

"She killed them?"

Simon shook his head. "Already dead. It was horrifying. We'd never seen anything so gruesome. We were all on the verge of being killed."

Something within Marie crumbled. A knowing crept in. "Where is Serah?"

The silence grew thick. Simon fidgeted. "We were scared."

"I've known you to be a lot of things, Simon Faubert, but I've never known you to even once be thrown off your game by fear."

"I never had to choose between the lives of people who mattered to me," he said. "All I could see was a gun pointed at one of our heads and I tried to figure out what mattered more."

The echo of those words choked Marie. "Where is Serah?"

"At the Mother House." Iné stepped back into the room. Yara followed. Marie waited for something more. Instead, the women raced to pack up the notebooks and box. "It's what they used to call Fontevraud Prison."

"Outside of Saumur?" Marie remembered. "What's there?"

"I'm sorry, Marie," Simon interrupted. "She'd been with us for a long time running reconnaissance on our missions. She was the youngest, the ablest. We thought we'd lost her."

She stuttered and hesitated. "Please tell me you didn't send my daughter out there."

Simon's eyes narrowed in angst. Iné stopped her work. Marie circled the room. Finally, she stopped in front of the fire. She took the poker and moved the hot coals around.

"Four hundred and eighty days." Marie broke the silence, her voice clear and deep. "Every one of those days a girl was shot in the head or howled in the night from the gangrene they injected into wounds. I watched a mother's daughter die. Every day a warden ripped the dress off a young woman and forced us to watch. Every day another train car full of women was sent off, their hollow eyes firmly imprinted on those who remained. All that kept me alive was knowing that Serah was not at Ravensbrück. I enabled Nazis, ran rescue operations, did horrible things for the slightest chance I could come home. That I wouldn't have to watch her die."

"Marie." Noam walked in.

"You bastard." Her head shot up. She turned to him. Then, she punched him in the face. "I guess this is what you meant when you said there were no good men left."

Marie ran for the stairs to the storage room. Noam held his jaw and raced after her.

"Please," he said. "We can still get her back. Don't do this."

"Don't do what? Let you lie to me? Make me believe you have no idea where my daughter is?" she asked. "Was he right? Was Philip right? Did you kill Jules too?"

"She's not dead, Marie," he said.

"How the hell would you even know?" Marie scanned the walls in search of markers to get her out of the caves. She raced past the hanging meat, bins of potatoes, onions. She stopped at the crates, scrounging for a weapon. Marie came up with a knife and a pistol, along with a box of bullets as Noam approached.

"You can't just shoot your way into a prison."

"Maybe not." Marie shoved the knife in her belt, loaded the gun, and headed out into the night. "But, it looks like I'm all Serah's got."

Chapter 37

PHILIP

MAY 6, 1945
THE HILLS BEHIND CHÂTEAU AMBOISE
AMBOISE, FRANCE

Philip could hear shouting beyond the crest of the hill that defined the ramparts of Château Amboise. He scrambled up the embankment. Less than five hundred meters away, he spotted Noam Marchant and the source of the shouts—Marie Guerrant. Was Marchant chasing after her, Philip asked himself? Had Marie figured out that her daughter had taken the Mona Lisa and vanished without anyone's knowledge, even the Maquis? His leg burned. Philip didn't want to examine it, avoiding the chance that he might have to stop. Marie was getting close to figuring all of this out. She would lead him to Serah Izem. He had to find a way.

Phillip scanned the surrounding area and checked his watch—0500 hours. How had so much time passed? A hint of daylight split the horizon in two. Injured soldiers were just starting to come out of the drug-induced haze. There were so many dead. Diebitsch was nowhere in sight, and Philip needed to keep it that way.

Marie and Marchant had stopped moving and began arguing again near the crumbling wall that once separated the castle grounds from the servant's walkways and countryside beyond. Philip knew he'd have to keep below their sightline. Every ten yards or so he lost sight of them, but their conversation kept him aware of their position. What had Marchant told her that caused her to rage like that, he asked himself? Marie was livid.

The path suddenly dropped off. He slid deeper into the ravine. The Nazis hadn't been ousted but a month earlier. Rotting bodies were piled up in the low parts. It reeked of death and decay. The vomit rose up. He lost time trying to keep himself steady in the overwhelming stench. He focused on the shouts. Marie's voice clung to him. The rage in her words pulled him through it all. He scrambled out of the muck and found them inside the castle walls, headed toward the silos.

He retched. Marie whirled round.

"Dammit." Philip knew he'd given himself away. He pulled back to hide, hearing a third voice. Another man approached.

"I miscalculated. We've got to go, now." Philip heard the man say.

"I'll go alone." A woman's voice, it had to be Marie, Philip thought. "It'll be easier for one of us to get in."

"Not now." The second man spoke again.

"She's my daughter. I'm going."

Philip's senses lit up at Marie's words. She was, despite everything, right where he needed her to be, accomplishing what he wanted from her. He moved out of his tight position and pointed his pistol at the three of them. They backed up. Philip saw Marchant turn just enough to make a run for it. The others were injured and old, but Noam was ready for an escape, crouched and tense. That wouldn't do. Philip fired his gun, purposely missing. "Get down on your knees."

The three of them put their hands up, but none of them followed his command. He fired again, closer to Marchant. "Get! Down!"

Behind him, the voices of men charging up the hill rankled Philip's concentration. Distracted by it, he hadn't noticed Marie and Simon easing away toward the safety of a crumbling edifice that appeared to once have been the statue of Venus. They were gone, Marchant running through the rocks and debris piled up along the old walkways of the castle courtyard.

Philip fired his gun again and missed. His leg burned. The pain raced through him, stiffening his back. He winced, limping down the path, pushing himself to keep moving. His frustration with his leg grew until he was forced to rest on a bench near an alcove. He could only watch as Marie, Marchant, and their companion maneuvered down a winding set of stairs that lead inside the castle. Movement at the edge of the wide, walled courtyard caught his eye. Cloutille came racing along the north edge toward him.

"Can you move?" she reached him and propped Philip upon her shoulder. He nodded. "There's a small opening by the statue of Mary. I suspect they are trying to get to the docks."

"Why?"

Cloutille ignored him. She wove her way along the broken paths until they reached a narrow wooden door and the bottom of a shallow set of stone steps. It creaked open as if it had been unlocked in advance. Philip took note but couldn't waste a moment questioning his luck. Within fifty steps of entering the lower corridors, he and Cloutille hit an intersection. Marie and her men were less than one hundred feet in front of them.

Cloutille drew her gun. "Stay low."

Philip had no space in his mind for rest. As soon as he steadied, he broke away and moved ahead far faster than he planned, stumbling. Cloutille followed and yanked him back and they rammed into each other. "Quiet, or we'll never take care of this."

Aside from the two of them, the corridor appeared abandoned. Philip began to shake. He was losing control of this. The Sibyl was his. He'd find her and destroy her. He patted the picture in his pocket. Her destruction would make life bearable again.

Suddenly, someone charged them from a side corridor. Philip took a blow to the stomach. Cloutille spun and fired at their assailant. Philip was down and the corridor grew quiet again. He caught his breath and spotted two pairs of feet, just the toes, sticking out from an alcove, just out of view. He inched closer. A sack was on the floor nearby. He spotted a leather book cover amongst the notebooks. It was one from the Louvre, one of Melzi's.

He scrambled closer. A whisper. A man's voice.

"I never intended to hide her from you." It was the old man with Marie.

A pair of feet moved. Philip guessed they were Marie's.

"Well, now you're going to help me get her out," she said.

Just as Marie spoke the final syllable, a shot came from behind Philip. He drew his knife and reached for the bag.

"Go, Marie!" A voice screamed. The old man leaped for the bag. "Allez! Allez! Allez!"

No one else, however, moved. Philip held the knife at the man's throat. Marie stood just feet from him, paralyzed. Cloutille held Noam at gunpoint.

"Simon Faubert, I thought you were dead," Philip said. "Did you think the Sibyl was yours?"

"She is for no one. You should know that by now."

"Always the purist, eh, old man? You know as well as I do, it's like a genie in a bottle for the one who finds her first. He who controls the oracle . . ."

"We could be on the same side, Philip," Simon said. "Neither of us wants her under the thumb of a tyrant."

"Ha." Philip pressed the blade harder against Simon's throat. "Every man is a potential tyrant."

"She doesn't need to die," Simon continued.

Marie stepped forward, her breath catching as Philip's knife drew blood. "We'll all be dead if you don't stop. The Sibyl is a curse."

"Then we agree." Philip said. "We are both here to destroy what remains of this evil. Do you not want the myth that dismantled your life burned to dust?"

Philip watched Marie's eyes grow dark, her temperament turn hard, her arms moving behind her as her shoulders stiffened and straightened. He couldn't read her. Was she conceding? Was she . . . A glint flashed behind her. Iné Soudier eased out of the darkness and slapped a knife into Marie's hand. "You bitch!"

Marie lunged at him. He dodged the swipe and sliced across the back of her left arm. She hissed, distracting Cloutille long enough for Noam to break away.

"Everybody move," Iné shouted.

Simon dove for the bag of notebooks. Philip dropped a knee on top of his hand. Simon howled. Marie tried to pull him back.

"Iné, get those two out of here," Noam shouted.

Philip's attention shot across the corridor, then back to Marie. She was just inches away. He flipped the knife in his hand to reset his grip and swiped.

The old man jumped between them. He yelped and reached down. Philip's knife was in his side.

"Simon!" Marie shouted.

Philip pulled out the knife and spun around. They were nearly eye-to-eye, bent over, when Iné pulled Marie back down the corridor and they ran.

"Can you get us to the front silo just past the ramparts?" Marie shouted.

Philip gave chase. Cloutille had been right. They were headed for the river. He pulled his gun from the holster, aimed, and fired. His feet hit the ground like a metronome. He fought through the pain shooting through his leg. He could only hear the slap of his boots on the stone. The women were only a yard or so in front of him. Philip ran past part of a white shirt swinging from an old iron hinge that jutted out from the wall. It was dark with blood. Marie was injured, he thought.

He heard Iné shout. "This way! Do not hesitate!"

Philip fired. One bullet. An empty pistol.

The women cleared a level of broken stairs. Philip launched himself down them, anticipating his feet hitting the hard stone floor of the silo tunnels. He hit nothing but air. He fell. Fast. Through the dark. He landed on his back in several feet of water. He gasped for breath, the wind knocked out of him. Turning his head, he saw Iné and Marie in the water less than twenty feet away.

Philip got to his knees while Iné and Marie slogged through the black sludge until they reached a metal gate. He couldn't catch his breath, forced to watch as Iné ratcheted the bars up. On the other side, the Loire rushed by. A single boat bobbed in an eddy. Philip got up and ran awkwardly toward the women, dragging his bad leg. He forced himself out onto the grass, then the dock. The boat was waiting for them. How could they have known, he wondered? Before he could sort through his thoughts, the women fired up the outboard motor and moved up the river.

Philip spotted three soldiers rounding the bend on a path leading from the commune streets. "Fire until your guns are empty."

He kept shouting as the women slumped below the low wall of the flat-bottomed boat. It sped up. Two heads popped up. The soldiers missed their marks.

Philip gripped his leg. He had a new gash from the fall. He ripped a strip off his shirt to bind it. His men stood at attention, waiting for orders. Cloutille walked out of the cave with Simon's sack of research tossed over her shoulder. She held up a notebook. Philip tossed his hands in the air, waiting for her to stop making him guess

"Is that Dr. Guerrant?" She pointed at the boat nearly out of view on the river. Philip rolled his eyes and nodded. The pain in his leg made him draw hissing breaths. Cloutille helped him to sit. She slid the book over to him and tapped the page. The notes, in Simon's handwriting, detailed a Maquis plan.

"Pack it up." Philip ordered the soldiers. "We're going to Fontevraud."

Chapter 38

MARIE

MAY 6, 1945
CANDES-SAINT-MARTIN, FRANCE

Marie leaned over the side of the boat headed for Fontevraud and dry heaved into the Loire. Her left side burned. She looked down. She had tightly bandaged her right arm with torn pieces of her shirt. Still, a trail of pink and yellow seeped through.

"Well, at least neither of us was shot." She laid back on the boat bottom and waited for Iné to answer. Eyes closed, Marie tried not to move. How long had they been on the water? She lost track with bullets soaring past them as they pulled away from Amboise. "How are you?"

"Grazed. It's not deep." Iné maneuvered the boat through the misty curtain of early morning light. "We'll stitch it at the prison."

"Are we there?" Marie hadn't expected to be eighty kilometers away from where she started.

"We've got a ways to go after we get to the dock. It's going to be slow," Iné continued. "How did you know the boat would be there, in Amboise?"

"I saw them along the shore on the way to Simon and Yara's yesterday. I was just hoping you could get us close to one." Marie sat up. She waited for her head to settle. The pain in her arm was only slightly less than the pain in her side. When her eyes steadied, they landed on her bloody patch-up job on Iné's right shoulder and reached out to touch it. Instantly, a flat bottomed boat seemed to appear, crossing the river so close that Marie could see three women, one who appeared to be cloaked in velvet.

Iné pulled away from her and the boat faded into the fog. "Thankfully, those Brits are bad shots."

Marie knew she ought to take the moment to settle. The quiet of early morning on the river wouldn't last long. The prospect of breaking into France's notoriously brutal Fontevraud Prison to get Serah out blunted any peace she might have found in the cormorants feeding along the shoreline or the coquettishness of the pair of swans splashing one another in a shallow eddy.

Prison.

The panic surged through her.

Prison.

An, ki, lu, munus, kur, geme, sag, kag, ninda. Her mind ticked through ancient Summerian words to calm herself down.

Prison.

Each word she whispered distracted her from the terror of being forced behind bars. Again.

"I need you with me." Iné shook Marie's shoulder. "We've got a lot to do, and there's more you need to know."

The boat idled in a small cave where light filtered from under the water and illuminated the stone above what looked like an underground, watery causeway beyond. On the left, Marie spotted the remains of a boat tie-off and a small stairway beyond the rocks. "Where are we?"

"Candes-Saint-Martin. We've got to get to the top of the hill."

"How's your pain?" Marie reached out again, a jolt of air forcing her to gasp as soon as her hand laid upon Iné's shoulder. Her sight was forced beyond the woman to the waterway. The same flat-bottom boat pushed out from the darkness, the light from below casting a soft glow upon the craft's occupants. The woman in velvet turned to her and locked eyes.

"Serah?" Marie swore the woman was her daughter, but somehow not.

Iné took her hand and the vision released its grip on her. "I'm fine."

As they stepped onto the stone dock, Iné went rigid and teetered. The effort to keep them both from tumbling into the river worsened the fire in Marie's side. "That bad, eh? Let me see if anything is broken."

She tried to reach down and reassess Iné's injuries, but got swatted away. They made the slow ascent up an old stone path. Shallow gullies and bare roots complicated the climb. She stayed back while Iné waved down a ride. It seemed foolish for the woman to think she could just flag down a truck and they'd hop in. Yet, the driver stopped.

Iné argued with him for a moment, then held out her arm. Marie spotted the tattoo she'd seen on the first day they met. It was simple, distinct. One single line. A crescent moon on either side. The bickering ceased. Marie hurried over. They climbed next to heavy farm tools stored under tarps.

Marie poked her head out. Her ribs flared up every time the truck hit a bump. The twisting dirt road brimmed with life. The truck paused often as chickens or goats crossed. She waited for the smell of ersatz soap. The click of a gun. The familiarity of it all unnerved her. She pressed her eyes closed, lips repeating the alphabet in Attic Greek, "Alpha, beta, gamma, delta, epsilon . . ."

The morning warmth was soothing. Finally, at ease enough to speak, she looked at Iné. "What does it mean? Your tattoo?"

Iné rolled up her sleeve as the truck bumped down the road. "The prime meridian. A balance between the two halves. Justice and equanimity."

"Sometimes you talk like you are a thousand years old."

"Five hundred, actually." Iné smiled for the first time. She unhooked the chain from around her neck as they remained on their bellies in the back of the moving truck. Iné handed it to Marie, who let it drop into her palm. "It is very ancient, with me since . . . I've been looking forward to passing it on."

Marie propped herself up on her elbows under the tarp and studied Iné for a moment, hoping she'd explain, but the woman slumped back as if the necklace had been keeping her from relaxing until that moment.

"Go on," Iné said. "See."

Again with the odd language, Marie thought. However, she focused on analyzing the piece of jewelry. The cylinder was no more than an inch long. "I've seen this before. The Sumerian presentation scene with the goddess. Hematite."

"Indeed it is hematite and the goddess, but not quite Sumerian. I know you have concerns about the Sibyl, but you must . . ." Iné held her hand out to stop the conversation. "Damn, Second Dragoons."

"Troops?" Marie peeked through a split between two tarps that hung on the left of the truck. She scanned the area. A hundred yards back, a platoon of French soldiers in gas masks marched along the roadway. Her nerves frayed. "That's going to complicate things."

"They guard the forest around the prison's perimeter," Iné said.

"Then, we should stick to town."

"Agreed."

Chapter 39

MARIE

MAY 6, 1945
FONTEVRAUD-L'ABBAYE, FRANCE

Iné banged on the truck bed and the farmer sped up. Within minutes, he stopped the vehicle near a side gate just past the commune church outside the prison gates and drove off as soon as Marie and Iné jumped out onto the dirt road.

"I'll go try to round up some supplies." Iné disappeared inside the vestibule. "There's a little walled-off area by the church. Wait there, I'll be no more than a few moments."

Marie limped over to a bench in the alcove to keep her from being seen from the street. The ancient monastic village held much history that she knew well. It had been the primary site where illuminated manuscripts were illustrated by enlumineurs. Stories of this artistic service and devotion to the abbey were commonplace. It once held the reputation as home to generations of Abbesses who wielded more power than any man in Europe. Just as she settled, the blare of alarm horns took her mind right back to Germany. "Dammit. Why?"

As her eyes settled on the walls of the prison, her body stiffened. She couldn't stop the memories of guard towers above row upon row of barbed wire, guard dogs, and floodlights. The flashes of beatings, of starvation, of blood kept coming. Gun fire beyond the prison walls reverberated inside her head. The bandages on her arm oozed a rusty brown. She kept counting, this time in Sumerian. "Aš, u, geš, geš-u, šar, šar-u, šar-gal."

She realized she still had Iné's necklace and secured it around her neck. A breeze wafted across the courtyard. Pink roses climbed the trellis of the stone walls behind her. There was the smell of gasoline, overheated machinery, and perfume. Her eyes fluttered. The courtyard shimmered like a mirage in the morning sun. The desire to sleep took over. Where was Iné? Marie slumped against the wood bench and let her eyes close.

A spider skittered on her shoulder. Marie watched it until it dropped off the tip of her finger and rappelled to the ground.

Suddenly, the church doors opened and she was startled to her feet. Each step seemed as if Marie's legs had turned to air, carrying her without the security of the ground beneath her.

Out filed a procession of women dressed in plain, white-collared shirts and ankle-length navy skirts with the same type of cylinder as Iné's around their necks. They moved in silence, as if lost in prayer, and formed a line in the street, then turned at the bend of the main road. Marie could not see their faces—no eyes, no sense of breath, not even a whisper.

"Iné?" She waited. No response. Not even a turned head from the crowd. She attempted to move, her legs buckling. "Mademoiselle Soudier!"

She cut herself short, too exposed, sitting out in the middle of the village. Marie turned to sit back down on the bench, but somehow got swept into the crowd of nuns. The twenty or so women were enough to blend into, allowing her to move unnoticed and find Iné. They moved past a side gate to the prison. More women streamed out from doors at the back of the church. Still half-dazed from the pain, Marie wove into and out of the crowd, searching alcoves and small buildings.

Iné's absence unnerved and irritated her. Yet, a melodic chant of women's voices rose as they continued their slow procession. The hymns vibrated in the air. The skin on Marie's arms tingled. She scanned a small garden patch for Iné and spotted the carved wooden door to a round, ancient building with eight tall chimneys and as many turrets. The scale-like shingles on the outer roof matched nothing else in terms of the style and age of the rest of the complex. It was attached to the prison, yet outside its walls. Each one knelt before the entrance before disappearing inside.

"I know this place." Her mind sharpened. She pushed on the latch and stepped inside. Marie recalled news reports her father had saved about French architect Lucien Magne working on this building, trying to restore it. He never finished, distracted by the supervision of the building of Basilique du Sacré-Cœur forty years earlier. It looked abandoned and in a state of mid-restoration. Past the outer scaffolding, the stone and carvings proved well-preserved and intricate in their craftsmanship.

She stepped inside.

Eight fireplaces.

Circular designs.

Ancient motifs of medieval crosses.

She peered at the intricate, blackened ceiling above. Flues for the fires remained open to the sky, like the dovecotes of the sixteenth century, kept by the wealthy of France.

Her eyes flickered again. High above her, modillions depicting ancient queens were carved into the circle of stone. She felt the strangest sensation—as if they were calling out, but no one was there. She was wholly alone when a skirt hem fluttered in a doorway. Marie moved toward it and found stairs that led downward.

The chants grew louder and more clear. The sound enveloped her. She could not resist the urge to follow the women. She stepped down and then panicked. The darkness swallowed her. The voices grabbed hold. The songs transformed. Elohim, Alláh-U-Abná, Maranatha, Gayatri. All of the same hymns she'd heard in the grove at Amboise.

Marie shot her hands out to the side to catch herself, felt for carvings in the way Iné had shown her in Amboise. There they were. The lines. The guides. She felt for them, then stopped. One single line with a crescent moon on each side. The same as Iné's tattoo!

Marie thought of the conversation she had with Iné in Amboise where the woman called herself a Ba'alat. Sorceress. She moved her finger clockwise around the carved symbol and the room shimmered with a dim light. The outlines of figures emerged from the shadows. Before her, one became clear. There stood a woman in velvet robes. The one from the boat. The one who looked like . . .

"Serah?"

Chapter 40

AESMEH

MAY 1, 1519
CHÂTEAU AMBOISE
AMBOISE, FRANCE

W e had to get to Melzi, and moved along the ridge behind Château Amboise like silent specters. Master da Vinci tip-toed like
a child while Maurine and I followed behind, blades in hand. I lingered
on the candle-lit rooms of Clos Lucé to the west. Gaillard stood, dark and
quiet, to the north at our backs. The waters of the Loire raged to the south
beyond the castle. The servants' routes allowed us to get from the paths
covered in blooming wisteria at Gaillard to the lush gardens of the castle
filled with lush lavender and roses without the chance of running into
Tommaso. Maurine's eyes searched the landscape.

"You are distracted." I took her hand as we walked. I did not need to
take my gloves off and touch her bare skin to know what she withheld.
"What happened with Tommaso?"

"I got caught up in ... I'm afraid this may be my doing," Maurine paused.
"We just wanted to be together."

"What could you possibly have done that proved so grave?" I doubted
the dramatics.

"I did not intend," Maurine stuttered.

"Stop already. You are frightening me."

She paused for a long while. "I tried to leave."

"Pourquoi?"

"Out of Amboise, to Italy."

"You are bound by your vows." I stated the obvious.

"Not if I vanished. We could marry, I would disappear into society," Maurine continued. "But, it became more than just sneaking away for him. I never thought his ambitions . . ."

I shook from the revelation. "Oh no."

She nodded. "I taught him the technique—how to cleanse spaces—so we could leave without anyone able to trace us. I did not intend to betray you."

"And now?"

Maurine's tone turned abrupt "I thought I had ended it in time to stop this."

I found myself furious. However, I knew as well that I could very well have been Maurine. My love for Melzi had left me endlessly contemplating my vows and plotting the possibility of breaking them from the moment I met him in Milan.

"A broken heart is infinitely more powerful than I could have ever imagined." Maurine finally interrupted our silence.

I held her hand tighter than ever. There was no comfort I could bring, no easing of her mind. If Tommaso's heart was at the root of his betrayal, how could she know she'd risked our very existence in breaking it. I knew I must focus on getting Melzi out of the dungeon and our Dear One finished. Entering the temple on time had become imperative. Only then would the future of the Sibylline be secure.

The Amyntas met us at a narrow passage hewn out of stone. I found the imprint of a wheat husk carved into the walls and knew our route to the supply stores. Amongst the clean bed coverings, tapestries, and vast stock of unused furnishing, the maids, valets, and page boys worked. The room full of people offered anonymity. All were too busy to question our presence. In a single chamber reached only by a narrow set of carved stone stairs, we saw Lady Marguerite deep in her reading. Maurine whistled to catch her attention. She rose, put away her book, and came down the stairs to meet us.

The Amyntas spoke with her. I could hear nothing. In an instant, they whisked Master da Vinci, Maurine, and I away down another of the servant passages. This one led along narrow stairs which headed downward. Only the light of a single torch carried by the smaller of the two Amyntas allowed us not to turn a heel or catapult end-over-end down the steep stairwell. The Master had gone far ahead. I spotted nothing more than his silhouette at the bottom of the stairs, and asked myself how many times he had traversed this very path on one of his quests for information, company, or wine. Our success in reaching the lower levels of the catacombs went unnoticed by castle garrisons and proved swift.

As we entered the damp air of the dungeons, Master da Vinci clicked and cooed like a bird. We all snickered, but within moments the call was returned. At every turn, he navigated with the call and return, until we stood at a cell with a heavy wooden door. He pointed at the door.

"How do you know?" I whispered.

The Amynta who carried the torch passed it to Maurine and attempted to pick the lock. Her thick fingers made it a struggle. The Master handed her a thin piece of metal from his pocket and demonstrated how to manipulate the mechanism. Success.

Melzi was within. I resisted launching myself upon him. He greeted us with a warm smile, and took my hand. Master da Vinci intruded, checking his apprentice over for wounds, more out of curiosity, it seemed, than out of a true concern for Melzi's condition.

"Where did you find him?" Melzi's voice shook.

"Under the fountain." With my hands on my hips, I took Master da Vinci to task.

"You were here all along?" Melzi forced him to back up.

"I left you a note." Master da Vinci shrugged and whistled at a servant boy. The child swiftly returned with stockings and shoes.

"And you." Melzi ignored everyone but me. "How could you have thought I would do this?"

"She needed you gone." Master da Vinci broke in. "Heartache makes us all a bit sick in the mind."

"What is your excuse, old man?" Melzi smiled at him. "You could have simply told me you were leaving."

The Master shrugged. I cringed. Maurine and I set ourselves upon a path from which we might never return because of love.

Melzi wasted no time. "La Joconde?"

"Still there," I said. "He has not finished her."

Melzi glared at his Master and spoke, "The hand?"

"Maybe." Master da Vinci pointed at me. "Ask her again why she did this to you. Let us focus on her."

My guilt kept me from giving the speech I painfully prepared.

"Such a good ruse by Tommaso. He found me gone and thought this all up," the Master continued. "I might have thought it dim-witted."

"Had it not worked." I finished his sentence.

"Well," Master da Vinci said. "You were rather quick to send our dear Melzi to the dungeons."

Maurine, and even the Amyntas, nodded.

"I never expected you to stay with me," Melzi said. "This is a bit much, though."

Master da Vinci elbowed him in the side. "Good thing she found my note."

Melzi rolled his eyes. "I told you to stop leaving those."

"Are you not glad I did? Otherwise, this evening's bedfellows would think your ears a snack." Master da Vinci picked up a squealing rat by the tail. "Let us take care of Tommaso's treachery someplace with wine and a warm coverlet."

"I cannot believe he is capable of this." Melzi sighed, looking straight at Maurine.

"This is my responsibility to make right," she said. "I will go to him."

"No, I should have known." My heart ached for all of us.

"Why?" Melzi said, looking at me as if I might have simply overlooked a message or forgot to kiss him goodnight. "Did you not trust me? Have I not earned the right to be counted amongst those who serve the Sibylline?"

"You have. And now we desperately need your help."

Chapter 41

MARIE

MAY 6, 1945
THE KITCHENS
FONTEVRAUD-L'ABBAYE, FRANCE

Marie fought it and kept her hands on the carvings along the wall. The light narrowed. The woman rushed past her, up the stairs. She followed. Ten steps up. Ten excruciating steps that seemed as if she would never arrive at the top. Marie was on her hands and knees by the time she made it back to the circular room with the eight fires.

Iné burst through the door. "I left you too long. I hadn't meant for them to call for you so soon."

Two women wearing nun's habits rushed in with blankets. Marie tried to focus. For a moment, Iné and the two nuns stood above her in a chamber painted with red and gold, the modillions along the ceiling fresh and clean. Her vision remained blurred, the women translucent, as if the light in the room poured through them. Marie reached for Iné, and missed, skittering back toward the wall. "Serah, I found her."

"No, my friend." Iné remained silent as she unhooked the necklace from around Marie's neck and wrapped her in the wool.

"She was here. Down, over there." Marie motioned, but as her eyes cleared, they found no staircase downward, not even a door or a passage. "I . . . I don't understand."

"We're both exhausted." Iné sat down next to her. The nuns brought them both a steaming mug, from which they drank.

"No, it's . . . I followed a group of women here."

"I'm sorry, there's no one else here."

Marie looked around as she sipped what seemed like tea with herbs such as peppermint, possibly verbena. The round room was crumbling, colorless, and dank. A rickety scaffolding held up a part of the wall that would otherwise be in pieces. She and Iné sat in the cool dirt and shook her head at the realization that her mind had deceived her again. "I don't know why I thought I saw Serah."

"You're her mother." Iné's thoughtful tone surprised Marie. "You are worried."

"That's just it," Marie continued. "It's the second time. Before, at Amboise, and now."

Iné's gaze shot through her, an eerie sense rising up in Marie that the woman understood pieces of this she had not yet deciphered. So much had surfaced in the last day. It all was too much, she thought. The Sibyl, Serah, all of it was too much. She had to focus on the one element she could control.

Marie forced herself to block out anything that seemed even mildly off-mission. Her mind cleared. "What are our options for getting inside the prison?"

One of the nuns pressed a hand-drawn sketch of the complex out on the ground in front of them and pointed to what looked like a gate in the high stone wall. It was along the edge of a forest on the other side of the complex.

"Hmm." Marie considered the recommendation. "Crossing town we risk being spotted. What is there?"

Iné looked at one of the nuns for a long moment, as if the Sister was relaying information. "Supplies."

"You're positive Serah is inside the prison?" Marie asked.

"Yes. We are working on pinpointing her location."

Marie tapped her finger on the map, considering "That gate is too exposed with the forest behind it. What day is it?"

"Sunday."

"Are there machine shops? Anything like that?"

"Why?"

"Inmates won't work on Sundays." Marie stepped in with her working knowledge of prisons. "Guards log fourteen-hour shifts on weekends. They can barely stumble into their beds by shift change. They'll be slow, but punchy. We've got to move with care."

Marie noted an outbuilding just in front of the prison wall.

"What is it?"

"Food stores. We can rest there. If I am right, those buildings are almost never locked." The implications were clear to Marie. Fontevraud was a fortress. "I've seen it. No one would dare enter or leave without permission."

"That's a lot of ground to cover." Iné said.

Marie thought for a moment, then eyeballed the nun's habits. "No one is going to harass a holy person on her way through town."

The two plain, thin women looked at Iné and nodded once each before beginning to disrobe. Marie helped Iné as she struggled out of her torn, filthy pants and gingerly handed them to a nun who slid off her wimple to reveal her short, blonde hair. Iné offered an apologetic look for her bloodied body and filthy condition. The nun raised a hand and pointed down to her feet. She had on a fresh pair of pants and military boots, which she slipped off and passed along.

Marie took note of the obvious dichotomy of sisters wearing military gear under their habits and approved of the sedition. She peeled off her blood-caked clothes and tied them up in a tight bundle. She handed it to the second woman whose right arm bore a long scar as if once sliced open. The remains of her tattoo, just like Iné's, marked the awkward wound.

"Do you have weapons?" Marie asked.

"Preferably a knife," Iné winked.

The nuns left, returning with a small metal box. Marie opened it—a Luger pistol, a switchblade, and a long butcher knife were inside. Neither woman spoke, which irritated her, but they didn't exactly roam the Earth unprepared either, which left her impressed.

"It's Avoir Voix Au Chapitre," Iné said. "That is why they don't talk."

"The rule of silence? Like the nuns a thousand years ago?" Marie asked. "I suppose you are going to tell me you were one of them."

Iné let out an uneasy laugh. "Not in the way you are thinking, but Fontevraud is still the most sacred of places. They are silent so they might all hear the Great Mother speak."

Marie found Iné's newfound piousness disconcerting. "Or kill themselves."

"It's meant to find peace."

"Peace, right." Marie said. "In my experience, the most severe punishment is always what it takes to silence a woman."

Iné offered a low grumble. "The prisoners here are bound by it as well."

"That's terrifying." Marie scanned the roadway for soldiers.

She tried to block out memories of silent women being tossed into tiny shacks with muzzles on, only to be cut down from the rafters in the ceiling a day later. What did they do to the men at Fontevraud to keep them from saying a word? Was the Vichy no better than the Nazis? Did all men torture those they couldn't control? She had returned to hell.

Marie loaded the Luger and passed it to Iné. She put the switchblade in her pocket, straightened Iné's habit and wimple. "Let's go."

Iné watched her. "This is not the first time you have broken into a prison, is it?"

"Into, yes. Out of, no."

"Might I just say, you continue to astonish me."

Marie grabbed a woven basket from a doorway in the village, buried the butcher knife beneath the cloth inside, and moved toward a vegetable stand. She and Iné bought onions and spring lettuces.

"I helped women escape from work camps," she said. "This part is easy. Plus, there are no guards in the village to shoot us."

"Not yet," Iné said. "Risky, breaking women out of those places."

"Not as risky as staying in them."

They agreed the best cover was to hide in plain sight. When two men in gray wool chore coats left the market, Marie instructed Iné to follow her lead. They lingered close behind, moving as the men hauled baskets of early greens, radishes, and spring potatoes from the market stand to the trucks. The men tried to shoo them off, but the women waited and pushed further and further down the hill in silence. Finally, the farmers filled the basket with food. Marie and Iné skittered off toward the woods without anyone taking note.

"I can't believe this is working," Iné said. "It is like the men don't even acknowledge the nuns."

"Shame," Marie said.

Iné looked confused.

"Everyone here knows what happens inside that prison. They're ashamed. Ashamed that they deliver guns to the guards. Ashamed they know someone inside. Ashamed they get drunk to drown out the screams at night," Marie continued. "Feeding the nuns and sending them on their way is their penance."

"You seem to have thought a lot about this," Iné said.

"No one likes to acknowledge that they help cruel men. They look for anything to relieve their guilt."

Marie's words were followed by silence. A garrison from the Second Dragoons moved up the road. The women skittered into a sliver of green space between a tavern and an old boarding house. The path led to a short hill that ran along the high wall of the prison. The gate the nuns had pointed out was about five hundred yards beyond them. The sound of guards yelling commands echoed from inside Fontevraud. For a moment, Marie thought she heard another sort of scream, distinct and familiar.

"She knows you are coming for her." Iné seemed to hear Marie's thoughts. "She knows we are here."

Chapter 42

MARIE

MAY 6, 1945
FONTEVRAUD PRISON, FRANCE

The supply shed was unlocked and packed with canned goods and rations, just as Marie suspected. She began to wonder if French forces had either collaborated to guarantee food deliveries or stormed Nazi strongholds just to raid their cupboards. It was a single room no bigger than Marie's tiny apartment in Paris. The women shed themselves of the nun's habits and dropped on top of crates to regroup. Marie took a tin of sardines from a box and passed another along. Iné gripped it but could not peel the lid back.

"You're really hurt," Marie said.

"It doesn't matter."

"Don't tell me that." She opened the other tin and gave it to Iné. "Can I take a look?"

The woman recoiled and shook her head.

"Stop. There was a doctor from Strasbourg in our barracks." Marie pulled Iné's bandages back. "She taught us all . . . Well, we learned to take care of one another."

Iné nodded. They didn't speak. Marie peeled back another layer of cloth. Iné's shoulder was split open just above her clavicle. The blood had congealed, but the wound was yellowing. A second long cut where Philip had attacked her in the tunnels ran across her shoulder blade. Marie pressed Iné's fingernail beds and waited. It took almost half a minute for the pink to return.

"The circulation in your arm looks bad. How are you not in shock?" she asked. "I've never seen anyone get up and move around after an injury like this."

"I just need some water."

"You need a doctor. Sutures. I thought that's what you had gone for earlier."

"There have been a few distractions," Iné said.

Marie caught a faint scrape of shoes on cement outside the building. She reached for Iné and pressed her to move back behind a tall set of crates marked with a swastika. A figure came out of the shadows and into the room. Marie noticed the perfect, auburn victory roll. On her hands and knees, she crept along a path that led parallel to Cloutille, matching moves with the woman above. Marie came up behind Cloutille with the butcher knife. Iné pressed herself above a crate, her gun aimed at her mark.

Cloutille shook her head and lowered her own weapon. "You're not as soft as I suspected."

"You bitch." Marie took the gun from her. "You led me into a trap."

"You took the bait, that's all we needed," Cloutille remained stiff, her hands up. "Our friend the colonel is deep in nasty matters that couldn't be ignored. You were the only one who could draw him out. You were already deep with Philip, and we knew he'd tap you because of her."

"You're a spy?"

"Agent Cloutille Seydoux, British Special Operations Executive. I couldn't tell you back at the museum."

"You used me?"

"Don't be so indignant. That's what we do," Cloutille said. "Leverage our assets. Let situations play out so we can complete our mission."

"You would have let me die?"

"You got the photos, right?" Cloutille asked.

"It was you. Are they from Serah?"

"She tapped into my network. That's how we learned about Philip."

"Why didn't you just get her out?"

"She didn't tell us where she was. She just handed off the marked pages and told us you needed them. Colonel Millar isn't working for anyone but himself. We had to see the mission through. We still have to see it through or we lose everything."

A pounding from below startled the women. Iné jumped up from behind the crate. Marie pressed the knife into Cloutille's back until she dropped to her knees.

"Well, push it out of the way already," Cloutille told them.

"Why? Who the hell is on the other side?" Marie asked.

"Just do it. No one who wants to kill you is going to crawl out of a hole."

"Don't be so sure," Iné said.

"Look," Cloutille said. She pointed to a trap door on the floor. They tried to move the crate off of it as the banging continued. Iné's injuries and Marie's exhaustion made it difficult. Marie pried off the lid. It was filled with Rinderbraten.

"You do it," Marie made Cloutille empty the contents onto the floor. A loud slam against the hatch from below sent the mostly empty crate flying. A man popped up from below.

"Holy Mother!" Marie kicked Noam in the shoulder as his graying curls and bullish shoulders came up out of the underground passage.

Cloutille rushed over to pull Noam out of the hole. They shook hands and stood in front of Marie and Iné.

"You knew Serah had informed on Philip?" Marie asked Noam.

"Cloutille made contact with the Maquis after Serah went dark last week."

Marie found herself a pawn. "I don't care why anyone else is here. I'm here for my daughter."

"Aren't we all," Cloutille winked at her. "Do your job. Get the asset out. We'll do ours."

"You're not going to explain this?" Marie was indignant.

"You're on a mission, now," Cloutille said. "Follow your orders."

Noam motioned for Marie and Iné to head underground with him. "We're clear."

"You've got to be kidding me?" said Marie. "Why don't you just . . ."

"Look, the colonel is here, right now, hunting for you, Serah, the Sibyl. Don't do this," Cloutille said. "Or we'll lose."

Marie wanted to fight her, but all she could think about was Serah in the hands of that bastard.

Noam helped Iné down into the underground passage, then took her hand. "Just let us get her back for you."

"Fine." Marie knew he was right. Whatever anyone had hidden from her, they were at Fontevraud ready to help save Serah. Her anger couldn't cloud her judgment. Her fear, though, could.

She stood just beyond Noam and Iné and looked into the darkness, again. Four hundred and eighty days it had taken her to get out of Ravensbrück. Another few steps and she would put herself back behind bars. The thought of Serah locked away in such a hell hole, hunted by men for whom life held no value, kept Marie focused and her fear in check.

Serah always kept her steady.

Chapter 43

AESMEH

MAY 1, 1519
CHÂTEAU AMBOISE
AMBOISE, FRANCE

A haze of sun shone through the windows of the hunting lodge at Château Amboise. I entered through the guard's room where two men played chess at a wide, wooden table. They dared not glance up from their game. The Abbess waited for me under the stone arches at the far end of the room. I stepped into the hall. The scent of orange and cinnamon tickled my nose. My stomach rumbled, and I could not recall the last time I took a meal.

The Abbess yolked my arm and we walked, attempting to appear unassuming. After releasing Melzi from the dungeon to go complete the painting, we had concocted a scheme to catch Tommaso in the act of betrayal and set the situation to rights. We reached the drummer's room where the old cavalry finery was stored. I weaved my way through poles that were hung with the violet standards of the king and a maze of drums and horns. Lady Marguerite entered and locked the door. Maurine pushed open the hatch to the servant's passage and joined us.

"Let me talk to him," she said.

"No." The Abbess's stern declaration stiffened us both. "You will do nothing more to provoke him."

The ache in my chest almost crippled me. There was no time for mistakes and her assessment was prudent. I could, however, sense Maurine's loss, her need to make amends. We had to figure out what Tommaso planned.

"La Reine," Master da Vinci greeted the Abbess with a deep bow. "What an honor it is to serve you once again."

"No time for vanity." Her eyes showed fierceness that befitted a woman who no longer needed kings to assert her authority. She laid a strong hand upon Master da Vinci's shoulder.

"Ma bella . . ." He grinned and snuck off. A deep grunt from one of the Amyntas who had taken up at the door alerted us to men moving through the passageway just beyond. Without a moment to mourn the circumstances, we rushed straight to an alcove outside the great hall.

Maurine stayed at my side. She whispered in my ear about the Amyntas who followed us. "Are there more in the wings?"

"The rest are leaving with the Abbess. Let us hope we don't need them." I paced the length of the wall to ensure the royal garrisons did not listen in. We took up a position just ahead of the great hall where King François gathered his court. We stood for a short space of time. Master da Vinci returned and stepped out onto the balcony with The Abbess. They watched the boats laden with wheat, young apples, and gold come ashore near the silos at the treasury for storage after arriving in Amboise. Maurine and I stood back, holding hands. The weather had taken a tumultuous turn. Rain pummeled the workers. The clop of horse hooves upon the stone of the towers and the jolly arguments of men from the dining hall should have soothed. Instead, they punctuated a bitter homecoming.

A voice we knew well spoke from the King's war room. "Mon Roi. I am now beyond measure in my concern."

"Go," The Abbess ordered Master da Vinci through the servants' passage to the other side of the great hall. "I think we are about to learn Tommaso's fate."

"What else did you turn up?" François's voice echoed.

"I'm concerned about your sister. Maybe it is time to consider ending this."

My shock grew as Maurine gripped my forearm. What was 'this'? When had Tommaso become powerful enough to plot in private with kings, and against one's family? I returned to eavesdropping.

"I only mean that she always takes great pains to protect Master da Vinci along with the Sibylline," he continued.

"We all have. Will those bastards ever accept that they have chosen to serve France?"

I bristled. We'd done no such thing.

"Of course, Mon Roi. However, the Sibylline and Master da Vinci have hidden much from all of us."

"They would never betray their king."

"Yet the King of Spain is preparing to raid Amboise. My men say that the Sibylline Amyntas stand guard at his side. I believe the Abbess and your sister may have negotiated with both sides."

Lady Marguerite grew red-faced, her lips thinning, eyes sharp at the words as she stood at the door with me and Maurine.

"What are you saying?" The king's voice grew indignant.

"Do you know her loyalties?"

"I know my sister."

"Sisters betray." Tommaso paced around the room as we watched. "What will happen if Aesmeh rises? How long do you think any of you will rule? We've seen what they can do. Your sister is high within their ranks. Her presence here, Aesmeh's presence here, risks our lives and the future of France."

The Abbess pulled her robes closer to her chest as the wind battered at the windows of the alcove just beyond our position at the door to the king's chambers. "I feared an even deeper betrayal was afoot," she said.

She rushed down the hall in the other direction. Tears ran down Maurine's face. She and I remained to see if any other details might be uttered.

"Please, forgive me," she whispered.

"Forgive yourself," I said. "Our heads must be clear, free of whatever we have mistaken. The Sibylline requires our full attention."

Maurine nodded and gripped my hand.

The king and Tommaso whispered and moved out of earshot. Doors slammed. The noises of the castle grew soft and routine, nothing more than a crackling fire in the hearth. I picked up my skirts and moved toward the chamber doors.

Lady Marguerite stopped us before we entered. She waved us over to a storage room. There stood Melzi, grief stricken.

He pointed. Split into dozens of pieces on the floor was La Joconde. I nearly collapsed at the sight. "I went back to finish the painting."

"No." Master da Vinci poked at it. He pulled up piece after piece of the wood she was painted on. "No, no, no. Melzi, this yours, not mine. See, your sfumato is almost perfect. Always my most talented."

We all breathed again and searched the room. Master da Vinci nosed in places none of us dared until he found a length of linen. Under it were the remains of other paintings. An eye here, a background there, all of them of some version of La Joconde that Salaí and Tommaso had painted over the years.

"Where did he get all of these?" Lady Marguerite asked.

"Oh, Great Mother," I said. I had not accounted for Tommaso shattering the paintings into pieces when we laid the trap for him.

"Why would he destroy them?" Maurine continued.

We tensed at the sound of men coming back from the other side of the castle. The Amyntas knocked as a warning. Melzi and Master da Vinci slipped out the servant's door. Maurine and I rushed behind heavy velvet drapes.

Tommaso and another man stood at the edge of the room. "Tell Charles everything is ready. All of the traitors will be easily rounded up when the Sibylline pilgrimage begins. You cannot touch the one they call Maurine. She is mine."

I stiffened. Tommaso, I realized, had not told anyone about La Joconde. Did he intend to betray France? Rome? Keep the real painting for himself?

I snuck out onto the terrace. Maurine stood there, her face wet, in silence.

"This is what you found out, why you left him?" I asked her.

"The Amyntas raided several locations. I knew of his pandering to both sides for some time."

"Why would he do such a thing?"

"Why not?" The Abbess rejoined us. "A man must make the most of his talents. His were not born of a canvas and brush."

"He is trying to kill me?" I asked.

"He is trying to rid himself of me," Maurine said.

"Let us go." Melzi came up from behind us, startled at the sight of the Abbess. Maurine used it as a moment to skitter away.

"You must go as well," the Abbess said. "You must enter the temple tonight."

"I cannot."

Melzi rushed back and hurried us over to a side hall and pulled a rendition of La Joconde out from behind his back. I slid my gloves off, grazed a finger over the still-wet glaze, and waited for the glimmer to rise up. Master da Vinci painting, brush in hand, appeared before me.

"Dear One! Where did you find her?"

"With the others." Melzi forced all of us down the servants' passage. The painting was tucked under his arm.

The Abbess waved us away. "Finish what you can, then meet us at the temple. Aesmeh can tell you the key."

Melzi turned to me, "Are you prepared?"

"Of course," I said. "You are the only one any of us trust."

"Then I shall insert it into the painting at the last moment," he said. "Tommaso cannot win once you are the Sibyl of Amboise."

Chapter 44

MARIE

MAY 6, 1945
FONTEVRAUD PRISON, FRANCE

They walked twenty-five meters through the nave of an old priory that had been buried by time or war or possibly on purpose. She spotted remnants of frescos and stone modillion brackets carved with women's faces along the walls where they met the ceiling. At the other end, they climbed yet another set of stone stairs. The door pressed up and open. It was the upper level of the church. A false floor and temporary walls had been installed in the choir. Beyond it was a long room filled with machinery.

Noam helped Iné and Marie up. "Cover your faces."

Marie coughed, choking as the stench of bleach and chemicals hit them. It was the textile factory. It made her sick to think that the French were just as capable of using forced labor as the Germans.

Noam moved them through the humid stench out into a dirt courtyard. In the middle stood a metal awning propped up with poles. Iné collapsed to the ground.

"There's a spring just past that brick wall," Iné sputtered. "I need a drink."

"What about the guards?" Noam asked.

"It's Sunday," Marie said. "Remember?"

They helped get Iné around the corner. The crumbled mass looked as if it had once been the north wall of the old cloister. Noam knelt to push a heavy slab of stone aside. Marie watched as water bubbled over and out onto the ground in a steady stream. The water tasted like vanilla and lavender as she drank. Next to her, Iné did the same.

"We need to clean her wounds," Marie said. "There are usually medical kits in the foreman's office of these factories."

The women wiggled out of what they still wore of the nun's habits while Noam went to fetch a medical kit. He returned with three navy-blue one-piece workers' uniforms, as well as sheets, alcohol, a needle, and thread.

"We need something more to clean these wounds," Marie said.

Noam handed her a flask. "Gin, I think."

She smelled it. Marie snatched it from her and poured some on the gashes, then handed it back. "Drink the rest."

"No, use the water," Iné told her.

"That's not enough to cut the pain."

"Just do it, please."

Marie flushed Iné's wound with water and checked for any red lines of infection running up her arm. Iné flinched, but the water cleared the puss and blood within a few breaths.

Once she stitched up Iné, the wounds appeared markedly better. Marie went to treat her arm with a salve, but the graze wound had closed. She'd need to rinse it again and put fresh dressings on, but it looked far better than it had in the supply hut. It was odd. She lifted her own shirt. The entire left side of her ribs was purple and wondered if she should pour that spring water on it. Instead, she got into the work jumpsuit as Noam came back with ration packs, a pair of metal cups, and a set of keys.

"That's nice work." He looked at Iné's stitches. "You took up sewing in Germany?"

Marie rolled her sleeves up and cuffed the long pants. She showed him her healing arm while Iné dozed. "Are you sure that's just water coming from that spring?"

"Holy water?" He twisted up his face and raised his hands to the sky.

They laughed. Noam paused as if wanting to say something, exhaled, and then paced before speaking. "Cloutille's man reported in. Serah's in the hen cages. Near the main cloister underground."

"How far in?"

"Pretty far. One of the guards is old Maquis. He said they've kept her in solitary."

"How do we get there?"

"We don't. She somehow got inside as a political prisoner. They are guarded around the clock," he continued.

"I thought you said there are Maquis inside."

"Sure, but--"

"You should be glad." Iné interrupted. "There are nearly two thousand men in this prison."

"How many women?"

"Four, including the two of us and Cloutille."

Marie sucked in a hard breath and tried not to panic.

"Serah's here and we know where. That's all that matters." Noam gathered anything that might give away their presence and shoved the stone back over the spring.

"We must get the Sibyl out," Iné said.

"Is she with someone else?" Marie whispered, eyes closed, teeth clenched.

"We have orders," Noam said.

"There's only one person that matters." Marie wanted to shout in rage, but she pushed the anger down.

Noam tried to take her hand.

"Don't. Not now. Not after everything." She felt her mind slipping again. Her voice cracked. She pounded on her thighs. "I'm not compromising now."

"That's not what we're doing," Noam said.

"What the hell are we doing, then?" Marie asked. "No piece of art is more valuable than my daughter. Screw the painting. Screw the Sibyl."

Marie felt Iné's eyes bore down into her. Men's voices echoed. Door chains clanged.

"Dammit." Marie knew her outburst had alerted someone. Philip. Of course, she thought, he would have thought to search the Madeleine first. Marie started to suspect Cloutille of telling to draw him out. At Amboise, he could hide behind his role with the Allies. At the prison, he couldn't play British hero and Nazi collaborator at the same time without getting caught. It was a risky gamble, one Marie didn't savor. She looked around for places to hide. They hustled inside the factory. The machinery was too big, the space between, too narrow. Pressing the map out onto the floor, she plotted a route out. "We'll have to make a run for the main cloister and hope that they haven't sealed off the entrances. Are we agreed? Serah first?"

Three men in prison guard uniforms, boots crunching against the gravel in the courtyard, came around the corner, stopping Marie from arguing. She yanked Iné out the back of the factory toward a gate, while Noam tried to lock the machine shop door with keys on a ring he had retrieved from the infirmary earlier. None of them worked.

"If they don't fit those doors, maybe they fit that one." Marie pointed toward a massive, twenty-foot door along the back wall of the compound. "It's our only shot."

They scrambled down a short ramp and out a side door and ran for the gate. The first key stuck. No luck. The second slid in and twisted, releasing the padlock. They slipped through the door, eased it shut, and stood at the edge of a forest of towering oak trees. Carpenter bees buzzed nearby.

Iné's legs buckled beneath her the moment she stepped into the forest. She grabbed at her throat. Marie went to catch her as she fell. Her hands closed on empty air. It was as if they passed right through Iné before the woman hit the ground. Marie skittered back. She sorted through everything the woman had told her; of being five hundred years old, being a Ba'alat; of how she dismissed the confession as the rantings of a woman whose help she needed, but whom she never quite trusted. "What are you?"

"Do you have the necklace?" Iné shot a glance over to Noam.

It was in Marie's pocket. She'd taken it off of Iné to patch up her arm. Marie handed her the chain with the cylinder on it. Iné slid it over her head and shuddered. Her strength returned in an instant. "Okay, let's go."

A sudden whir and flap. They all jumped. A pheasant shot up from the bushes along the tree line and reeled in the sky. Then, quiet.

"How about we go back inside?" Noam spoke slowly, carefully. He pushed Marie into a darker area along the wall. "Move."

Marie ignored him and kept backing up. She tripped. She turned and looked down. The bulging eyes of a man stared up at them. Marie recognized him. He was one of the farmers they'd gotten vegetables from earlier.

"You need to run!" Marie jumped to her feet.

Noam and Iné blocked her view. Marie could hear their guns cocking. Whipping around, she bolted into the forest. She caught the scent of ersatz soap. A single voice barked orders. The same single voice followed her, shouting through the trees.

"Yes, run Fräulein Guerrant. Run, and we'll see who catches you first."

Chapter 45

PHILIP

MAY 6, 1945
FONTEVRAUD PRISON, FRANCE

Philip stepped through the front gate at Fontevraud and smelled death before he saw it. He'd crossed into one of the dirt court-yards where the prisoners were released from their cells to walk once a day, but only in silence. One lay in a pool of blood, a bullet to the head. Firing squad. That sort of death had a distinct odor, as if dishonor had its own stench.

He knew the reputation of the prison. Men who raped. Men who murdered. Men who turned traitor. More than two thousand were locked in what were once the cells of peaceful nuns and monks. The irony, he thought, of the evil that lived in the most sacred of places.

His capture in Belgium played like a horror film in his mind. The face of that creature, how it unleashed the fire that burned his sons to ashes. Other men, shot in the head just like the inmate in the courtyard. The weeks the war raged on as he sat in his vomit, chained, day after day, reliving the moment Henry and Benjamin vanished from this earth.

Philip sucked in a hard breath as two young officers approached.

"We're clearing the barracks," one reported. "Some of the machine shops are locked down though."

"Why?" Fontevraud was more than a prison. It was money. Textiles and machine parts. Idle machines equaled no cloth, which equaled no French economy. That, Philip thought, made no sense.

"It's Sunday."

He'd had enough of false piety. "Tell the Directeur that he can either have his men conduct a search or I'll make sure he spends more than every Sunday with his God."

He walked past the body of the man who'd been shot for his crimes. His face was unrecognizable. It curdled his stomach. He pointed his soldiers in another direction, stepped into an empty cell, and puked. The cell, simple and cool, offered comfort untouched by war. He closed his eyes and breathed.

He remembered the night Allied planes dropped bombs on the prison the Germans had locked him in. He learned later it wasn't the target. They just scatter-bombed anything in range. Allied troops who moved in after the raid pulled him from the rubble. He'd nearly lost his leg in the shootout with the Nazis that followed.

He'd gone back to Belgium after recovering. Everything was gone. Bodies turned to ash. Henry and Benjamin burned. Nothing to bury. Nothing to remember them by. Nothing to do but place headstones on empty graves. The world was horrifying. The dead man outside reinforced his need to correct that. He imagined himself setting the Mona Lisa aflame, taking out his pistol and shooting Serah Izem in the head. This quest for the Sibyl would end with him. He'd make sure his boy's lives were worth it, Philip repeated the promise just as he did every day.

He looked up. The prison directeur stood in the doorway.

"We'll set up HQ here." Philip straightened his jacket, wiped his mouth. His stomach still churned, his mind on his sons. He stammered a bit, shouted to keep from sounding weak. "And maybe remove the dead once you've gotten rid of them."

Two guards pulled the body out of sight. A third rolled in a wheelbarrow and shoveled dirt over the blood.

"Any problems opening up the machine shops, Directeur?"

"Non, monsieur."

"English, Directeur. My troops speak English."

"Of course, Colonel." The prison warden's face lacked expression, Philip thought. It seemed carved of wood. His willingness to concede to demands, Philip knew, demonstrated that he understood the gravity. "We have started at the old Madeleine."

"What's there?"

"A textile mill. It's at the edge of the wall." The directeur paused. "We may have more serious matters, though. My men in the watchtowers have spotted German activity in the forest. It might serve us better to call on the Second Dragoons."

Philip regretted not properly tending to Diebitsch and his men after the incident in Amboise. He hadn't considered the consequences of walking away from an enemy he'd kept so close. "Do you have nerve gas?"

The directeur stared at him in silence, hands crossed in front of his chest.

"I don't care why you have it or who you got it from. I want gas deployed in the forest. Now."

The directeur raised an eyebrow. With the point of one finger from him, two broad shouldered French guards saluted the colonel with orders in hand.

Philip heard Cloutille outside taking men to task for letting Marie and Iné evade capture. "Find out how they are always ahead of us. There must be a leak in our ranks. Plug it."

She'd changed into chocolate brown trousers and a crisp white shirt with a black silk scarf tied at her neck. Philip couldn't remember a time he'd seen her in anything but a proper suit. Cloutille was lovely, her hair always in that perfect victory roll. He shook his head, distracted. Cloutille tossed a big box down on a table. "We've got friends in the wrong places."

"Germans. I know."

"You still trust Diebitsch?"

"Do you?" He knew that if the man got inside Fontevraud, Philip's troops would be shot without hesitation. "Go through the maps. Figure out the most likely place where Serah Izem is."

"How are you handling him?"

"Don't go into the forest without a mask," Philip said.

Cloutille looked at him approvingly and nodded, then returned to the work in front of them.

They pored over architectural drawings. Fifteen minutes passed. Philip turned his attention to the door. A young British private fought two others as they wrestled him into the room. He stood shaking in front of the table where Cloutille and Philip worked.

"Him?" Cloutille asked.

Philip noticed the look in the young man's eyes. He was looking at Cloutille as if she might offer him some sort of relief.

The soldiers nodded. "The others saw him out by the textile mill talking with a man who fit the description of the one you're after."

Philip rolled his eyes, sighed, nodded. They hauled the young man into the courtyard. He pulled his pistol out, walked up to him, pressed against the soldier's temple. One shot. A heavy thump.

"Can anyone tell me where this goddamn woman is?" He slammed his hands down on the table and looked up. Across the courtyard, a small, thin prisoner was being escorted in a group led by guards. Philip zeroed in on the shaved head and chestnut eyes. "Who's that?"

"Which one, Colonel?" The directeur asked.

Philip ignored him. He walked into the rising heat of the day, and yanked the prisoner's head back. "Hello, Serah."

Chapter 46

MARIE

MAY 6, 1945
FORÊT DE MORTE
FONTEVRAUD-L'ABBAYE, FRANCE

Marie's feet pounded against the softening dirt of the rugged forest path outside Fontevraud. She'd run without paying the necessary attention to markers like downed trees, a pile of rocks, or standing water. Now, she was lost. Rain slicked the rocks. The voice of Diebitsch turned to sharp hollers that cut through the storm. A man whelped in the distance. She knew what a knife wedging a person's side sounded like, begged for it not to have been Noam.

She skidded off the path and into a mossy pine grove, crouching low to rest. More hollers. Too many. Unless the German's started killing each other, someone was fighting the Nazi Werwolf squad and fighting hard. A rumbling came through the forest behind her again. She darted into a clearing and tried to catch her breath. Marie needed to get oriented, put as much distance between herself and the soldiers as possible. Her eyes traced the tree line, looking for the angle of the light, but the thought of Serah with a knife in her side made her turn around.

She ran back toward the prison wall. Her feet moved with their own will. The sky blackened and opened up. It drenched her as she stumbled. Her legs barely held her upright as she tried to find the prison. At every turn, nothing but forest. No walls. No drone of the voice from the old Fontevraud bell tower blaring announcements and commands. It was as if she'd stepped into nothingness.

Anything but silence, she thought. The lack of sound sent her heart racing. Her breathing sped up. Her head grew light. Her lungs started to burn. Her bruised ribs shot bolts of pain up her spine. She scanned the flat terrain, desperate to rest. She hadn't realized how late it was. The rain stole any remains of the day. The dense forest swallowed all light with which to navigate.

Iné's voice came into her head, "Not sight."

Marie closed her eyes, stretched her other senses. A smell of burning garlic and horseradish wafted up. It stung her nose. "Dammit."

She knew that smell. Mustard gas would take hours to kill her, but the blisters and lungs filling with fluid would cause an agonizing death.

"Forêt de la Morte." Marie spoke the words she had seen labeled on the map earlier. It was a forest of death and she was going to die.

Her best choice was to move deeper into the thickness of the night. She had failed Serah, again. If she went back, she'd die. If she stayed, she'd die. She moved as fast as her exhaustion and weakening lungs allowed. The darkness within the forest seemed to pulse. Uneven waves of searchlights coursed through the brush. Soundless. Menacing.

Marie fought the urge to call out for help. She dropped to her knees and felt her way along the ground. She remembered the Canadian soldier that had gotten her and three-hundred other women from Ravensbrück to Paris, the shovels they dug holes with to save themselves from German troops. She wanted to bury herself to stay alive. If only she could stay alive.

Marie's hand landed near a massive oak. She yanked herself off the path, beneath the roots of a tray laid bare by erosion and dug herself a hole. She crawled in and willed her heartbeat to quiet. The searchlights passed over her six, seven, eight times. They quickened in succession. Her chest pounded.

Then, voices, muffled as if they were wearing masks. The men were almost on top of her.

She patted her side. No knife. No gun. The men were close. She scanned the underbrush, and tried to haul a long, felled tree branch up to use as a weapon. Her arms couldn't get it. Again, another. Too stubby. A third had a series of branches broken off and was more like a spiked club. It hurt to lift, but she could defend herself with it. The gas grew thick, and she started to cough, but stood with the branch in her hand.

A soldier came out from behind a tree and she swung. He dropped. Marie heard a gurgle. The branch had lodged in some part of him. Marie didn't care which one. However, she had nothing left with which to fight. Another soldier charged her.

Suddenly, a figure stepped onto the path. Light from men's flashlights caught flecks of the royal blue. Was it a cloak? The velvet? Like before. Marie wondered if the gas had infected her mind. The slim, strong hand of a woman urged her to stay low. For a moment, she swore it was Iné. Finally, a shot rang out and the second soldier collapsed.

"Serah?" Marie called out. It was her, but not. The woman with jet black hair and obsidian eyes wore a cylinder around her neck as well. She offered a slight smile for Marie, who sensed relief. Then, a wide, masculine hand reached out.

"Nice work." Noam shined the flashlight on the man she'd taken down. Marie had gotten him right in the chest. She ripped the gas mask off the dead man, as Noam took one off the guy he shot.

"Where's Iné?" Marie asked.

"I heard screams. I ran toward them hoping you were out here."

"We can't stay in the forest." Marie slid the mask on, but she knew she'd already sucked in too much of the gas. "It's phosphene. It might not kill us, but could come damn close."

"I'm sorry, Marie," Noam said. "I thought we'd have Serah back by now."

"Just stay with me," she continued. "I think I can get us out of here."

As soon as she turned his flashlight into the woods, Marie scanned for any sign of the figure that had appeared just before Noam. A layer of yellow gas blanketed the ground beneath the canopy. It shifted and flowed while more poured in at ground level. "We can't go that way."

They watched as the layers of fog and gas mixed.

"It's right through the trees, then," Noam said.

The pair hiked their way into the thick underbrush, moving east until Marie's breathing became too labored.

"Why the hell are they gassing us out?" She started to slur as they dropped down into a low gully where the toxic gas had dissipated. They moved along, rustling through dead leaves until a boulder blocked the path. "If we die, they get nothing."

"I don't think it's the Nazis." Noam took a labored suck of air.

"Philip. He wants them out of the way." Marie coughed to try to clear her lungs. Her attention shot up. She was sure, for a moment, that voices shouted in search of her and Noam somewhere in the forest.

"You should go." Marie couldn't get up. She pushed Noam back from her. "One of us . . . Just get out of here and get Serah."

"I'm not going to leave you out here alone," he said. "Don't make me into the one that lived."

"Well, good news then. Neither of us is going to survive out here together."

"Cloutille will find us."

"She can't break cover for this," Marie said. "All these years, I thought the Germans were going to kill me. Turns out, it's my own insanity."

"You're not insane." Noam took her hand as their breathing slowed.

"Oh, really? For the past three days, I've been seeing Serah everywhere."

Noam cocked his head and frowned. "There's plenty about what's happening that I can't explain either."

"Please, not the Sibyl."

"Marie, there's more to this."

"It would seem this whole prophetess nonsense has corrupted all of us."

He pulled her close. "Sometimes you have to suspend all belief in reality to make sense of the horrors people do to each other."

"That suspension of belief is now going to kill us." Marie knew that neither of them had the strength to move. She just wanted to keep talking.

"Maybe, but what if the Sibyl is real? What if there were more women like her, an entire society?" Noam asked. "That's incredible."

"It's also bullshit. I study and deduce and authenticate. I don't . . . "

"You don't what? Buy into the theories that there may have been societies that were deliberately erased? Are we not living through a time that proves it's possible to wipe out an entire civilization?"

"Yes, proof. That's the key. If I can't prove it, it's not real." She felt herself fading and grabbed for anything on the ground to hold and feel, to maintain her senses.

"I agree, but what about what we both saw tonight? Your hand passed through Iné. For a moment, she wasn't there. You can prove that. It happened. It was real."

Marie swallowed hard in the silence. Could Iné really be five hundred years old? A Ba'alat soldier left behind to protect a relic from another time?

"Some of us get the chance to uncover truths no one could have ever imagined until witnessed," Noam offered. "For whatever reason, your chance is right now."

"How would you know?"

"You're the one who survived." Noam took her hands.

"I don't need you to do this," Marie said.

"What?"

"Some ridiculous dying declaration of love."

"To be honest, you're pretty hard to warm up to in that way." Noam coughed long and hard.

Marie gave a guttural laugh. "Good thing you figured it out before I lured you in."

"We're going to get out of this. We're going to get Serah back. We're going to see La Joconde hanging in the Louvre once again. But, you have to stop fighting the Sibyl."

"You can't possibly think she'd now become all of my hope." Marie started to cough. Her lungs ached. She couldn't get enough air.

"We all could use some hope."

"Too late." Marie wheezed. "So, should we end it all side-by-side like Pompei lovers?"

Noam chuckled and coughed again. His eyes watered up. The moon broke through the trees and lingered on them. Marie heard the rush of the river, then saw it. The sandy, low banks of the Vienne River seemed to light up less than fifty meters away. She and Noam had somehow made it almost to the narrow waterway that flowed into the Loire less than a kilometer north of Fontevraud.

"If I'd just done what I was supposed to, none of this would have happened," Marie said.

"Or all of it would have happened anyway." Noam took her in his arms.

They both laughed uncomfortably. Marie regretted her emotions bubbling up and settled against his neck. Their breathing eased in unison.

"One last adventure." Noam kissed her forehead. "For Serah."

Marie sobbed. She let her eyes close. "For Serah."

Chapter 47

AESMEH

MAY 2, 1519
TOUR HERTAULT
AMBOISE, FRANCE

I waited in my chamber at Tour Hertault for the Abbess to return from her latest round of secret meetings. The results would determine how to continue in light of Tommaso's duplicity. Melzi had hidden away, along with Master da Vinci, to finish La Joconde. Maurine had left me to rest. There was no need for any of us to rouse suspicion that we had figured out Tommaso's plan.

The rhythmic coo of the pigeons sleeping upon the window sill of the tower shook me from my stupor. They gathered in the morning sun; I stroked the feathers of these divine creatures and stared out upon the wildness of the Loire River. The three pairs of pigeons had never been together in one place. For the last thirteen years, one was always in the air delivering letters between myself and Melzi or ferrying clandestine communications for the Abbess. To see them all in one place might have once given me joy in the light of us all having come together in the same place. Laying eyes upon the six gentle birds cooing at that moment delivered only a sense of dread that our time was near its end.

I brought them in just beyond the sill and set a pair on a length of cool silk. The darlings were in a state of torpor from the heat and the owls would come calling if I left them out. I stroked the back of one, sensing myself the dove and the men around me, the owls ready to attack. My protective instincts took over.

I watched their eyes flutter as they rested. Their peacefulness was a balm, for the revelations of Tommaso's duplicity had rocked us all.

The Abbess, so anxious for me to make my way to Amboise two days past, now stashed me away in the room at the top of the tower. Until she set the pieces of our plan in place, she told me, I remained unable to change anyone's fate. What was my fate? I pressed my hand against the cylinder around my neck. A scene of the goddess leading men to stand before the Sibyl rose up, and then vanished when the door to my chamber opened.

"You have taken up with the beasties now?" Maurine asked. She stood in the doorway of the small space.

"They may prove less likely to try to kill me."

"Such a quandary. It is, however, up for debate."

We laughed, a necessity after the chaos of the previous day. Gathering the pigeons one-by-one, Maurine moved them onto the warm straw of their cages at the back of the room. "Are these the mated pairs?"

I choked back a sob. Since the day Melzi and I had separated in Milan those dear creatures had ensured we traded out letters. We shared everything from longings to Master da Vinci's mad theories, to everyday goings-on. It was the closest a woman of my position would ever come to marriage. "Thirteen years they are in our service."

"How many letters have they possibly delivered?" Maurine asked, smiling softly as she handed me a sack

I opened it and beamed. I loved her for her sentiment of the heart. "You saved them? You painful romantic!"

"Melzi did as well." She showed me. The bag included his replies. My heart grew heavy.

"How is he?"

"As well as any man in hiding."

"And Master da Vinci?"

"They commiserate together, back under the fountain," Maurine said. "It shall not be long. You ought to prepare."

A knock at the door interrupted us.

"Enter." We said it at the same time.

"Désolé, Sister Maurine," the servant girl said. "But there is a bit of a scene at Gaillard."

"Why do you call on me?"

"The Amyntas asked me to find you," The girl paused. She was not to look a woman of the Order in the eyes, but she dared to now. "They require your attention."

"I see." Maurine gathered herself.

"I shall go," I said. If it was at Gaillard, I knew it had to be about Master da Vinci.

"No." Maurine forced me back. She handed the girl the key to my room. "Bring the Great Mother a hearty meal. Veal. Potatoes. Wine. Keep her warm."

"You cannot trap me up here."

"As sure as the heavens I can." Maurine pointed for me to sit before continuing with the girl. "I shall need wool blankets."

"I have them bundled by the entryway," the servant girl said. "Along with a compress of chamomile, and your tinctures."

"For Master da Vinci?" I panicked. "What is happening?"

"The meal," Maurine told the girl. "And whatever else the Great Mother requires."

As they left, the Abbess swept through the door.

"It is set," she said.

"What is going on at Gaillard?"

The Abbess appeared uneasy.

"No one trusts Tommaso," Lady Marguerite said as she entered. She set out a written agreement from a series of lesser dukes "At least a handful on both sides have agreed to deal with him accordingly.

"Then you will prepare immediately to enter the temple," the Abbess ordered.

"No." I could not believe she would relegate me to such a minor task when I knew Tommaso better than nearly anyone. "He will trust me."

"I doubt that almost entirely," the Abbess continued.

"Let me make the arrangements. You shall have your man and the Sibyl."

Lady Marguerite took the Abbess by the arm. I knew they discussed strategy and longed to find myself included in such matters of men. Yet, I also understood why they kept it from me.

"She is the only one." I heard Lady Marguerite whisper. "The Harimtu logs clearly demonstrate he has not yet realized . . ." It trailed off and I stretched my ears to collect her words.

"This leaves Aesmeh prone. I will not risk it," the Abbess replied.

"If we do not end this deceit, she will be dead long before the Sibylline can regain any modicum of control." Lady Marguerite's words proved correct, I estimated.

The Abbess shook her head. Lady Marguerite retreated to the doorway, giving her a nod.

"It seems you are," the Abbess turned to me, "the only one who can properly end this with Monsieur d'Arced."

She turned to walk away, then spun around to take my hand, "The speed of the Great Mother be with you, Aesmeh. I will see you again when you have taken your vows."

The glimmers began again. It was time for me to pen a letter to the future Sibyl.

"I thought we agreed not to find ourselves in one another's company until I was done." I looked up briefly from my writing, but not long enough to note the visitor coming through the door of my room. "I have made arrangements."

"For what?" Tommaso slid a plate of candied oranges onto the desk, pilfering a handful before sitting on the divan. The pigeons cooed behind him.

"Tommaso, I thought you were . . ." caught off guard, I concocted a lie. How had he broken through the Amyntas guard? A foursome of soldiers filed in behind him. "I thought you were the Abbess."

"Not unless I have unknowingly developed a bosom. There is a bosom under that habit, yes?"

"Monsieur d'Arced, such blasphemy." I tried to remain light and playful.

"I've always wondered why you have never donned the habit of your Order," he spoke to me as if old friends remained untouched by the politicking, despite the guard. Where were my own? I perked my ears for any hint of the state of the Amyntas.

"Disguises have never served either of us well." I tried to grin and wondered if he knew we had been listening in earlier that day. "I still do not understand how Melzi's treachery slipped past all of us."

"His private dealings most assuredly secured him loyalties beyond our reach," Tommaso continued, sitting down at the table where he set the food. "And now we have far greater problems than a missing Master da Vinci and a faltering apprentice. Your safety."

I resented the ease with which he lied. Yet, I found myself just as comfortable in the task of deceiving him.

"Only a madman would try to kill a Sibyl." I straightened my robes before moving to the window. I remained deeply concerned over the rush in which Maurine had departed and my vanished Amyntas. Were Melzi and Master da Vinci safe? I started to concern myself with my present company and searched the grounds for assurances that any of the Amyntas, who had arrived that dawn in advance of the procession to the temple, stood guard. They were nowhere to be seen, which I knew was a near impossibility based on the concern the Abbess had taken with my safety. Something was amiss. Had the Abbess been wrong to heed the advice of Lady Marguerite?

"Please tell me you have decided to serve the king," Tommaso continued.

"Is that why you've come with your men?" I paced the floor. "Much has come about since Fontevraud." I paced.

"I come at the behest of King François himself. Indeed, you are in the most profound danger."

"From whom?" Stopping mid-way through the room, I found myself unable to contain my outrage for Tommaso's actions.

"Must we go over the threat yet again?" he asked. "Charles is closer than ever to an assault."

"What does he even know of the Sibylline?"

"What does he not? Let me negotiate peace with you at my side."

"You are but a boy. These men will not gather at your request."

"This boy you speak of, has the very ear of a king." He remained seated, but leaned in over the table toward me. "Diplomacy, my friend, is simply keeping all of the parties engaged long enough for them not to notice you have already declared war."

"War? Is that what we declare?"

"Do you not want to win?"

"I want to serve."

"Then, this is all we have left."

A knock at the door interrupted us. I rushed to answer. At the entrance, a chambermaid bearing the green undergarments of the Harimtu glanced at my gloves. Remove them. She spoke with her mind.

I took one off and knew in an instant the letter was from Melzi. I did not have to read it to know what had transpired. Summon the Abbess. Call the Amyntas to her side. I gave her the order.

"I shall replace the drinks if they are not suitable." She spoke nonsense to give me time to return the glove to my hand.

"Do so. I have guests."

I slid the letter into the sleeve of my gown, trying to keep from alerting Tommaso to my knowledge of what he had already ordered done. My head spun.

"You look tired," Tommaso said.

"It has been much to deal with." I fidgeted with the cylinder around my neck.

"I shall leave you then. Shall I call the femme de chambre back to turn your bed down?"

"Yes, please."

"Good, then. Please, consider what we have spoken about." He stood and kissed my hand. "Good day, Great Mother."

I nodded, unable to respond.

As soon as Tommaso had gone, I tore the parchment open and wept.

Master da Vinci is dead.

None of us could have foreseen what this moment might bring. We all trusted Tommaso far too much. I fear he has put us all within an arm's length of death.

Amboise is under siege from within.

We must finish the task he set out to accomplish for the Abbess, for the Sibylline, for you.

Do not linger.

M

Chapter 48

MARIE

MAY 7, 1945
FORÊT DE MORTE
FONTEVRAUD-L'ABBAYE, FRANCE

When she took her next breath, Marie found herself floating in water. The contaminated spring at Amboise sprung to mind and she fought to escape, thrashing at the water, only to give in as a gentleness overcame her. Whatever held her up seemed to warm her body.

"What are you doing?" She pleaded. A gentle shake settled her. A hand lifted to quiet her, then moved in a circle overhead.

Marie's sight remained weak, but the sense that women surrounded her, even supported her in the water, allowed her to give into ease. The hymns she'd first heard in Amboise filled the air. She couldn't move, hands held her still. She cocked her head to the side. Had she made it to the Vienne River? A touch alighted upon her palm. Then, another drew a brilliant light in front of her and down. Each set of hands performed this same action as if stealing light from the full moon which lit up the black night and placing it into Marie's body. The air began moving more and more clearly through her nostrils and lips. She gave in to the intoxication, wondering if she'd died.

Yet, her energy grew. In the last of the moonlight, just as dawn broke, Marie found herself strong. Whatever had stiffened her earlier released her at that moment. Her vision cleared and the face of a woman closest to her came into focus.

"Serah!"

"Mother, are you okay?"

"Are you alive?" Marie begged for the woman in front of her to be her daughter.

"I think she is okay," another voice piped in. Iné appeared in the water beside Serah.

"Are we all alive?" Marie hesitated, yet found herself filled with joy.

She powered her arms and legs to shore. Her feet held her up. She breathed in, deep. No gas. No blisters anywhere on her. She turned to look at the river. It was quiet. No sign of Serah or Iné. Her heart sank.

Onshore, two women in tan overalls, delicate flower-print blouses, and gumboots nodded at her as they left blankets and a change of clothes next to a steaming mug of herbs that smelled like valerian, devil's claw, and a type of mint Marie once had at a garden party. Noam was sitting on a rock a few feet away sipping a mug of his own.

"What just happened?"

"I have no idea," Noam said. "The tea is pretty good."

"Did they, well, do that light thing on you?"

"The Sibylline," Noam pointed to the women in the overalls, "had you in the water for a long time. I didn't know whether it was about clearing your lungs or getting the poison out. You were right. It was gas."

The two women nodded again, one with dark hair as short as hers motioning for Marie to drink.

"You called them the Sibylline? Who are they?"

Noam twisted his face and didn't answer as he wrapped himself in a wool blanket. Marie made her way over and slumped down next to him. He wrapped his arms around her and kissed her head.

Marie wanted to resist, to deny, to abandon any sense that she and Noam had, yet again, narrowly avoided death thanks to women who had gifts beyond an average person. However, there seemed to be no other explanation.

"Was Serah really with them?"

"I never saw her. Only Iné and the other women."

"How long have you known?"

"Serah figured it out. She's connected to them somehow. That may be why you keep thinking you are seeing her."

Marie thought of Philip's obsession with the Sibyl. "Millar thinks she is hiding the woman."

"That's why she separated from the Maquis. I think she thought she could keep us safe that way."

"Then why send for me, like Cloutille said?"

"You're her mother."

The tea dulled Marie's aches, but not her emotions. She wanted to question everything, but the time for caution had passed. She tossed it back and down her throat and began fading in and out of a haze. A woman came to check her pulse. As she did, Marie shoved the sleeve of her blouse up.

"So, you are Sibylline," she said. The tattoo was the same as Iné. There seemed to be Sibylline everywhere at Fontevraud. Marie couldn't believe she had conceded to believing everything she'd long insisted was a myth. The events of the last two days had forced her to question her preconceptions. They made her question what she believed more than Ravensbrück had. However, Serah and these women were connected. She let go of the woman's arm, stumbled to the bank of the river, and puked.

Noam grabbed a cloth from a pile left nearby. He wet it with cool water and placed it on the back of her neck. "That drink didn't settle very well."

"Something like that." Marie pulled the cloth down to wipe her face. The sun was high in the sky. "How long have we been here?"

He shook his head and helped her up onto a rock where two pairs of khakis, black combat boots, and plain white T-shirts sat in a neat pile. Next to them, a gun and a knife.

Marie realized she was in her underwear. "We need to get these Sibylline to help us find Serah."

"Are you suddenly becoming a believer?" Noam got dressed.

"We did walk into a gas attack and survive."

"You killed a man with a stick," Noam said. "But, honestly, I've never . . ."

"I was kind of hoping I'd just dreamed it," Marie said, slipping on pants and tying up her boots. "Maybe we should just tell everyone we got gassed by nuns."

They both laughed. Noam nudged her with his wide shoulder, easy and comfortable in his manner. "Or maybe we should find Iné."

"And Serah."

He took her hand. "And Serah."

The pair trudged up the path back into the forest. Within fifty feet, they'd crouched behind a tree after catching an echo of footsteps. Marie moved around the back of a hooded figure. Noam drew his gun. The figure froze up near a set of stone stairs. Marie once again had her knife pressed into the back of a woman.

"You have some explaining to do, Mademoiselle Soudier," Marie said.

"Save it." The woman spun around.

"Yara!" Marie found herself without additional words. Her mother's oldest friend stood in front of her in thick head coverings and military fatigues, a Luger in her holster and a rifle in her arms.

Without a word, the group moved down a long set of stone stairs into an underground chamber.

Yara finally spoke. "It's time to get our Dear One out of here."

Chapter 49

MARIE

MAY 7, 1945
THE CATACOMBS
FONTEVRAUD PRISON, FRANCE

Marie watched Yara. The woman silently led her and Noam past the threshold of an inconspicuous doorway in a low, weedy section of the forest outside of Fontevraud Prison. The effects of being caught in the nerve gas the night before had entirely subsided. However, Marie's concern over what was unfolding before them grew. She considered the recent hallucinations, the experience with the women in the river, and wondered what Yara was possibly leading them into.

In the field gear, Yara looked thirty years younger and ready for a fight. Her gray ringlets caught what little light there was. She took Marie's arm and gently squeezed it, her eyes soft and loving. Marie wanted to hold her and cry over the loss of Simon, but grief seemed to have no place in such a moment.

Yara stashed her weapon in a shoe-sized box near a wooden door at the end of the cool, gray tunnel. Prime meridian. Two crescents. The markings on the box had become so familiar to Marie. Yara pulled navy linen from a stack of cloth beside the box and draped the covering over her head like a veil. Marie followed suit. The thick linen left her face in shadow. The door opened.

"No men." A woman with startling green eyes pushed back against Noam's chest. Her walnut-colored skin was deeply creased as if carrying the memories of a thousand years. She wore a floor-length gown of saffron silk. She did not look like a nun. She looked like a priestess. Around her neck was a cylindrical medallion made from moonstone. Marie found herself longing to touch it, feel its weight. The woman's eyes glimmered like emeralds against her dark complexion.

"He is one of ours," Iné said from inside the room. "Give him a veil. We cannot leave him in the corridor."

Noam draped the cloth over his head.

Marie smiled at him. "Sœur Marchant. You've finally found your calling."

They laughed at the reference to Noam as a nun until Yara cleared her throat.

"This is Rafidah Qabbari." Iné made introductions.

"Another Ba'alat?" Marie asked.

Iné smiled. "No. She is an Asu Priestess, our librarian of sorts."

"Where is Serah?"

Rafidah ushered them into a simple, round room that was carved from the tufa stone of the earth that the abbey sat upon. Stacks, shelves, boxes, and enormous chests lined the walls. Over a single table, an enormous lantern in the shape of a teardrop illuminated the space with a golden light.

"Why are we wasting time?" Marie asked.

Iné didn't answer. She pulled out a chair from the table and sat down. Marie took one, pulled out another for Noam.

He raised a hand and retreated to a corner. "I think I'm better as an observer."

"Yesterday didn't go quite as anticipated," Iné started right in. "But, now you know."

"About the Sibylline?" Marie had expected an apology or an explanation. "I reached for you and you weren't there. Noam and I almost died in the woods."

"The Heliade are talented or you would not be here right now," Rafidah said, tapping two fingers to her left shoulder twice, her lips once. Marie looked at Noam. She found herself an outsider in this circle.

"Fontevraud is not how any of us remember it." Iné kept up with her own line of conversation. "That is why our Dear One is where she is."

"You found Serah, then?" Marie lit up.

"Possibly, but we are cut off," Rafidah said.

"Millar? The Nazis?" Marie continued.

"Diebitsch is not working for the Nazi's," Iné said.

Marie's breath caught at that comment, but she did not pause to question what surely was a lengthy conversation no one had the time to undertake. "You've got maps of the tunnels?"

Rafidah stepped forward and slid on a pair of cotton gloves, handing Marie a pair as well. Then, she produced a set of weathered pages from a leather satchel.

Marie unfolded the parchments. Each was written in a different format. The first was in Middle French and faded. The markings clearly showed an underground network and a legend with elements including water, fire, amaranth, and a crown, just like the ones carved into the walls that Iné had shown her. She oriented herself by looking for the markers that looked like Iné's tattoo. They were at the southwest edge of the monastic complex, labeled as the kitchens. There were tunnels beneath. That was where she had collapsed, Marie thought.

"The mark on your arm is so you can find your way back to the kitchens?" she asked.

"The fires," Rafidah said. "Where the flame of the Sibylline Order once burned."

"Where do we think Serah is in relation to that?"

Rafidah pointed to the kitchens. "Beneath the fires."

"What is there?" Marie found the coincidence of her earlier vision unsettling.

"Catacombs," Iné said. "Once you told me about the marking on the photos in the SOE file, I knew that's where she had to be."

"So, let's go." Marie stood and moved toward the door.

"As I said," Rafidah offered, "we've had some trouble getting inside the tomb."

"What do you mean? I was there yesterday, at the top of the stairs."

"The entry point from the kitchens was sealed hundreds of years ago," Iné continued and spread out two more recent drawings. They were a cluster of intricate cartography, each one showing different routes, sometimes walled up. "There are other ways in, but maps aren't always accurate."

"So, how do we know what else is blocked?" Marie asked. She thought about Noam's tunnel from the food storage to the Madeleine. "Do we have any undocumented routes?"

"It's all trial and error. We'll need to split up."

"That doesn't sound smart," Marie said.

Yara took Noam's arm and tugged, eyeballing him. "We can start with the first several maps while you two track the others. We'll meet back here in two hours."

"What about Philip? Diebitsch?" Marie asked.

"The gas got the Germans as far as we know. There hasn't been a peep," Yara said. "As for Philip, you'll need to be ready. Cloutille's men left weapons and other gear in the corridor."

"What about the prison directeur. I'm sure he has orders to shoot on sight," Marie asked.

"The directeur isn't going to have us killed." Yara winked at everyone. "Now, go."

Marie nodded and headed off with Iné into the corridor. She took a knife from the crate in the corridor. Iné handed her a gun and bullets as well, which she took without question.

"You know, I've never met anyone like Serah," Iné told her as they walked. "No one has come close to her bravery, her sense of what is right. She reminds me a lot . . . "

"Of the woman, Asfoora." Marie finished her sentence. She couldn't avoid these conversations any longer, and she had too many questions not to engage. "You think Serah is the modern Sibyl."

"Aesmeh de la Rose, and yes, I do." Iné pressed her hand against Marie's arm. "She knows, Marie. She's already very powerful."

Marie choked on her own breath. Her eyes filled with tears. For a moment, her mind's eye offered a vision of Serah and Iné walking the corridors together as they were doing now. This woman had been at her daughter's side, maybe even fought at Serah's side, when Marie couldn't. She had loved Serah when a mother could not. Marie's emotions, raw and cutting, bordered on love for Iné. All of her logic told her she was wrong, but her heart spoke a different language. "How long have you been at Amboise?"

"I'm not even sure I remember a time when I wasn't there."

Marie smiled at her as they reached another door. "Thank you, for saving us in the forest."

"The Heliade did that." Iné lifted the ancient, weighted door mechanism to release a latch.

"Rafidah used that word earlier," Marie said. "What is it?"

"The women at the river. They are healers, but with energy and light."

"That's impossible."

"Is it?" Iné pressed her hand on Marie's chest, her warmth penetrating Marie's spirit.

"You were there though, right? I meant just before Noam and I found each other out there? With Serah?"

"Well . . ." Iné paused and looked at her with knowing eyes. "You're welcome, Sister Marie."

The words somehow seemed to seal the bond between them as they stepped into a chapel fit for a troglodyte. The room was burned on one side, the murals still vibrant with gold and glaze that brought light to the gloom. Pieces of the ceiling had fallen. Stairs to another door had nearly collapsed.

"It is amazing that this is still intact," Marie said.

"Over here. It's the only way in."

"To where?"

"Come." Iné pushed on a seal of the medieval cross, which triggered another latch and the women dipped down into a cavern.

At first, Marie saw nothing but blackness.

The pair moved quickly into a room already lit by candles burning in sconces every two feet, lining the walls. Shelves were carved into the stone. Marie noted worn carvings that appeared Celtic. Inside the cabinets, books, files, and other documents were preserved.

"Looks like someone knew we were coming," Marie said.

Iné remained silent.

Above them, the sound of the prison guards on bullhorns fractured the silence.

Marie pointed upward. "How is it that you can keep so much hidden from them?"

"This is just one set of archives. There are similar repositories such as this all across Spain, Greece, even North Africa." Iné showed Marie the filing system. It was ordered by which Abbess was in power rather than by date. She pointed out several scrolls locked away in glass and wooden cases that could not be accessed.

"All of this is . . .?"

"Sibylline, yes," Iné said. "I have to deal with other things. So, I'll leave you."

"I thought we were looking for the entrance to the catacombs?"

"We'll start here."

"What am I looking for?"

"You'll know it when you see it," Iné interrupted.

"What about Serah?"

Iné locked the door behind her and was gone.

Marie had so many questions, her mind filled with half-truths, or half-knowing of actual truths, or something like that. Surrounded by what were surely undocumented historical archives, she was curious, but trapped. Marie expected her anxiety to kick in. Instead, the room left her with a sense of the familiar, like a place deep in her own experience that she had only begun to remember having been.

She thumbed through the collection. She peeled back page after page. What did she need to find? Many of the documents had elements at least a thousand years old. It occurred to her that maps and other guides for getting around the underbelly of the abbey might be amongst the papers, and drove her to read on.

Marie yanked at several pieces and spread them out. She knew better than to treat artifacts like this. Yet, she was frantic, possessed.

Within fifteen minutes, she sat wedged between the wall and a tall, narrow cabinet that held rows of scrolls and palm-sized manuscripts. Her hands seemed to have a will of their own as she went through two sets of tiny books decorated with elegant illuminations.

Next, a stunning parchment, written in Attic Greek, fascinated her. A second, with the same mark upon the cover, had the same words written in Arabic, forcing her to pause.

A third in Hebrew.

A fourth in Latin.

A fifth in French.

All translations of the same words. All with the same tattoo mark. She was tossed into panicked wonderment. These were documents, no, one document, in particular, translated over and over. There was only one reason to do that—to preserve it from destruction.

Iné stepped back through the door. She stared at Marie and twisted her finger through the black hair that had escaped from her cap.

"You didn't bring me here to find maps, did you?" Marie asked.

"No. I just thought you should read this on your own."

"It's . . . incredible."

"I have one more for you." Iné handed Marie a folded parchment. It was written in Middle French. The looped handwriting seemed familiar. Where had she seen it before? She searched her mental archives but gave up as she realized what the document was. Her feet suddenly weighed more than a dozen bricks in anticipation of Iné's next words. The unquenchable sorrow and hope behind Iné's eyes startled Marie. She sensed that what she was about to read mattered more than just about anything else up until that moment.

"What is it?"

"A letter from Melzi's Asfoora. To Serah."

May 2, 1519

Dear One,

How awkward this must be to have a dead woman about to declare the direction of your life. It is unclear to me, even at this crucial moment, how I should address you. Alas, as time can no longer keep us apart, let us dispense with being strangers and begin.

I am the Sibyl of Amboise. I died here. You have arrived in this tiny commune because of a five-hundred-year-old pact to find you and bring you home.

As I write these words, I wonder what you know of my kind. Do you recall the names Hypatia and Lubna? Does history speak of Shushandukht and Shajar al-Durr? Or, are the Sibyls little more than mythological prophetesses painted upon the ceiling of the Sistine Chapel? In truth, we are ancient, once powerful, and nearly vanished.

Born of the Great Mother's very womb, each Sibyl's sight gave men a glimpse of what might come. We predicted wars, warned against the rise of tyrants, shed light upon the fates of many. In the great capitals of Badari, Olmec, Xi, Khemet, the Jiroft, even the wilds of Scythia, we served humanity for more than eleven thousand years. And, then . . .

What do you know, Dear One? It pains me. What kind of world did my failures leave you? In the glimmers of your time, I saw only fire and death. Power is a seductive demon. Without the Sibyl, men know not the cost of their acts. Have I left you with the tyrants?

I must assume the world is well enough that Sister Maurine stands at your side in fulfillment of her vow as your Ba'alat, your watcher. My regret is not being there beside you as well. You are the hope of the Sibylline. I was once too—the first to complete the training and enter the temple in more than one thousand years. Such care was taken to protect me. However, a malicious enemy lived amongst us. By the time I knew, my throat was nearly slit. It lays upon you now to do what I never fully could—to rise and serve the world.

Yes, Dear One, your coming has been foretold for five centuries. In those fifty decades, such knowledge has hung in the halls of the men who thought us eradicated. They celebrated that sublime smile, all without the fortune of knowing whom they kept safe. You are the oracle they could never burn, lying in state until this very moment.

Listen, Dear One. Listen without fear. Your life is an amalgamation of so many others. As you gain the sight, Amboise will return our memories to you. You shall reclaim them as your own. You may feel as if you have gone mad. Know that you are but coming alive. This is where your service begins.

In the moments to come, others will attempt to strip your sovereignty. Such war is inevitable. You must prepare for it. Train. Fight as a warrior. You must remain devoted to your purpose alone. Do not concede.

Then, call the Sibylline to your side. Step beyond the seven bridges of paradise and into hell in the forest beyond Gaillard. There, in the temple of the Sibyl-

line, you shall rise and take my place at Amboise. That you might watch over humankind in beauty and justice as the Great Mothers before you intended.

Eternally in your service,

Aesmeh de la Rose

Marie translated the letter over and over, looking for any possible signs of it being a fake. She could not push her mind beyond the historical record she knew so well. The text: Middle French. The handwriting: definitely a woman. The medium: sheepskin. The ink: oak galls rather than carbon, gum, and water—she could tell, just from the shading of the letters.

"The Nazis were right. Melzi's Asfoora was the Sibyl," Marie spoke the words as a matter of fact.

Iné nodded.

"And La Joconde, she is the Sibyl too."

"In a sense, but no."

Rafidah entered the room. Marie studied the old woman, her face creased like the parchment in front of her.

"Do you confirm? It is five hundred years old? One person's script?" Rafidah asked. "No doubts anymore?"

"It looks authentic, but I cannot confirm anything here without . . ." Marie paused, her suspicion growing that she'd fallen for yet another con. "Why do you care what I think?"

Iné was trying to get Rafidah to stop talking when the woman blurted out, "You are the only one who can decipher the old writings, to tell us . . ."

Marie was in shock, ". . . The name of the next Sibyl."

The magnitude of such a declaration hung between them. It trapped Marie like a prison. The Sibyl was starting to feel very real.

"Please, we are not using you," Iné said.

Marie kept her guard up, but everything that had transpired in the last day meant she gave Iné the benefit of the doubt for the moment. "You don't know who she is?"

Iné touched her necklace. "I can't force this upon Serah if it is not her."

"Only our Dear One will tell us if we are right," Rafidah said.

Marie had lost her bearings. Everyone, everything really, was leading her to this oracle. "How could anyone think the name of a Sibyl would survive in a painting for five hundred years?"

"We're not meant to understand," Iné said. "We're meant only to believe."

Chapter 50

AESMEH

MAY 2, 1519
AMBOISE, FRANCE

I swept down the wide stone stairs of Clos Lucé, prepared to race out into the sweltering night. A figure ran through the gardens toward me. I dashed behind a tall holly hedge and watched. A man, I deduced. He moved in silence. His right foot fell harder than his left. Must be carrying something large on that side. He grunted. I knew that grunt. He ran past me and I flung myself out of the bushes. "Melzi!"

He did not even try to return to his feet, remaining on his back where I had put him, stunned and sobbing. "You must have gotten the note I sent with the Harimtu. Thank heavens you are alive."

"What has transpired?"

"He is dead. Aesmeh, they killed him. Master da Vinci is dead."

"Was he not with you?" I stiffened at the sight of a covered canvas laying on the ground on this rainy night. "Oh, Great Mother, is that La Joconde?"

He scrambled to get it covered. "They ripped the door down. I only had seconds. He kept screaming at me to run, run, run."

I frantically searched the gardens for friends and foes. We rushed toward the side entrance from which I had just come out. "Let us get our

Dear One to the workshop."

Melzi followed in silence. We crept back up the stairs. He set the painting down on an easel and whisked the cloth away. Only the lower right quadrant was muddied. He tried to smooth it out with a finger.

"Fix it later. How did you get out?"

"'You have to survive it. That is all Master da Vinci said."

"And then what?"

"He dove at the men. Right onto their blades. Gave me enough time to snatch up the painting and run."

"He sacrificed himself?"

Melzi had collapsed onto the wide table in Master da Vinci's workshop.

"Has no one gone to retrieve him?"

"Amboise is teeming with soldiers. I had only the time to save La Joconde."

I was battered, capable of nothing other than fury and sadness. I considered burning the letter I had penned for the next Sibyl just before Tommaso's arrival, even held it over the flickering hearth. Melzi snatched my hand back just as the flame licked the lower edge. He tamped it out with the sleeve of his doublet, I sobbed and folded it with care, placing it in Melzi's pocket. The room stank of carved wood and varnishes.

We could not contain our nerves, therefore we moved into the dining hall where I mixed some herbs for a warm tonic.

Melzi drank it fast and eased back. We sat for a long moment in silence, staring at nothing, until he finally stood and returned to the easel in the workshop. He pulled on a painting shift and started in on the remaining work.

The tears welled up in my eyes. "How much more? Is she not so beautiful already?"

"I have not slept since we found out." Melzi looked like a ghost. He gathered brushes and mixed powders. "Is it wrong to tell you that every move of my brush on the canvas feels like an offering?"

"I thought it might be torture."

"Sweet pain. Now, not just for you, but for all of us. With you here, I shall insert the key this evening."

As we stood, only hours before I was to head to the temple, we knew every stroke of Melzi's brush sealed our fate. His was to return to Italy and take over as head of the Melzi family. Mine, to lead the Sibylline in their return to the world. In this test of our devotion, we would succeed. Yet, his other hand, holding mine, told me another story. This glimmer that shot up revealed Master da Vinci splayed upon a sword, La Joconde—the future of all Sibylline—unfinished, and both of us drowning in failure.

I longed to change such fate, to embody the very Sibyl within me whom I denied in many ways until that very moment. I took the cylinder around my neck and breathed as the Abbess had instructed, awaiting a future glimmer I could reveal, then reverse.

I watched Melzi as he laid a layer of glaze over the painting. It ran over the edges and onto the floor. We both stood, breathing, forcing ourselves to treat these final steps in as proper a manner as possible.I probed my mind for glimpses of tomorrow. Time vanished. The threat of our deaths drove me to want to push Melzi harder and harder. He began to mumble to himself, thinning the layer out bit by bit. "How could he? After everything I . . .?"

"Who could blame Tommaso?" My voice shook Melzi out of the daze and he knocked over a jar of oil. He fumbled to clean up the mess. "What did he even have before this? Rejected by his family. Left to fend for himself. When Maurine left him, he had only . . .'"

Melzi shot up. "His honor."

I had not meant to spit out a laugh in one sardonic, sick burst. "What honor is there left inside any man?"

Melzi kicked at the unfinished painting. "Do you not require my help? Why do you keep making excuses for him?"

I knew why. Had it not been Tommaso, it might have been us. "I would have taught you how to cleanse a room, how to sense others, so much more if it meant we could have stayed together. Had I not returned to Fontevraud when I did, this moment might be because of our broken hearts."

Melzi's face twisted as if he had not considered the very same thing.

I took his hand, "Tommaso is hungry for admiration, but you know it is not from other men. Tell me you would not sell your mother if such a transaction gained you my life."

"Love provokes a terrible hunger." Melzi stroked my cheek. "Why use my heart against me in such a way?"

I considered all the foolish actions undertaken by us in the effort to win each other's love. It was time we stopped questioning and completed our task.

"Where are we at with the other details?" he asked.

"I have ordered Maurine to Fontevraud. We cannot risk Tommaso's broken heart being pushed to even greater depths of depravity if provoked by her presence."

"Wise."

A woman behind us cleared her throat. Lady Marguerite stood in the doorway. "We have other concerns. I can no longer guarantee the loyalty of my brother," she said. "He has gone, well, a bit mad with all of this, declared the Sibylline an enemy of the kingdom at dinner last night with all of his men in attendance."

Melzi paced, his composure lost. "Is there no one left to trust?"

"The game is in play. We cannot interrupt it now," Lady Marguerite continued. "It seems as if the Sibylline are to be forever hunted."

She slapped a letter into my hand. "That we might all slit our own throats."

I read it allowed:

By the time you receive this, I will have relieved myself of Amboise as all men with any sensibility must do to save what remains. The Sibylline—those evil sorceresses you remain devoted to without cause—are now the property of the men to whom they owed their very existence, and we have you to thank for all of it.

It is too late for the Sibyl, too late for all that any of us might have once believed. However, let it not be too late for those of us with the power to return greatness to the Empire to step forth and rid ourselves of all the Sibylline left in their wake.

The time has come for you to see the error of your misplaced loyalty.

In The Service of the Empire,
Tommaso

"Tommaso!" Melzi shrieked. "You bastard."

Lady Marguerite shot back one of my tonics that was sitting on the table. The Amyntas rushed into the workshop. They stood in the nun's habits they had been wearing as cover.

With that, I pushed back the black veil I had donned in preparation for entering the temple and gulped down my tonic. I wiped my face with the sleeve of a simple, obsidian silk gown.

Lady Marguerite paced, agitated with indecision. "Will you not hunt him down? Does he not deserve to die for this?"

"Tommaso's death is worthless to us now." I blazed with fury, yet stopped short of declaring a Sibylline war against the men amassing in the streets below. "Every moment must be spent preserving our own."

"How long until you can enter the temple?" Lady Marguerite asked.

"The Sibylline are already in the procession," the Amyntas said. "The Abbess is expected by dawn."

"Then, we shall finish La Joconde at the temple." Melzi snatched his great coat from a hook.

Lady Marguerite stopped him. "You shall stay right here, entirely removed from the game. We cannot risk Tommaso learning of the arrangements we have made."

"How will the Sibylline protect themselves if we remain holed up in the workshop?" My skin burned.

The Amyntas glared at Lady Marguerite. They cinched weapon belts around their waists, covering the blades with black tunics. I plotted shooting out into the hallway and launching myself upon the treasury to fight. Maurine stepped into the workshop. Her face was gaunt and gray.

"Are you not supposed to be at Fontevraud?" I panicked at the sight of her.

"Lady Marguerite," she bowed a bit too formal in her approach, and then turned to the Amyntas. "I beg you to come with me."

The Amyntas stiffened. Lady Marguerite blanched. "Remain here until everything is in place for the ceremonies. Promise me."

I nodded, without recourse. Maurine, Lady Marguerite, and the Amyntas rushed out of the room through the servant's entrance. I questioned my instincts, the ability to read a situation. Tommaso had stood less than a leg's length from me. Did he know I lied? Did he resent the Sibylline so deeply he would send men to recapture La Joconde with orders to kill if necessary? At that moment, the loss of Master DaVinci overwhelmed me. I watched Melzi continue thinning the layer of varnish, manipulating the colors. I watched how the light fell upon the woman in the painting. I might not survive this. She, however, had to. Even if the Sibylline had to wait, they had to know of her.

"We cannot stay here," I told him.

"I know. Such idleness is suicide."

We did not have to debate where to take her. Melzi packed up the tools he needed and removed La Joconde from her perch. We walked out the front door of Clos Lucé, across the gardens and straight to the smithy's shack at Gaillard, all without coming across another soul.

The hot breeze of the forge would set the varnish faster. We would be safe there.

I had not thought through what happened next. We should not have risked it. Yet, there I stood, a woman shattered by grief, bound by duty, and with my love for just one more moment. Melzi stepped across the threshold of the small shack near the edge of the Amasse River and pushed away the sheer black veil from my forehead.

By the light of the low-burning forge, we stared at what sat upon the easel.

"How long Master da Vinci waited to complete this precious work," Melzi said.

"Then, let us finish it for him."

"You know the key."

I nodded, took up a position to the right of his palette and paints, and we began. The painting was too wet. The wait stirred our senses. The sweet pauses, lips upon breasts, Melzi entering me, the pulse of merging and parting. I laid my hands upon him and let the memory of all that we had been flood my mind. The rush penetrated the depths of all that remained. As I caught my breath, we continued. Inside my mind, the landscapes of Rome, Amboise, the Royal River revealed the path of our life together. Melzi took me. I called out, lingering upon him. As the moon rose high above Gaillard, we lay skin-to-skin.

"I want this forever," I whispered.

Melzi heaved and pushed me away. I knew he was right to, yet the finality of it stung.

"I shall go find us some repast," I said.

"Should we not finish her first?"

I opened the door and waved a hand toward the orangery just past the fountain where we had found Master da Vinci. "First, oranges. Then, the key."

"You thief." He laughed at me. I stepped outside the smithy's shack, wrapping the folds of my gown around me in the cool of the dawn. Melzi reached out and ran a stained thumb across my cheek. I pushed away and tiptoed across the garden of Gaillard.

I turned around to see him waving at me from the smithy shack doorway. Melzi stood in his white under-tunic, his hose at his ankles. I could not help but laugh; he looked like a drunk after waking up in an alley. My spirit hummed from the renewal of our bond. There he was, my Dear Melzi. Our night together would last me for one hundred lifetimes.

I glided up the stairs of the orangery. I watched as his hair caught the last light of the moon. He shimmered, almost iridescent against the night. I snatched a pair of oranges and stuffed them in my pocket, then turned back to show off my prizes.

In that instance, Melzi was yanked into the darkness. Five men wearing the colors of the Spanish King Charles charged up the banks of the river, forcing him into the smithy shack. Silence fell as if Melzi had never existed.

I held back a scream, gripping my hands over my mouth. I latched the door to the orangery and twisted around.

In one night, I had lost Master da Vinci and Melzi.

Had I lost La Joconde too?

Chapter 51

MARIE

MAY 7, 1945
THE CATACOMBS
FONTEVRAUD PRISON, FRANCE

Anxiety gripped Marie as she finished reading the letter from Aesmeh for the third time. Her breath grew labored. She stammered and considered the evidence that had been set out before her in the subterranean room filled with cabinets, books, and files where Iné had taken her. Melzi's journals, the markings on the photos in the SOE file, now an actual original letter from Melzi's Asfoora—Aesmeh de la Rose—led to Serah. Very little could be done to deny it. Yet, she also knew that Philip would stop at nothing to capture her.

"You must read the key." Rafidah gathered the original letter and locked it away in an ancient cabinet carved into the stone and concealed with carved wood covers. Dozens of other documents and manuscripts were carefully fitted into the openings.

"All I want is Serah."

"Serah has brought you here to read the key," Rafidah said. "The Great Mother has seen fit to bring both of you to us."

"What if I refuse?"

"We acknowledge all that you have been through," Iné said. "But, those men out there are either going to kill Serah or imprison her for this. She is your daughter."

"And what will you do to her?" Marie asked. "The Sibyl has driven men mad in search of her power for thousands of years. What guarantees will you make me that you won't kill us both once you have what you came for?"

"It's time." Rafidah collected the maps and packed them carefully in a leather messenger bag. "You have a duty."

Marie's fury exploded. "I have a duty to sacrifice my child?"

"Her death is not our plan."

"Everyone who touches this is dead," Marie's voice cracked as Noam and Yara returned. "Maybe the Sibylline need to stay dead."

The group stood, aghast, in silence.

Marie glared at the women. "It's too much."

"No, you need to open your eyes," Rafidah told her.

"I don't want to see it."

"It's too late for that."

"Is anybody not using me at this point?"

"Enough!" Iné pulled back her veils. Marie gasped at the sight of the face of an ancient being, translucent and pure. "Too many lifetimes of loss and grief have passed for this to continue."

Marie softened. "What are you?"

"A guardian," Iné nodded and took the cylinder from around her neck. "It's the Seal of Amərətāt, one of the nine Seals of Annach that give power to the Sibyl. When a Sibyl is gone, the Ba'alat protect them, keep them safe until . . ."

"For God's sake." Marie's grief nearly choked her. "You're telling me you've been under orders to protect all of this for five hundred years?"

"By order of the Sibyl of Amboise herself."

For the moment, Marie suspended her disbelief. "No one else knew?"

"Others knew. No one made it out."

Marie broke, the tears welling in her eyes.

"You were the one that survived." Noam looked at Iné. He slid back his headdress and pulled his fingers hard and slow through his hair. Marie stepped up next to him and took his hand.

"That was my duty," Iné said. "I promised Aesmeh the night she died."

"How long were you in the temple?"

"A long time."

"So, what?" Marie asked. "The Maquis found you?"

"Serah did. She found the tunnels."

Marie's eyes grew wide. "You thought I knew?"

"A misunderstanding," Iné said. "I am a refugee of the most horrific moment in the history of my people, Dr. Guerrant. So are you. I'd hoped you would see me as kin."

"And now?"

"You are here, and I fear you are only modestly convinced."

Yara interrupted everyone. "We found a way in. Come."

She led Marie, Noam, Iné, and Rafidah as they rushed, single-file into the dark, narrow corridor. The walls seemed to close in more and more as the five moved even deeper into the stone caverns.

"Is that water?" Marie whispered about the constant rush above them.

"We're below the aqueduct that feeds the Loire. Hurry," Yara told her.

The hallway grew warm and dry; a breeze from the outside wafted in. They climbed over what looked like boulders of tufa stone that had been rolled aside. Then they entered into a short hall. Along each wall, the tombs of dozens of women were meticulously carved out.

"The big torch, please," Iné said. "Good work. Now, out."

Marie shuddered. Carvings on the wall and the floor all included the strong middle line and the two crescent moons of Iné's tattoo. She could see a crypt full of sarcophagi through the remains of a door in front of them. The world of 1945 seemed to have vanished.

Marie walked up to the first of the ornate tombs that formed a circle around the perimeter of the room. She read off the name of the inhabitant of the sarcophagus. "Audeburge of Hautes-Bruyères. She founded the abbey near Stonehenge in the twelfth century."

"By that point, women had grown to control the entirety of England, France, even Spain. While men fought and fucked, the women quietly went about the governance of their world." Iné said.

"Mademoiselle Soudier," Marie said. "Who knew you had such a foul mouth?"

They laughed softly.

"We had long served to position the Sibylline to renew their vow. Every vision, everything, has a ripple. We cannot control chaos, but we were there to stop its waves from overtaking humanity. Each of us was a thread through it all."

"And you?"

"My ancestors held Fontevraud after Madinat al-Zahar fell."

"Spain?"

"Hardly Spain, but, yes. The Protectorate forged east, founding Fontevraud to train and protect the Sibylline as we rebuilt."

"It was never an abbey?"

"Of course it was. Every place has an outer life and an inner life. The sœurs prayed and learned some of the skills of the Sibylline such as speaking with their minds, communing with the dead, and governance. The Protectorate trained and took their vows at Fontevraud." Iné paused to gaze into the sunlight that peeked through slits in the stone above them.

"How long were you here?"

"I learned the sword by the fountain at the upper gardens, gardens that were filled with lavender and mint, red amaranth, and helianthus." Iné seemed caught in her visions of the past. "We'd sneak up and walk along the high walls above the raspberry hedge to earn a single glimpse of the Abbess and her women."

"Brittany, Flanders, Burgundy, Blois." Marie read off the French towns on the grave markers. "These women came from all across the kingdom."

"Each Abbess was initiated into mysteries far older than any religion. The original Sibylline."

"So, a pack of powerful women with some powerful friends gets nuns to commit mutiny and then gets wiped off the face of the Earth for it?"

"You're never going to ease up on me, are you?"

"It's ridiculous." Marie let out a conciliatory snort. "But, I can no longer figure out how to deny you my loyalty."

"I'll take what I can." Iné paused in front of a tomb. The engraving read: *Tommaso d'Arced. May 2, 1519.* She ran her fingers over the name etched on the tomb.

"Who is he?"

"There were many attempts at harnessing the Sibylline power. The Cosmati built floors that harnessed ancient geometry. Gutenberg tried to dilute our knowledge by replicating it. An attempt less than one hundred years ago to use the power of the Great Mother herself against us to control our words. Prayer books, reliquaries, ossuaries. They tried everything, even putting our bones on the altar."

"Ah, a plague of the mind."

"A plague of the mind." Iné tapped the letters with her finger. She pressed another rolled parchment onto the table. It was sealed with red wax and bore the mark of the Sibylline:

May 2, 1519

My Dear Maurine,

I fear this may be the final time I press my quill to paper and etch your name. I have learned, as I'm sure you have as well, that Fontevraud has fallen silent. The Abbess, like Master da Vinci, is dead.

Without her protection, we are exposed to all that Tommaso's deceit perpetrates against us. I see now that my place should have been at the front of the Sibylline, blocking those blades, in defense of all we are.

I am going to fight as a warrior. The Sibylline already await. I hear their sparrow-hawk calls in the night. They remind me of my duty.

I did not choose this moment. However, I refuse to forsake our people.

Both of us now are bound by duty, not by our hearts, Dear Maurine. You once asked how you might serve our friendship and our Sibylline until the end of time. That day stands before us, and I require your service, forever my champion.

Death will come for many. However, that must not be the end of the Sibylline. Instead, it must become a call to renew our vows and reaffirm our duty to humanity.

Do not mourn me. Promise me not to let yourself succumb to corruption. The world of men is ruthless. This is the division they want. Instead, we must move into action as one.

Fight for us.

When one man begins the work, others will follow.

Train those who come after us as warriors.

Train those who come after us as healers.

Train those who come after us as seekers of knowledge.

Train those who come after us in the truth of their hearts.

Train those who come after us to see beyond the veil laid over the world in attempts to enslave us.

And, when the time comes, train them to rise from the ashes of all that burns in the coming days.

Let the world find itself captivated by a single focus. Keep our Dear One safe. Let her be the one that preserves us until we can rise again.

Me-kädmen anina il'ati,

A

Marie looked up from Aesmeh's final letter to Iné and stared at her as they stood at the table in the crypt below the kitchens. They both cried.

"You are Maurine?"

Iné nodded. "It was I who brought Aesmeh's killer to her doorstep."

"Tommaso? You loved him?"

"Beyond words," she continued. "His father insisted that Master da Vinci make something out of him. That's how Tommaso ended up in France with us. He adored Melzi, as I did Aesmeh. We committed ourselves to them, and each other."

"What made him turn?"

"Me. We thought we could run away together. When I told him I could not violate my Sibylline vows, he betrayed us."

"How do you win against that?"

"We didn't." Inè waved her hand to show the crypt walls.

Marie dusted herself off and read through the inscriptions. "There are dozens and dozens here, all with the same date"

"Yes, May 2, 1519."

"All because of Tommaso?"

"We didn't know until he'd nearly succeeded."

"How bad was it?" Marie read over the inscriptions on the tombs, again.

As she worked her way through, she noticed two places where it looked like handles had been carved out on either side of Aesmeh's crypt. "La Joconde. Sibyl. Mother. House?" Her eyes cleared. Her mind settled. "This is it."

"I don't understand," Iné said.

"The codes. It was Serah. She got me the pictures, the message in Paris. She wanted me to find her. That's the only explanation for them. Serah must have gotten the photos to me. If I was Serah and I knew about all of this, I would stash La Joconde with Aesmeh. She was the last Sibyl, right?"

"Yes."

Marie pointed out the finger hold at the ends of a long stone slab slightly out of alignment. She jimmied one side out of position, then the other, and yanked hard. The slab came off right away. She almost toppled over from its weight. She got back to her feet and peered inside. There was a crate slid into the spot behind the removed stone. Marie paused, unwilling to open the crate. For the first time, she wished she wasn't the one to find La Joconde. "You keep calling her the Sibyl. Did Aesmeh ever rise as the Great Mother?"

"Not while she lived. I was ordered into the temple at Amboise and remained inside with the Seal of Amərətāt. Ba'alat across the world did the same."

Marie looked around for something with which to wedge the crate open. "Tommaso really caused all of this? How could such powerful women be destroyed?"

"He took advantage of a situation more serious than a broken heart."

Marie had no idea what Iné meant.

"We were leaderless and had been for nearly two thousand years.

Sibyls are rare, born only twice a millennia. Each one can live for a thousand years. It used to work well. One would rise, another would be born in the middle of their service to the world and would train with the Great Mother until she was ready to rise."

"What happened?" Marie found herself overwhelmed with Iné's telling of the history as she slid the painting out from the thin slot.

"We call it The Schism. More than fifteen hundred years ago, men plotted against and murdered the Sibyl of Alexandria with no heir. None had ever died in such a manner, and only twenty years into her reign. It broke the Sibylline. Two women who had trained at Hypatia's side attempted to lead us. But, we had no knowledge of the Sibyl to come, no way to find her. A group of us served Shushandukht. The Amyntas went east to train with a Sibylline named Damarah. We retreated underground and rebuilt the Orders."

Marie tried to remember the ones she'd learned of. "Let's see, Heliade are healers. Harimtu are spies. Ba'alat are seal guardians. Amyntas are warriors. Metradora are . . ."

"No," Iné grew serious. "The Metradora were never with us. The Amyntas, well, we don't speak of their kind any more."

As Marie removed the cover, she saw familiar eyes in La Joconde, the ringlets of obsidian hair, the thin smile. She hesitated. "All this time. I honestly can't believe it."

"Why is it so hard?"

"Do you know what Diebitsch did to women at Ravensbrück?" Marie showed Iné the scars on her back, her left thigh cut open and badly healed. "The Nazis were crazed for blood. Every day, they drained the veins of hundreds of women until the women were at the edge of death. I swore I'd destroy it all."

"To protect every woman on Earth," Iné said.

Marie lifted the painting. Her heart surged. "Now, if I destroy the Sibyl . . ."

"You destroy your daughter," Iné interrupted.

The two of them locked their focus on La Joconde. The world stilled. They waited as if to see if it would speak.

"The key, it's in the eyes," Iné said.

Marie pulled out magnifying glasses and tools from a pack Rafidah had given her earlier. She settled in to examine the painting she knew so well. The faint details set themselves apart from the rest of the eye only by their lighter shade of gray. Five hundred years hanging on the walls in king's castles had made the patina dull and muddled.

"What do you see?"

"You hovering over me, breaking my concentration," Marie said.

She checked the known elements to ensure it wasn't a forgery. No signature. That was fortunate. Few knew that da Vinci never signed the piece. La Joconde's eyebrows had not been touched up. Another clear sign. However, Marie had one sure way to know if the piece was the one she'd packed up and sent to Chenonceau in 1938. She flipped it over. There was the hint of a green triangle she'd drawn herself on the back of the poplar board it was painted on. It was her.

Marie worked the magnifying glass around the painted eyes. Each shift in the light and magnification and La Joconde seemed to gaze in a new direction. She spent more than an hour examining every millimeter of the eyes.

"There's nothing." She heaved a sigh and conceded. "If there was a key, it has been painted over or is too blurred to recover."

"That's not possible."

"That's it." Marie half wanted more and half loved that her belief that the modern Sibyl was a myth was right. "What can I tell you?"

Iné's voice went quiet, "They would never have left it to chance like that."

Marie clenched her fists. "I'm so tired of all of this."

"Not too exhausted, I hope." A familiar throaty baritone barked his inquiry from the corridor leading from the kitchens.

Philip Millar shoved someone through the door of the crypt. Marie leaped back and stared. For a moment, she couldn't figure out who it was. Shaved head. Thin build. Prison clothes. Then, their eyes connected.

"Serah!"

Chapter 52

AESMEH

MAY 2, 1519
AMBOISE, FRANCE

I shot myself across the lawn of Château Gaillard, blinded by what I had just witnessed: the abduction of Melzi. Upon reaching the smithy's hut, I pressed myself flat against the cool stone and crept around to the open door. A hint of morning hovered on the horizon. I stole inside, retrieving the knife Maurine had given me earlier, and which I had left along with most of my clothes near the entrance. There she was, La Joconde, under the arm of a wiry soldier dressed in the colors of the Spanish King.

He stared right through me, as if I should not exist, and thought nothing of walking right past me with the painting under his arm. My fury mounted as the glimmer from the knife set my mind ablaze. Maurine's pain, her abject loss at the betrayal of Tommaso, surged up in me. I shot my blade out and up. The soldier collapsed.

I carefully covered La Joconde with one of my black veils and ran.

I stumbled back to Clos Lucé. I locked La Joconde in the workshop, and myself in Melzi's room. In my bloodied underdress, I perched at the edge of the bed, the fire of a warrior who'd taken life in service to the Sibylline coursing through me. I wept thoroughly and gathered myself. Less than an hour had passed. The ease with which I murdered a man thrilled and horrified me. For the first time, I understood why the Abbess kept the Amyntas from us. I cursed myself for not having fought like this the entire time, without hesitancy or remorse. I moved to Melzi's desk, penned what I knew would be my final letter to Maurine, and prepared for battle.

Suddenly, a pair of Amyntas burst into the room. "The Abbess has been killed," one reported.

"When?" I could not comprehend the speed at which our lives unraveled.

"Just moments ago. We were ambushed on the way here." The Amyntas were bloodied, their armor torn.

"Men killed Amyntas?" I questioned. Our warriors had never been bested before. "Where are the Ba'alat? The Seals?"

"The Abbess had already sent them away." The Amyntas stood at attention. "All of the Seals of Annach other than that which hangs around your neck are in hiding. We must get you to the temple, Great Mother."

Still half-dressed in nothing more than a bodice and shift, I knew I could not leave behind what I had killed a man to save. "I need a moment."

The Amyntas retreated with haste.

I raced across the room toward the workshop and fished out La Joconde from a corner. I would have to attempt to place the key into her myself. I tried to recall the techniques the men repeated day after day for so many years. Yet, my mind turned up blank. We faced one another, both unfinished, both fugitives. I stepped back and turned to set up an easel. Then, I felt a knife pressed at my neck.

"You might as well do it," I said. "Go on. One fast, deep cut, and I will drop on the floor and drown in my blood. I beg of you."

"I would much rather be sipping wine and eating pheasant with you,

Great Mother, in a king's service thanks to me. However, you cannot be left unmanaged."

"You find me so threatening, Tommaso?"

He spun me around and we saw one another for the first time. He unraveled a rope. "I find you problematic, tedious."

"I believe I am not the only woman whom you find so troublesome." I looked up at La Joconde on the easel.

"Have you known all along, then?"

"You had many fooled for a short while."

"Not anymore, though."

"Not since you killed Master da Vinci and the Abbess."

He removed the knife from my neck and shoved me toward a chair. "I would never do such a thing."

"No, but you would put other men to the task for your gain."

Tommaso forced me to sit and cut the strings of my bodice with his knife. He ran the blade across my chest just hard enough to draw a bead of blood. "Out whoring around last night?"

"What would you know of love?"

"Very little, it seems." He traced my thigh with the blade.

"At least run me through like you pretend to have any honor at all."

"Put some clothes on." Tommaso tossed one of Master da Vinci's painting smocks at me. "I would not desire many believing I violated you before . . ."

"You are playing a fool's game with forces you shall never control." I slid into the white smock stained with ochre and violet, buttoning the collar.

"I would have to if Master da Vinci had not served my soul to the devil."

"You brought this upon yourself, dear friend." Tommaso tied my arms and legs with the rope. "All of these years, thinking me nothing more than an errand boy, nothing more than a glorified slave."

"I am here to offer you mercy, Tommaso." I remained bound, but hopeful that I could turn him. "The men you move around your board like chess pieces will not be so generous."

"That I might fall prey to the wiles of such a woman. Those men rely on me to rid them of you."

"Men indeed!" A shout came from the doorway. There, Maurine stood, hooded in black, blade in hand. "Tommaso, this is not you."

"Oh, but it is." He kicked my knees, forcing me to drop to the ground. "You should know. You created this."

"Is that what I did?" Maurine asked. "With my arms around you, my heart filled with you, my devotion to you?"

"Do not lie, whore."

Maurine's expression remained steady as she stepped closer and closer to him. Tommaso gripped the blade, his knuckles turning white.

"All I ever wanted was you," she said, one hand up, the other reaching for me.

"That's why you abandoned me?" Tommaso turned away.

With two moves, she had my hands unbound.

"I left because I loved you too much, and you loved me too little," Maurine said.

Tommaso flipped back around, his face flushed red. "We could have disappeared."

WOMAN ON THE WALL

"Enough! The painting, now." He grabbed me by the back of the neck and forced me toward La Joconde. I tripped over my own feet and slammed my head into the stone floor

Maurine flinched at the blood trickling from my forehead. She snatched a flickering taper from one of the candelabras. "Let us finish this."

I got to my knees as she moved toward La Joconde.

"So, you are with me?" Tommaso asked Maurine.

"Not even for a moment," she replied.

"We trusted you with everything." I stood. How I understood Tommaso's ache, the rage of ending up on my back at the mercy of my own heart. I also hated him for turning it against us.

His ferocity turned bitter. "I was nothing more than a useless appendage."

"The Sibylline are not meant for men to love, you fool." Maurine set the candle down.

"Yet, you lure us all the same."

Tommaso lowered his dagger and charged at me. I saw Maurine's eyes widen. Her hand shot to her weapons belt and up. Terror. Three quick jabs. A swipe. The pain seared. In an instant, I was on the cool floor of the workshop. Tommaso was splayed out across from me, his neck slashed.

Chapter 53

MARIE

MAY 7, 1945
FONTEVRAUD PRISON, FRANCE

The women scrambled as a pair of soldiers filed into the crypt flanking the group. Marie leaped up to pull her daughter close. She ran a hand over Serah's scalp. Her deep-set eyes, that soft smile, and stunning nose. It was eerie how she'd grown, transformed.

"Are you all right?"

Serah interrupted. "Mother. Oh, my God. You got my message."

"You could have been a little less cryptic."

"This is quite the reunion." Philip strolled over to La Joconde, which was propped against Aesmeh's tomb. "All this fuss from you. You could have had your daughter back if you'd just done your job."

"You didn't fool anyone, Philip," Marie said.

"I didn't really need to, did I?" he continued. "So, who is it, Dr. Guerrant? Tell us, is our dear Serah the next Sibyl?"

Marie pushed her daughter behind her. "The key doesn't exist."

"You're lying."

"No, really, there's nothing here." She showed Philip with the magnifier, pointing out the obvious. "All of us were wrong. La Joconde is just another painting."

He drew his gun on Marie as the two British soldiers in combat gear set up the painting on a table.

"I know you found it." He snatched her up by the hair.

"Mother!" Serah tried to help. One of the soldiers, baby-faced but brutal, yanked her back, ripping her shirt. She skidded across the floor.

"Shut up, you little bitch," Philip said. "You better get your mother to talk, fast."

He gripped Marie's short curls with one hand, pointed a gun at her head with the other. "If not, you're both going to die here."

Marie realized Iné hadn't even tried to stop it. She shot a look at her. The woman seemed frozen, her eyes locked on Serah who sat on the floor, her shoulders bared.

"Philip, it's nothing!" Marie tried to stay still. The blood coming from her split eye stung. "A myth, just like I told you in Paris."

"Really?"

The soldier wrestled Serah, half naked, tears running down her face onto the table right next to the painting. Marie stared at the gun pressed against her daughter's temple and panicked.

In a flash, her mind seemed to reorder. Marie wanted to save Serah, but what she saw left her unable to even breathe. She turned to Iné. That must be what she saw too, Marie thought.

"Dr. Guerrant, tell me who the Sibyl is," Philip ordered.

Serah's face, the length of her nose, the chestnut of her eyes, the very shape of her lips was as if the two women were painted side-by-side in the exact likeness of one another.

"Do you see the marks?" Iné whispered.

The birthmark on Serah's left shoulder formed a perfect reverse letter S. The river in the left quadrant of the Mona Lisa formed a perfect reverse S, Marie thought.

A second marking on her right shoulder was from the forceps that pulled Serah out, at least that's what Marie had always believed.

There it was, though, just above the clavicle. One. Two. Three complete arches, with a half arch at the front. It was a bridge—no, Marie thought, the bridge above La Joconde's right clavicle in the painting.

"Shoot her," Philip said.

Iné took another breath as if to speak. Instead, she leaped toward Serah. "Me-kädmen anina il'ati!"

The soldier released Serah and turned the gun on Iné. Her chest caved. Her body collapsed. A ghostly form shot up toward the ceiling and then settled near the body that was bleeding out on the floor. Serah ran.

"Secure the girl." Philip gawked, wild-eyed, as the specter took the shape of a veiled woman.

Iné's words echoed in Marie's ears. She snapped her head to make sure Serah had gotten out of the crypt, then the ethereal figure collapsed on the ground in front of her.

"Don't let the witch touch the doctor," Philip said.

A soldier pinned Marie's arms back.

"You have no idea what this Sibyl beast is capable of," Philip said.

"She's not the Sibyl, Philip. Leave her!" Marie shouted.

Half-wrenched over, Iné pushed herself to standing and lunged at him. Philip pulled his gun. A spark lit the room. Iné convulsed and separated into two. They spasmed. Their expressions contorted. The bodies twisted. Philip fired two more shots.

Marie kneed the soldier holding her and rushed over. She dropped onto the ground.

Iné could barely speak. Her spirit seemed to stand beside her, pensive, waiting. "Your daughter. It's got to be there."

"Stop." Marie stroked Iné's hair.

"Check the river."

Marie tried to plug Iné's wounds with her hands. "Stay with me, please."

Iné tried to nod. She struggled to breathe. "The key. Check the river."

Marie wiped the blood from Iné's cheeks.

The soldiers hauled her up from the ground. Another rushed Serah at gunpoint through the crypt door. Shouts of prisoners to machine gun fire broke out. Then, Silence. Suddenly, orders in German echoed.

Philip checked his gun. He stopped a soldier. "Give me your weapon. Lock Dr. Guerrant in the cell in the north corridor. Bag and burn the body. I'll deal with her once this is finally done."

Chapter 54

AESMEH

MAY 2, 1519
THE SIBYLLINE TEMPLE
AMBOISE, FRANCE

Maurine carried me over her shoulder. I knew what my wounds fore-told. The pain in my side nearly blinded me. All I could do was try to breathe as she moved me and our Dear One across the yard at Clos Lucé.

Three times I crossed the gardens that night. This time, I knew, would be the last.

"Let us hurry." Maurine bowed in front of me.

An Amyntas approached. "Me-kädmen anina il'ati. Melzi is safe."

"How?"

"The Amyntas found him in the woods."

"Is he hurt?"

"A bash on the head. Nothing more."

"That was a lot of blood back there." I tried to joke with her.

I spotted the other Amyntas who had come with me from Fontevraud. They hauled a cart up the hill from the lower gardens. As soon as they reached us, Maurine put me in it. She rolled me over to assess the wounds and flinched. I watched her. It was no time to joke. She had just killed the man she loved most in life to save me.

"He used us," Maurine spoke to me the way the Abbess had before I left Fontevraud—without a word. "He used me."

"You cannot blame yourself for this." The air caught in my throat. I coughed up blood.

"I tried to let him come to terms with our lives apart. To ignore him. I did not see what he had become, until now."

"And now that our eyes are forced open?" I passed her the sealed letter.

"We fight."

"No." I took the cylinder from my neck and handed it to her. "That is exactly what you cannot do."

Maurine's face had gone white. She picked up the bloodied clothes and put them in a bucket. She tried to stuff more cloth in the knife wound on my side. "You will not die."

"You know none of us die," I told her.

"You are the only one who can accomplish that."

"No, you are just as capable. I must beg something from you." I grabbed her forearm.

She shook me off. "I cannot enter the temple."

"If it were not me, it would have been you. Now, though, you must enter as a guardian."

"I am not a Ba'alat?" Maurine had trained as one of the women who could protect the sacred Sibylline pieces in a time of crisis but had yet to take her vows.

"You must do it, for the Sibylline. Take us to the spring. We cannot both die here tonight."

"I must get you to the temple."

"The spring, now. You must take the vows. Our future outmatches your heartache."

"I am not capable of such a task," Maurine said.

"Do you think me unable to understand your devastation? I am asking that which only you are truly capable."

Maurine watched me. Her eyes filled with loss. "Is this my penance for loving him?"

"No." I took her hand. "It is your greatest act of love."

I paused. We had reached the spring. Two Sibylline postulant girls rushed in. Maurine took a tincture from one and poured it down my throat. In an instant, the pain vanished. However, it brought the extent of my injuries into clear view.

"Lay her in the water. Heal her," Maurine ordered the Asu Priestesses who approached.

"No!" I shouted. "I am too far gone."

"Step into the spring, Sister Maurine," one of the Asu guided her.

The postulants propped me up in the wagon. I coughed blood and wheezed. Lady Marguerite appeared at the edge of the water and I nodded.

There the Sibylline gathered and sang. Elohim, Alláh-U-Abná, Gayatri. Their voices swelled up as the light of the Great Mother descended upon Maurine and infused her with the long life of the Ba'alat.

I took the seal from my neck and placed it around hers. "Me-kädmen anina il'ati."

In an instant, the clear crystal turned to black stone carved with the inscription of the goddess. The Seal of Amərətāt would be safe until the Sibyl came again. Once the ceremony proved complete, I ordered the Amyntas up the hill. "Take me to Melzi."

Maurine raced behind me, but I would not let them stop.

"I am at the end, dear friend," I spoke to her with my mind. "I can smell the fires burning on the hill above Château Amboise. We have to get the key into the painting. Then, you into the temple or the Sibylline are lost."

The cart stopped as shouts pierced the dawn. We were struck motionless as the rainclouds drained the midday sun from the sky. The ramparts of the royal residence filled with soldiers. Charles' troops had crossed the Amasse and begun their attack.

Maurine gripped down on my arm. "Allez. Allez. Allez."

The Amyntas ran, hauling the cart behind them so quickly that I doubted they would recover their strength once we reached the inner courtyard of Gaillard.

Howls echoed—I knew the cries too well. Men attacked the Sibylline procession. Women died in the streets trying to get to me.

As the gates of Gaillard opened, Sibylline women flooded inside.

"The Great Mother is in the cart. Take her to the temple." Maurine ordered anyone who would listen.

There, in the fetid, storm-laden light stood Melzi. He took my head in his hands and kissed my forehead.

Lady Marguerite arrived and confirmed to Maurine the attack had begun. The trio moved me with hasty silence through the corridors. We were lost in all that remained undone. As they pressed open the front gates and maneuvered out onto the path above Gaillard, fire lit up the streets. My vision became reality.

Melzi, Maurine, and Lady Marguerite pressed tight against the tall stone walls along the route to the temple. The fires that stank of blood and bones turned the streets into funeral pyres. I sat up. We watched, helpless, as bodies sheathed in the robes of the Sibylline were thrown from Tour Hertault. Each hit the road below. The horror and depravity of men bent on murdering the Sibylline ripped my very soul from me. Children screamed for their mothers and wept on the road. Their fathers and brothers locked the doors. Soldiers ripped at throats with their blades; no woman was spared.

Maurine heaved in sorrow. Tears poured down her face. "I have to fight."

"We have lost today." Life started to leave me. "We cannot lose tomorrow."

Melzi's knees buckled. He clutched the painting against his chest. Blue-robed Amyntas swooped out from the darkness. They snatched us up and pushed us through a small hatch in the tufa rock.

There, inside the temple, the Sibylline who remained stood firm. They encircled us, these queens, wives, maidens, whose devotion allowed the Sibylline to maintain for eighty generations. It left me in awe.

Maurine laid me on the stone table in the middle of the circular room. In my last moment in this world, I could not fail them again.

The past years with their secrecy and solitude drained from me.

I had lived so long as the one whom tens of thousands sacrificed to birth forth. At that moment, I tried to consider how I could have seen my fate and stopped it. It was the curse of the Sibyl—I could see the future, but not change it.

"Immortalize her." Lady Marguerite pushed Melzi's shoulders square in front of the canvas. "She must draw the attention of all who lay eyes upon her."

"Chet, Resh, Samech," I whispered.

"Serach," Melzi translated. "The wise woman. How beautiful."

He painted the Hebrew letters I spoke into the bend of the river in the left quadrant: סרח

With turpentine and oils, he completed his purpose. As my dearest Melzi raised the soft bristles, I knew each stroke brought me closer to life after death. The key had been inserted.

La Joconde, we named her—caller of the sparrowhawks, keeper of the key, the Sibyl the world would not know for five hundred years. She carried with her secrets that her visage alone could reveal.

Maurine lifted the painting so I could see her, complete in every way. Then, as I drifted, she left to take her place in the temple, locked behind the alabaster stone, a gatekeeper until the time came again.

Lady Marguerite swore to me that, after Amboise quieted and men moved on, she would carry the wood and canvas forth into the world and deliver this future Sibyl to the side of the men who would otherwise think the Sibylline defeated. "La Joconde will be the oracle they will never be able to burn," she declared. "Lying in state as the prophetess once again prepares to rise."

Chapter 55

PHILIP

MAY 7, 1945
FONTEVRAUD PRISON, FRANCE

Philip panted and ached. His men were getting picked off by the German snipers who'd overrun guards and taken over tower positions. He tried to regain composure as he rushed through the corridor his men had blasted through. Serah Izem was in custody. By all measures, he had shot the Sibyl, exacted the necessary retribution for the death of his sons. Yet, in the Grand Moutier of Fontevraud, his people were dying. He was on the verge of defeat. A nagging sense of dissatisfaction drove him back to Marie.

Philip stood in front of the cell where his soldiers had locked her up. Maybe this was done, but he needed proof. He stared through the tiny, barred window in the heavy metal cell door and took stock of the woman inside. Philip hoped to find Marie shaking, panicked, willing to confirm to him, finally, the identity of the Sibyl. He needed the doctor far more than he wanted to admit. However, Philip knew he'd already destroyed any trust that would make this easy.

His throat stung, voice hoarse, worn down. The flashlight beside him gave out an eerie, dim glow. He unlocked the cell and shook Marie's shoulder. "Come on. Get up. The Nazis are on top of us."

Marie tried to run out of the cell and up the stone stairs but tripped over a body.

"Watch your step. I ran out of flares." He didn't want to explain how Diebitsch survived the gassing attempt in the forest, how the Germans had easily infiltrated the prison, or how many of his own men died in the process.

"Sorry for the game," Philip said. He led Marie into the crypt. His soldiers had done most of what they'd been told to do. They'd emptied every cabinet and cubby. Iné's limp, gray body sat propped up against the north wall. He winced at the sight. The Mona Lisa was crated and nearly ready for transport, propped up against a tomb. The cover remained ajar, as he'd instructed. "Didn't mean to leave you in the cell that long."

"Quite the ruse." Marie said dully. She thought of Cloutille and the other ruse playing out, possibly without Phillip's knowledge.

"I knew what these bints were trying to do to you." He offered his hand. "You figured it out too."

"That you intended to take my daughter prisoner because of some ridiculous story told thousands of years ago?"

"They were the ones trying to imprison her. They're evil, Marie." Philip worked on her weaknesses. He knew she hated the Sibyl. He pushed. She was falling for it, her face reddening, her breathing growing heavy, the sweat beading on her forehead. He continued, pointing at Iné, "It wasn't about getting to you. It was about getting to her. You were doing just fine. I figured another few days, and you'd join the team without question. She, however, wouldn't give up."

"You knew Iné had discovered who you were." Marie said. Philip saw she had noticed the Mona Lisa.

"I knew I had discovered who she was."

"Why didn't you just kill her back in Amboise?"

"I needed proof. I meant this to be easier, or at least less of a mutiny on my part when it came to you." He used his quiet, calm voice. He was trying to get inside her head. He searched through several bags left on the table. "But, Serah. Your daughter's a traitor."

"I get that you are very, very afraid of these women," Marie said.

Philip's eyes lit up. "I hoped once you saw what the Sibylline were capable of, then you'd . . . Just tell me the key."

"I don't know it."

"Bollocks." Philip had lost his patience. He considered what additional pressure he could put on her to force the situation.

"I told you before, there was nothing in the painting."

"You're a terrible liar."

Did Marie forget he had trained as an agent, understood the art of the fake, he condescended.

"People are going to find out what you've done," she said.

Philip laughed. "You think too much. Men don't care what you've done when you offer them power."

"Like Diebitsch?"

"Such devotion from a woman who two days ago couldn't get past her own grief," he said. "I do the work no one else is willing to."

Philip grabbed her. "No more questions. I just need this to be done."

"And then what?"

"All I've ever done is try to protect you."

"I don't need protection, and you are courting your death."

He slapped her across the face. "You're no freedom fighter anymore."

"You're betting on the wrong horse, Philip," Marie said. "There are men in this world whom even you wouldn't want to spend eternity with in hell."

"You hate me so much." Philip walked away, then whipped around. "I wish you understood what we are trying to do. We limited your exposure until it was necessary."

"Exposure to what?"

"Goddamn, Marie, for a woman who stared Nazis down face-to-face in the camps, you're still so naive," Philip said. "We'd have taken care of this a long time ago if you had just . . ."

Philip slammed his hands on the table. "Stop delaying. This is a race."

"You son of a bitch." Marie tried to break away from him, but Philip snapped his hand around her bony arm, controlling himself from breaking it.

"Serah was never going to survive this without me," he said.

"Or with you either, I suppose."

He let go of her arm, unholstered his pistol, pointed it, and fired.

Marie waited for the pain, the blood. Nothing. She turned. A soldier in a gas mask crumpled to his knees in the doorway, blood blossoming on his khaki shirt.

"You shot your own man?" Marie said.

Philip stripped the soldier's mask back. He cleared the documents from the table. He stuffed them into a leather satchel and moved to the door. The smell of ersatz soap wafted up. "Damn, I didn't expect this."

"Are there more than two sides in this scenario?" Marie asked.

Philip relieved the man of his gun. It weighed heavy and cool in his hand as he took a dagger from the soldier's belt. He offered the gun to Marie.

"Why?"

"Because I need you alive."

"I'll take the knife, then."

Philip nodded and traded her, snorting at her inferior choice of weapon. Shouts from above echoed into the crypt. The commands were in German. He stiffened and shoved her back.

"Nevermind. Just. Stay put." Philip closed her inside the tomb, locking the door behind him.

Chapter 56

MARIE

MAY 7, 1945
FONTEVRAUD PRISON, FRANCE

Marie's chest pounded and sunk all at once. Philip had left her in the dark with a crypt full of dead women. She collapsed next to Iné's body, holding her, sobbing. "What the hell am I supposed to do now?"

She allowed the rage and sadness to flow through her. After everything Marie had survived, losing Serah this way stole the last of her will. Back flat upon the cool stone floor, Marie listened to the battle playing out above. The fighting in the prison took on a brutal tone. Guns shot. Men screamed. More whelped. She knew the sound of a man stabbed. A voice cried out in that final howl of death. She silently begged for Philip to return and put a bullet in her head.

Marie tried to focus on the walls. Holding the stiff hand of Iné, she steadied herself by translating the old prayers carved into the stone circling the room. She kept reading. The carvings on each tomb were in the native language, she assumed, of its occupant. Her voice echoed as if she offered last rites to herself and Iné as well as to the other women, long dead. French, Latin, Hebrew, Arabic, Farsi, Runes. They lulled her into a state. She would die in the crypt. That seemed a guarantee.

The translations quickly became a tome, a chant, a prayer to the dead until a single inscription transfixed her. The name, in Latin, once again jumped out: *Tommaso d'Arced - 1499-1519.*

"Here, with the others." Marie pressed Iné's hand against hers. She remembered all that this woman spoke of having transpired because of the love between them. Then, she recalled her last words, "Check the river."

Marie jumped to her feet and rushed to where La Joconde remained, took her, and placed her on the table. She fumbled through her pants pockets, nothing. On the floor under the table she spotted the remains of her magnifying glass. She found a shard big enough to use. The light was almost non-existent. She scrambled, searching for Iné's flashlight and found it wedged under a sarcophagus.

"The river," she whispered to herself. Yes, the marks on Serah's arms matched up oddly close to the marking on La Joconde. She'd also taken on a remarkable resemblance to the painting. Marie hesitated. Did she want to confirm what seemed evident about her daughter? She flicked the flashlight on and began again to examine the painting.

The river on the left side of the painting had always been a mystery to experts. Questions, she knew, had existed as long as the painting hung on the walls of kings. It was as if da Vinci had painted two, even three different settings behind the woman in the foreground. She meticulously searched every stroke laid down in the creation of the left quadrant background. Growing more and more tense, she came up empty with every pass, until . . .

"Chet, Resh, Samech," Marie read the Hebrew symbols out loud. She double-checked. It couldn't be. "Chet, Resh, Samech."

There it was, the Hebrew name of Serach. She was the Hebrew guardian of the collective memory, the bridge from the ancestors. Could it have been that obvious? Would they have inserted her actual name into the key? It seemed inconceivable. In modern French, one of its many translations was Serah. "The wise woman, how?"

A blast from the other side of the crypt created an opening.

"Move!" Philip ordered her before turning and fired his gun just beyond. The single shot echoed loudly.

Marie recoiled from the painting and grabbed the knife she'd set beside Iné. She scrambled toward Philip and followed him up the stairs that had fractured from the fighting. The entire space smelled like shit and blood.

Philip had tucked La Joconde under his arm, using the dead men along a stairwell as a means to get up to the surface. They launched themselves onto the gravel at the southwest end of the commune. Marie thought to run, but Philip shoved her through a small entry in the prison complex wall. Her shoes left bloodstained prints along the route. The complex was in an uproar. Philip pulled her across an open courtyard, pressing her head down to keep her focused on moving.

As they ran, Marie saw prisoners crushing themselves against the heaving doors of the refectory dorm where they were locked. Others climbed up into the choir. A man cried out for mercy. Another yelled that he'd slit the throat of anyone who came near him. A pair, upon spotting her feminine form, belted out vile intentions for what they'd do to Marie once they broke out. Prisoners pissed from the windows. Guards shot at them. Marie couldn't tell who fought who.

"Where's Serah?"

"Worry about yourself." Philip gripped her elbow.

"Please, just not her."

"Shut up and move."

Shots ricocheted, yelps followed. Marie and Philip pushed to the edge of the main cloister, the Grand-Moutier above where they had initially entered the crypt. She expected it to be filled with British soldiers and prison guards. However, the old cloister stood abandoned but for two privates and two other soldiers in gas masks.

Philip handed off the painting to the privates who disappeared down a set of stone stairs and sealed off the entrance they came through. The others were already buttoned up tight. Marie stared at the shorn head of the woman on her knees in front of them. Their eyes connected. Oh, Great Mother, she thought. She resisted looking again into her daughter's deep brown eyes. They were so familiar, but in new ways, having grown bright and more fierce. Marie fought the urge to kill every soldier in the cloister. There was one shot at getting Serah back. She had to play this just right.

"Now, we have all of them," Philip said. He took back the knife he'd given Marie and forced her toward the soldiers and to her knees beside Serah before putting on a gas mask himself.

Marie wondered, for just a second, if she'd given in to him willingly in order to spend this moment with her daughter. That was until she smelled the gas starting to fill the air. She knew she couldn't concede to emotion. Marie took stock of her assets, anything she could use against him to at least get Serah out.

Serah appeared docile, maybe even drugged, as the soldier tied Marie's arms behind her. The young woman's eyes kept jutting down and to the right. Was she having a convulsion? Marie thought. No. It was something else.

"Once more, Dr. Guerrant," Philip said, ordering one of the soldiers to aim their gun at Serah's head. "Who is the Sibyl?"

Marie worked her binds as she'd learned in training. They were loose enough that she could slip at least one hand out. She watched Serah again, trying to get a better look at where her eyes went. There was a switchblade, Marie spotted, under Serah's right leg. Her pant leg was turned up. The Cross of Lorraine was stitched into the cuff. Marie glanced at the boots of the soldiers holding them. Black boots. Trouser cuffs turned up.

"The Sibyl, or your daughter is dead." Philip said.

Serah's eyes rolled into the back of her head. Marie slammed her body into her daughter's and toppled her, grabbing the switchblade.

The soldier on the left kicked Marie out of the way, raised a gun, and fired. Marie tossed herself on top of Serah.

Philip jolted back. Marie spun around on her back to see the guard behind Serah shooting at him. The soldier yanked off the gas mask. Marie saw a flash of auburn hair. Red lipstick. Cloutille whipped out a long-blade dagger. It caught the low sun as the agent slid it to Marie.

Philip grabbed Serah. She bucked and kicked to break free. He cinched his elbow around her throat and pressed his gun against her head. "I'll kill her."

"You've never been that brave, you bastard." Marie launched herself at Philip. Elbow, neck, knees, waist, ankles, shoulders, she whispered her father's words. "That requires you to believe in something that matters."

A yelp. Metal into flesh. Philip dropped to one knee. She heard the sickening sound of blood gurgling out from the folds of his shirt as she pulled the knife from his stomach.

Marie reached over to her daughter. Serah tried out a weak smile. She was gray and shaking, covered in Philip's blood as he laid beside her in the cloister.

"I see both of us learned how to fight in the last two years," Serah said.

Marie pulled her close and looked over her shoulder. The second soldier pulled off his gas mask. There was Noam.

"Did you know that oaf was behind me?" Marie asked.

Serah nodded. "Wasn't quite sure we'd pull it off though."

"Brilliant girl," Marie held a hand to Serah's face. "My goddamn brilliant girl. You had to be out here, fighting with Noam."

Serah gave a short laugh and nodded. "Couldn't have you take all the glory."

"I see you got father's common sense."

"And my mother's brains."

Marie pulled Serah close, and they sat in the cloister holding one another.

"Sorry, we had to do it like this, you two." Cloutille kicked the weapons away from Philip's reach and nodded at Noam for assisting them in the take-down. Philip curled up on the ground, gasping for breath, shuddering in and out of consciousness. "It was the only way to draw Diebitsch and Millar out, and get La Joconde and Serah back in safe hands."

Marie looked toward her. "Agent Seydoux."

"Doctor Guerrant." They exchanged a relieved smile.

Yara came out of the old church and into the cloister. She carried the painting tucked under her arm. Marie could see the evidence it was the original—the carved frame, markings on the back. Yara saw Philip laying in a pool of blood. "Good riddance. But, now, let's get out of here."

Marie dug through Philip's pockets, searching for keys to his Jeep. She found them, along with a single bullet on a keychain and a creased photo. The two uniformed young men in it stood with their arms around each other's shoulders in the bright sun. She studied the photo. She hated him, and yet she understood what he'd lost.

"Love and devotion drive a person to their best or their worst." Yara took the bullet and picture and tucked them back into Philip's pocket. "He's with his sons now. Let's go."

"Iné is dead," Marie said as she gathered Yara, Noam, Cloutille, and Serah. They began to head for the north wall in fading light of early evening.

"She knew the risk." Yara passed her a canteen, but didn't miss another beat.

"Did you know the key was Serah?" Marie felt herself falling apart. Yara remained silent.

Marie turned back to her daughter. She wondered if she ought to not just destroy La Joconde to protect the young woman in front of her—or preserve her to do the same. Everyone was moving toward the Jeep when Marie's hearing perked up. The distinct sound of German being shouted from what sounded like inside the prison walls interrupted everyone. "What happened to Diebitsch? Can anyone confirm that he is dead?"

"Why?" Cloutille asked. Marie circled her finger in the air to get her fellow agent to listen in. From the south end of prison came the shouts of Diebitsch, the thunder of rattling bars. The sirens in the old bell towers wailed and guards charged into the cloister.

"Dammit," Cloutille said. "We've got to go."

The prison directeur burst through the doors into the cloister, heaving for breath and bleeding. "He's not far behind me." He motioned to Noam to help him chain the doors shut. "We'll hold them off best we can, but you need to get that painting and yourselves out of here. If they catch you, I will have no choice."

"We'll never get La Joconde back to Paris in one piece if we have to make a run for it." Cloutille turned to the directeur. "Can you keep the Germans out of the crypts?"

He nodded. Three soldiers came up behind him and he signaled for them to follow her orders.

"I'll stay with it," Cloutille put her hand on Marie's arm. "Get out of here. Serah has to survive. I'll make sure the painting does too."

Cloutille scooped up La Joconde and vanished beneath the prison. Noam, Yara, and Serah waited for Marie to call the next move. A gun fired from above. Yara's eyes went wide. She sank to her knees. The old woman tried to reach for Marie, but the blood rushed from the wound in her chest. Her expression went blank.

Marie spun around. There was a sniper in the bell tower. "Move!"

Bullets whizzed through the air. Marie dropped to the ground. She yanked Serah behind a bush. A German soldier rushed to Philip and heaved him over his shoulder. He shouted, "Feind extrahiert."

Enemy extracted. Marie knew the phrase. She spotted her knife in the gravel, crawled over to it. She waited until the soldier turned, then took two slashes at his calves. He dropped within an inch of them. His watering eyes stared deep into Marie's as she jabbed him in the side with her knife and pulled up.

The soldier writhed on his back. Serah grabbed his pistol and shot him twice. Philip and the dead German lay side-by-side as mother and daughter stood over them, weapons in hand.

Another shot fired from above. Marie and Serah bolted through the cloister garden. The directeur stumbled and collapsed. Serah turned, aimed, taking out the sniper.

"Christ, what a shot!" Marie shouted.

They ran. Another bullet from nearby almost hit Marie's head. They dove flat as layer upon layer of bullets rained down. Face in the dirt, Marie caught sight of the chapel and an open door nearby that led out to the woods. She pointed it out to Serah. They jumped to their feet and sprinted without stopping.

Marie led Serah toward the river, trying to remember the course she took before. The shooting began again. One. Two. The third bullet struck a tree inches from them. Marie tried to stop but was catapulted through the underbrush.

Noam pulled her down. They huddled beneath the roots of a massive oak. The gunfire let up.

"We have to get to the river," Marie said. "As long as we are in the forest, they have the advantage."

Serah reloaded her gun. Noam moved into the brush behind them as they raced along cut paths. Marie knew it was too risky.

"We have to get off the trail." She waved them into the bush. "Off the . . ."

Marie spotted the soldiers dropping from the trees. One charged Noam. The force knocked him along with Serah into a patch of blackberry briars. Serah dropped to her knees, pivoted, and fired. Noam's assailant collapsed, but others were moving in. Serah arms were caught in thorny briars. Marie scrambled across the dirt on her belly toward her.

"I have no idea how many are left." Marie shoved another loaded handgun at Serah. "Fire it at anything that doesn't look like us."

Noam was just down a gully. She could see his chest moving up and down, the blood on his shirt shoulder. He was alive, and that would have to do. Marie's eyes shot back to Serah, then just beyond. They trained on a lone soldier as he crept through the forest, his gun drawn. She seized up. It was Diebitsch. Marie couldn't make a sound. She moved around until she was just behind him, lifted the gun to fire.

He turned in the direction of Serah. Marie shouted to get his attention and skittered back behind the tree. She tried to aim again, but lost sight of him.

"Where's your daughter, doctor? I can't wait to see what she can do." Diebitsch's voice echoed from behind the other side of the tree.

Marie holstered her gun and took her knife from its sheath. She considered his position.

Diebitsch called out in a lilting, grotesquely playful voice, "Seraaaaah. Your mother needs you, Serah."

A rustling came from the underbrush. He cocked his gun. Marie shouted, "Serah, no!"

She swung around the tree and caught Diebitsch's arm as the gun fired. Elbow, neck, knees, waist, ankles, shoulders, she thought of her father's words. She stabbed Diebitsch in his right side with the blade and yanked up until he started to gurgle. He grabbed her around the throat and pressed her hard against the tree. His hand tightened until there was no air. Marie searched the forest for Serah, her eyes frantic.

A single gunshot echoed in Marie's ears. Diebitsch slumped, his hand dropping away from her neck. She gasped and choked, sucking in air until she could breathe normally again.

"Mother." Marie heard a voice, weak and cracking. Serah stood, propped against a tree just feet from where Diebitsch laid dead. She was shot, her shirt and pants shredded from tearing out of the brambles. She had a gun in her hands. "Is he dead?"

Marie nodded.

"Noam, he's in the ditch."

"You're my concern." Marie hoisted Serah up and grabbed her under the armpits. She tried to keep her daughter conscious, repeating the alphabet in Attic Greek out loud to keep their minds focused. Blood ran everywhere.

It began to rain. Serah stumbled, legs failing as Marie moved her, slow and deliberate. The rain fell in hard sheets. They made it through the trees until the river came into view. Marie eased Serah down onto the sandy bank of the river and propped her up against a downed log. Her breath grew shallow.

"I won't let you die." Marie shook. "But, you're right. I have to get Noam too."

She ran back into the forest, searching, when a man came into view. Marie had nothing, no weapons to defend herself. Yes, going back for Noam was the right thing to do, she told herself. However, Marie had no plan. She should have never left Serah at the river, she thought.

"Got any boulou on you?" the man spoke.

"Oh hell." Marie exhaled hard and ran to Noam. His arm was limp at his side, his right eye split open. She steadied him, propping him up with her shoulder. They made it to the riverbank. Serah was almost unconscious at the edge of the water in the growing darkness.

Marie eased her arms beneath her daughter and waded into the river. She felt Serah's consciousness slipping even further. The freezing water stung. "Serah, just let the water hold you up."

"Marie, what are you doing?" Noam shouted. "We have to get out of here."

"I can't," Marie told him. "I am a part of all of this. My daughter is a part of this. We are . . . Sibylline."

She tried to recall the rituals and chants that saved her and Noam a night earlier in the haze of mustard gas. That's when Marie heard the voice that had called out to her at Amboise, the same one that sang on the banks of the Loire and in the forest behind the castle. Marie's chest grew still as her breathing slowed. Her skin felt like it was someone else's. She began to sink with exhaustion. She tried to release everything she'd endured. It was no longer about winning. It was about saving her daughter, and the Sibyl, from dying.

In a vision, Marie stood back from herself, watching her body alongside Serah's floating in the middle of the Vienne River where it flowed into the Loire. A trio of women in silken, midnight-blue robes rushed into the water. She watched as the Heliade pulled the light from the sky into her body once again. Serah's as well. Then, the hood of one of the women's capes fell back.

"Me-kädmen anina il'ati!" Marie could only use her mind, but all of the women looked up and toward her in the vision on the shore. They nodded and returned to their work, harnessing the light in silence as the storm turned into a steady rain. Their constant chant, a single tone, filled the air. She knew then what the words meant—in service to the Great Mother.

The river steamed and cleared, a blue-green glow ebbing. Marie's vision ceased. She'd returned to her body in the river. With each pulse, she grew stronger. Finally, Marie sat upright. The Heliade walked with her and Serah from the water, then they were gone.

On the shore, Serah and her wrapped themselves in a blanket. Women treated Noam's wounds. Marie stretched the stiffness out of her shoulders and back. She placed a hand on her daughter's shoulder. If she had been shot, there was no evidence of it. Feeling returned to her limbs. She fell into the embrace of those arms. Marie held Serah tight as they sobbed. It was an intimacy she'd never experienced, baffling and connective, which latched itself onto her spirit.

Marie watched her daughter who seemed to light up the night. "What are you capable of?"

"I'm only just starting to learn." Serah's voice echoed without her saying a word.

"Do you have the sight?"

Serah held out her hands and jolted as Marie held them. A deep pain overwhelmed Serah's face and she broke down.

"You saw it all," Marie said, "from Ravensbrück? Didn't you?"

Serah trembled and held her mother's face in her hands before pressing their foreheads together.

"I'm sorry, Mother," she said.

"For what?" Marie thought Serah only a hero.

"That I couldn't relieve you of the responsibility of discovering my fate. Your courage . . ."

She realized Serah had already accepted what Marie had wanted so profoundly to reject for so long. Her daughter was not a victim at all, but a warrior, a Ba'alat, even a Sibyl.

"I did nothing more than uncover the truth," Marie said. "It is you who are so very brave."

Chapter 57

MARIE

MAY 8, 1945
FONTEVRAUD-L'ABBAYE, FRANCE

Marie spent the morning that followed moving in and out of awareness of who her daughter might be. Belief was slow to come, but it had come. The Sibylline had saved them both.

There was much that required handling. Cloutille was dead. They'd found her in the crypt next to two German soldiers who'd been shot in the head, the painting secure as planned. She'd been stabbed. Marie knew what had happened. Cloutille stayed with the asset, completed her mission. She would have done the same.

The mission, she thought. Marie was finally done with her own personal quest. Yet, nothing felt finished. She stood in the modest bedroom of a safe house in the village well outside the prison walls. A light breeze blew through the open window, ruffling the white linen curtain. Marie wanted nothing more than to just vanish with Serah, the two of them never to be seen again. However, she knew that Serah and her would have to return to Fontevraud if they were to reconstruct the world of the Sibylline. That was only proper. Serah needed to know who she was. Iné deserved to know she'd restored her honor.

Serah slept in the single bed across from hers. Marie shot looks at her, trying to get her to wake up. She watched the air move in and out of her lungs. After scribbling a few notes, Marie laid her head sideways on the desk at the window. The young woman's strong shoulders poked out from beneath the yellowing cotton sheets. Outside, the small commune of Fontevraud-l'Abbaye bustled with life as villagers shopped for vegetables at the open market and children played ball on the street. How could Serah sleep? Marie found herself jealous of that kind of peace.

"Mother, stop staring at me," Serah said without even opening her eyes or lifting her head from the pillow. "I need you not to treat me differently. I'm not quite ready for this whole Sibyl thing yet."

"Neither am I." Marie found herself relieved that Serah was hesitant to accept what the painting had revealed. "Is that why you took off with La Joconde?"

"I left because, if I didn't, I thought everyone else would die," Serah said. "And, they all still died."

"I don't think either of us could change what happened."

"At least it gave me time to find you."

Marie could not stop analyzing all that let them survive, once again. "Your gift, it's sort of amazing, isn't it?"

"It makes sense of a lot of things."

"What do you mean?"

"In the war, I had a sixth sense about where people were, what was going to happen. The Maquis, they started to rely on me," Serah said. "For a while, I thought it made me tough. I killed a lot of people, Mother."

"You can't blame yourself for what happens in war." Marie put her arms around Serah.

"Like you?"

Serah's words hit her like an accusation and Marie wondered if she had seen her regrets, her wanting to give up and die in the camps. Marie had watched so many women slaughtered at Ravensbrück. She had done what was needed to survive, to get back to Serah. Reconciling with that with herself, much less with her daughter, would be a Herculean task.

"I'm exhausted." Marie didn't want to talk anymore and knew she would pay for her restlessness when Noam returned from making arrangements with the prison directeur to help with the final recovery and transport of La Joconde. They had to get moving again. She stretched out on her bed. The pillow was cool, calming. Maybe she could rest for a few hours if only she could just shake the visions of what had transpired. Yet, they haunted her.

Serah crawled back into her bed and fell asleep. Marie tried but gave up on rest. She needed to move. Taking the knife Noam had left on her side table, she stepped out into the cool of the morning and down past the village church. There was no need to sneak onto the grounds of the prison this time. The guard at the main gate stopped her and pointed her in another direction.

"Monsieur Marchant is over at the kitchens." The guard said. "You know the way?"

She nodded. Never would Marie get used to being free to come and go. She breathed deep to calm herself and moved quickly. The prison grounds had once again settled into a disciplined state. Inmates worked in silence. The only sounds were the machines and the voices of the prison guards shouting announcements and orders.

Noam met her at the top of the stairs in the kitchens. La Joconde had been placed in a plain wooden crate with nothing more than "FRAGILE" stamped across it along with the roundel of the Free French Forces. Philip's Jeep sat parked just outside the building on a road that led toward Saumur and then to Paris.

"Four hundred and eighty days." Marie shut the crate.

"Well, four hundred and eighty plus another month," Noam said. "I can't believe you put yourself through all of this. It must have been utter hell."

"I survived."

Noam stared at her for a long time, finally pulling her close. "Do you think it's really Serah?"

Her daughter with those radiant dark eyes, that enigmatic smile, her simple beauty, was, undeniably, the woman La Joconde foretold in the upturn of her mysterious smile and the wonderment of her gaze, Marie thought. Now, though, it was even more. The Sibylline were no longer a myth and they required a mother and daughter to do the work of bringing them back from the brink of extinction.

"Where is Cloutille's body?" Marie asked.

"The directeur is having it handled."

"Yara and Iné?" Marie wiped her eyes and got back to work.

"We're taking the bodies back to Amboise before heading to Paris," Noam said.

"To the temple?"

"Beyond the seven bridges of paradise and into hell." He nodded as he repeated the words from Aesmeh's letters. "You should go see your Asfoora before we leave."

Marie was startled at Noam's knowledge of Aesmeh, but found it satisfying that this incredible woman, lost to history, lived again on the lips of those who knew her truth.

She made her way down the steps and into the crypt. The doorway at the bottom of the long stairway had been cleared of rocks and bodies. The fresh bullet holes in the tufa stone looked rather natural, she thought. Inside, she traced the lines of carvings with the same mark as on Iné's arm. As she moved into the crypt, she nodded at Tommaso's grave marker, understanding it as a reminder-- not everyone can be trusted with secrets. She admired the Sibylline. Then, she made her way to the most prominent of the group with its stone effigy of Aesmeh carved into the lid of the sarcophagi. She ran her fingers over the inscription: Aesmeh de la Rose: unknown-May 2, 1519.

The second tomb beside it only confirmed what she had grown to understand. Melzi and Aesmeh had shared a devotion most people could never even imagine. They served the Sibylline and each other until the very end. *Giovanni Francesco Melzi: April 15, 1491- May 25, 1570.*

Serah appeared in the doorway, a field thermos in hand. She passed it to Marie. "Coffee should fix you right up."

"You are magic." Marie unscrewed the top and poured some into the lid, then passed the rest back to her.

"Brewed it myself," Serah winked. "What are you going down here?"

"I'm trying not to close myself off. To not overthink why so many had to die for this to happen."

"You can't blame yourself for what happens in war." Serah repeated her mother's words from earlier. She set the coffee down and pulled her close.

"This is excruciating." Marie held her tight. Tears streamed down Marie's face. "Nothing is what I thought. I've been fighting against the Sibyl for so long. Now the door is open, and I cannot ignore any of this. To turn away at this point would be the final, terrible act of abandoning Iné, Aesmeh, you, myself."

"We've got a lot to sort through, that's for sure."

The prison directeur limped into the crypt and cleared his throat. "Monsieur Marchant wanted you to know that you can leave for Paris within the hour."

"Merci," Marie said.

"We also found this on Iné Soudier. I thought you might want it." The directeur passed her a leather satchel, nodded, and made for the door. "Me-kädmen anina il'ati."

Marie smiled at his loyalty to the Sibylline. She unlatched the buckle and pulled out the cylinder necklace that Iné had called the Seal of Amərətāt along with a single piece of parchment paper with the mark of the Sibylline on it. "I think this is yours."

Serah slid the necklace over her head. In an instant, the dark cylinder transformed into a radiant, clear crystal hanging around her neck. The pair didn't speak. Instead, they pulled up two chairs at the table in the crypt. The tomb and all of the women in it seemed to encase them, like a stone cocoon as Aesmeh's final words settled in:

Dear One,

Only now do I understand such devotion. None of us are free, yet it is freedom for which we do our duty.

You now know the Sibyl lives. It is up to you to find her within yourself. That I could not reveal it to you in person proves my most mournful regret. I can only hope now that Maurine is still at your side, and that we might once again rise and bring justice to the world.

Me-kädmen anina il'ati,
Aesmeh de la Rose

Chapter 58

MARIE

JUNE 16, 1945
PARIS, FRANCE

Marie and Serah stared up at the rosy Parisian sun. Hand-in-hand, they moved toward Peré Lachaise Cemetery. A baguette and a fresh bunch of muguet crowded the basket on Marie's arm. Baked goods and blooms had brought them back to Paris.

Serah knelt and placed her hand on her father's gravestone, reading it aloud: *"Non sire, ce n'est pas une révolte, c'est une révolution."*

"Well, La Rochefoucauld got something right." Marie helped her up. "This isn't a revolt. It's a revolution."

"So?" Serah asked, squinting in the afternoon light. She poured a cup of coffee from a thermos and pressed it toward Marie as they stood amidst the canopy of trees that shaded the grave.

"You realize we're walking away from any sort of normal life if we go back to Fontevraud?" Marie asked.

"We owe the Sibylline as much," Serah said.

Marie plucked a flower from a bush and slid it into her daughter's raven hair. "I rather blame them for everything."

"Like proving my life is a five-hundred-year-old coverup?"

Serah's words struck Marie. La Joconde had lived within its boundaries of Paris for half a millennia with little interruption. She had served her purpose as Aesmeh had intended. The portrait of an unknown woman was the Sibyl hiding in plain view, able to captivate men so intently that they cherished her, even revered her, without ever knowing what secrets she harbored. The Sibylline had found a way to straddle the past and present from beyond death.

"I guess we should go deal with all of this then." Marie took Serah's arm and they headed for the subway.

Mother and daughter hopped off the metro at Palais-Royal. Marie paused as they passed the Basilique Notre Dame des Victoires. The Great Mother had granted her prayer just a month earlier. The return to Paris with Serah at her side proved miraculous. For a moment, she wondered if the Blessed Virgin Mary might have been Sibylline too.

They walked in silence, even as they got caught up in the crowds gathered just beyond the entrance to the Louvre. Heels clicked against the tiled floor of the museum. Marie and Serah gripped one another's hands until they found themselves at the doorway to the Grand Gallery. The pair waited arm-in-arm as the crowd moved into the hall.

The curator stepped into the wide corridor filled with repatriated artworks and smiled. He held out an arm for Marie to take and escorted her inside. Serah nodded and smiled as the tall, gangly man helped Marie up onto the low platform. Men wearing press hats and holding bulky cameras squeezed in as the curator offered brief remarks. Marie looked up and found Noam at the back of the room. His left arm was around Serah. They waved.

Finally, the curator pulled the sheet back. Marie stood for a long while as the workers mounted the painting back onto the wall in the exact place she had removed it from seven years earlier.

There, da Vinci's masterpiece hung—La Joconde—hands gently folded over one another, gaze locked on the crowd, and Marie's heart ached. Behind those pensive eyes lived the knowledge of an entire civilization nearly wiped from the Earth. Behind those pensive eyes lived those of her daughter. The woman on the wall had returned Serah to her. In the days to come, she and Serah would begin the task of returning the Sibylline and their sight to the world.

"Ready to go?" Serah whispered, taking her mother's hand.

Marie heaved a sigh as the crowd scattered. "I just needed to be sure we all found our way back home."

* * *

ABOUT THE AUTHOR

Robin Rivers is an award-winning writer who guides young authors as CEO of Quill Academy of Creative Writing. She has always been fascinated with stories of lost times and nerds out in the realm of all things historical, fantastical, female, and mythological. As a result, she spends her days in a literary universe best described as slipstream — a mix of historical, magical realism, and haunting romance.

Robin lives with her husband, daughters, and their sphynx cat Hypatia on the unceded territory of the Coast Salish Peoples, including the territories of the Musqueam, Squamish, and Tsleil-Waututh Nations in Vancouver, Canada.

Woman On The Wall is her debut novel.

COMING FALL 2023

A mother's devotion.

A daughter's determination.

An ancient terror's obsession.

The Mother House
THE SIBYLLINE CHRONICLES BOOK 2

Sign up for exclusive advance content at
www.thesibyllinechronicles.com